BOOKS BY REX PICKETT

SIDEWAYS NEW ZEALAND

SIDEWAYS NEW ZEALAND

THE ROAD BACK

REX PICKETT

**BLACK
STONE**
PUBLISHING

Printed in the United States of America

First edition: 2024
ISBN 979-8-212-18026-9
Fiction / General

Version 1

Blackstone Publishing
31 Mistletoe Rd.
Ashland, OR 97520

www.BlackstonePublishing.com

To my special needs cat, Max

INTRODUCTION

Given that it would soon land like an atomic bomb in California wine country, it is hard to remember that upon its release, *Sideways* was one of the great mishandled works of American literature at the turn of the century. Miles, a down-and-out author and the protagonist of the story, however, would have been reminded immediately of Herman Melville after the ruinous publications of his critically reviled novel *Moby-Dick* and his final work, *Clarel*. Not only was the latter remaindered—written off and sold to sellers for a few cents—but when readers proved unwilling even to pay pennies for the book, Melville's publisher forced him to sign, personally, the form ordering the book's pulping.

Moby-Dick and *Clarel*, of course, survived the caprices of the publishing industry, and so too has author Rex Pickett's masterwork, *Sideways*. The novel owes its rediscovery to Alexander Payne's film of the same name, and its literary longevity to the authenticity oozing from every page. Miles knows wine because Pickett knows wine. Miles knows the pain of the publishing world because Pickett knows that pain too well. And anyone who has ever loved and lost can experience the paralyzing pain and loneliness felt by Miles in the aftermath of a collapsed marriage and an ex-wife moving on with her life.

Sideways moved mountains in the wine world, not because Rex Pickett set out to change the way we think about wine, but because he tapped into an unrecognized truth about wine's place in the human experience. One need not be a wine connoisseur, own a EuroCave, or recognize the name "Riedel" to know instinctively that after a wedding ceremony, you raise a glass of champagne to the newlyweds. The first miracle of Christ was turning water into wine. The first thing Noah did after stepping off the ark was plant a vineyard. Wine was inseparable from the birth of philosophy in ancient Greece. On a first date at an expensive restaurant, the wine list becomes a leather-bound minefield; what one chooses says as much about his or her character as the conversation to come. Rarely has ordering the cheap stuff by the glass been considered the safest path to a second date.

Regardless of one's country or culture, wine has always been fully integrated with our lives, yet few have managed to capture in literature why that is or what its implications might be. When *Sideways* the novel and *Sideways* the film caught fire, Merlot was, at the time, having a moment on the wine scene. It had become the inescapable grape dominating restaurant menus after the "big Napa Cab" had exhausted our palates. Pickett, through Miles, asserted that the emperor had no clothes and, more importantly, humanized an alternative. Pinot Noir, said Miles, "enchants me, both stills and steals my heart with its elusive loveliness and false promises of transcendence. I loved her, and I would continue to follow her siren call until my wallet—or liver, whichever came first—gave out."

No novel before or since has so fundamentally transformed the $64 billion American wine industry. After Miles snarled famously—both in the novel and on film—that he would storm out of a double date if anyone ordered a bottle of Merlot, Pinot Noir grape growing in California rose over 650 percent over the ensuing years, while Merlot decreased. Economists called it the "*Sideways* Effect." Twenty years later, Pinot Noir outsells Merlot by hundreds of millions of dollars in the United States, the exact opposite of things before Rex Pickett had his say.

The reason, on some level, is obvious. Never had anyone so romanticized a grape and, by extension, its wine. Indeed, *Sideways* introduced many casual wine drinkers to the idea that varietals yielded wines of different character. Moreover, Pickett's prose ripped down walls and made wine an egalitarian pursuit. After *Sideways*, the domain of fine wine no longer belonged exclusively to some monocled aristocracy. Rather, he gave wine back to the common person—the people to whom it always truly belonged. Vineyards are just farms with the same John Deere tractors, country music stations, and manure-covered boots found on Kansas cornfields. And if Miles, a lonely, starving writer one week away from eviction, could so relate to wine—could, indeed, find a momentary transcendence for which each of us in some way pines—then perhaps, too, could we through wine.

Beyond the bottles sold, the blockbuster film, the Academy Awards, and the transformation of Santa Ynez from "the poor man's Napa/Sonoma," as Pickett described it, to a thriving tourist destination, a word must be spared for the undeniable literary achievements of *Sideways*. It is a beautifully written novel: sensitive, evocative, and sparing, with dialogue at once genuine, joyful, awkward, and moving. Pickett's darkly humorous prose captures the pathos that underlies life—that, indeed, makes life worth living. We are going to die, each of us, and every good conversation, lively or muted, jubilant or melancholy, is driven on some level by that one simple fact.

But not yet. And so we reach firmly for the corkscrew and grab the bottle by the neck, and twist the one into the other. Beneath that two-inch cork is an elixir sublime, that in turn can fuel sublime experiences. That is what Rex Pickett understood when writing *Sideways* and what readers learn with each elapsing page of one of the great literary works of our age.

—David W. Brown,
wine essayist and
author of *The Mission*

And what if one of the gods does wreck me out on the wine-dark sea? I have a heart that is inured to suffering and I shall steel it to endure that too. For in my day I have had many bitter and painful experiences in war and on the stormy seas. So let this new disaster come. It only makes one more.

—Homer, *The Odyssey*

CHAPTER 1

"Dear Miles, I hope this finds you well. I don't know if you remember me, but this is Milena Ernst. I'm the woman you met at L'Auberge Hotel in Del Mar, California, some two decades ago . . ."

I closed my eyes and sighed through my nostrils, breathing slowly in and out. Images flash flooded over me, spreading across the arid plane of memory, geologically buried deep below the bright strata of consciousness. After reading the lengthy, disturbing, heart-stopping email, I closed my laptop, set it on the coffee table, and straightened from the couch in the splendor of the Prophet's Rock Winery guest cottage, located three miles up a winding dirt road and perched sentinel on a knoll in Central Otago, New Zealand, where I had been bivouacked for the past year and a half. Wandering—staggering is more like it after the shocking email!—over to the amber-tinted windows, I was focused both inward and outward. Inwardly, I kept trying to conjure Milena. Yes, the name resounded in me, clamorously and sonorously at the same time, an arrow launched from a past across vast oceans to a present where I have often found myself in purgatorial limbo. Outwardly, I gazed in stupefaction at the mountains in the distance. Snow draped over the Pisa Range like a gigantic tattered white throw tossed haphazardly on the back of a colossal brown sofa. Below me and to the right stretched vineyards, their deciduous rootstock denuded of their summer verdancy, a bronzed barren patchwork of vines glinting in the wintry afternoon sunlight. Two years ago, with the help of an aspiring Kiwi publisher, I had accepted a fellowship to teach creative writing at the University of Otago in Dunedin, located on the South Island, and to set to work on a new book, a quasi-sequel to a successful one I had written a decade before, which had been adapted into a film that had brought me a sliver of ephemeral fame. *Ephemeral* being the key adjectival modifier. My whole life was riddled with modifiers.

I fell in love with the south of the South Island, and fed up with the US and the barbarous film business, I had gone out on a limb, cashed out some 401(k)s before their maturation, and invested in half a hectare of Pinot Noir vines in the Bendigo region of Central Otago and named it Miles's Lot, not unaware of the irony. When the semester had ended, I had an opportunity to continue working on my book at the Prophet's Rock Winery guesthouse, situated next to my half hectare of precious vines, thanks to the serendipitous meeting of a woman winemaker. I had officially become an expat in New Zealand. With the Kiwi publisher on board to publish my book and a modest advance in hand, I wrote and loved and prayed my Pinot Noir would one day produce greatness. A year and a half flew by. Perhaps the happiest of my life. That the balloon of my happiness would be punctured by one email had seemed inconceivable only moments before.

At the window I sucked in my breath and then let it all go in an exhalation that fogged the glass: the leg-vibrating news in the email that found me halfway across the planet in a rare moment of peace and tranquility; the winter pulchritude of Prophet's Rock; my first book in years in the process of publication; and the new uncertainty all of the above would entail that was about to rain down on me. Outside it was no more than forty degrees. Below my hilltop perch unfurled vineyards and scrubland suffering in these mica- and quartz-rich schist soils broken down over millennia from metamorphic evolution. I was existentially unmoored, once again without a true home, adrift in the New World wine region of Central Otago, fifteen miles outside the placid, scenic town of Cromwell. South of me lay Queenstown, an Aspen sister city so assailed by cyclonic winds jetliners often had to abort and re-attempt landings more than once, sometimes even having to divert to nearby Christchurch or, God forbid, return to Auckland. South of Queenstown was flung the end of the world, the jumping-off point to Antarctica. I found solace in the realization I was close to the end of the world, a forbidden icy realm radically different from where I had grown up (San Diego) and where I had suffered for my writing, like my vines for their grapes, and despaired so much (Los Angeles, Hollywood, whatever you want to call that abominable megalopolis where moths to the flame had fluttered for a century, only to have their improbable hopes and dreams thwarted, silenced, derailed, or crushed in the heart of their selfsame yearning, and at one time unspoiled, soul). Here at Prophet's Rock I had discovered, like the gold prospectors who came and perished in crude limestone hovels centuries ago, a singular purity, a cleansing, an expiation, if you will, of all my transgressions, all my regrets, all my loathing of a world that had crawled to the precipice of everything despicable certain human beings could exact on one another, a world clinging to the friable edge of an impendent violent revolution. I had come of age in America's most prosperous time, and over the years I had watched it slowly crater, terrifyingly devolve into a country obsessed with greed, fame, hypocrisy, and worse. Its swaggering toxicity had riven my soul, and when I was vouchsafed an opportunity to move to New Zealand to teach and to write a book that had been annealing too long in the intracranial theater of my imagination, I leaped tangle-footed and headlong at the chance. And then I met a woman, as love would unexpectedly happen, and my life both grew richer and became complexified, but in magical ways that reinvigorated my cynical spirits with wellsprings of new hope. Ella—more in a minute. But the email from . . . Milena . . . was crucifying me on the cross of a distant past as I frantically cycled through the rhythms of remembering, desperately trying to fit this woman into the jigsaw puzzle that composed the unsettling vicissitudes of my roustabout, if at times colorful, life. No matter how far away you go, in this modern, technological age, you can't escape your history.

"Dear Miles," I started rereading from the beginning, still in a state of shock and disbelief over my first read, this time from my iPhone before a knee-weakening view that could have been a million years ago, the landscape was that pristinely beautiful. "I hope this finds you well. I don't know if you remember me, but this is Milena Ernst. I'm the woman you met at L'Auberge Hotel in Del Mar, California, some two decades ago. Now and then I have wondered whatever happened to you. I followed your success with your book and your movie. Stung to realize you were still married when we found intimacy by the beach (O, the crashing surf of Del Mar!), but that was long ago, and hopelessly fated to come to nothing (distance, expectations)—it doesn't matter now. I see from your rare social media posts you're in New Zealand, teaching, writing another book. I hope it's going well . . .

"You're of course wondering why I'm reaching out to you after all these many years of silence and lives lived apart. Fear not, I'm not after any of your celebrity. Nor am I reaching out to simply say hi. There's something important I need to tell you . . ."

I rose again from the couch I had drifted backward to, disoriented. In the refrigerator I pulled out a bottle of Prophet's Rock Chardonnay, made by my winemaker friend Paul Pujol working with grapes grown at the Kopuwai Delta vineyard on the valley floor abutting Lake Dunstan. I poured half a glass and admired it in the light. It was two hours before my self-imposed allowable first pour, but I needed its anesthetizing anodyne, its liberating properties that would assuage all revelations, no matter how distant or from someone so far—and so briefly—in my past. Disinterring the memory of Milena, and the news she felt compelled to tell me across oceans and continents and time, was going to take courage. Chardonnay from Central Otago is as unique as any from Burgundy. In these nearly infertile soils, composed of only 3 percent organic matter, vines struggle to find sustenance, shooting their taproots deep on a quest for water and nutrients, hurtling all their propagating properties to their sole destination: their fruit. The vine suffers, its leaves etiolate, turning ocher and yellow as the clusters of berries intensify with phenolics and sugars, then, if it's Pinot Noir, coloring a dark violet, a lustrous black, and extracting all the life the soil can afford to surrender, as if it were their only purpose, but in truth, by planting them here they had become enslaved plants, not wanting to live this cruel existence in this harsh climate for the sole purpose of satisfying the palates of oenophiles thousands of miles away. But they do. And if they were sentient creatures, like my beloved special needs cat, Max (more in a minute), I would feel ashamed to be a vineyard owner in this forsaken land where Pinot Noir, like me, knows that suffering and hardship yield the most sublime fruit for the alchemization known as wine. "They don't want to live this life," Rudi Bauer, the legendary winemaker of nearby Quartz Reef winery, lectured to me, telescoped forward over a bar table at the Bannockburn Hotel's restaurant in an intense conversation where I was trying to learn about growing Pinot Noir in Central Otago and he was intent on explaining why nothing should be grown here, obsessed as he was with the suffering of all living things, sentient and plant life, as if they were married in some kind of holy matrix. But I digress.

Where is Max? I wondered to myself. "Max man, where are you?" I set the glass of Chard down, its razor-sharp, acid-driven, stellar fruit lingering powerfully in the midpalate, the same as the email I had yet to finish the painful act of rereading, which I prayed would end differently than on the first perusal, and which I wished had never found its way to my inbox. I discovered Max dozing by the floor-to-ceiling windows in the cat hammock Ella had custom-made for him, resting where the last rays of the sun were slanting in and where he enjoyed a diorama of avian and rodent life that came and went. Was he frustrated he couldn't go out and prey on them? Or, like me, did he prefer fantasy over reality?

Max is a special needs tabby. He was rescued meowing plaintively in a ravine near Prophet's Rock by my winemaker partner of over a year, Ella. She drove him in a snowstorm to a feline shelter, but not before I got a heartbreaking look, his large, terror-stricken, dilated, soulful brown eyes burrowing into mine. I hadn't cared for a pet since I was in elementary school and didn't want one for fear it would yoke me to the earth and compromise all my precious time. Writers only have precious time, borrowed time, time usually without remuneration, time wasted by mountebanks and master swindlers, time, time—"All I want is free time," I ranted to my eager-eyed students at the University of Otago in a sermon on the perils of writing, in an auditorium crammed with creative-writing majors, glassy eyed and glancing distractedly at their phones, hoping to steer them away from the life I had led to one that promised a more secure existence. But dreams die hard in the youth. "I don't care about money, I only care about free time. If I can't exercise my imagination in the pursuit of a book or a screenplay, then I don't want to live," I concluded fatalistically, hoping to rouse them from the mesmeric charms of Instagram and enjoying little success.

When Ella and I first moved Max up to Prophet's Rock, his back legs would occasionally collapse on him, and he would locomote by pulling himself with his front legs and crawling desperately to wherever he was trying to go. It was tragic. One heroic journey to his litter box fogged my eyes with tears because, God bless him, he was a fighter. I loved him more for his infirmity than for his being the sweetest cat I had ever met. When Ella and I learned his condition wasn't neurological, that it was a metabolic bone disorder—something about an absence of vitamin D and rickets—and that a supplement, calcitriol, administered orally every night would afford him a relatively normal life, we adopted him unhesitatingly. His care was expensive—parsimonious Kiwis would have put him down. However, the traumatic episodes with his collapsing back legs gradually subsided, the cushiony cat steps we bought to assist him climbing onto the couch, where he curled up next to me and helped me write, were proving to be a success, and now I couldn't imagine a life without Max, I couldn't imagine a world in which he didn't exist. At night when I woke, the dread of loneliness and eternal homelessness weighing down on me, I would grope my way in the dark and find Max in his favorite bed, gently lift him up, and rest his warm body on my chest. As the winter winds howled outside on this exposed hilltop location, exacerbating my sense of alienation from the world, Max's contentedly loud purring would comfort me. The current of feeling that coursed from him to me and back to him was as unsullied a stream of emotion as any I had experienced with a human being.

He had transformed my life. Friends derided me, Miles, the passionate wine-guzzling cynic, the guy who irreverently gave the middle finger to the conservative existences and pursuits of others, for going soft—cat pictures in texts?—for losing my edge. How could they fail to realize I was always a romantic at heart? That I believed in the inscrutable vagaries of love—on my terms—as much as anyone? And if I found it with a special needs cat and a winemaker who lived across the lake on her modest vineyard property—because we couldn't live together; it was too frightful a thought for both of us in the beginning due to traumatic breakups and overall relationship circumspection; we would eat each other alive with arguments over late frosts and vine fungi—on the south of South Island of Aotearoa New Zealand, then, I guess . . . well, that's why I called my half hectare of Pinot Miles's Lot.

I stroked Max's silky fur from a squatting position, but the email boomeranged back to me in a torrent of dismay and confusion, its appearance in my inbox haunting me. It would now never evanesce like some unbidden fantasy because there was no way I could archive this one, there was no way I could ever forget the words I had read and was now rereading in order to know I hadn't hallucinated it in my penchant for catastrophism. In the past year since I had been caring for Max, he alone—not even Ella—knew of my own hopes and dreams, my frequent anxiety attacks, my rants (out loud) inveighing against enemies and perceived enemies, charlatans and people who had ripped me off, monetarily and emotionally. Once, when I was swept up in an irate stem-winder, I glanced down, and there was Max staring up at me, wide eyed, ears pointed ceiling-ward in cat consternation, with that fey expression of awe and wonder he often wore. And that look of his silenced me, cut me off midsentence, often had me tumbling into self-deprecating laughter at the absurdity and ineffectuality of my ranting monologues. His innocent face, with his round unblinking eyes, was worth a milligram of Xanax washed down with a glass of Central Otago's finest Pinot. He had unwittingly become my emotional support animal. I didn't like the term, I didn't like its label slapped on an animal by a human, but Max, with his disability, always made me feel grateful for whatever I had achieved in this at-times terrifyingly unorthodox life I had led, and if it took Max's startled expression to halt an out-loud, lunatic, mounting diatribe in its tracks, then he was my electroconvulsive therapy, he was my straitjacket and Thorazine, he was my hope I wouldn't go barking mad. Nothing made sense to me anymore. Max made sense to me. An email from halfway across the world from a woman I hadn't been in touch with in a quarter of a century didn't make sense to me. I was shattered.

"I'm glad you appear to be thriving with your writing," Milena continued. Drip drip drip, the awful disclosure was rearing up again, beseeching: don't pretend it'll be different this time. I couldn't hear her voice in my murky memory because our wild, physically depleting, no-boundaries affair was rushing back at me in a cataract of transgressions. It had been conducted so long ago it seemed but a distant star transmitting a light generated far in the past that was just now reaching me, a dying brilliance, grunion spawning on a high-tide shore. Was her voice a bit high in register when she was distraught? I couldn't remember. I did remember she was tall, indefatigable in that seaside hotel room, our bodies a perspiry pretzel of limbs pursuing new frontiers of insatiety. "I think about you often, Miles," the email went on. "At a time when I was going through a lot of personal self-esteem issues, you made me feel like a woman—wanted, adored, desired—and I'll always cherish that about our short time together." A disembodied hand had seized my heart; I was choking on the knot of a memory. "But I didn't write you to tell you that . . ." And then she dropped the bombshell. I finished reading the final sentences and unthreatening request for the second time in a blur of shock and dismay, it all sinking in now with the weight of shoveled earth. And then I looked up and it was night. How did that happen, this ellipsis of time? A moment ago the sun was slipping over the mountains and the snow was gilded and the lands were dark, and now it was night and my hand was clasped to my mouth, and I had no words for what I was feeling, what had now shattered the placidity of my newfound sacred aloneness.

CHAPTER 2

"What do you mean, you're going back to California," Ella raged. "Are you out of your fucking mind?" We were standing in my half hectare of Pinot Noir adjoining the Prophet's Rock guesthouse. The air was cold and our exhalations visible, opposable fogs intersecting at the acrimonious space suddenly between us. In Ella's mirrored Ray-Bans I could make out my hirsute face, flecked with gray. Nests of wrinkles crinkled at the edges of my eyes, making me disquietingly realize I had crossed the tropics of life and was closer to death than to birth. Ella wore a black watch cap over her thundercloud-black hair. She was bundled up in a knobby navy-blue sweater slung over a pair of fitted jeans. When she lifted her Ray-Bans to the top of her head, her dark-brown eyes bore into me with a laser-vectored fury. She snorted air through her nose in an exclamation of reproach. In anger she tore off her watch cap and raked a hand anxiously through her hair, striated with grays—which she blamed on me—that fell over her shoulders in a riot of crisscrossing waves.

"Put that down," she commanded, referring to the battery-powered electric pruner I was unwittingly brandishing in my right hand.

I lowered the pruner and let it hang at my side. I couldn't meet Ella's eyes; I couldn't bear to confront the contempt protruding from her puckered lips. Staring down at the barren schist soils that mirrored the desolation of my soul at that moment, I shook my head in lieu of an answer to her question. I half expected a stinging slap across the face.

"Huh?" she insisted, hands planted on her hips, rooted to the ground and refusing to go anywhere until she dredged an explanation from the muck of my inscrutable, and seemingly insensitive, words to her about my having to possibly return to California, knowing full well I might not be able to return.

I slowly winched my head up to meet her glowering gaze. Early forties, mistaken for younger, her face was only slightly weathered from years as a vineyard manager before she graduated to the winemaker of her own label. We planned to have her produce my scant few barrels of Pinot Noir from Miles's Lot in a small facility she shared with the winemaker across the lake at Pisa Range Estate. My Pinot would be harvested by hand, carefully sorted—half destemmed, half full cluster— and lovingly crushed in a new sophisticated computer-operated wooden basket press that had cost me a small fortune, but I would do anything for Ella because I truly loved her with all my heart. She was one of the finest unknown winemakers in all of New Zealand, and I was fortunate to have crossed paths with her at a lecture I gave at the university titled "The Disappearance of the Sui Generis and the Rise of the Low Common Denominator." Enamored at first sight, both of us lonely and unattached, we collided together like meteors in the sky. But instead of it being a glancing hotel-room affair, as was the case with Milena, she accepted me into her world, heart, body, soul, and wine. My longtime best friend, Jack, who I had reconnected with recently, chided me for my indulgence of Ella's vintner whims and my special needs cat, Max, arguing they would bankrupt me by educing this generosity from me, but I didn't care. I wanted both of them to have the best. I wanted my small-batch Pinot to be the most soaring expression of Central Otago, something to be remembered by because I had never had offspring, I was a failure in marriage, my literary fame was fading. At least that was the dream. It was never my intention to hurt Ella. We were passionately in love. True, we didn't live together, but with my visa running out, we had plans, inchoate as they were, to buy a double-wide or an ADU and mount it above my half hectare. But in the interim, with my writing taking precedent, we had chosen to live facing each other from opposable ranges. Her mornings began when the sun climbed over the hills and engoldened the vineyards, and mine began when its rays slanted through the windows, and my pour-over Gesha coffee and the blank page on my laptop were beckoning me like Lorelei. I wrote; she tended vineyards and vinified grapes into the kind of sublimity I hoped to achieve with words. We both took our ingredients—she what the land and weather had given her; me what the dominion of my imagination had vouchsafed me—made subjective choices and produced, and lived with, for better or worse, our creations. We had much to look forward to together. The new book was done, and the vines were in winter hibernation resting up for spring budbreak, which meant Ella had a lot more time on her hands, which meant she had her full focus on my explaining to her why I had casually dropped, on the eve of a book-tour departure that had been in the planning stages for some weeks, that I might have to return to California at tour's end.

"Huh?" she barked, standing her ground, waiting for a reply, which I couldn't find in the skies where a hawk swooped, wheeled in circles, and scanned for prey, and prey was profuse for these raptors here.

I *had* no reply. That was the tragedy. That was the rift that was about to rive an unbridgeable abyss between us where, hours before, we were a blissful couple, she teaching me how to prune vines, me pointing her to the great literature she always wanted to explore. Now all our plans were shipwrecking on the shoals of my recalcitrance. My stomach churned, the shocking email from Milena recrudescing in my mind, a scar slashed open. When I met her fiery eyes, all I could manage was: "Like I said, I might have to return to the States."

She shook her head at me with an expression of malign disbelief. "Why?" she said in a rising tone, her cheeks colored crimson with anger and the frigid air.

"It's too personal, Ella."

"Another woman?"

"Not in the way you're thinking," I pleaded for understanding. "I could lie, but I promised I would never lie to you like I have to other women in the past. I never wanted our relationship to be founded on untruths." I nodded up and down, hoping this would placate her. It didn't. Her eyes burrowed into me, still blazing with an adamantine incredulity.

She shook her head again, back and forth as if trying to promote the seed of another way into the buried explanation of my announcement, and stared off at the scenic vista, its splendor marred by my words. "I mean, the New Zealand book tour, great," she started, seeking footing, "but you realize you've overstayed your visa since you gave up teaching, which I advised you not to do?"

"I know," I said, shamefaced. "But teaching creative writing does not beget creative writing. And I had a book to write."

"And you had someone new in your life."

"This is something surreally out of left field."

"If you fly back to California—for reasons you'd better tell me if you want me in your life!—you won't be able to return to New Zealand. They will detain you at customs, then deport you!" Her hand gripped her mouth, and she looked away in pain at a landscape growing increasingly desolate in her being. "And I'll lose you. And you'll lose me. And all our dreams of . . . of . . . this." She swept an arm circumscribing my minuscule lot of grapevines, the tortured souls that would produce my first vintage this coming year, the enterprise that bound us together, the half hectare she had brokered with her Kiwi citizenship on our mutual behalf, the cushy arrangement she had negotiated with the owners so I could stay at Prophet's Rock, finish my book, and then make the commitment and finally move in together and subside into each other's love. Now, it was all slipping through her mittened hands, and I couldn't tell her why and reassure her I wouldn't go unless I could make my way back, because if I did she would crucify me on the cross of a past I'd thought was merely a forgotten marker in a life's chronology that had numbly found me its victim.

I nodded in resignation at her damning conclusions, my tongue caterpillaring over my upper teeth in a thought bubble not forthcoming with a reply. "I'm not a hundred percent sure I'm going back because there're issues waiting for me on the other side"—I sounded lame in my equivocation—"and I . . ."

"What? I thought you had resolved your problems with the tax authorities?"

"I have," I said, fearing she was accusing me of lying. "Uncle Sam and I are like this." I crossed my index and middle fingers and shook them defiantly, comically, but the attempt at humor was lost on her.

"What is it then?" she said, cocking her head to one side, her anger undiminished.

"I can't tell you," I said in an exasperated tone, reflecting back on the email I had read last night whose wound had not subsided, whose arrow was still embedded in my side.

"*Why* can't you tell me?" she said, her head telescoped forward threateningly, our foreheads nearly touching, our lips inches apart but a thousand miles from kissing.

"I haven't even processed this . . . this news, but I wanted to let you know I might have to go back. *Might* being the operant qualifier."

"Oh, you were considering not telling me, and then when your book tour ended in Auckland you were going to hop on a plane and jet off, and what? Write me an email?"

"No, Ella."

"It's another woman," she said, convinced. She had speared me with such accuracy my heart raced. Yeah, it was another woman, another woman from my distant past, but how was I to explain why she had written me out of the blue?

I shook my head. As always happens to me in emotionally awkward moments, a smile incongruously disorganized my face, disconcerting whoever was on the receiving end.

"Why are you smiling?" she reproached me, regarding me now with contempt. "That's when I know you're lying."

I shook my head to efface the awkwardness and with it, I hoped, the smile. But like a sudden affliction of hiccups, it wouldn't leave my face. The news that had landed in my inbox was so absurd that I still didn't know whether to believe it. Debating confessing, I feared telling Ella. She wouldn't let it go. She wouldn't understand. It wasn't the right time. "I should have flown to Melbourne and gotten my visa extended,"

I muttered, hoping against hope to shunt the conversation away from the thorn now lodged in her heart.

"Yeah, you should have."

"I suppose I figured we would become a legitimate couple when we moved in and that would sort itself out, you being Kiwi," I said, trailing off.

"Oh, you were going to marry me for the visa?"

"No. Come here." I dropped the pruner to the ground, stepped closer to her, reached out my arms, but as my hands touched her shoulders she recoiled from me, and in my imagination I glimpsed the fissure widening and the two of us physically, literally, and metaphorically drawing farther and farther apart.

"I can't believe you can't tell the woman you love, and have made plans with, and many other promises, you can't tell why you might have to return to the States, knowing fullfuckingwell we're finished," she said, fuming.

"It opens a Pandora's box I can't deal with right now. You'll know in due time. I would have hoped you'd understand. Obviously, I horribly miscalculated."

"Obviously. You leave me in limbo."

"You have to trust me."

She barked a laugh. "From the author of a book that was all about lying men!" She glowered at me. "If you're not going to tell me why you *might*," she mocked, "have to go back to the States, then I'm ending this before you end it in your . . . your wanker Yank way." Her narrowed eyes signaled a seismic shift in the relationship. It all came unraveling: the happiness I had found at Prophet's Rock, the untrammeled vistas, the unmolested silence to write, the spiritual beauty that inflamed my being, everything I had wanted, found, put a stake in the ground, was now dying on that selfsame hill, an unspoiled hill that had bestowed on me a serenity I had never known, a hill that was now persecuting me, a team of oxen dragging me inexorably down its dirt switchbacks to its basin and a fateful road back to the US.

"I know you think I'm being unreasonable, and I wasn't going to tell you," I started haltingly, "but the only reason I had to bring it up is because if I do have to go back, I'm going to need for you to take care of Max." That I had shifted the conversation from what this news portended for our future as a couple to Max incensed Ella in a manner that flat-out nonplussed her.

She threw a backward glance to the guesthouse where Max was ensconced. Max's expression was probably still wide eyed, sensing his world was about to change. Ella turned back to me, shaking her head in disgust. "I love Max, but he's your cat, and you're not abandoning him with me and our memories," she said, clutching a hand to her face to cover her eyes, which, judging by the quaver that had disturbed her voice, I imagined were blurred with tears. In a trembling speech: "When my mother went in for the triple bypass and suffered the awful stroke that plunged her into an irreversible coma, you were there for me every day in the hospital, Miles." She now openly wept. "And when we had to let her go, you were there. The eulogy you wrote for her was beautiful." She forearmed tears from her sodden eyes and stared at me angrily. "It's like you're a different person now, Miles, someone who doesn't need me. Cold. Indifferent. Aloof. A monster! You can't tell the woman you love what this news is that you might have to go back to the US for? I can only suspect the worst."

I grabbed her elbow with the feeble fingers of a desperate man on the verge of a breakup with an intelligent, one-of-a-kind woman, one I had searched my whole life for, one who got me on almost every level, one who I had used as a sounding board for my new book and who had listened patiently and produced ideas I had implemented. She complemented me in every way, making me better as an artist and human being. "Ella."

"Let go of me," she said, twisting her elbow out of my grasp.

"I have a nice dinner planned."

"Well, now I'm not so hungry."

"Come on, Ella."

"Miles, I drive all the way over here to have a nice evening, talk about our first vintage of Miles's Lot, and you inform me you might have to fly back to California, knowing full well you won't be able to get back into this country and that we might not see each other ever again. And you say it casually like it's not the end of the world, like you've got a plan to get back, when I know you don't, because I know you and plans, so I can only conclude you're in love with another woman and you've been doing some . . . some . . . internet whatever, and it's reached the tipping point . . ." She collapsed into sobs.

"No, Ella, it's not that at all. It's not another woman, not exactly . . ." I stammered.

"It *is* another woman!" She rose up from the headstone of her despair. "I know it, and you've gone back to your motherfucking cheating, lying ways. Book tour? You're returning to Hollywood because you've got some lucrative movie deal lined up, and you can't wait to get back and start whoring all over again!"

The switch had flipped in Ella and she had transited like many distraught and aggrieved partners in a relationship into the intransigent, the irrational, the inconsolable. I had sent her somersaulting over the edge. This was an Ella I had never witnessed before. Her wrath was both uncontrollable and justified.

"We're done," she said, red faced and eyes muddled with tears. "You knew this all along when you dropped this on me, and you didn't care or think about my feelings."

"No, I didn't, I just—"

"If you just got it out and got it over with, whatever this news is, we could have talked it out. But, but," she sputtered in her tirade, "You leave, for whatever *fucking* reason, I'm done! Forget about moving in. Forget about marriage." She looked at me with eyes blazing, two miniature conflagrations burning in her skull.

I couldn't meet her eyes and that spoke volumes of tragic poetry.

She reached down and took possession of the pruner and shook it in my face. "You're doing it all wrong. I told you we want four canes out of these spurs instead of two for protection. And we want three shoots out of each." She started pruning the winter vines, attacking my mistakes with a vengeance.

"Ella?"

She stopped a few vines down the row, scowled at me, then held the pruner up at the sky, prepared to shoot whoever it was who had dropped this anguish on her. "I'm keeping these. I don't want you fucking up these vines." She spun away from me. "Enjoy your Hollywood whore," she said as she stormed out of the vineyard in the direction of her SUV. The driver's-side door slammed. I heard the engine rev like it had never revved before, and the all-terrain tires churned dirt and gravel out of Prophet's Rock in a pinwheeling fury, spitting them back at me with the ire I had engendered in her. It wasn't the first time a woman had left me like that, leaving me all alone, standing empty, hands thrust into my pockets.

But Ella I sincerely loved, and this breakup hurt me to the core. The shocking news I had received, and which I had no control over, like the seas rising inexorably because the ice sheets of Antarctica were melting four times faster than even the most pessimistic of climatologists had ever predicted, the news that had twisted a knife into my heart, the news I couldn't bear to divulge to anybody for fear of judgment or recrimination or, worse, feigned commiseration or, even more pathetic, sanctimonious advice, was the cross I now had to bear, the decisions regarding it all my own. Were Milena's words even true? I half wondered. My world was in a vortical turmoil.

It was growing bitterly cold, so I returned to the guesthouse and squatted down next to wide-eyed Max slumped on a pillow on the floor with his scent on it. I wanted to deliquesce into his innocence badly. He immediately broke into a calming purr when I stroked his fur. "Come on, little guy," I said, lifting him up. I carried him over to the couch, lay down, and set him on my chest, hoping for the soothing, painkilling magic of his purring. I nosed his whiskers the way he always craved, and he craned his neck to gain the full effect of my human touch. It didn't escape me how complicated my life was and how uncomplicated his was, despite his disability.

"I guess I pissed Ella off, little Max," I said out loud, realizing I was talking to a cat who could only make sense out of my dismay and not the fraught, weblike complications of the source of the dismay. "I came all the way to the bottom of the South Island of New Zealand to find you, my little friend. I bought a lot in a vineyard and started to write the book this Kiwi publisher had commissioned me to write, figuring it would one day wend its way to America and a publisher in my home country, where I had had several book proposals turned down and my agent had gone AWOL. It's finally coming out and I should be proud of that, right, Max?" I nosed his whiskers again, and he leaned his snout into me so we were pressed together, fused for a heavenly moment, hominid and African wildcat, comrades in the ongoing battle against debilitating anxiety. I kept nosing his whiskers because it comforted me. Ella leaving in a state of rage and unimpeachable hurt had left me with the vacated feeling in my stomach that came when all was lost. That feeling that invades your stomach and retches it. What would Ella do now in her pique of anger? Go fuck the hot Kiwi vineyard manager at one of the neighboring wineries and inform me she had started up with someone anew? If she thought I had another woman waiting for me in LA (laughable as it was to me), a retaliatory relationship could spark up.

We had been together a year and a half, but in that time we had intimated lifelong plans, plans that would be set in motion when I finished the new book and it had set sail. Well, the book—*A Year of Pure Feeling*, a confessional novel of sorts—was finished, and Ella was no doubt eager to set those plans in motion. And so was I, wary as I was about living with someone for the first time since my marriage. I had found peace in New Zealand, a publisher, a teaching position I could return to anytime, a half hectare of Pinot, a beautiful, soulful woman. What more could a middle-class, middle-aged guy like me want?

"I don't know, Max man," I said, shaking my head. "I couldn't tell her I found out I had a daughter, you know, because this is pretty shocking shit to learn after two and a half decades. I know you're a cat and your only fear is my leaving the door open and you darting out and some raptor swooping down and attacking you"—I shuddered at the horrific image—"and I don't know what I would do because, other than Ella, I love you more than anything in the world, little fella." I drew Max closer and hugged him for dear life. "We're at the end of the world, little Max man. The polar ice caps are collapsing into the seas. We're past the point of no return, and then I find out . . . I have a daughter? My own flesh and blood?" I shook my head back and forth, unable to inter my disbelief at the email still impaled in my side, a spear hurled from the darkness of a forest I was forever in danger of growing lost in.

It had fallen cold inside. I considered lighting a fire; however, that would require returning to the cold and fetching more kindling from the woodpile, but I was too poleaxed with grief to be bothered by such quotidian tasks. A yawning ennui had settled over me, paralyzing me, sending me spiraling to suicidal fantasies, which had plagued me since I had awakened to the world with a fierce desire to etch my mark on it. I couldn't move. Death yawned invitingly. The power of cerebration—once my forte—wasn't ameliorating this convoluted morass I had suddenly found myself in, as if I had stumbled into an open well on a pleasant walk and was now enveloped in a vast darkness of gloom, a bottomless plummet to an uncertain landing. The prospect of taking Max with me on the book tour, and then across the equator, over the vast expanse of the whole of the Pacific, back to California, suffused me with dread. But I couldn't give him up either. I held Max closer to my chest and noticeably shivered. I debated hopping in my car and driving around the lake and up to Pisa Range and spilling the truth to Ella—fuck the consequences—because to lose her would be to lose the purest love of my life, the woman I envisioned myself buried next to. But before I could act on that improbable impulse, a notification banner appeared on my phone. It was reminding me of my Zoom with Jack.

CHAPTER 3

"I've got a stage-four clinger," Jack announced in his recognizable southern drawl, without immediately elaborating. "It started with a toothbrush."

Jack looked at me under a warm key light that illuminated his face theatrically, his long, straight, side-parted hair thrown back and making him appear more and more like a dissolute Brad Pitt. A new opportunity had arisen in his world; vanity had taken over his actor's persona; he had thrown himself back into the gym with a vengeance, was swimming laps with the ardor of an Olympian, and even hired a private trainer to push him to new post-middle-age heights of physical conditioning. We'd been glancingly in and out of touch for the past five years, Jack dreadful at email, me reluctant to pick up the phone. My two years in New Zealand had put a damper on getting together in person. It had taken Jack a while to warm to Zoom—whereas I preferred Zoom to actual interactions—but once Jack, postpandemic, realized this was now the new norm, that even auditions were being conducted on Zoom, he had embraced it.

"What does that mean, Jackson?"

Jack raked his fingers through his hair and combed his scraggly locks off his forehead, now furrowed with concern. "She's a former theater actress—well, she doesn't think it's *former*, if you know what I mean."

I shook my head, not interested in the elucidation but waiting on it to humor my friend of thirty years, the one guy who had my back, the only person I could count on for their unwavering loyalty, the sole person in my life who could keep a secret, and that's saying something for someone who had plied his trade in Hollywood! "With theater shut down and just now getting back up and running, her libido has needed other, how shall I say, outlets?"

"I see." An image of Jack in bed with a theater actress forced me to suppress a laugh. The faking had to have been competitive!

"And she just went all in, brother. I don't know what I said . . ."

"Probably that you loved her and wanted to marry her," I interrupted.

"No, no, no," Jack said. "She's Aussie. Even if she's living in Byron Bay, they're never too far from the bush or the penal colony." He shook his head in bemusement. "Problem for me is she's the producer of my new show."

Purely by coincidence, six months ago Jack had received an unexpected call from his theatrical rep—this surprised me because I thought he had been dumped—that a pathetic reality TV show he had been featured on titled *Washed-Up Celebrities*, which had been scuttled by the impatient streamer after a year, had found an unexpected cult following down under—in Australia *and* New Zealand—and some Aussie producer (the stage-four clinger) wanted to reboot the show with Jack, who had found a following as the host on the ill-fated US version. Jack knew it was a pitiful coda to a career that had never effloresced into the one of his dreams, but it was SAG legit, would pad his pension—something I didn't have—and he found himself in Melbourne in preproduction. Naturally, it didn't take him any time to hurtle himself headlong into a relationship, fuck the consequences and the conflicts of interest, and now he had a "stage-four clinger" with a "toothbrush"—and no doubt a suitcase clutched in one hand—bearing down on his rented oceanfront condo with a mind to sap him of what little energy he had, forget the fact he probably had other women vying for his attention, especially now he was a, well, washed-up celebrity in a land where he was American, where he was fresh meat. And no doubt Jack, like me, knew the

world was imploding and had at the penumbra of his brain the possibility of relocating to a region all the media was advising was the place
to be when the revolution came to right the wrongs of all the wealth in-
equality afflicting us Stateside. And the madness. And the biblical floods
and fires. We weren't getting any younger, the sands in the bottom of
the hourglass outnumbered the ones in the top, and even if I viewed this
as a positive—not afraid to die; in fact, looking forward to it, I often
joked—Jack was deathly afraid of his mortality. I had my one novel that
would be my legacy, even after I returned to carbon, but Jack, as always,
only had the moment. And this is the problem with people who only
live for the moment. They're scared to death of death.

"They have a thing for Yanks," he explained, "and, well, I have a
thing for Aussies. They're more liberated in the . . ."

"You didn't tell me she was the producer of the *Washed-Up Celebrities* reboot."

"I didn't want you to think I was fucking my way back to the top."
He grinned sheepishly.

"Jack. I'm not a judgmental guy. I sincerely don't care how you get
to where you're trying to get. It's Hollywood, man, everyone's got a
price. Even me."

"Even you," he mocked. "I could buy you for a case of Burgundy's
finest, a new set of golf clubs, and—"

"Okay, okay," I halted him midsentence. "So, why are you telling
me about this stage-four clinger?"

Jack pulled on a can of Aussie craft beer. His face had grown florid
in the time we had been online, and that smiling rubicund countenance
had washed over him, and there was that impish twinkle in his eyes so
unmistakably Jack when mischief was brewing in his inveterately determined quest for new adventures in the tunnels of perdition we both
were intimately acquainted with. "I know I said I wouldn't be able to
make your book tour, but I'm having second thoughts. I need to blow
this pop stand here in Byron Bay until the actress-turned-producer—"

"What's her name?" I chopped him off.

"Amanda."

"Amanda. Okay. Let's try to pay her a little respect. After all, presumably, you are inside her most nights."

Jack drew a hand across his haggard, handsome face. "The production has been pushed a few weeks, and the timing is, how do you say, Miles, in your brilliantly scholarly way . . . ?"

"Fortuitously prescient?"

"Fortuitously prescient! *Exactement!* You've always got the right phrase for the right moment, Miles."

"Lately I've been googling words I knew were once up there but suddenly are galaxies removed from their appearance on the page."

"You could work with half your word palette and still deliver the goods."

"Okay, Jack, stop your blatant inveigling. What're you saying here? You want to come on the trip now?"

Jack scratched the incipiency of a beard. "You're going to need backup, brother."

"For a book tour?"

"It's winter here, Miles. More so where you are."

"I'm fully aware." I glanced out at the snowcapped peaks in the distance, now scintillant in the lowering sun, where, it occurred to me, Ella was now stewing. A pang of guilt scampered across my brain, insects over open wounds.

"And, well, we haven't hung properly for, what is it now? Five years? I'm sure you've got some deep truths to lay on me."

"All the deep truths I've laid on you in the past fell on tin ears." Jack smirked at the riposte. "Especially the ones that ended with a plea for money."

"Well, I haven't exactly been flush myself, brother."

"With you, Jackson, between truth and money lies the Grand Canyon."

"The money's coming, brother, the money's coming." He paused and studied his can of beer with thoughtful eyes. "There's something you said in particular a while back I will always remember," he said, punctuating his provocative opener with another chug of beer.

"What's that?"

"You said to me: 'There's one thing money can't buy.' And then you waited on my response. And you knew what it was going to be (happiness). And I fell for it because I know you're a sly fucker and you would never drop a cliché on me like that without a deep revealer lying in ambush. 'There's one thing money can't buy.'" He paused and pointed an index finger at me. "'Immortality.' And I had to think about that one. And you know, you're fucking right, Miles. I thought I had that with Babs. That money, or marrying into money, would buy me happiness. Or security. Or something to keep me from the ranks of the unsheltered. And it did buy me happiness. In a way. But you were right—it wasn't going to buy me immortality."

"When you marry for money, you pay for it every day."

"Hear, hear, brother. Hear, hear."

"We've both witnessed money take down some big players."

Jack grew thoughtful. "What's going to buy me immortality?" he inquired, slurring a little, hobbling his words and muddling them.

"You're going to anchor this reboot of *Washed-Up Celebrities*, Jane Campion or Taika Waititi is going to recognize your buried talents, they've got just the project for you, they direct a film starring you in all your washed-up glory, it nabs Oscars and BAFTAs and you get cast in what turns out to be the most memorable version of *True West* ever staged on Broadway, it's filmed, you're immortalized as the Brando who came out of the chrysalis of middle age to find everlasting fame."

Jack nodded up and down and narrowed his eyes at me. "And fuck you, too."

"It's better than dreaming of moving invoices and cashing out your 401(k)s."

"Amen, brother. Amen."

We shared a cathartic laugh. I needed it for reasons I didn't want to divulge to Jack. God forbid I would tell him my secret and not Ella and Ella found out! Ella had never met Jack, and it would likely only happen if we got married—Jack, of course, in a reversal, would have to stand in as my best man, should a second marriage warrant such a traditional ceremony, otherwise I would risk alienating him.

"So, you're saying you want to be my über-factotum on this book tour."

"I don't know what *über-factotum* means, Homes, nor do I want to, but you said it was the Stagecoach bus and boutique hotels up the east coast of all of New Zealand. I can dig that."

I was warming to his proposition. Conditionally. "I don't want you fucking your way through my fan base."

"I'm sincerely disappointed to hear you say that, Miles," Jack snorted. "As if I need *you* to draft off of."

"I'm just saying."

He put on his histrionic face of harried perturbation to seal the deal. "Look, it's been a wild couple weeks with Amanda. I need a break from her," he said, practically in tears. "Plus, I've heard Kiwi women aren't into casual sex like the Aussies, so I don't think they're going to be coming on to me."

"I wouldn't know, Jack. I'm a one-woman guy. I believe in committed relationships."

"For a couple months."

Laughter rippled out of me. "That's pretty good, Jackson. I'm going to use that."

"You've been making a living using me as a foil in your fiction your whole life." He pointed an amiably accusatory finger at me.

"You are one colorful dude, and I have exploited your likeness and real-life foibles, it is true, but other writers have met you and they haven't. I'd like to believe you have some modicum of respect for what little talent I possess to bring you to life with only the words on my admittedly vast lexicological palette." I gestured to my laptop monitor until we were dueling with finger-pointing. "With only words, my friend."

"And I respect that," Jack said, a tinge of desperation creeping into his voice. Hearing a noise, he threw a quick backward glance, fearing a new drama erupting at any moment, it appeared. Relieved, he turned back to me. "So, what do you think? A little road trip reunion?"

"I have to talk to the publisher and my publicist."

"You have to talk to the publisher and the publicist," he mocked. "Oh, bullshit. You're the author. You're calling the shots."

"I don't know if they'll spring for your accommodations. And we're not bunking in the same room like we did at the Windmill on that now-infamous road trip I made famous," I said, referring to my legacy work. "Those days are history."

"I don't want to be awakened by your snoring either."

"And we've got to go light on the grape."

He made a face. "That's your Achilles, not mine."

"Achilles' heel," I corrected.

"Don't be correcting me, Miles. You know I don't have your vocab—"

"Sorry. Bad habit. It's cost me a few girlfriends."

"I'll bet it has!" Tilting his can of beer skyward, he drained it in one long pull. He left the screen. Off camera I heard a pop-top on a can puncture open. The stage-four clinger must have been putting him through the wringer. He returned with his beer poured in a glass mug this time, an inch of white foam cresting it, his face tinged with a lively red. "How's Ella, by the way?"

"She's fine." I nodded, debating my next words. "Or was until this evening."

"What happened?"

I glanced over at Max. Chin on his forepaws, he was dozing in his cat hammock by the window, and I wished I could transpose myself into him. "I got some news, and I might have to return to Cal-i-for-ni-a."

"What news?" Jack forearmed foam mustaching his upper lip.

"I can't tell you. It's personal. It's private. It's dismaying, and I'm still processing its concussive consequences."

"And you didn't tell your honey?"

I shook my head. "I can't tell anyone except my little buddy Max."

"Max being your special needs cat, right? The one you text me pictures of, you sentimental fuck."

"Yep."

"You can tell a cat but not your current girlfriend, let alone your best friend of three decades? Come on, Homes."

"I can't tell you, Jack. Sorry. Like I said, it's deeply personal shit. I'm still wrestling with it. It's so seismic I couldn't even tell Ella when she confronted me after I told her I might have to go back to California, and she flipped out and maybe even just broke up with me, so I'm dealing with that shit."

"Sorry to hear that."

"Yeah, I mean, I've overstayed my visa here. If I fly back to California to face this thing, there's a good chance I won't be able to return. New Zealand's already a difficult country to get into. Ella will probably take my half hectare of Pinot and graft on Merlot in a kind of vintner version of a revenge fuck. But of course Merlot doesn't ripen down here in Central Otago, so that would be both a death sentence and a humiliation, a sorrow beyond words."

Jack chortled and smiled. "This news must be pretty heavy shit," he commiserated in a rare, but not unprecedented, show of feeling.

"It is."

"And only Max knows?"

I nodded. "And you'd better get used to him because he's coming on this road trip."

"What?"

"Ella won't take him. Not because she doesn't want to care for him but because it's her only hold on me, I'm psychoanalyzing."

"Max is coming with us?"

"That's right."

"And how's he doing?"

"He was doing fine until I told him."

Jack barked a laugh and spit a mouthful of lager.

"Don't laugh. He feels shit. He can't articulate it, but he feels it. He curls up next to me and purrs when I'm stressed."

Jack nodded, not wishing to alienate me with his coming on the book tour on the line and everything. Despite what some negatively assumed about Jack—the goatishness, the phony social butterfly extrovert, the profane womanizer—he was an immensely feeling guy. If something was awry in my world, he'd be the first to stomp down the doors, clear the room of the riffraff, and roughhouse me out of there to safety, even if it imperiled his own well-being. He'd done it before. He'd taken me to the depths, and he had pulled me out of the depths, the nepenthean depths. Figuratively and literally. You don't forget this shit. It's what bonds men together for life.

Until an Amanda materializes.

CHAPTER 4

I drove out of Prophet's Rock Winery on a washboard dirt road that snaked downhill to Highway 8. The heater hadn't warmed yet in my Prius rental, and I could still make out my breath. On the passenger seat to the left of me—I was driving on the right side of the vehicle and on the left side of the road here in New Zealand, and I still had nervous moments where I wasn't sure if I was on the correct side of the road or not—was a hardcover of my novel *A Year of Pure Feeling* that Hugh Martin Press had just issued. It was a fledgling imprint and I was their first title. "Hughie," as I had come to know the publisher—with whom I had only communicated virtually—was proud he had scored an author of my ostensible fame for his debut release. Like my legacy work, *A Year of Pure Feeling* was a confessional work that married truth and fiction. More comedic than its predecessor, but still very much a sequel, it was a meditation on where my life had taken me, the countries I had visited, the search for a semblance of home as, the *puer aeternus* I admit to being, I had never settled on one place to live. Until the blowout with Ella, I thought I had found a tiny sliver of heaven at Prophet's Rock, as far away from humankind as I could get. I couldn't remain at the guesthouse forever now that the book was finished and the owners were gently pushing me out, but with Ella's and my plans to park an ADU high up on a hill on a patch of dirt overlooking my half hectare of Pinot the good folks at Prophet's Rock had offered me, and move in together, I had fantasies of becoming a gentleman vintner/viticulturalist and continuing to write the books I wanted to write that Hugh Martin Press seemed eager to support. It was small, but it was something, a new start after the naughty days post-literary-movie success. But that was all thrown into chaos with one email. Fucking internet!

Mount Pisa in the distance was covered with a fresh blanket of snow. I noticed it had snowed lightly at Prophet's Rock, but not enough to remain on the ground. As I descended to the valley floor, snaking through the defoliated vineyards, I kept thinking of legendary winemaker Rudi Bauer's comments about the suffering vines. A mostly mammal-free country until recently, here and there rabbits, an invasive nonnative species, darted jaggedly across the dirt road when they heard my approach. At great expense, we were obliged to cover the rootstock with plastic sheathing from the ground to about a foot up the vine to prevent the rabbits from gnawing their way through the tender shoots and deracinating them. These were still young vines, not yet producing grapes of elegance and power, but promising one day to soar to epiphanic heights. Glancing out the window, I noticed vineyard workers silhouetted against the blinding sun, pruning the vines, like I had been doing with my half hectare, in preparation for spring budbreak, and training the canes along guide wires. More suffering for the vines. There was something pure in this glorious marriage of air and land. I wanted to somehow become one with it, lose consciousness, grow oblivious to all the havoc consciousness wreaks on us. I don't know if it was me or if it's the fate of humankind's evolution, burdened now with a massive ego-consciousness that gets in the way of everything that is pure nature, or what, but I glimpsed storm clouds on the horizon. That unbidden anxiety welled up inside me and held its hand clutched to my throat. Why couldn't I be happy in this starkly beautiful paradise known as Central Otago, with my half hectare of Pinot, my winemaker girlfriend, my special needs cat, Max, who radiated unadulterated love? How had it come about I had contaminated it all with a lacuna of my youth? If whoever created us was not a cruel numinous being, why did they continue to oppress us with the past? Why couldn't we escape the past or have it calve off into the ocean as we ascended to greater heights? Age, I ruminated philosophically, yokes us irremediably to the past.

I stopped at the intersection of Highway 8 and the dirt road I had dreamed my way down and adjusted my rearview mirror. I had let a beard grow in because I had little interest in my appearance, and Ella claimed she liked it. Tiny discolorations speckled what remained of my face. The brow was knitted in perpetual apprehension, but it always had been because worry had never left me for more than a few days at a time when, at the age of seventeen, I gave up marijuana and surfing and woke to the frightening reality I wanted to be a writer and nothing else. My eyes were clear now that I had cut back on the drinking—liver; crucifying hangovers; unfamiliar hotel rooms with women who only came into focus when they recited their names for the benefit of my befogged memory. Age had coarsened my face into statuary, the temples were frosted gray, but the books were still coming, my one religion: art. There was still a coruscation of hope in my eyes. I was down—down under!—but I had not given up. The ideas for books continued to burble up from deep wells of lived experience, and I still felt a creative obligation to bring them to life.

What if I had told Ella the truth? I wondered. Would she have flipped out? Launched into an inquisition? Disbelieved the truth as my flickering memory recalled it? Maybe she would have accepted it, gone into problem-solving mode, figured out a way I could get back into New Zealand if I had to decamp to California to face the music—I had a daughter (!). Then, too, was there a part of me who wanted to embark on this book tour, return to the US, and leave my life behind at Prophet's Rock? I had burned bridges, and I kept burning bridges because somewhere deep inside me there existed the truth that change was the *via regia* to the next book. Did I, in fact, see the email as my escape route and was fantasizing its inevitability? Could I heartlessly do that to Ella? But if I told her I had a daughter—shaking my head at the revelation—I would no doubt be barraged with all manner of questions, speculations, doomful prognostications about our future. Better to keep it on the down-low, let her wrestle with the unknown, cruel as that sounded, and see how it played out.

I readjusted the mirror, turned onto Highway 8, and headed in the direction of the small town of Cromwell (quaint, pleasant, friendly; no doubt hiding darker truths). Every time I came off a dirt road, I had to exhort myself to turn in to the left lane. Once, at the last moment, I saw an eighteen-wheeler bearing down on me and veered sharply out of its path as a horn blared indignantly. To my right sparkled Lake Dunstan. Formerly a river, it had been dammed to generate hydroelectric power. Seeing the wide body of water with birds floating peacefully on it, it occurred to me New Zealand was far from the megadrought crisis afflicting California, a drought that was causing uncontrollable Nagasaki fires, biblical flash floods during now-frequent thunderstorms, not to mention crop failures, Lake Mead shrinking to a puddle, a revolution brewing as the desertification of the densely populated Southwest of America grew increasingly alarming. And still the rich demanded Eden in the hell of the apocalypse. Did I want to return? (I was on another one of my monologuing rolls! Where was Max?)

It was a tranquil drive along Lake Dunstan into Cromwell until I glanced down at the book that had caused me tremendous anguish to write. The pitch for *A Year of Pure Feeling* had been turned down by every publisher in America. My agent, who pressured me for a sequel to my legacy work, grew disenchanted when I told him about the Kiwi opportunity and the four-figure advance. She argued that because my first book had been adapted into a wildly successful movie, she could have easily gotten me six figures. Was I insane? "Do you not like money?" It was all about brand recognition, sequels, cannibalizations of intellectual property, an economic reality I wanted no part of. More reflections along Lake Dunstan. Craning my imagination back to my youth, the books I read, and the movies that transported me that would never get written or made today, I felt a deep sorrow for the artistic losses we would never know we had lost because they had never seen the light of day.

My agent ghosted me and I negotiated the deal with Hugh Martin Press for the pathetic amount of $5,000 with blah blah if it was ever issued in paperback, with more blah blah if it was ever adapted into a movie or a TV series. I was elated to see it in print. It was never about the money for me; it was always about the work. If, in this tsunami of content, only a few thousand people read it, it still existed as a literary record of whatever value. It would go into my archive. It would be there if anyone wanted to discover it one day. But Hughie Martin had big plans for it. He saw a book tour as potentially churning excitement and sales. "It has limited series written all over it," he enthused from his offices in Wellington, which I later learned were in a wing of his compound in a wooded bedroom community. But the book tour required coordination, planning, and that's why I was driving into Cromwell on this cold June morning. I was en route to meet my publicist.

I parked in the Cromwell Heritage Precinct, a charming restored enclave of craft shops masoned out of stone and dating back to the mining days, and strolled across the street into Grain and Seed Cafe.

"Hi, Miles," greeted a young woman who worked behind the counter pulling shots for flat whites. "What brings you in today?"

I held up my book. "Fresh off the press. Getting set for a tour to promote my new book."

"Wow, I want to read it," she trilled.

"I only have the one copy, but when I get more, I promise to bring you one, Rosie, and autograph it."

"I'd love that. What would you like? Flat white?"

"Flat white is fine, Rosie," I said, glancing around, searching for my publicist, whom I would only recognize from a picture Hughie had emailed me. I clatteringly pulled out a wooden chair at a table situated at the window. An elderly couple was parked across the opposite end of the small café engaged in a conversation I couldn't make out. This time of year the only tourists on the South Island were in Wanaka and Queenstown, a moneyed crowd jetting in to ski and snowboard, drink and fuck, social media their exploits to phantasmal fame and fortune.

I glanced out the window. A faded red Subaru Outback pulled sharply into one of the parking spaces across the street, its tailpipe wheezing and rattling as the driver killed the engine and the vehicle coughed and choked to a stop. Out of the driver's-side door a young woman uncoiled to a standing position, her eyes wedded to a cell phone, both hands cradling it as her thumbs bounced up and down in a flurry of keystrokes with a proficiency—while striding purposefully across the street!—I had never been able to master. No more than twenty-seven, I guessed, she was wearing tapered jeans; a black, vintage military frock coat ornamented with brass buttons open to a long-sleeve T-shirt; and incongruously incandescent white leather tennis shoes.

The woman from the Subaru blustered into Grain and Seed with an anxious look. When she saw me, her face exploded into a smile with pronounced white teeth offsetting middle-parted, curly black hair that cascaded over her shoulders. Her brooding lips were painted purplish red, her black eyes were almond shaped, and her nose was wide with flaring nostrils. Judging by her extraordinarily distinctive physiognomy and skin color, she was unmistakably Māori. Her military jacket and penetrating gaze lent her a more imposing aspect than her New Zealand–accented voice would make you picture if your eyes were closed and you were dreaming her—and in my halcyon youth I would have because she was that striking; but alas (sad emoji). She pounded across the planked floor and thrust out her hand. "Hi, I'm Hana Kawiti. You must be Miles."

I nodded. "Nice to meet you, Hana." I held her hand in mine. It was cold to the touch from the chill of the outdoors. When she shook mine in return, she crushed the delicate birdlike bones of one of my writing hands, perhaps in an effort to show me she, as well as our relationship, was all professional. "That's quite a handshake, Hana," I said. "Sit down. What would you like?"

"Mineral water is fine."

I crossed the room and conveyed Hana's order to Rosie, then returned to the table, trying to disguise the aches and pains of standing and sitting lest Hana have doubts I was fit to take on New Zealand's East Coast in the dead of winter. Out of her large purse Hana had produced an iPad and was swiping around on it, ready for business.

"So," she began.

"Hana," I said, "hold your horses. Let's just ease into this, okay, converse a little bit."

"I loved your book," she exulted. "Self-effacingly personal."

"Thank you."

"You have a lovely way with words."

"Hughie told me he had to have his dictionary at hand."

"Not me," she said. She leaned forward a few inches. "I especially like your confessional honesty. Is that hard to write?"

"It can be. When you risk the personal and you get rejected, it hurts more than if you wrote a, I don't know, serial killer thriller."

She smiled warmly and met my eyes. Beauty and intelligence whorled in hers. "It's not commercial fiction, and I admire that. You capture our country vividly." She leaned closer and lowered her voice. "Is Helen based on a real person?"

I smiled a reply. "All my characters are based on real people. Until they disappoint or no longer inspire me."

She laughed. "I hope it works out."

Bringing up the fictional Ella, Hana unwittingly drew me into a dark silence. "I suppose we'll find out in the next book. If there is one."

"There will be." She leaned back in her chair.

"You didn't find my story depressing?" I wondered self-consciously, self-deprecatingly, which was my wont.

"I found it uplifting."

"Because the author was so despairing?"

She crinkled her nose at me, trying to figure out what I meant. "Your despair gave me hope. Your humor leavened your despair and delivered it to me like an arrow to the heart."

I jolted back in disbelief at her lyrical, trenchant critique. Not what I expected coming from a publicist. "You sincerely thought that?"

She nodded with widening eyes.

There ensued an uncomfortable silence. The awkward moment was rescued by the arrival of our drinks. She poured a local sparkling water brand into a glass. I sipped my flat white. Without meeting eyes, we studied each other. From my jaded perspective, she seemed impossibly young for a publicist but had all the sand in the world in the top chamber of her hourglass, thus her wickedly optimistic smile. I had all the transgressions and mistakes of my past loaded on my shoulders and more than half the sand in the bottom chamber.

"You're young for a book publicist," I remarked.

"Am I?" She sounded defensive, and her lips curled outward in defiance.

"Have you had a lot of clients?"

"A few," she said. "But none as famous as you."

I smiled, colored red at the compliment, and looked away from her radiant youth out the window and to the lake shimmering beyond. "I'm not that famous," I said. "I had to come across the equator to the end of the world to find a publisher."

"You're not alone, Miles."

"Oh, I'm quite alone."

"You are famous, though. In the wine world particularly, I'm told."

I turned back to her. "I want to stay away from the wine world as much as we can, even if it trails me like a stray dog."

"We're going to stay away from the wine world then," she said, parroting what I wanted to hear.

"You're Māori," I said matter-of-factly.

"Yes. My iwi's on the North Island." *Iwi* was Māori for *tribe*, and there were a hundred and three of them in Aotearoa New Zealand, all with their own distinctive rituals and idiomatic ways of speaking.

I nodded. "How'd you get into book PR, Hana?"

"I majored in marketing and communications at Victoria University." Her professional tone suggested she feared I was interviewing her and that her job was hanging in the balance.

"I don't know the Māori language at all, but I know it's used interchangeably a lot, and I don't want to be insensitive to that fact."

"Don't worry about it. I'll help you."

"Thank you." I inhaled through my nose, then leaned forward on both elbows. "Look, Hana, I have an irreverent sense of humor. I've matured a little, but not as much as some would like." She giggled and glanced away to hide her embarrassment at my admission. When she turned back to me, we locked eyes. "I'm not interviewing you, Hana. You've got the job. If Hughie thinks you're right for this, I'm going with his judgment. I like what you said about my book. My biggest fear in meeting you was learning you hadn't bothered to read it."

"Of course. How could you think I wouldn't?"

"You should meet some of the publicists in the States."

She snorted a laugh. "Never been. Want to go someday. See LA."

"You'd hate LA."

"Would I?"

I nodded emphatically. "Unless you'd like to be stuck in gridlocked traffic for two hours trying to buy groceries and meet guys who are all writing screenplays."

She laughed again. "I was a little nervous to meet you."

"Don't be. I'm the one who's nervous. I've got to be on for these book-signing events."

"I'll get you through them." She turned back to her iPad. "I wanted to brief you a bit on the schedule."

"Okay."

She returned a hand to her iPad, planted forearms on the table, and telescoped her head across it. "Hughie told me to get creative. I decided that readings and signings in bookstores are old school, past history. No one shows up at those." She raised her eyes to mine. "What is hip here in Aotearoa is book clubs."

"Book clubs? Hmm."

"They're more personal, we make more on the book sales, and they spread the word."

"Book clubs?"

She nodded enthusiastically up and down with brightening eyes. "Yes. Book clubs. And I've got some fun ones lined up."

"Do you?"

She nodded, a smile brightening her face. "Do you want me to run down the schedule of events with you?" she said, unconsciously swiping through screens on her iPad. Page one of her screen featured the cover of my novel, a lone man silhouetted against a lowering orange sun, gazing off at the horizon, where doom and gloom seemed to loom. I loved it!

"Enlighten me on the first one," I said. "I don't want to have a panic attack."

She laughed. "Have you ever heard of the Tough Guy Book Club?"

I shook my head. "No. Tough Guy Book Club?" I narrowed my eyes at her in mock suspicion.

Hana grew animated. "They originated in Australia. They bill themselves like a fight club for the mind, a book club for the thinking tough guy."

"Seriously?"

"Aotearoa's chapter is in Oamaru." She threw an arm toward the window in the general direction of the Pacific. "The only chapter in New Zealand. They ordered a dozen books, and Garret, their president, who confirmed, said they have 'questions' for you." She held up both hands in air quotes.

"I've got questions for them."

Hana chuckled. "I'll bet."

"That sounds cool. Unique. A book club for tough guys."

"Book clubs are big in New Zealand. They're going to be our friend."

"Is it in a home or a . . . ?"

She shook her head rapidly back and forth. "No. Fat Sally's Pub and Restaurant."

"Fat Sally's Pub and Restaurant in Oamaru." I enunciated each word. "You can't make that up."

"No. It's very Kiwi."

"Tough Guy Book Club, huh?"

"They bought a dozen units."

"We're off to a rousing start."

"Hughie's delighted."

"I bet."

"How's Max?" she inquired.

"How'd you know about Max?"

She pointed at my iPhone where the home screen featured a photo of Max gazing soulfully into the camera lens. "I read your blog, Miles."

"You're probably the only one."

"Oh, no. I've run analytics. You get some serious traffic."

"I do?"

She nodded up and down. "I'm excited about this trip, aren't you?"

"The Tough Guy Book Club, what author wouldn't be? That's creative, Hana. Was that your idea?"

She beamed. "Yes. You told Hughie you wanted the offbeat; the weirder the better. Material for your next book maybe?"

"You're a prescient young lady."

"And then after the Tough Guy Book Club . . ." she started, eyes back on her iPad, forefinger swiping to a spreadsheet.

I held up my hand. "That's okay, Hana. I want it to be a mystery."

She looked up from her screen. "Okay. A mystery it will be then."

I inhaled through my nose and gazed out the window, holding the air in my expanded lungs. The road was calling again, and soon it would be real.

"Is there something wrong?"

"Slight change of plans," I said to the window.

"What's that?"

"My friend Jack wants to come on the trip."

"Jack Manse. From *Washed-Up Celebrities*?"

I turned sharply to her. "You know him?"

"Miles," she said, leaning forward again, "I've read everything I could get my hands on about you. I know you and Jack are great friends. I've read he was a model for the character in your now-famous debut novel." She leaned back. "I think this is fantastic he's coming. We've got you covered," she said without elaborating. "Text me his contact info."

"Okay."

"Right now."

I picked up my phone, ready to comply. I tapped Messages and started to scroll through my contacts. My eyes failed me. I fished around in my left pocket for my reading glasses case.

Hana extended an importuning hand. "Give it to me, and I'll do it."

"No, it's okay, I'll get it." I knew she could do it five times as fast, but I feared if she tapped the wrong icon, pornographic photos of Ella and me might blossom on the screen. "What's your number?"

"Just AirDrop it to me."

"I don't know how to do that?"

"Settings. General. AirDrop."

I did as she instructed. We exchanged more fumbling back and forth until I had sent Jack's contact info successfully over to her.

"One other thing," I said. She waited, the young publicist, antennae eternally quivering, trained to extinguish fires before they raged into conflagrations. "Max?" She waited. "He's coming too."

She swallowed hard, pivoted. "That's great, Miles! An author with his special needs cat. We're going to get serious pub out of that!" Her delighted reaction took me aback. American publicists I'd worked with would have greeted my admission with *Hell no*. Hana laid a reassuring hand on my wrist. "Do you have a tracking collar?" I shook my head. "You need to get one. Don't worry." She wrote a note to herself on her iPad. "Tracking collar, and a carrier, and . . ." She looked up at me. "What kind of food does Max like?"

CHAPTER 5

After Hana chugged off in her battered Subaru, I walked up a flight of moss-covered stone stairs to Objects of Art, a cramped and cluttered workshop run by master jeweler Les Riddell. A month ago, I had ventured into the shop and inspected the samples in his anteroom and was deeply moved by his one-of-a-kind jewelry creations. I struck up a conversation with him, told him how much I admired his work and that I needed an engagement ring, but I didn't want it to be a crass, prosaic diamond, but perhaps something indigenous to these schist soils my Pinot vines were struggling to gain a foothold in. Les had a brainstorm about creating a ring in a rare quartz. But things had changed. An about-face of epic proportions had occurred. Ella had dumped me. The surprise was now tainted.

"It's good to see you, Miles," Les said. He was a dapper Canadian in his fifties, fit, and often sartorially attired in suits and loud, colorfully illustrated ties. Today he was sporting a burgundy vest over a long-sleeve black shirt accessorized with a red tie dotted by white spots.

"You're looking sporty, Les," I said. "You know, I've only worn a tie once in my life."

"When was that?"

"My wedding," I said, smiling wryly at the fossilized memory. I settled onto a stool. Les had spun his away from his workbench and faced me, champagne flute in one hand, an uncorked bottle of champagne on the bench.

"Can I offer you a glass?"

I shook my head no. "Too early in the day for me."

"Your ring is done. Do you want to see it?"

I closed my eyes and audibly sighed. "No, that's okay, Les."

"What's wrong, Miles?"

I ran a tongue over my upper teeth. "A confluence of unforeseen circumstances has left me a little poleaxed." I looked up at him. "I don't think the proposal is going to happen." He stared at me fixedly. I kept nodding up and down, wondering what to divulge to Les, one of my few friends in Cromwell—we had golfed when the weather cooperated. "I might have to fly back to California. And because I've overstayed my visa, my chances of returning are going to be fraught, if not nonexistent."

"Not if you marry her."

"I wouldn't want that to be a condition of my proposal. It makes it seem . . . transactional."

Les shrugged. "I did it. And it wasn't transactional. It was practical. And we're still together, going on two decades."

"That's nice to hear, Les. Where I come from, two years is verging on a record."

"I can sell the ring . . ." he started.

"No, it's okay. I ordered it. I'm going to pay for it, take it, hold on to it, see if things change." I raised my eyes. "Is there any way you can add a chain so I can wear it around my neck and maybe rub it now and then for good luck?"

"Of course, Miles, whatever you want."

Les rose from his stool, crossed the room, removed the finished ring from a box lined with black velvet, and handed it to me. It was a light-pinkish quartz stone mounted on a sterling silver band. I stared into its scintillant eye. Ella's face materialized in it out of the wingbeat of my imagination. And then it just as quickly evanesced. I nodded introspectively, still wounded by her impulsive, explosive—but justifiable—breakup with me. The thought of losing her devastated me.

"It's beautiful, Les. Stunning."

He retrieved a sterling silver necklace from a nearby workstation, threaded it through the ring, then deftly looped it around my neck and clasped it closed. "In case you change your mind, you'll always have your proposal close to your heart. These things go in cycles, Miles."

I nodded, reluctant to encourage conversation. I was still trying to grapple with the news: the imminent book tour; my young Māori publicist, Hana; the Tough Guy Book Club in Oamaru; Jack deciding to jet over for a reprise of our ill-fated bachelor trip to a little-known California wine region back in the day. "Storm clouds are converging on me from all sides. I knew New Zealand was too good to be true," I muttered. I fingered the ring now dangling on my sternum and stared into its microcosmic universe, the one I had fucked up. Was it sentimentality that I wanted to wear it around my neck or a good luck charm ensuring I would make it back to where the quartz was quarried: an abandoned mine above my beloved Miles's Lot?

With a heavy heart, I drove along Lake Dunstan back to Prophet's Rock, the engagement ring bobbing sneeringly on my chest. Untrammeled vistas were suddenly unsettling.

Max greeted me with incessant meowing when I came inside. Having missed me, he rubbed his whiskers against my pant leg. I prepared his dinner, which he attacked with alacrity. Shortly afterward he disappeared into the spare bedroom where his litterbox and toys resided. I followed him in and watched him, hunched over with arched back, defecate. This didn't bother me. In fact, it was as much of a relief for me as for him because, in the early days of his disability, he had trouble going. But now I viewed it in a different light: How would he do this in a Stagecoach bus? Would I leave him in the bus when Jack and I checked in to our hotel rooms, or would I sneak him into the hotel room with me? And where would I leave Max when I was hosting my events? Having never had children nor cared for a pet since I was a kid, I was woefully at a loss in these caregiving matters. And there was no Ella, who had fostered many ferals, to consult.

I stacked split logs in the fireplace and managed to kindle the beginnings of a warming fire. Max padded back into the living room on wobbly legs. Instead of retreating to his bed, he climbed his cat stairs to the couch and curled up next to me. I rubbed his whiskers and let my thoughts run. Max rested his head on my thigh, dreaming away the moment as I catastrophically envisaged the future. I glanced down at *A Year of Pure Feeling* resting on the glass-top coffee table. It wasn't the bawdy, comic novel my fan base was no doubt clamoring for. It was a sardonically bleak vision of the future enveloped in a love story that was now, it appeared, more fiction than reality. Ella had read it and claimed to have loved it, but you never know with those close to you what their true feelings are. It was our story, and it truly had been a year of pure feeling. Now it wasn't our story because of one email flung from halfway across the world, over an equator and nineteen fucking time zones. If there hadn't existed an internet, my life would be different. Milena, the woman from my past, would never have been able to track me down. Fate is different now, I thought, as I continued to stroke a contentedly purring Max.

My cell rang. Hughie Martin's face blossomed on the screen. He was a bespectacled man with a head of thinning hair, a lover of life, a believer—*in* life, unlike me—and an ardent fan of books, especially the one that had brought me a modicum of fame, if not fortune.

"Hi, Hughie," I said as soon as I tapped the green button.

"How's it going, mate? Heard you met Hana today."

"Yeah. Smart, upbeat woman. You've got good taste in both litera-ture *and* employees, Hughie."

Hughie chuckled. "How did you get on?"

"Cracking," I said in imitation Kiwi parlance. "She walked me through the opening day."

"I heard about your bringing Jack along. That's brilliant. Jack's going to bring another level of excitement, Miles. *Washed-Up Celebrities* was a big hit here and across the Tasman in Aussie land."

"I heard. I don't know what that says about Kiwis or Aussies, given it was canceled after one season in the US, but I'm glad you approve. Not that I'm dancing in the aisles about the cross-promotional association."

"Hey, it'll be two guys on the road, just like before." Like Hana, like Jack, Hughie preferred to view everything through a lens of positivity.

"I'm not sure what it'll be, Hughie. If nothing else, Hana's idea about book clubs instead of boring readings at indie bookstores is inspired. The book looks nice."

"Thank you," Hughie said. "David did a bang-up job." David was David Hedley, an erudite, refined bookseller in Masterton.

"I hope we sell a lot."

"I'm sure we'll be into the fifth printing by the end of the tour."

"What was Hedley's initial print run?"

"Two thousand," he said, as if I would be impressed. "At nearly five dollars a copy, I'm out ten thousand."

I wasn't interested in his complaining about money.

Hughie sensed it and got off the subject. "You're in capable hands with Hana."

"I have a good feeling about her. She seems like somebody you wouldn't want to betray or fuck with."

Hughie laughed.

Two years ago, when I was struggling, Hughie Martin, a successful businessman, had wanted to find fulfillment in life, so he naturally turned to the arts and founded a publishing company. A fan of my legacy work, he contacted me out of the blue and wondered if I had another book in me. One that might be set in New Zealand. I did, sure. Who wouldn't want to jet to New Zealand and write a book? I told him. I fielded these emails all the time, and usually they turned out to be charlatans wasting my time trying to hustle me to write a sequel to my now-iconic-first-novel-turned-into-movie fame. But Hughie hung in there, got me the fellowship and the visiting professorship, and soon I had reinvented myself in New Zealand, looking for a way to morph my rejected pitch for A Year of Pure Feeling so that it would bring New Zealand into play. It was when I met Ella and landed at Prophet's Rock that it all dovetailed. That novel, the one gleaming on my coffee table, had been written in a true cataract of creativity. I figured a New Zealand publisher, even if fledgling, coming out with my book would galvanize international sales, the US now being international—me, Miles, now officially an expat.

"I'll be dipping in and out to see how you're doing, Miles," he said in his rat-a-tat-tat manner of speaking. It still felt weird that all this time, with all that had gone on, we had never met in person. As I traipsed his country in search of a book, he stayed headquartered in Wellington.

"Okay, Hughie," I said. "Thanks for everything. I appreciate all you've done. I look forward to finally meeting you when I cross Cook Strait." I didn't have the heart to disclose I might have to fly back to California and wouldn't be able to return for the broader tour he was brainstorming that included Australia. I needed the second payment, due upon completion of the tour, a tour I had my doubts about, given that such book tours had been scuttled a long time ago by budget-minded US publishers. And who came to book signings anymore unless you were a famous celebrity TV chef or some scumbag high up in scandalous politics or an actor penning an autohagiography letting the world know what a genius you were? But New Zealand boasted a high literacy rate, independent bookstores were prospering, book clubs and wine were all the rage, so what did I know? With Hana's creative book club itinerary, maybe my cynicism would be upended. Maybe books *had* a future, and content consumption wasn't all social media and superhero films and video games and MMA. We used to massage and grow our brains with words; now we clobber them with violence.

Max purred as I roared in my head.

CHAPTER 6

I had spent my penultimate two days before the book tour at Prophet's Rock circumambulating the property, inspecting my dormant vines, no sign of Ella, deep in thought, when in the distance, I saw a funnel of dirt pouring out of the back of a tall, blindingly white, giant vehicle climbing the hill in my direction. I stared at it rising toward me on the serpentine dirt road that led up to the guesthouse. Who could it be? The winemaker and his cellar master had gone home with nothing to do, the first fermentation completed, secondary malolactic not yet underway. I kept thinking the gigantic vehicle would bend off on one of the dirt roads that branched off to other reclusive properties, but it kept barreling toward me. The late-afternoon sunlight seemed to be following it like a klieg light held and directed by a fierce and powerful god, because the closer it drew to where I was standing, the brighter it became. Hughie? No way. Someone wanting to . . . camp? On the property? Squinting into the angling sun, I saw the vehicle veer right at the final fork, following the signs to Prophet's Rock.

A few minutes later, I stood at the front door, mouth agape, as the twelve-foot-high vehicle lumbered into the parking area and braked to a halt, crunching gravel. The automotive leviathan revealed itself to be a camper van. On its side, in blue lettering, it read "Pacific Horizon." Its blue-and-red spinnaker-designed logo promised smooth sailing in equatorial zephyrs. The driver cut the engine, the heavy driver's-side door swung open, and down a rubber-treaded side step bounded Jack, grinning broadly, as if the world had descended on him in the most beatific way. He perched one foot performatively on the side step, tented his eyes with a flattened hand, pretended to scout the landscape surveyor-like, and then his eyes alighted on me standing below him in histrionic stunned disbelief.

"Is that you, Miles?" he said, always the actor, washed up or gearing up for his close-up; it came naturally to him.

I didn't say anything, stared dumbfounded, disconcerted, dismayed, all the words that begin with *dis*, including *fuck me* and *what the hell in Jesus's name?*

Jack leaped down onto the gravel. He crunched forward and enveloped me in his arms. He smelled of booze and bonhomie.

"It's good to see you, Homes," he slobbered into my ear with his beer-scented breath.

I pushed him back at the shoulders. In the fading light of day he looked more youthful and vital than he had on the Zoom call. Looked like he'd spent a fortune in the tanning salon. His long straggly hair was professionally tinted, and his stomach was tight as a drum pressed against my slightly burgeoning one. He was wearing faded jeans, fashionably scuffed rattlesnake cowboy boots, and a worn and holey black sweater, his rent-the-thrift-store uniform du jour, his *I don't give a fuck what you think of me, I'm Jack Manse, lover of women, lover of life, here for a good time, not a long time* zeitgeist.

"I cannot believe you pulled this off," he enthused in a booming voice. "God, I love how you operate in the shadows, Miles!"

I had no clue what he was talking about. I crooked a forefinger at the camper van. "What. The fuck. Is that. Jack?"

"Your publisher didn't tell you?"

"Tell me what?!"

"When he heard I was coming on your book tour, he thought it would be awesome if we went full Kiwi, camper-van style. It's a New Zealand tradition."

I stared at him incredulously. Trying to imagine the two of us sleeping in the camper van together had me fingering the vial of Xanax in my left pocket, and I hadn't resorted to that crutch in a while.

"Check it out," he said. "Awesome, dude!" He telescoped his oversized jaded-movie-star face into mine. "We're going to get seriously off the grid in this. Forests, lakes, remote beaches . . . You love beaches, Miles. Your window to an absence of anxiety, I think you once told me. And that's exactly what the doctor ordered." He straightened up. "This fucker's totally kitted out." Jack wheeled around the front and disappeared to the other side. "Come on, bro, check it out." His voice boomeranged around the camper van. "Our crib for the next few weeks. Or longer, if this tour takes off!" He grinned with anticipatory excitement.

I shuddered at the suggestion, then circled around the rear of the vehicle, giving it a wide berth, eyeing it suspiciously, still in a state of near catalepsy. Where Jack leaped in heedlessly, tangle-footedly—affairs, bad TV roles—I required hours, days, to process change, especially change of this magnitude. When I got around to the other side, Jack had thrown open the passenger-compartment door and had accordioned out a single-step metal ladder.

"Step on up, Miles, and check out our new home." Jack, still beaming that klieg-light smile of his, threw out a welcoming arm. It's possible he feared my questioning circumspection and was hoping to paint a rosy picture of this B-movie scenario, or it's possible he thought I would be on board with his unfeigned exuberance.

Shaking my head in ever-stomach-tightening trepidation, I climbed up the retractable step into the passenger compartment, Jack trailing. As I swept my eyes over the cramped space, Jack stood, fully erect, near the cockpit, inspecting the bed that was positioned over it.

"Do you want the top bunk or the one in the lounge?" His blithe tone suggested he truly had no clue what I was grimly picturing in my mind. "I know with your fear of heights you prefer to be closer to the ground."

I shook my head back and forth, back and forth, with no brakes. "How'd this all go down?"

Jack clapped his hands excitedly together. "I got a call from your publisher guy, Hughie; he told me the change of plans. I got excited. He got excited. The camper van was waiting for me in Queenstown. I flew in, and some Kiwi winemaker dude checked me out on this baby"—he slapped the upper bunk cushion with his hand—"and here we are. Two guys in New Zealand. On the road. Into the wild. Just what I needed to get away from the SFC!"

"SFC?"

"Stage-four clinger."

"Amanda, right." I was still shaking my head in annoyance, trying to imagine the unimaginable. This did not appeal to me at all. The tight quarters, absence of privacy . . . Instead of the promised Stagecoach tour, we had gone back in time to our college days.

"Check this out," Jack said, sensing my lack of enthusiasm and eager to shore it up. He addressed a black screen the size of an iPad mounted above the door. He tapped it to life, then, with great flourish, swiped back and forth to different screens and selected a light bulb icon. "Here's our mood lighting," he said, grinning. A warm golden light, toggled by a dimmer switch, illuminated the passenger compartment. It indeed was calming, if you had already accepted the premise this rig was going to be your home for the next however-many weeks. "It's got mobile Wi-Fi, satellite TV, full-on audio system, backup solar power, the whole enchilada, all on a Mercedes chassis." He turned and swung open the sizable refrigerator. Inside, it was distributed neatly with drinks and other provisions. "And they stocked us up." He ran his hand over the convection stove. "And you can cook your special fish recipes." He pinched my cheek and wiggled it until I swatted his hand away. "Check this out." He slapped the counter.

I glanced at the convection stove. It had two burners, and it did appear one could whip up a meal if they were possessed of the insane inclination as we hurtled through the night or were parked next to a roaring coastline. Jack unlatched cabinet doors, uncovered cutlery, flatware, dry goods, kitchen supplies, towels, toilet paper. He produced a water kettle. "And you can do one of your elitist pour-overs while I drive," he said, shaking the kettle in my face like a large maraca.

"That's not going to be happening."

Ignoring my misgivings, he threw open a door with a full-length mirror. Inside was a toilet. "And get a load of this shower-toilet combo. A little tight, but we can get our three *S*'s in without leaving the vehicle! This is an incredible rig." He rambled on, excited, as if he were the company's salesman on the showroom floor and I were the rube about to take out a third mortgage.

I stared into the toilet-shower combo, picturing myself slumped on the throne, head in hands, as Jack piloted us to the next book club event. I kept shaking my head to the point where it had become a clapper in a church bell, ringing out a doomful peal warning the citizenry of New Zealand: Miles and Jack, two guys on wine, were about to career through their country, face down in Pinot, hell bent on another narrative hardwired for perdition.

Jack, realizing I was fraught with reservations, eased up on the pedal of his elation and regarded me with a concerned expression. "Did you honestly want to be staying in hotels?"

"Yeah, I kind of did. But that isn't the issue here."

"What's the issue?"

"Hughie's trying to save money on this tour. When he knew I had a cocaptain, he rented this fucker"—I slammed the door to the shower-toilet combo with my hand—"not thinking to run it by me because he knew I would nix it."

"That's not what he said to me."

"The guy's a piker, okay? The publishing business is in the shithole, and a camper-van book tour, though it sounds romantic, is taking the budget route. The original print run was supposed to be five thousand, but he downgraded it to two. I see this as more than a demotion. It's a humiliation."

"He views it as a publicity opportunity."

"More like a publicity stunt," I said in a rising tone. I shook my head in dismay. "I wonder if Hana knew about this when I met her yesterday."

"Who's Hana?"

"My publicist. The woman who spilled the beans about your coming."

"Whose bunk is she going to be in?" Jack said in an insinuation of lechery.

"Jack. The woman's in her twenties. She's not going to be riding with us in here. And by the way, she's fucking hot, and if you even so much as flirt with her I will coldcock you. Keep your desecrating mitts off her." I looked away.

Jack raised both hands in surrender. "No need to insult me, bro. I've got my hands full with the SFC, trust me."

I scratched my beard in contemplation, my cinematic imagination working overtime. "She'll probably be trailing us, is my guess." I wheeled on Jack. "Assuming I agree to this cockamamie bait and switch." I massaged my temples. From the email from a woman out of my befogged past with heart-stopping news to Ella's breaking up with me and tarnishing Les's exquisite bespoke quartz ring, to Jack materializing up a dirt road in a camper van instead of in the back of a sleek Stagecoach piloted by a professional driver, I had been ignominiously assailed on all fronts. Once again. And millions aspire to be writers. I wished my creative-writing students could see me now.

"What're you doing, Hughie?!" I practically screamed as I stepped out of the camper van and made my way back into the guesthouse, phone in front of my mouth, Hughie's voice crackling over the speakerphone. Inside, I drifted over to the window. Espying Max asleep in the last remaining sliver of sun shafting in through the windows, I realized he, Max, was also going to be extremely compromised by this camper van. Where would he fit between Jack and me? Who would be the first to step on the poor little guy and send him to the vet?

"What do you mean?" Hughie said, his words garbled by a mouth stuffed with no doubt his favorite hogget pie.

"A camper van? Are you fucking insane?"

"There's free camping everywhere in New Zealand. And some great campsites if you need hookups." He had done me a favor to scuttle the promised Stagecoach bus, he babbled on, the con artist in him rising to the surface.

"If we need hookups?" I pressed a fist to the picture window and searched the darkening skies. A storm had scudded in from Antarctica over the Southern Ocean and was wreaking havoc on the South Coast. An icy wind whistled through the sturdy beams of the Prophet's Rock guesthouse. The fire I had lit was still glowing with embers but evanescing with my hopes. I gazed out at the hardscrabble landscape and tried to picture myself in a camper van with Jack, hoping my mood would perform a one-eighty.

"I'm talking to a New Zealand TV production company about doing a series about this tour," Hughie said in a blatant effort to placate me.

"Oh, great. A shot of Miles Raymond, thigh high in gorse, taking a leak on a pristine beach in between incandescent bursts of lyrical inspiration," I exploded. "Fuck the TV show, Hughie. You know what my problem is, what my problem always is? Why did you spring this on me and not tell me? And you didn't have this idea *after* you learned Jack was accompanying me on this trip."

"It was all last minute. I was lining up a driver when Jack—"

"Bullshit!" I chopped him off. "You were going to put me in that camper van all alone." He went silent in chagrin. "I can't believe you would pull this on me without asking," I said, now ineffectually, knowing the die had been cast, knowing my only recourse was the scorched-earth one: to call off the book tour.

"Isn't it beautiful?" he said. I didn't say anything. "Custom built on a Mercedes sprinter chassis," he boasted.

"Yeah. Jack told me. What did it cost to lease? Hotels would have been cheaper. Diesel on that is going to be a bitch."

"I got it for free," he confessed. "Hana's going to be doing some social media for the company. She'll fill you in."

"Oh, now you have me set up for some influence peddling? Here's Miles Raymond with his Pacific Horizon camper van. And of course Hana'll get me to produce a blazing smile as I cruise the coast of New Zealand, happy as a clam. I'm doing advertisements now, is that what you're telling me? You're selling me off for fucking spare parts? Here's author Miles Raymond taking a dump in his camper van. Watch it flush!"

I tapped the red button and ended the call with Hughie. Air streamed from my nostrils in a lung-emptying sigh. I squatted down to pet Max because he was looking a little worried after bearing witness to my elevated voice. "It's going to be okay, little guy, it's going to be okay. No one's going to abandon you."

I heard Jack shuffle into the guest cottage. I straightened and faced him.

He swiveled his head all around and broke into an appreciatory smile. "This is nice." He turned to me. "This is where you've been holed up all these months?"

"Yep. And now I'm apprehensive about leaving. Except they're kicking me out, so I don't have any choice," I muttered.

Jack instinctively drifted toward the open-plan kitchen. I heard a screw-top crack open, heard liquid poured into two wineglasses he had slid out from an overhead rack, heard footsteps approaching me from behind, glimpsed a glass of garnet-colored wine floating over my shoulder, an angel waiting to land. I hesitated with another lung-emptying sigh, then accepted it from him. Jack clinked glasses over my shoulder. We both grew tacitly philosophical. The years had annealed us both in the cauldrons of our discrete ambitions. I had fared better than Jack, but he was felicitously perched on the cusp of a third act, and even if it was an embarrassing reality TV show with him headlining as host, it was, as he rationalized, "coin in the pocket." "My ticket to retirement." I had no designs on retirement. I didn't know what retirement meant. I had been a storyteller all my life: novels, movies, plays; I had done it all, not always successfully, and I was not entertaining pulling down the shade with *The End* written on it as Jack was envisioning.

"Hughie says he's in touch with a New Zealand TV crew to make a series out of this," I said to the window in a disdainful tone. I threw Jack a backward glance. "Was that your cerebral hemorrhage of the imagination, too?"

Jack shrugged, sipped his wine guiltily.

I pointed my wineglass down at Max. "You realize Max is coming with us."

Jack grew an expression of alarm. "I know. You told me."

"Not when I knew it was in a camper van."

"Can't you leave him here with folks at the winery?"

"No. I'm not leaving him with people he doesn't know. That would be cruel to him. He wouldn't understand. He would miss me."

"And you can't talk Ella into it?"

"Now that she and I have broken up, she doesn't want him because he'll remind her of me. Plus, I'm attached to the little guy. We're bonded. I need him. And he needs me. He's the only one who'll listen to my stem-winders on the death of literature nonjudgmentally."

"That's a relief," Jack said.

"It is. Otherwise I would have gone insane up here on this mountaintop hideaway."

"Otherwise you would go more insane, is what you mean."

"Touché."

"You spend too much time alone, Miles. You need to get out more." He swept his arm around the universe that surrounded him: the stark hills, the leafless vineyards, the cloud-mottled skies. "You've been missing from the world, your fans, man."

I shrugged, the weight of all that had upended me in a short few days crowding in on me.

"What're you going to do with Max if you decide to fly back to California?"

"I don't know," I said, fingering the now-worthless engagement ring hanging from the chain hooked around my neck. I sipped the Prophet's Rock Pinot Jack had uncapped. The wine helped. Sometimes the wine didn't help. Right now it was magical.

"'Cause I don't see you on a transpacific flight for fifteen hours with a cat," Jack said.

"I never did either." My eyes went to the floor, where Max was observing the birds outside. I gazed out at the gathering storm, paused as another gust of wind convulsed the cottage and rattled the tin chimney on the roof above us. Rain started battering the windows. "You'd be surprised what some people would do for the love of an animal. It is as pure and unadulterated as any love I have ever experienced," I confided, fearing Jack would think I had gone soft and was no longer the laugh riot of the past, the past he wanted to re-create on this book tour in a fucking camper van.

"Max is more comforting than this Pinot?"

"Give me a moment."

Jack barked a laugh that drew a twist of the head and a wide-eyed, unblinking look of curiosity from innocent little Max. In the lacuna of a few seconds, Jack and I had reunited after five years, camper van aside, and the three of us, Max included, were momentarily, euphorically, in heaven. As the storm clouds whorled and amassed and the skies ruptured black, I glimpsed a fulguration of hope from somewhere in my bleak being, as if there were still new galaxies to be discovered, in tow with Jack, another road trip beckoning.

CHAPTER 7

The storm that had blown in from Antarctica raged all night. Spectral noises permeated the sturdy wood-beam cottage. It rocked like a boat on tumultuous seas. I floated in and out of phantasmagorical dreams, all of them featuring me at the end of the world, homeless, destitute, suffering deprivations of one ignominy or another. Once something growled (a badger?) and it startled me awake. I slipped out of bed, found Max asleep in his bed, brought him to my chest, and lay back down. His purring calmed me, submerged the disquieting dreams back down below the level of consciousness.

In the morning, sipping a cup of coffee, I stood at the picture window looking out. Heavy snow had fallen overnight and the crests were now covered in white. Somewhere on that hill slept Ella, or perhaps she was already up and tromping through Pisa's vineyards. In my foggy brain, I was still trying to bring into focus the camper van, Jack, Max, this New Zealand winter, the book tour / road trip, the return to the States after two years abroad.

I heard the shuffling of feet and turned. Jack had emerged from the back bedroom and slipped into the bathroom. A moment later the shower ran. On the kitchen island, two bottles of Prophet's Rock's finest stood empty and a third had been opened but was largely untouched due to a rare moment of prudence on Jack's and my part.

Today was day one of the book tour. According to Google Maps, we were looking at one hundred and forty miles to Oamaru and a rendez-vous with the Tough Guy Book Club. Allowing for the slower speed of the camper van, and the narrow, curving roads, I calculated we were no more than three hours from our destination. But the gathering storm facing me out the picture window discomposed me. I glanced at my weather app. It showed it was thirty-five degrees outside, complete with alerts of snow and gale-force winds, with paradoxically cute animations to underscore the warnings.

I brewed two Kenya pour-overs and handed one to Jack as he finally emerged from the bathroom, unshaven, wet hair a mop on his head, smile incongruously broadening his outsized face. He blew on his cup of coffee and glanced over the rim out the window, his eyes narrowing.

"It's pretty raw out there," I said.

"We'll be fine. We're heading north, where it'll be warmer."

"Not north. East, Jack. And we're practically in Antarctica right now."

"Before I got into acting, I drove big rigs. Eighteen-wheelers. It's been a while, but that camper van to me is like a single-engine Cessna to a 787 pilot."

"And you're the 787 pilot?"

"Called out of retirement." He patted me on the shoulder reassur-ingly. "Just for you, big guy."

"Are you packed?"

"I am. Are you ready, brother?"

I gazed out at the fury of the skies and exhaled through my nos-trils. "As ready as I'll ever be. Fuck me. Fuck this book tour. I'm too old for this shit."

"No last-minute thoughts on Max and your gal friend Ella?"

"I'm not leaving Max here alone, Jack."

"Okay."

"I still can't believe you jumped in the cockpit of that beast without calling me. I promise you I would have straightened this out. I would have threatened to bail and the Stagecoach bus would have been up here in a heartbeat."

"I know. And that's why I decided to surprise you. This is going to be fun," he reassured me. "Under the radar. Off the grid. Wherever the fuck we want to go."

"That's what has me doing Saint Vitus's dance."

Jack raked a hand through his curly locks, unable to disguise a troubled, inward look.

"Something bothering you?"

"The stage-four clinger was texting me incessantly this morning."

"Jackson, you shouldn't promise these women shit in the heat of passion."

He threw me a lopsided grin. "I know. But in that moment I actually mean it when I say *I love you.*"

"Hope can be hell with those three magic words."

"Hope can be hell," he echoed. He noticed the rose quartz ring dangling on the chain around my neck, touched it with thumb and forefinger. "What's this?"

"Engagement ring for Ella. But that's off, obviously."

"Shit, man, I'm sorry. Maybe you can sell it."

I turned sharply to him. "You have no sense of sentimentality. It's a keepsake of what we had. I'm not selling it." I mollified my anger. "It's cool, man. Fate is incomprehensible."

"You never know," he said with a tone of compassion.

"I'll wear it for good luck." I met his eyes. "Because we're going to need it out in that shit." I pointed a finger at the storm closing in all around us with a darkening menace.

A rapping of knuckles sounded at the door. "Are you two decent?" a woman's voice called out. Before we could answer, Hana entered, blown in by the squall of the inclement weather. She was wearing the same fitted jeans as when we had met, a moth-holed black knobby sweater, a cashmere scarf, and a pair of Red Band boots, or wellies. She appeared prepared to do battle with the elements. "You guys ready to go?" she demanded more than asked.

I looked at Jack. Jack shrugged a *yes, I guess* gesture. "The world hates a coward."

"Amen," I said. I flung out an arm to Jack. "Hana, meet Jack. And vice versa."

Jack took one long, lingering look at Hana and glimpsed Edenic shores that were a chimera, and he knew it in his head, if not in his fantasies. "Hi, Hana. I've heard a lot about you," he said, offering his bearish hand.

"Only good things, I hope," she said, taking his hand briefly and shaking it.

"Things best left unspoken," he flirted.

"Jack?" I said sharply.

Jack smiled wryly. He knew she was out of his league. He shook off the early-morning image of this indigenous Kiwi beauty who had been hired to be our monitor and publicist—a daunting proposition for anyone who possessed even a scintilla of a clue of Jack's and my ignoble history. "We're going to need to stop and fuel up," Jack said, pretending to be all business.

"We'll stop in Tarras," Hana said. She crossed the room to where Max was sniffing the window. She kneeled down beside him and hooked a bulky collar around his neck and fastened it loosely. She took care to adjust it so Max felt comfortable wearing it. When she was satisfied with her handiwork, she stood and turned to me: "I need for you to download this app on your phone, Miles."

"Do we have to do it now, Hana? I'm still processing that monstrous automotive beast out there," I said, casting an arm in the direction of the dreaded camper van that awaited its driver and once-famous writer now, according to one early review of *A Year of Pure Feeling*, "gone lyrically to seed with the fictional memoir of a failure." I couldn't decide if it was a backhanded compliment and I was on the fast track to a Booker or if it was a snarky vilification.

"Give me your phone," she said, stepping toward me.

I surrendered my phone to Hana. "Just don't open Photos or Messages," I cautioned. "Or WhatsApp."

With both thumbs a blur, Hana commenced downloading the app for Max's new location collar. "I'm not interested in your personal life,

Miles." She waited a few seconds for the download to complete, punched in a series of security codes, then handed the phone back to me. "Tractive GPS. Best on the market. I put the monthly subscription on the corporate card even though Max wasn't budgeted," she said in understated triumph.

"I appreciate that."

"Let's go. We have a book event tonight, guys."

"The Tough Guy Book Club?" I said.

"Right. The Tough Guy Book Club."

"You weren't joking, then?"

"No! I told you. Hughie urged me to get creative because bookstores are still a little wary about opening to live events. I've gone all in on book clubs. Do you know the Pulitzer Prize winner *Tinkers*?"

I shrugged and shook my head.

"Turned down by every publisher, even small imprints. Then, in a miracle, published by a tiny imprint. Publicist pushed it hard through book clubs. Grew a following. Won the Pulitzer for fiction."

"Underscores how ignorant the publishing industry can be," I said, reminding me of my own failure-turned-success.

"Proves how smart and diligent that publicist was," Hana said, defending her profession. "She made the difference between a Pulitzer and a remainder in a bargain bin."

"And a writer nursing a pint of vodka on a desolate beach, peeing in his pants."

"You've got a twisted sense of humor, Miles."

"He does," Jack said, hooking an arm around my shoulders. "That's why we love him."

"Thank you for that upbeat story, Hana," I said. Jack nodded in concert. "We're going to need it for that out there." I crooked a finger to the threatening skies that had charcoaled the landscape in an omen of what was yet to come.

We gathered up our luggage. Hana and Jack hauled it outside while I placed Max in a carrier, furnished with his favorite blanket and an assortment of chew toys. I lugged him out to the camper van, his eyes pressed anxiously to the mesh-wire enclosure. I was debating where to place him. In the back? In the space between the driver's seat and shotgun?

Hana was already in the passenger compartment when I came out, scoping out the space. "This is nice," she said to me as I stood outside the flung-open door, the buffeting wind knifing through me, snowflakes spotting my knockoff navy Harrington Steve McQueen jacket. "Bigger than I thought."

"Where do we put Max?" I said, not sharing her enthusiasm, an image of Jack squatting on the toilet, legs bent ninety degrees in the passageway, miasmic odors permeating our purchases and possessions, disabusing me of the romance of a thousand-mile road trip up the two islands of New Zealand.

Hana, hair flying, swiveled her head all around, then decided the floor mat between the two cockpit seats would make Max feel most at home. "You can reach down and give him some pets," she suggested. She walked through the passageway to the cockpit and plopped down in the passenger seat. From a tote bag she produced a holder she mounted on the dash with a provided adhesive. In it she placed a sophisticated electronic device rabbit-eared with two rubberized antennas of unequal height. She fiddled with the buttons on it, then turned to me, still in the back—still unsure, growing anxious—and Jack now behind the wheel, a kid in a go-kart.

"This is a two-way radio." She pointed to one of the buttons. "This is the press-to-talk button. It must always be turned on. When you want to reply to me, or shout out something, press this button, okay?"

Jack and I nodded, our befogged brains only half listening.

"It's also got GPS, so one of you needs to take it with you all the time. Not only so I can communicate with you, but in the event you go off on some nutty walkabout, I know where you are. Okay?"

"This is shaping up like a military operation," I said.

"Aotearoa is no joke in the winter," Hana said. "Take a wrong turn in this weather and this guy's going to save you," she added, tapping the device for emphasis. "And these were rented, so we can't lose these"— she held up her companion unit—"or Hughie's out a thousand dollars." She swiveled her head from me to Jack and met our eyes.

"Sounds serious," Jack said.

Walkie-talkie in place, Max's position for the trip selected, Hana scrolled and swiped through her phone. "Thirty kilometers, in Tarras, there's a gas station." She looked up from her phone. "Follow me."

Hana leaped out of the passenger-side door, and I stepped gingerly over Max and settled in next to Jack. Through the giant front windshield, I could make out Hana striding through the freezing rain/snow, which had been coming down unrelentingly all morning, climbing into her Subaru, and turning the engine over. The tailpipe rattled and spit diesel exhaust. Bald tires spun slightly before engaging on the slick gravel.

"Let's go, blokes," her voice crackled over the walkie-talkie.

I pressed the button to speak. "We're on your tail, Hana. Don't get too far ahead of us."

Jack commandeered the wheel and I rode shotgun, Max on the floor between us. "She's pretty hot in those Wellingtons," Jack commented.

"Do not go there, Jack."

"It's just an observation."

"An unseemly one. That ship has sailed."

"What's your problem, Miles? Aren't you psyched?"

"It's snowing. I'm freezing. I'm in a camper van, not a town car or the kitted-out Stagecoach bus. My partner just told me to fuck off. And my best friend of thirty years is slobbering over a woman in her twenties leading us to God-knows-where on the South Island of New Zealand. Next stop, the Doomsday Glacier, if we take a wrong turn. I've come full circle in twenty years, and I fear the worst is yet to come."

"The tent goes up; the tent comes down."

"I guess."

Shaking his head, Jack turned the diesel engine over. It grumbled to life on the first turn. "Ready, dude?" A crooked smile creased his face.

"Not really," I said. "New Zealand, here I come. Be gentle."

Jack laughed, switched on the windshield wipers in intermittent mode, dropped the shift lever into drive, and pressed his foot on the accelerator, and we started off. We coasted out of Prophet's Rock. The back of the van started rattling as we rode over the washboard-rutted road, following Hana in her Subaru, a funnel of dust and gravel in a vortical plume pouring out from behind her, obscuring her rattletrap.

"The book's good, man," Jack said.

"You read it this time?"

"Don't condescend to me. I may not have read Jung, but I've read Dostoevsky."

"*Anna Karenina?*"

"Yep."

"Dostoevsky didn't write that. Tolstoy did."

Jack twisted his head in my direction with a burning look.

"Watch out," I shouted. In that one extended second he had glowered at me, the camper van had veered into the scrub. "Jesus, Jack. Keep your eyes on the road."

"I've got it under control. Relax. Okay?"

I didn't say anything. The rain/snow slush beat down on the windshield as we wound our way out of Prophet's Rock. In the rearview mirror I could make out the diminishing image of the cottage where I had spent the last year and a half writing a book, falling in love, acquiring a special needs cat who comforted me on those evenings when I woke with night terrors. The thought of returning to California unnerved me. Would I be able to face the shocking news from an old fling who had barely registered on the radar of my memory?

"Still won't tell me what's in California?" Jack said, staring fixedly at the sinuous dirt road in front of us.

"It's personal, Jack. It transcends the bounds of our friendship right now. And I don't need you getting all philosophical on me. You'll find out soon enough. Plus, I'm still processing this departure in this, this"—I slapped the dash with my hand for emphasis—"fucking camper van."

"I respect that," he said. He switched on the slow wipers as the snow landed more profusely from the closed-off skies that seemed to have lowered and were now barely overhead, obscuring the world.

"Sad to be leaving Prophet's," I mused.

"I can imagine," Jack said with feeling. "Beautiful up there. I'd go crazy, but then, I need people. You're a lone wolf, Miles. I wish I could be you sometimes." Jack nodded at something liminal and unexpressed, no doubt the stage-four clinger and the drama he had left behind in Byron Bay.

"And knowing I might not be able to return," I said, nodding to myself. "It hurts physically." I turned to Jack. "This is a spiritual place down here in Central Otago, and you know I don't employ wellness-crap words like *spiritual* lightly."

"Cynical to the bone." Jack patted the top of the cat carrier resting in the passageway between us. "But you've got Max. I think he's humanized you."

"That's predicated on the fact I'm not a humanist."

"You know what I mean," Jack said, his feelings singed.

"Yeah, I've got Max." I bent down and glanced inside Max's carrier. His snout was pressed up against the wire-frame door and he was sniffing the new accommodations. "You okay in there, buddy?" I gave him a few whisker scratches, then raised myself back up. "I think he's okay."

Jack slowed to a stop at the end of the dirt road where it intersected with Highway 8. Snow glazed the empty road. Jack turned right in the direction of Hana's fleeing car.

"Woman drives fast," Jack said, depressing the accelerator in an effort to catch up with her. Now that we were finally on asphalt, the passenger compartment and all its cabinets and drawers stopped rattling, and my nerves settled a little. Visibility was low, however, and the shoulderless highway treacherous. All of a sudden, out of the fog, a truck was barreling down right at us. Jack whipped the wheel and swerved into the left lane, responding instinctively to the scolding of a blaring horn. The velocity of the passing truck caused the camper van to list left for a terrifying second before it righted itself. It was never in danger of tipping over, but it felt like a boat on choppy seas smacked by a lateral swell.

"Fuck!" Jack said.

"Left side of the road, Jack."

"I know, dude. I live in Australia. Just blanked."

"It's cool. I've done it. Always freaky to turn in to the left lane, but once you get into the flow of traffic, it feels normal."

"We'll be fine, brother, we'll be fine." Jack leaned over the steering wheel and blinked at the blurry windshield. "Where is Hana? We saw her turn right, didn't we?"

"Did we?"

Jack threw me a glance. "Don't fuck with me. I don't see as well as I once did."

"I had a retinal detachment in Italy and the ophthalmologist put on a different lens than the one in my right eye." I closed my right eye. "Left eye is fifty millimeter." I reversed the closing of my eyes. "Right eye is thirty-five. Ditto: shitty depth perception."

"Good to know when you take over the wheel," Jack said. He started to lift up his undershirt. "You want to see my road rash scar?"

I held up my right hand to stop him from displaying his war wounds. My pinkie wouldn't straighten. It looked like a hook. "Flew off a curb walking home in Santa Monica after an epic Pinot tasting." I shook my head at the memory.

"That's gnarly, Miles."

"Thank God I can still type."

Jack reached for his left knee. "Tore my ACL at a softball game rounding third and heading to home for the winning run. Crutches for three months. Bitch getting off painkillers."

I nodded. A silence descended. "I have a neoplasm in my groin."

Jack whipped his head in my direction. "What? What's a neoplasm?"

"Tumor. I don't want to talk about it, Jack."

"Go see the doctor, man."

"I did. They wanted to biopsy it. I had a book to write, said fuck it."

"Go, man."

"I don't want to know. Plus, I don't like doctors. Past forty all they want to do is poke you with needles."

"Neoplasm sounds . . . like cancer."

"Yeah. And it could be curtains. Or could be nothing. Fuck it. The shitstorm's coming and all we've got are windbreakers."

Jack chuckled. Then, the more he pictured the two of us in the fatalistic image I had conjured, the funnier my comment became, and he laughed harder until tears sprang to his eyes. "We are fucked."

"I'm glad you're finally coming around to my view."

"Let's make this one for the ages," Jack said, still laughing uncontrollably. "Let's go out in style, what do you say?"

We tore on through the unending curtain of rain and snow, the weather gods undecided about how barbarous the lashing should be. Passing cars sometimes washed us with rainwater from the narrow one-lane rural highway. The winter beauty of Central Otago was shrouded in ghostly gray drapery. I glanced at Jack. His face was gullied by nearly six decades of a life lived, like mine, on the edge—part-time acting and directing gigs, too many (him) or too few (me) women, and definitely too many wines—inhaling the fumes of hope, clutching at dangling carrots, false promises, projects—and paychecks—that more often than not never materialized. We both had floundered in the Hollywood universe of repeated and humiliating rejection. We still believed in the hope of success because we had once whiffed its perfumed roses, its dancing exultation, its wine, and its women, but we were unmistakably, ineluctably on the declivity. ("On the declivity," Jack repeated my words. "I like that.") We still had something to live for, but there wasn't as much to give as there once had been.

Hana's voice interrupted my thought dominoes, crackling over the Garmin: "Pull over at the gas station on your right."

In the tiny, tiny town of Tarras, Jack steered the camper van off the highway and braked to a halt at the pumping station. We climbed down out of the camper van. A fierce, icy wind sliced through us, and we buried our hands in our coat pockets.

"Go in and take care of this, and I'll fuel us up," Jack said.

"It's New Zealand. You can start fueling before paying. No pump and dash here!"

Jack gave me a thumbs-up and reached for the fuel hose.

Turning away, I noticed a flotilla of vehicles pulling into Tarras, congregating around the pumps in a chaotic fashion. They were disgorging wraithlike from the east out of the mist like battered tanks retreating from a battlefield that ended in defeat. A flurry of activity had broken out. Disparate, unintelligible voices—Kiwi accents, wind, vehicular noises—floated around me through the clotting curtains of snow. I ducked into an adjacent building named Tarras Country Café. Inside I found a casual breakfast spot crowded with stragglers swarming in from the cold, warming themselves in the heated dining room. Puzzled, I accosted a Kiwi guy—about my age, with a florid face hidden by a ginger beard—and asked him what all the vehicular commotion was about.

"The pass is closed," he said.

"Pardon?"

"Lindis Pass is closed." He drew me over to the window with a calloused hand gripping my shoulder and pointed east toward the pass. "It's snowed in. They just closed it. See all the cars turning around?"

"They closed it? Just now?" I said, incredulous.

"Yep, mate."

"We need to get to Oamaru."

"Good luck." He roared with laughter. "Where're you coming from?"

"Just down the road at Prophet's Rock."

"Unless you've got a helicopter, I'd recommend going back, lighting a fire, and turning on the telly."

"You're kidding? There's no other way to get there?"

"Whole South Island is closed down."

"What's your name?"

"Rob."

"Rob. I'm Miles. I've got a book club event in Oamaru I need to get to," I babbled. "You're telling me I'm snowed in?"

"You're an author?" I nodded. "You're snowed in, mate. Tell them to reread the book and reschedule. Excuse me." Rob with the alarming news broke away and went back to his seat at a table where a group of men was drinking coffee and reading actual newspapers. Apparently snowed-in, closed Lindis Pass was nothing to get excited about.

Feeling dispirited, I braced myself and ventured back outside. Hana, thumbs dancing on her phone, approached me through the slanting sheets of snow.

"Pass is closed," I told her. "What're we going to do?" Hana didn't respond immediately, intent on her phone. "Guy named Rob said there's no other way," I said in a voice loud enough to compete with all the idling diesel engines. "Advised us to return to Prophet's Rock and light a fire."

"Robfuckingwho?" she said, glancing up at me from her iPhone with blazing eyes. Hana displayed the screen of her phone to me. "Yeah, the pass is closed, but there's an alternate route."

"Rob claims there isn't."

"In New Zealand, there's always afuckingnother way," she said, a propensity to hamburger profanities in between her words.

Jack ambled over, arms crisscrossed against his chest, shivering. The snow blew across us with greater intensity, gravely decreasing visibility. "What's up?"

"The pass is snowed in," I said, pointing to the ghostly mountains rising in the east.

Jack craned his neck and gave the Lindis Pass a backward glance. "What does that mean?"

"Some bloke named Rob said we should pack it in," I said. I opened my hand to Hana, who was pinching her phone screen and traveling routes on Google Maps. She looked up from her phone with a smile incongruously brightening her face.

"Fuck Rob. We're taking the Pig Route," she announced.

"The Pig Route?" I said.

"I checked it for closures. There aren't any. It's a little longer, but we should make it in time." She shoved her phone away in her coat pocket.

"It's sleeting," I protested. I pointed in the direction of the blizzard obliterating the pass from view. "And at elevation it's blizzarding."

"Don't be a dick, Miles," Hana said. "I worked myfuckingassoff to get this book club, and we're going to make it." She turned and marched off. "Come on, follow me."

Jack turned to me. "I've been taking the Pig Route my whole life."

"Indeed you have."

He clapped his hands together. "Let's boogie."

CHAPTER 8

Spitting gravel and mud, Hana performed a fishtailing U-turn and headed south on Highway 8. Jack lumbered after her in "the Beast," our affectionate sobriquet for the six-ton automotive leviathan Hughie had fixed us up with. I lifted Max out of his carrier, set him on my lap, and stroked his fur. His body was tensing, and I tried to calm him with pets and whispers in his ear. "We're going to Oamaru through the Pig Route," I said soothingly.

"You talk out loud to your cat?" Jack said, turning the wipers up to full speed as the sleet pelted the windshield with renewed fury.

"Max knows everything," I said.

"Max?" Jack said. "Why does Miles have to go back to California?"

Ventriloquizing through Max, I said, "Because he found out he has a daughter."

Jack darted me a look, then turned back to the road. "No shit?"

"If an email from a woman I haven't heard from in over twenty years can be believed."

"Wow. That's heavy shit."

"It is."

"Wow. How old is she?"

"Twenty-five."

"You let one slip by the goalpost?"

"It's more complicated than that, Jack."

"I might have some insight for you if you let me in on it." He glanced at me with wide-open eyes and lifted eyebrows in a question mark expression.

"I'm still in shock."

"And you didn't tell Ella?" I shook my head. "I can only imagine what you're feeling, Homes. That's bombshell news. How do you feel?"

"Numb."

He nodded, his face showing genuine concern. "When you feel like talking, brother Jack is here."

"I'd rather not bring it up the rest of the trip."

"I hear you, I hear you."

"I appreciate that." I produced my phone, loaded Google Maps, and put in Oamaru as our destination.

"Continue on Highway Eight for fifteen kilometers," said the British-accented female voice.

"Turn that off," Jack said.

"Just in case Hana loses us."

"She's not going to lose us. She's got us on fucking GPS. Plus, she's your publicist. She loses you, she loses her job."

Jack turned to me. "If this Pig Route gets us there, you've got to give her credit. Whoever that Kiwi Rob is was clearly either fucking with you or had gotten an early start on his libations. Speaking of which, I'd love it if you got me one of those coffee drinks out of the fridge." He jerked a thumb over his shoulder.

I set Max down on the seat and took two steps into the passenger compartment. I opened the refrigerator and rooted out a can of cold brew, my feet spread wide apart in an effort to maintain my balance. The wind was gusting viciously, and Jack was jerking the steering wheel left and right to keep us on the narrow road.

I returned to the cockpit, opened Jack's beverage, and set it in his drink holder. "Fuck, man, this looks bad," I said. "Maybe I should radio Hana to book us a hotel tonight." I started to reach for the Garmin.

Jack stopped me with a hand on mine. "She's going to think we're a pair of pussies if you do that."

"I guess we can't use *pussy* to mean *coward* anymore," I said.

"We can do whatever we want and say whatever we want when we're out of earshot of those brandishing their iPhones who would dare to take down two—"

"Washed-up celebrities?"

Jack laughed. "That's us. Made it; never made it."

"And then you die."

"And then you die. Great line in your movie."

A gust of wind blasted us, and the camper van violently heaved to the shoulder, the shoulder that wasn't there. Flora raked the side of the van. Jack turned the wheel to the right and kept us on the narrow one-lane highway.

"Jesus, Jack."

"We're fine, Homes, we're fine. I've got the Beast under control."

Max looked up at me, alarm glinting in his unblinking eyes. Hana's voice screeched at us. "How're you guys holding up?"

I reached for the walkie-talkie. "We're getting knocked off the road, but otherwise we're fine, Hana. Thanks for asking."

"Of course."

"Maybe you should book a hotel given these weather conditions."

There was no response on her end.

"Don't ask her to do that," Jack said. "If word gets out we're hotel-ing it, it's going to be bad optics."

"To whom?"

"The Pacific Horizon people." He threw me a sly smile. "And I heard there might be a documentary in the works."

"That ain't going to happen."

Jack turned away, holding an expression on his face that suggested he knew something I didn't.

We crawled past the somnambulant towns of Cromwell and Bannockburn, then descended along the frozen lake into Clyde. The sleet slanted in curtained waves, and Jack had to gear down to forty miles per hour to keep us from getting blown off the road. Hana had slowed up and was keeping a watchful eye on us in her rearview mirror. She radioed us frequent updates in her upbeat spirit—"We're making good time"—even as the skies darkened ahead of us and the sleet that had

turned ominously to snow again reduced our visibility and whitened the surrounding landscape to a wintry desolation.

As we passed through Alexandra and angled northeast onto Highway 85 (the Pig Route!), the heavy skies surrendered to gravity and it began snowing hard. Jack leaned over the steering wheel and squinted at the disappearing road ahead of him, crow's-feet etched at the edges of his narrowing eyes. For the first time that morning, he appeared concerned.

"I hope this has some kind of four-wheel drive equivalent," Jack muttered. "The Pacific Horizon folks told me the Beast goes down into some pretty low gears."

"This snow is insane," I said, tensing, one hand bracing the dash, the Southern California born-and-raised boy in me not used to snow, let alone blizzard conditions and closed mountain passes. "Worse comes to worst, we pull over and get a hotel, and Hana has to reschedule."

"We're going to get there," Jack insisted. "Don't go all negative on me. Fucks with my resolve."

I radioed Hana: "Does this snowstorm concern you?"

"Does a bear shit in a church?" she radioed back.

Jack and I exchanged looks and chuckled.

"Woman's got a sense of humor," Jack said.

"There are no mountain passes on the Pig Route," Hana said. "It'll get warmer when we get to the ocean."

"We'll take your word for it." I turned to Jack. "And don't tell Hana what I told you."

"How long have we known each other?"

"Too long."

"Exactly my point."

The countryside flew past in all its rural beauty. The small towns we passed through bore the architectural feel of Hollywood western cattle towns. Jack and I settled into a rhythm. We reminisced on old times in between exchanges of concern about the howling winds and heavy precipitation that alternated between snow and sleet. Jack, God bless him, did not bring up my "California issue." He knew I was wrestling with something deeply personal.

At Hana's suggestion, we pulled over at a gas station in the tiny town of Omakau so we could refuel and I could take a leak.

Hana and Jack were conferring when I returned from the bathroom, but they stopped talking abruptly, so I naturally assumed they were gossiping about me. No doubt Hana was asking Jack about my welfare, how I was doing, since there was always general concern about my occupational negativism. If Jack bailed she would be left all alone with me. She feared me, the way others feared me, because in my voice was always the portent of an impending humdinger of a panic attack.

I threw up my hands. "I'm fine," I assured the bedraggled crew. "Looking forward to the Tough Guy Book Club." They broke into smiles of relief. "Assuming we don't wash away into the South Pacific and end up drifting on a raft to our doom because the roads are washed out."

"He's kidding," Jack translated to Hana.

"I'm sorry for the biblical storm, Miles," Hana said.

"It's not your fault, Hana. The book came out in winter, I couldn't wait until the summer to sell it, this is the book tour. You and my man Jack are going to get me there."

"It's all good. You're good. Let's go. We're cutting it close." She pivoted in place and strode back to her Subaru.

Jack and I climbed up into the camper van and resumed our cockpit seats. I fed Max a treat and whispered more reassuring words to him.

We barreled on into the freezing rain and the buffeting wind, the taillights of Hana's Subaru blearily visible through our blurred windshield. My A *Year of Pure Feeling* book tour was off to a *wobbly* start, as the Kiwis are fond of euphemizing. Jack and I had somehow found ourselves in a six-ton camper van on the "Pig Route," headed to Oamaru with a ridiculously young publicist leading the way. Gone were the days of flying from city to city, hunkering in Marriotts overflowing with courtesy gifts of wine and fruit baskets, gearing up to read chapters to a hundred-plus fans clutching my novel, eagerly awaiting my autograph. Fast-forward ten years, and here I was at the jumping-off point to the

Doomsday Glacier in a camper van in sleet and snow and barbarous winds en route to the Tough Guy Book Club. I shook my head and exhaled a laugh.

"What?" Jack said.

"I was picturing myself driving the Beast all alone, in this weather or, God forbid, with some hired driver who doesn't know me. I'm glad you finagled your way on board. It's good to have someone who knows me."

"I have a confession," Jack started. I waited. "Hughie had already made the decision. He knew we were friends, he knew I was in Oz, so he called me and asked me to come on the trip with you. He knew you would bail if you saw a camper van and a Kiwi driver you'd never met."

"You—and Hana—knew about this last-minute change of plans with this camper van?" I pounded my fist on the dash.

"Well, it wasn't last minute."

"It was to me."

"Sorry."

"What? Did he offer you money?"

"No. And I wouldn't take it if he had. He's trying to save money."

"He doesn't believe in the book?"

"He said something about how you had shifted gears and written something less commercial than the first one," Jack guiltily admitted.

"Let me get this straight: he's going to lose money on the book, but he's going to make it back on this documentary he's hatching?"

Jack stared expressionlessly at the road. "Something along those lines," he mumbled.

I turned back and stared through the windshield at the whiteout that greeted my dismay, seething. It wasn't the first time someone had thrown themselves at me with flummery and then sharply turned a corner when I dared to defy expectations and not repeat myself. "I don't fucking care what Hughie thinks," I said. "The book is published. It is what it is. It's the book I wanted to write. And remember, time is the harshest critic"—I wagged a finger at Jack—"not the naysayers massaging their worry beads and bemoaning their vanishing dollars."

"Amen, brother. Amen."

"Let's stop in Palmerston, guys," screeched Hana over the walkie-talkie.

"Palmerston," Jack echoed.

"Coming up," I said, staring at Google Maps.

Palmerston was on the East Coast of the South Island. Nearer to the water, it was a few degrees warmer and the alarming snow had stopped falling, but the wind and rain were as torrential and brutal as ever.

A bedraggled but determined Hana huddled with us in the convenience store where we purchased a few snacks. "We've got enough time for a meal at the Star and Garter," she said. "Google it, and I'll meet you there. I'm going to race ahead to check on things with Garret."

"Garret?" I asked.

"Head of the Tough Guy Book Club."

"All right, Hana, we've come through the worst of it. I think we can make it," said Jack.

"See you there," Hana said as she marched back out into the rain, no doubt questioning her newfound profession: book publicist in the twenty-first century, declining days of the Age of the Anthropocene, when books were being supplanted by social media, video games, dark web chat rooms, women dancing half-naked on Instagram and TikTok, and young men hurtling themselves off fjord cliffs in wingsuits. No time for Dostoevsky or Austen, let alone Miles Raymond.

"I like her spirit," Jack said, watching her disappear into the rain.

"Plucky woman," I concurred.

"You want to take over the wheel, Miles?" Jack extended his hand to give me the keys. "I need to go in the back and return some emails and take a snooze."

"No problem."

I climbed into the driver's cockpit. Max was meowing, so I removed him from his carrier and set him on the passenger seat. He stood on his haunches and tried to peer over the dash. For a brief moment, it appeared as though he wanted to get up on the dashboard for a better view, but with his disability, there was no way he was going to be able to launch himself on his spindly hind legs. And that saddened me. I glanced back through the passageway toward the rear. Jack was sprawled on the lounge cushions pecking away at his phone, raking a hand through his tousled hair.

"Stage-four clinger?" I inquired, sarcasm inflecting my voice over a backward glance.

Deep in thought, and without glancing in my direction, Jack answered with a thumbs-up.

I started the engine, which came to life with a satisfied snarl, and turned onto the main road out of Palmerston, remembering to drive on the left side.

Palmerston to Oamaru was an hour's drive on New Zealand's Highway 1. It wound in and out of the coast, featuring glimpses of windblown, white-capped seas. I needed both hands planted firmly on the steering wheel because the powerful, fickle winds would push the camper van this way and that of their own volition. There were moments when the wind caused the camper to lurch violently to one side, and I had to use all my driving skills from the million miles I had driven growing up in Southern California to keep it on the narrow one-lane highway. Even risking petting Max with my left hand brought disaster into the equation. Jack seemed to be rolling with the swaying of the vehicle, sans complaint, oblivious to the danger, not caring if we went off a cliff and plunged into the ocean. Jack and I had that sentiment in common. We had come through the worst of it—today on the Pig Route, and in the past in our respective "careers."

We were down, but we weren't out.

CHAPTER 9

We pulled into Oamaru as the sun was sinking somewhere behind ominous clouds, scudding and turning in whorls as if preparing for a new onslaught of beastly weather. Hana was waiting for us in front of Star and Garter Restaurant when we pulled up. She directed us to street parking she had blocked off with a traffic cone, and then Jack and I got out and followed her into the restaurant.

The Star and Garter was a homey place oozing with charm and Brit-themed bric-a-brac. We settled at a window table, exhausted and brain fried from the all-day drive. Outside, the rain poured down. The view window was rivered with rainwater. We came in with the cold, but the overcompensatory warmth of the restaurant had us shedding our outer garments.

Hana was working her phone with blurred thumbs. To the device, she barked, "They're going to be there; they're on time."

"What's the drill tonight, Hana?" I said as the server, a zaftig woman who had Jack's attention, dropped three menus on the table and promised she'd be back.

Hana manufactured a smile, the type of smile a publicist smiles when they're holding back delicate information. "They've read your book. They're going to ask you questions."

"They're called Tough Guy Book Club, but is that just a deflection from who they really are?" I wondered.

"What do you mean?" Hana said with suspiciously narrowing eyes.

"Are they *tough guys*, I mean like martial arts guys, or guys who hunt feral pigs and strangle them to death with their bare hands and light fires when it's not raining by rubbing sticks?" I said in exasperation, throwing an arm to the rain-slicked street.

"I don't know. I reached out to them because they're guys and you write about guys, mostly, and it seemed like a good fit, and Hughie was happy to sell them a dozen hardcovers, which you're going to autograph. They're not bikies, okay?"

I leaned my head back, muscle spasms clenching both trapezoids in painful knots. Tough Guy Book Club.

"Where are we camping tonight, Hana?" Jack wanted to know.

"I found us a free camping spot down by the water's edge." She turned to me with a manufactured smile. "Miles, you said you like the ocean."

"I love the ocean. In California. Where it isn't thirty-eight degrees."

"You and Jack will have that camper heated up in no time."

"While you enjoy the comfort of Oamaru's finest hotel?"

"Airbnb."

"Bone-warming hot shower."

"You've got a hot shower, too."

Jack and I exchanged glances. Jack nodded sarcastic reassurance. I shook my head, too tired to argue, too tired from the exhausting eight-hour drive in rain and snow to implore Hana to phone Hughie and get approval for a hotel on the corporate card. I wasn't going to let this parsimonious fucker get under my skin, start subtracting expenses until no royalties were forthcoming on my book.

On Hana's recommendation, we all ordered fish-and-chips. It came with a basic salad. British country fare. Jack and I ordered Three Miners Pinot Noir, a wonderfully mineral-forward wine that had migrated over to the Star and Garter from Central Otago. Hana sipped a nonalcoholic beer. Jack slammed the first Pinot down, smacked his lips, said, "Damn, that's good shit, Miles. You still know your wines." With a flourish of his index finger, he signaled the server to refresh us.

Jack and I were noticeably slaphappy as the three of us, bent forward at the waist, trudged together into the gale-force wind and slanting rain, arms braced against our chests. No words were needed, nor would have been intelligible in the clamorous weather. "Damn, it's freezing," was about all I could ineffectually utter as we followed a booted Hana bundled up in her black puffer coat to Fat Sally's Pub and Restaurant down a desolate Thames Street to meet the Tough Guy Book Club.

Fat Sally's is a large tavern with a welcoming ambience. Jack bolted straight for the bar to keep the wine continuum going, the dopamine from ebbing. With me, the talent, in tow, Hana addressed the maître d', a burly man with stirrups for sideburns.

Hana turned to me and spoke over the noise of the restaurant and the retro music pumping over the sound system. "They're in the back, still waiting on a few stragglers. Storm caused a few of them to cancel."

"Tough guys, my ass."

Hana laughed.

Okay," I said. "As my publicist, any notes on this event?"

"Be yourself."

I nodded. I don't know if it was the wine or not, but my spirits were lifting on the broken wings of absurdity. Hana had single-handedly navigated us here from the snowed-in Lindis Pass. I wanted to hug her. I weirdly felt like crying. Touched by the Three Miners Pinots, I spoke loudly over the atrocious music. "Would it be inappropriate to give you a hug for getting us here?"

Hana cocked her head to one side and smiled.

"I guess not. Okay. Cool." In the warmth of the pub, my spirits buoyed, I said, "You know you saved the day, Hana. That fucker Rob told me if we didn't have a helicopter we should have returned to Prophet's Rock."

"In Aotearoa, there's always another way. We wouldn't have made it as an island nation if we gave up too easily. Rob was fucking with you."

Our eyes locked briefly, and then she looked away.

"Come on, let's go back and say hi to the Tough Guy Book Club."

"Let's do it." I made a fist and pumped it.

Hana shook her head at me. "Silly."

Following Hana into the back room, I stopped at the bar and slapped Jack on the back, and he turned to me and grinned. "If it gets boisterous back there, come rescue me."

"You'll be fine, Homes. You've done the dog and Pinot show enough times you could perform it in your sleep. You'll be fine. Give 'em a show."

"Come on back and say hi," I urged Jack, grabbing him by the elbow.

"Okay, Homes, okay." Jack rose from the barstool and pocketed his phone.

Hana blazed the trail into one of the back rooms at Fat Sally's. The walls were constructed of red brick and were hung with photos and memorabilia: sports triumphs, large fish gaffed for photo ops, grinning Hemingwayesque men, and the like. Hana had already made the acquaintance of the club's president, Garret, a pug-faced guy in his early forties with a perpetual smile that seemed to be bursting out of his ruddy countenance in an expression that suggested amiability or sociopathy, it was hard to discern in the dim light and the cranial edges of cognition blurred by wine.

Hana brought him forward. "Miles, this is Garret, president of the Oamaru chapter of the Tough Guy Book Club."

Garret extended his hand. I took it in mine and shook it. It was meaty and damp. "Thank you for inviting me," I said.

"It's our pleasure. We don't normally conduct meetings with authors, so this is a first for us. The boys are psyched."

I turned to Hana, a single nod crediting her for the unprecedented opportunity. She glanced down, my acknowledging her success momentarily embarrassing her.

"And this is my copilot, Jack," I said, thrusting Jack forward.

Jack and Garret shook hands. "Let's get this show on the road," Jack said.

"Where do you want me?" I said to Garret in a rising tone.

"How about end of the table?" he said, throwing out an arm. "You're the guest of honor. Preside."

I turned to the long rectangular table, where a dozen men, ranging from late thirties to fifties, had congregated, all casually attired in

T-shirts and denim, all of them with glasses of ale stationed in front of them. A few rose from their chairs and greeted me cordially. As I pulled out a seat at the head of the table, I noticed copies of *A Year of Pure Feeling* had been arranged in front of the twelve men next to their glasses of ale, like sacred texts before a cult of literary-minded refugees who had returned from a seafaring voyage where they had lost a few to scurvy. Glancing at their weathered faces, I was heartened they had ostensibly read my semiautobiographical novel. Or had they?

Garret settled at the far end of the table opposite me. The server materialized in the gloom of the orange light, a drinks tray balanced on an upturned hand bearing sloshing mugs of ale. As she plopped them down on the table, she inquired, "Anything else, mates?"

Hands went up. Everyone who was more than halfway done with their beer ordered another. For some reason, in a sign of mutual solidarity, they all ordered Speight's Summit Ultra, because it either was on tap, was local, or had an extra kick. I quickly ascertained none of the assembled were teetotalers. This was a group whose low common denominator was inebriation and, incongruously, books.

The server logged all the orders in her intracranial notepad and disappeared back into the bar. Garret stood and called the meeting to order. "Okay, everyone, welcome to another edition of Tough Guy Book Club, the fight club for the mind and the soul of a group of sorry-ass men who have braved the cold of the South Island to come and meet Miles Raymond, famous author, who has a new book, which I see you all have brought with you."

Everyone turned to me and raised their glasses in a toast. The server returned and refreshed all those who needed refreshing. Glasses clinked and scintillated in the amber light as empties were exchanged for refills with alacrity. I raised an index finger and pointed to the nearest mug of beer, indicating I was moving on from wine to beer, *descending to the simian*, I wanted to joke, but wisely held it in check. A cheer went up from a few of the Tough Guy Book Club members who saluted my ale order. The conviviality of the moment wasn't lost on me; I was one of the guys now, not some wine-sipping, prissy author, but an ale man, a real drinker. Hana regarded me with narrowed eyes. No doubt Hughie had briefed her that I had gone off the sauce for a few years but was back on a self-rationed regimen so as not to disappoint the members of the various book-and-wine clubs I was scheduled to host. If I had to take one for the team, I would, humdinger benders be damned, author wandering lost in the night rectified by a Share My Location app toggled on and an underpaid beseeching publicist calling out to this lost mariner I was from time to time wont to become.

As everyone sipped their ales and forearmed foam from their mouths, Garret opened with, "We're going to go around the room. We want to hear what you've been doing, but we don't want it to be work related. Nothing about work. Okay?" Grim nods greeted his admonition all around. He pointed a finger at the man to his right. "Go ahead, George."

A bearded man with a stout physique, George cleared his throat and started in. "I'm George, and I've been hunting wallabies, a pest brought over here by our neighboring Aussies. I shot thirty last night. At seven a head, it pays the bits and bobs and keeps the wife in bitch diesel."

Laughter greeted his auto-thumbnail on his recent activities.

"Good on you, mate," Garret congratulated him.

"What's *bitch diesel*?" I inquired.

"What you Yanks call 'rosé all day,'" Garret interpreted. "Got our women—the few of us who cohabitate—through the worst of the pandemic, otherwise we would have all turned into savages," he psychoanalyzed.

George turned to the guy sitting next to him, a dark-haired man in his late thirties with hooded, deep-set eyes and a hawklike face to match.

"William here." He nodded his head up and down in contemplation of what he was about to confide. Words stalled on his tongue. "Returned home early from a trip," he began haltingly. His head bobbed again. It was difficult to read his eyes through his tinted eyewear, but his voice suddenly quavered with emotion. "Wife was, well, getting harpooned by another man."

Groans and "Oh man" echoed from the "Tough" Guys.

"One of my best mates."

In a chorus of empathy, "Oh no" and "That's rough" greeted his pitiful confession.

"Had to go to the court and file," he finished, tearing up, brushing his eyes with the back of the hand not white-knuckling the handle of his ale mug.

His terse recounting disinterred a memory in me of a girlfriend some years back who left to go to the store but forgot her purse. Curious, I rummaged through it, found a Flip Video cam. Recorded on it I found disturbing masturbatory sessions where she fingered herself off to her disembodied lover's off-screen salacious urgings. My stomach turned witnessing "Amy," head tossed back in performative delirium, her hand working her lush bush, her mounting moaning . . . I shook my head in a shivery motion and tried to expunge the lurid image, but it was scarred on my brain for life, fossilized in amber, and my once-annihilated heart went out to poor William. Tough Guy Book Club indeed!

"That's rough," Jack commiserated.

"Yeah," whimpered William.

Jack rose from his chair, gave me a few pats on the back, and disappeared back into the bar, uncomfortable with the direction the meeting was heading.

George drew an arm around William and pulled the latter toward him. William, the image of his mate fucking his wife still recrudescing in his perfervid, crucifying imagination, threw a hand to his aghast mouth and openly wept. After he had miraculously regrouped, he turned to his right and another Tough Guy member seated next to him, listing in his chair, more ales in than the others.

"Cooper here," announced the man, a twin bespectacled fellow, sporting a gray brush cut, possibly the oldest in the group. My eyes were still fixed on the wounded William, and I half thought Cooper was going to crack a joke to make light of William's cruel collision with infidelity because, well, they were the Tough Guy Book Club. But no, he turned empathetic. "I don't know what to say to make William feel any better," he said, "but it's happened to me, and it wasn't easy to get over. It took months, and I just want to say we're here for you, William."

Everyone raised their mugs and pointed them in the direction of the lachrymal William, wiping tears from his reddened eyes with twisting palms like warring scorpions.

I glanced over my shoulder at Hana, who, motionless, widened her eyes. Then, determining that the Tough Guy Book Club was more akin to a support group for emotionally damaged Kiwi men and not a horde of bikers out to gang-tackle me or pull me into a drunken impromptu rugby match, she left the all-male room to commune with her social media.

"I don't have a whole lot," said Cooper, in a valiant effort to right the ship of broken men clinging to busted masts. "I built a porch over the weekend before the rains came, and I look forward to sitting there and enjoying the view. I don't see much point in relationships anymore, for precisely that reason." He swung his head to his right.

The Tough Guy Book Club meeting circled around the table. William had set the tone, and everyone acknowledged his grief with reserved compassion. Most of them had mundane activities to report. One had gone out in his boat and pulled in some nice blue cod, a delicacy in New Zealand. Another had installed a new gearbox on his four-wheel drive, and that ate up his weekend. Halfway through, the server reappeared and everyone—and I mean *every*one!—reordered. Speight's for the lot of them, as if they owned stock in the company. Must have been a half-off special and Hughie was picking up the tab! What the hell, I thought. Hana no longer monitoring me, I raised my hand, too, and an animated cheer went up as William's travails and dark memories ebbed out to sea and were buried underwater in Davy Jones's locker as the beer liberated our collective desideratum to bond, pound drums, wail with our ales in the face of personal perfidies. Locked in communal combat with the plentiful repository of our bleak memories, we *all* wanted to forget.

As the torch was passed from one "tough guy" to another with their short stories of what they had been up to in the month since they had last convened, I came to the conclusion most of them were single, lonely, tenacious souls, longing for a piece of some illusional pie they couldn't delineate. By the time we ended on Lucas, a short, wiry man with a wicked grin plastered on his face, all my speculations about this book club were aimed wildly off the mark. I had showed up prepared to parry inanities but instead had come across a different breed of men.

Lucas raised his cell phone for all to see. He flashed everyone a dark and grainy YouTube video of a man scuffling with a tall bird standing on its two feet. Between bouts of uncontrollable laughter he explained it was an ostrich and it had fought him like a "mean motherfucker" when he entered the pen where it was corralled. His laughter grew more moronic as he played the short clip over and over. That was his month. And with that recitation I had whiplashed to my initial presupposition of who constituted the Tough Guy Book Club.

"Put it away, Lucas," Garret reproached him, worried I might form an impression of his club he didn't want disseminated in my blog or a future book. Hand firmly planted on the rudder, he said, "We're here tonight to honor Miles Raymond and his new book, *A Year of Pure Feeling*. How many of you have read it?"

"All the way through?" one joked.

A show of hands went up. I wasn't surprised to learn only half had read it.

Garret led off with his commentary. "I thought the book was slow in starting, but it built in a personal and comic way like his first one and demonstrated his ability to blend comedy with pain and depth. The pain and depth of a man now past middle age."

Finding that to be a fair assessment, I nodded. By the time I published a book, I had lost all perspective, and though I didn't need any disparaging perspectives to affirm I had spent the last however many years of my life wasting my time, I desperately feasted on affirming words I had touched someone in the dark on their e-reader or on their commute while they listened to the audiobook version.

"I found it moving," said a burly, bald-headed guy wearing a T-shirt that read "Jesus Has Your Back," along with an image of a long-haired, white-robed Jesus with a red-faced Satan in a jujitsu hold. "It deals with male friendship in a way we don't usually get from books." He grew philosophical with eyes looking into his beer mug. "Men, unlike women, sit on a bench staring at a fixed point. Their friendship is based on their mutual fixation on that point. If that point disappears, so too goes the friendship." I liked his metaphor. It seemed to sum up Jack's and my relationship, and why men, men different from one another, can maintain a close bond. "I like how it defied my expectations of a novel," he eloquently summarized his critique. "How much of it is true?" he asked me.

"Emotionally, hundred percent," I answered. "In reality, fifty."

"Brave of you. If I wrote my true story and it got published, I'd get booted out of Oamaru."

Guttural laughter was evoked by his self-deprecation.

"If you *got* published," said one of the Tough Guys.

Ale glasses were raised. The club members' faces grew more rubicund in the dark, and for a moment I imagined I was trapped in a Renoir painting. I had recently read a book that posited if alcohol hadn't been discovered civilizations wouldn't have evolved, and hunter-and-gatherer humans would still be ravening one another like savages. Here at the bottom of New Zealand, the drink was knitting these men together in a skein of humanity, keeping them sane.

"Mostly what I like is fantasy and sci-fi," said a guy self-introduced as Gerald, "so I found it uncomfortably too real at times." I didn't take this as a criticism but rather as an admission of his bias and why it had been a difficult read for him. "But it had a lot of moments I could relate to. Especially the pain of his infidelities, and the hopelessness of his loneliness."

"Does anyone have any questions for Miles?" Garret addressed the club members, a gimlet eye on his watch.

A thoughtful-looking man sitting in the middle raised his hand barely above his shoulder. Garret nodded at him. He turned to me: "Where do you get your ideas?"

I took a ruminative sip from my ale. "Real life," I replied. "Always real life. I write only out of reality because I use writing as an unwitting form of therapy, though I don't recommend it as a substitute for therapy because there's a good chance it'll hurl you into real therapy in the end.

And I'll spare you my jeremiad of the perils of being a professional writer."

Collective chuckling closed over my words. They seemed both excited and nervous to have a real, professionally published author at eye level, mug of ale in hand. Books for them were a *via regia* to something else, a low common denominator—that fixed point on the horizon— and a way to connect with one another.

Another hand shot up, drawing my attention to a goateed man at the far end of the table. His mind rubbed some ideas together and produced a spark. "You spoke earlier about the death of literature. Could you elaborate on that?" Beers were sipped in contemplation. They had started a club centered around books, and they genuinely must have felt my eschatological literary vision disconcerting, or paradoxical at the least.

"Well," I started, feeling large, "I believe in books as the savior of humankind because without reading we would have no way of growing cognitively." I tapped my temple with a forefinger. "I want to be clear on that point. I've given my life to literature and storytelling, but I'm witnessing a devolution in this Age of the Anthropocene." I held up my iPhone. "This guy, and the portals to the cosmology it unleashes to us, is destroying us." I could sense my discontent was being met with ambivalence and reticent alarm. Revved up on two wines and three beers, I concluded, "But here, in Oamaru, at the end of the world, at least to a guy like me from California, a dozen guys converge on a place named Fat Sally's Pub to talk about books. In this moment, I'm feeling a touch of hope. Because of the Tough Guy Book Club." I raised my mug in a toast to them.

Cheers, along with mugs, went up. I wasn't known among my friends for inspirational speeches, but it had been a bone-achingly long day in that camper van, these working-class Kiwi men had come together to read and talk about my new book, so why contaminate the mood with a stem-winder on the death of culture and the nearby Thwaites Glacier (a.k.a. the Doomsday Glacier) melting at an alarming rate, sea levels rising, little hope for planet Earth, let alone the millions of books soon to be suspended waterlogged in repositories resembling the lost city of Atlantis, gloomed faces of underwater archaeologists peering at them through full face masks and wondering what they were. Books, like arrowheads, I had thought while writing *A Year of Pure Feeling*, were only a blip, an evanescent scintilla of light, appearing on the four hundred eighty million years of planet Earth's embryonic experiment with existence and soon its horrible conclusion.

"And on that note," I said, pausing dramatically, "the drinks are on me!"

Another cheer went up. I felt a hand on my shoulder. I threw a backward glance and saw Jack looking down at me and grinning. "Way to wrap up, Homes. Didn't understand a fucking word."

"Well," Garret said, "I think that brings us to the end of another Tough Guy Book Club." He rotated his rosy-colored face toward mine and smiled at me through the phalanx of other ruddy faces and said, "We want to thank you, Miles, for visiting us here . . . *at the end of the world*"—mordant laughter caused him to pause, as obviously they didn't see their hometown as the end of the world—"and we appreciate your braving the Pig Route and the storm of the century to come grace us with your presence. So, now, as is the tradition when we welcome a new member, we're making you an honorary goon." He passed something to the member next to him, and he passed it along until it reached me. I held it up in the dim light. It was a decal of their logo: a skull with ominous black eyes and "Tough Guy Book Club" lettered in a circle around it.

I stared at it and said to the decal, "I'm honored to be inducted into your club. I'm honored to be an official goon. I'm honored you deigned to read my book and produce such insightful commentary. And I appreciate you bought a dozen copies. That might be all I sell."

Sardonic laughter exploded from the inebriated members. Mugs were raised in yet another toast. The members shuffled to their feet, splintered into small groups, and broke into conversations inaudible and, at times, due to the Kiwi patois, unintelligible to me.

I turned to Jack. "It went well."

"You're an honorary goon, Miles."

"What happened with the stage-four clinger?" I asked, assuming he'd slipped away to talk to his new girlfriend.

Jack's face grew stony and his jaw jutted out in defiance. "She wants to come join us."

"No, man, no," I said, alarmed. "You told her where we were?"

"Roughly. I had to. We're in a relationship."

"Wow, Jack in yet another relationship." I poked him in the ribs. "I guess her being an actress, you don't know if it's you or the booze."

"And I honestly don't care," Jack said, toasting me with probably his fourth or fifth glass of Three Miners.

The server reappeared for the umpteenth time and everyone raucously ordered more beers. I assumed they were all walking home in this small town, or were taking advantage of my largesse to pick up the tab.

"Where's Hana?" I asked Jack.

He held open both hands in perplexity.

More beers clatteringly arrived on a pair of trays, and Jack ordered another wine in the ensuing clamor. Some of the Tough Guy members sidled over to me and wanted to engage in conversation. One of them was deliberating writing a memoir, and I gave him my standard adage of advice ("If you have a backup plan, you've already sown the seed of failure"). Another invited Jack and me to go off-roading with him to see "the real New Zealand." I parried his offer with a promise to revisit it after the book tour with the excuse, "I sincerely do want to see the end of the world."

He grabbed my head with both hands and brought our foreheads together in some male-bonding blood pact out of another century. Through his beer-scented breath, he implored, "You need to get into the bush."

"Damn right I need to get into the bush."

Eavesdropping, Jack howled with laughter, and then so did the Tough Guy.

The mugs of beer kept flowing in from the server, who seemed to enjoy the attention. My eyes swept the pub for Hana, my savior, but she wasn't around. I thought about texting her, but in the lacunae when drinks keep imprudently coming and one isn't thinking in a linearly rational fashion, a guy self-identified as Cooper asked Jack and me if we wanted to go to another party and "meet a couple of birds named

Ashleigh and Shirley." "Shirley's a huge fan of your work," he assured me. From over his shoulder salacious chuckling underscored his affirmation.

Jack, fearing the oppression of his new "committed" relationship and buying a few days of precious freedom from it, hooked an arm around my shoulders and urged, "Let's go, dude. This could be fun. Plus, you're single now."

The next thing I remember, Jack and I were bouncing up and down in the rear of a jeep slicing through the desolate streets of Oamaru, caravanning with other members of the Tough Guy Book Club into the forbidding storm-ravaged night. Roads are unilluminated in most of New Zealand, and soon we were barreling down a dirt switchback lit only by the spraying headlights of our vehicles. More cans of beer were cracked open. Jack was whooping it up with the Tough Guys. He kept asking them about Ashleigh and Shirley, revving up his dimming, but still flickering, libidinous fantasies. Having had little to drink in the previous months, I could feel the booze hoisting me to another reality where the trapdoor springs, intemperance kicks in, and I'm once again in helpless free fall.

More alcohol-fueled gaps in my memory, and soon we crash-landed out in the middle of nowhere, rubbing our frozen hands, exhalations misting in pillars from our mouths. All the cars that had caravanned out with us were parked in a circle around a giant pen circumscribed by a waist-high split-rail fence, their high beams switched on, illuminating the football field–sized enclosure. All the members, only an hour previously contemplating the depths of my new literary work of genius, were now sitting on the hoods of their cars, popping open more cans of beer, foam geysering, laughter growing more rowdy by the minute. A staggering Cooper led befuddled Jack and me, playing along like good sports, through a hinged gate into the middle of the pen. My questions and protestations were met with, "Wait until you meet Ashleigh and Shirley," he shouted, bent at the waist, swinging his arms apelike.

Coming from Hollywood, Jack and I had seen it all. Or so we thought. It's a wicked place, with profane people climbing over the backs of one another with a desperate greed that knows no empathy. But this was a whole new fucked-up down here on the outskirts of Oamaru, on the south of the South Island of New Zealand, in the dead of the night—what time was it anyway?!—as a gate swung open and two ostriches, tall as humans, bolted into the pen, stopped, reared up, and blinked at Jack and me with enormous watching eyes. Then, espying the wobbly, discombobulated pair of men trapped in the pen with them, they sighted down their sharp aquiline beaks at the hapless two of us, frozen in place like the wax mannequins overimbibition had transmogrified us into.

"Meet Ashleigh and Shirley!" cackled a shit-faced Cooper as barking laughter erupted from various spectating stations on the split-rail fence occupied by the neoprimitives of this previously somber, male-bonding book club.

And then Ashleigh and Shirley—the fangirls Jack and I had come to meet—charged.

CHAPTER 10

"If you hadn't written that fucking scene about the ostrich in your first book, they wouldn't have had the idea," Jack said from his perch above the cockpit where he was swaddled in blankets.

"I made you famous, motherfucker," I said, standing below him at the stove, pouring water into the kettle boiler and getting ready to grind some beans with my hand grinder.

"That was twisted." Jack swung his legs over the side of the cushions, preparing to jump down. He shivered. "What happened to the heat?"

"I don't know. You were the one checked out on the Beast. It's fucking cold."

"I know it's fucking cold."

"Watch out for Max," I nearly screamed at Jack.

"Relax, Miles. Relax. You're a little jumpy this morning."

Max was pancaked on all fours in the space between the cockpit seats, scarfing his breakfast. Now and then he stopped, looked up, and weighed the lethality of an unbidden, mysterious sound that only he heard, then went back to eating. Rain lashed at the enormous front windshield, blurring the outside. In a small cup, I weighed coffee beans on my digital scale and emptied them into my grinder. "Do you want a Panama pour-over?" I asked Jack. "Gesha. Light roast."

"Gesha. Light roast. Fuck off. Yeah, caffeine anything. Head's pounding something fierce. We wouldn't have gotten into that situation with those guys if you hadn't overimbibed."

"It was a long day, and I felt like drinking, and I didn't see you trying to put the brakes on."

Jack opened the door to the toilet/shower combo and prepared to sausage himself inside.

"Please do not take a dump in there," I said. Even Max glanced up from his food bowl in consternation.

"I was checking it out for its shower possibilities."

"If the heater's not working, I doubt there's going to be any hot water."

Jack closed the door to the combo chamber and clambered his way to the dinette cushions and plopped down, raking a hand through his greasy locks. I ground my Panama beans and produced two perfect pour-overs, the only civil thing about the morning.

Jack wiped the fog from one of the windows and peered out, his expression grim. "Where the fuck did we park last night?"

"Hana rescued us from those guys who wanted us to box with those ostriches—don't you remember?—and said she didn't have time to get us into a proper campground, or it was closed or some bullshit."

Max began meowing, but not in a thank-you-for-breakfast way, but as if he sensed something beyond the reach of human audial capabilities.

"What's wrong, little guy?" I said as I sipped my coffee in the front seat as an unhappy, unbathed Jack wriggled into his street clothes in the back.

Max, growing increasingly agitated, replied with hissing and growling.

"Max man," I said, concerned, bending down to stroke his head.

The oddest sounds suddenly pierced the camper van. Shrill, high-pitched purring noises filled my ears, punctuated by cawing calls the likes of which I had never heard before. I turned on the windshield wipers. We were parked on a hill overlooking the Pacific. Fanning out before me were dark, knee-high shapes waddling toward the ocean.

"Check this out, Jack."

Jack swung open the passenger compartment door. "Holy shit," he said, eyes tented with a flattened hand, squinting into the harsh dawn sunlight.

"It's the blue penguins," I said.

"The blue penguins?"

"Remember those Tough Guy fucks telling us we had to wake early to see the blue penguins who live under these buildings here in Oamaru? The males head out in the morning to fish, return with their catch for the females and their nestlings."

"Don't remember that. I was trying to dodge a charging ostrich!" Jack stepped down out of the camper-van side door onto the street. I opened the passenger door and climbed down off the step and stood next to him. The rain poured down on us, but it was a once-in-a-life-time moment not to be missed, and we both sensed it in our shivery, wretched, post–Tough Guy Book Club, ostrich-encounter misery. The camper van was parked in a warehouse district on Humber Street. The two dozen or so penguins were marching toward a rising sun spilling a light fire onto the rim of the ocean. More animated now, they doddered across the road, over a winter-brown fescue-overgrown knoll, impervious to the pouring rain, vectoring to the Pacific, the source of their sustenance. There was something simple in their routine, something intrepid and unhesitating in their military-style march, knowing, as they trekked inexorably toward cold, deep waters, some of their flock would not return. It was equal parts fascinating and heartbreaking to witness.

"Surreal," was all I could muster. "That's how close we are to the end of the world."

Jack shook his head in amazement, then, arms wrapped around his torso, climbed back into the camper van. I hoisted myself back up into the front seat and reclaimed my thermos of Panama from the cup holder. With the high-pitched sound of the blue penguins in retreat, Max had calmed and resumed eating.

In the passenger compartment, Jack was swiping left and right on the control panel with an urgent index finger. "Fuck, I forgot to switch the heat on," he beat up on himself. He angrily tapped a few icons, rubbed his hands together, then said, "Get us an internet connection,

Miles, and where the fuck is our publicist? We need to ask her what happened last night."

I laughed in solidarity, mutual oblivion our raison d'être and bête noire. "We were TKO'd by a pair of ostriches before the opening bell and a club of lonely Kiwi men got the laugh of their lifetime at our expense, that's what happened. And one day we'll laugh about it, too, but I'm glad we made it back in one piece and they weren't some twisted fucks out to murder us."

"Hear, hear. They were still twisted fucks. Shirley and Ashleigh? Jesus. Miles, we've been around the block a few more times than many, how the fuck did we fall for that high school prank?"

"I don't know, man, but you were hot to trot."

"Yeah, I thought maybe they were rewarding us for your celebrity participation, but Oamaru? Jesus. What is wrong with us?"

"We lost our bullshit compass, that's what happened."

"I mean, for a minute there I thought they were all thoughtful and book minded and shit."

"They were, until they got half a dozen ales in their bellies and collectively decided *we* were now *their* prey."

Jack shook his head in his hands in mock self-disgust.

I switched on my mobile hot spot and threw Jack a backward glance. "It's on. Password is *maxthewritercat*, all lowercase."

Jack smiled and shook his head. "Okay. Good." He sipped his coffee. "Coffee's awesome. Not so much this camping site."

I texted Hana with a pecking finger.

"Be there in a few," she voice-texted back.

"Saw the blue penguins," I informed her.

She didn't text back. The new generation! Leaving us older guys suspended in apprehension.

"That was truly fucked up last night," Jack said to his importuning phone pinging with messages as soon as he logged on to my Wi-Fi. "And trust me, Homes, I've seen some fucked-up shit."

"They were just having fun. There were some intelligent comments about my novel, I thought. Until they went off the precipice."

"Hana went deep for that one," Jack said. "What happened to nice big lighted bookstores and your fans sitting in fold-up chairs, and more than half of them being beautiful, adoring women who think you're a rock star?"

"Those days are history. The chain bookstores are gone. It's book clubs now, I guess. Soon, authors will be chased down dark alleys by rats the size of golden retrievers as the youth sit in penthouses and spectate on huge screens like we're in a video game titled *The Book Tour*."

Jack chortled. "What's on the schedule for tonight?"

"I have no idea. I just wait for my marching orders. And like the blue penguins following their instinct, I go where I'm told." I placed my hand on top of Max's head. "I expect little from this life," I said. "I gave up everything for literature and film, and it's dispiriting to know I'm going out to sea with the blue penguins, a relic of the past."

"Pretty grim for seven thirty in the morning," Jack said.

"Seven thirty in the morning is grim, period," I said. "Just waxing a tad emotional, don't reproach me, it's been a lonely couple of years."

"Except for Ella."

"Except for Ella."

"And Max."

"And Max, true."

"You dwell too much on the past, Miles."

"If you had lived my past, you would, too."

"No, actually, I would do the opposite."

"It comes without warning."

"Like the shit last night," Jack said, shuddering to himself at the mortifying memory.

"What's up with the stage-four clinger?" I abruptly changed the subject.

Jack shook his head in disgust. "One of those Tough Guy fuckers, or our Hana, posted us on social media, and now she knows my precise location."

I laughed uneasily. "No, not precisely," I said, staring out the windshield at the bleak and barren frontage road at Oamaru's oceanfront edge. "We don't even know our precise location."

"Well, she seems to."

Knuckles rapped at the door. Jack rose, clomped two steps, and opened it. He backed into the lounge area when Hana climbed up into the passenger compartment and closed the door behind her. She looked bedraggled, like she, too, had had a rough night. I neither saw nor smelled evidence of a shower. Her black combat boots lent her an imperious look.

"How are you lads doing?"

"How'd you know where to find us last night?" I said.

"We did a Share My Location," she said, staring into her phone.

"When?"

"Last night."

"I don't remember that."

"Of course you don't remember. You were both pissed." She glowered at Jack.

"I'd had a few," I confessed. "I thought it went well, though."

"It did." She stared off. "Until it didn't."

"Until the fucked-up end," Jack said.

Sensing recrimination from Jack and waxing defensive, she turned sharply to face us. "Not my fault," she said. "If it wasn't for me, you blokes would be face down in the mud with ostrich poop on you." She thought the grand finale was hilarious and laughed at the memory.

"I'm not feeling the humor," Jack said.

"We appreciate you rescuing us," I said in an effort to smooth over the simmering rancor.

"Next time you go on a walkabout, take yourfuckingwalkietalkie, will you? Fuck, drove all around trying to get a cell signal." Hana looked up from her phone. She glanced back and forth between me and Jack. "Did you seriously think they had a couple of loose Kiwi women waiting for you out in the bush?" She shook her head and laughed uproariously. "Aren't you a little old for that?"

Jack and I both experienced a tacit moment of past-middle-age disgrace, our eyes cast downward, her stinging rebuke buzzing in the air.

"But tonight might be your lucky night," Hana said cheerfully.

"Why's that?" asked a curious, and now caffeinated, Jack.

With jumping thumbs Hana finished replying to someone via text, shoved her phone into her purse, then started toward the door. "We've got to get going."

"What's tonight?" I inquired.

"The Cougars of Christchurch Book Club."

Jack slowly broke into a smile. "Let the games begin," he said with the lopsided grin of lechery.

CHAPTER 11

The "storm of the century" had not abated. We were at sea level now, hugging the sublimely gorgeous coastline, and weren't facing any challenging mountain passes, so the threat of snow closing roads and sending us hurtling on another Pig Route had diminished, but the persistent rain made the going tough in the unwieldy camper van. The winds lashed at it. Provisions and kitchenware rattled in the secured cabinets and drawers.

"The Cougars of Christchurch Book Club." Jack couldn't stop laughing at Hana's title of the next stop on the book tour.

"Book tours have evolved, or devolved," I said, to Jack's bottomless mirth. "Wherever there are readers, there are potential sales," I rationalized.

"Brother, you are on some kind of literary journey," Jack bellowed through eye-watering laughter, unable to comprehend, or empathize with, the fate of the contemporary author. He shook his head in bemusement and adjusted the rearview mirror.

Riding shotgun, I had Max cradled in my lap and he had the gimlet eye on the windshield again. Every buffeting of the lashing wind startled him. After a year of the peace and quiet of Prophet's Rock, the strange noises of New Zealand's winter discomfited him. My hands gripped him tight so he couldn't dart into the back, where I feared he could get into trouble, lose his balance, hurt himself getting knocked around, or find some place to hide where we couldn't get him out.

"We're going to the Cougars of Christchurch Book Club, Max man," I said out loud to him, petting his head.

"You need to talk to him, don't you?" Jack said.

"He's my conscience. He keeps me on the straight and narrow. There's a current of understanding that emanates from him I can't put into words. He's the mirror I hold up to my soul."

Jack shot me a dismissive look. He hated when I waxed philosophical. "Didn't know you were a cat guy."

"I didn't either until I got Max. A lot of writers were. Chandler. Highsmith. Hemingway . . ."

"Okay, okay." He nodded, eyes fixed on the road ahead. "Amanda has a golden Labradoodle."

I shuddered at the image of the two of them with what I could only interpret as canine bling. "The neediness of dogs saps me of energy."

"I hear you," Jack said, the creases lining his face drawing him momentarily into the vortex of an uncharacteristically downcast look.

"Does the *Washed-Up Celebrities* hosting gig pay well?" I asked Jack, wanting to veer off the subject of pets and the sentimentalities they evoke.

"It does," Jack said, "it does. And if it gets picked up and they don't bump me for someone younger, then I guess I might be moving permanently to Oz."

"And the stage-four clinger?"

"I don't know, man." He shook his head in self-reproach. "She has a pretty nice pad in Byron Bay, and I can't deny I like it there. She's possessive as hell, but she also made this *Washed-Up Celebrities* happen, so give her credit. Of course, I didn't want to tell her—"

"You're shit low on cash and have no future?"

Jack smirked. "Something along those lines. She googled me on CelebrityNetWorth, and apparently I'm worth two million." Jack howled in amusement at the thought.

"I'm supposedly worth five."

"You should be. What if those CelebrityNetWorth fuckers saw us now?"

"I'm guessing we'd get downgraded. To reality."

"To reality," Jack echoed with emphasis. "What the hell is *reality*?"

The road from Oamaru to Christchurch snaked along the ocean on a winding, narrow road with few turnouts. Here and there intrepid fishing boats burned black dots against the enormous east of the Pacific. We lumbered by farmland and ranchland, sheep and cattle ubiquitously predominant, as one might expect in a country as verdant as New Zealand.

"Who's the mother of your daughter?" Jack said.

"A beautiful woman who lied to me."

"How so?"

"It's too painful to go into. I'm still processing that email and how it's upturned my life." I turned to Jack. "I don't want it to be a cloud hanging over this trip of ours." I patted him on the shoulder. "It's been five years, Jackson."

Jack smiled. "Yes. It has. Too long."

"I try to live alone to avoid complications," I began by way of an explanation. "Then you meet someone new, and like metal filings to a magnet, you're drawn inexorably back in. With their warmth. Their insight. Sometimes their inspiring presence."

"And their fuckability."

"A word I wouldn't use to describe our better half, but yeah, that too."

"That's the conundrum in a nutshell."

"*Conundrum.* Isn't that a ten-dollar word for you, big guy?"

"Wasn't that the name of the publisher who turned down your first novel, the one that *didn't* get published, not to raise a sore subject?"

"Yeah," I said ruefully. "Don't remind me." I stroked Max's head and scratched him behind the ears. "But back to the *conundrum* of women. It's wonderful at first. You feel reborn. But in my case, the next phase is always the makeover one." I turned to Jack. "You know that Maya—"

"The Santa Ynez Valley beauty?"

"Right. She advised me to burn the book that is my legacy work."

"You should have left the cunnilingus-on-the-golf-course part out, dude. Talk about shooting a hole in one!"

I laughed in spite of myself. "You know I bare my soul when I write."

"A tad too much sometimes," he said, shaking his head. "And I thought Maya had it going on."

"I thought she was everything, but I had to let her go on aesthetic grounds. And it hurt. But it hurt me worse she hated the book I wrote about our adventure. You know what she said to me?" Jack shook his head. "To my face, she said, accusatorily, almost irately, 'How can you be so personal?' Offended, I said, 'How can I not?' Isn't being personal the definition of art?" I said to the fur of Max, which I stroked unstoppably to keep him calm, more for my comfort than his, though I knew it comforted him, too.

"Grab me a beer back there. I need something to take the edge off. I'm still traumatized by those fucking ostriches." He exaggerated a shudder.

"Yeah, we won't go there," I said, laughing.

"Please don't." He wagged a finger at me. "And don't put that in your next book! It'll make me look bad."

"Don't flatter yourself." I set Max on the passenger seat, jack-knifed over into the rear compartment, and unlatched the refrigerator. I found Jack a Searchlight Brewery Thieving Bastard ale, which Hana had stocked, and which made me chuckle because I wondered if she was sending us a message in code. On the can with its riot of colors was featured a lizard-like dinosaur, its mouth hung open and its teeth bared as if readying to go to battle against another primordial creature of its cruel era. For myself I hooked a finger around the neck of a terpene soda and climbed back up into the cab, repositioned Max on my lap, passed Jack his beer.

"Thank you, man."

Out the windshield the clouds had been torn apart by enormous invisible hands, and the first patch of blue in days greeted our eyes and splashed the dash with a mottling of sunshine. We both instinctively donned our sunglasses, another first. In our camper van, all we needed now was a pair of sheep sweaters and some steaming mince pies and the expat conversion would have been complete.

Jack pulled on his can of beer with a quiet desperation. In his grooved expression he seemed to signal he needed it. Can half-emptied, his face was reddening perceptibly, and he crossed from the edginess of the morning to the bluing afternoon, where the selfsame burrs were sanded down with the fine grit of a low-alcohol beverage.

"What's that you're drinking?" Jack said with a quick sidelong look. His beard had come in and he scratched the side nearest to me.

"A terpene-infused drink," I said with deliberate inscrutability.

"A what?"

"Terpene. Compounds found in plants, including cannabis. Supposed to be healing."

"I thought you didn't believe in that wellness shit."

I pouched out a cheek with my tongue. A dark wave broke over me. "Ella said it might be good for the neoplasm." I turned to Jack. "Look, truth be told, I don't have the health insurance to take care of it. One of the other reasons Ella was pressuring me to get married. I could soak New Zealand's generous national healthcare system." I threw up a hand. "But that's out the window now. If it's cancer, I'm fucked, okay?"

"Get it biopsied, man. I'll pay for it."

I shook my head.

"When's the last time you looked at it?"

"I don't remember. I only know it's burgeoning and darkening at the gates to my gonads."

"Miles, man," Jack wailed, "I can't lose you."

"If it's malignant, I wouldn't be able to go on this book tour." I turned to Jack, slapped him facetiously on the knee. "And I wouldn't have missed this for anything."

"Fuck off, Miles, this is serious shit now. You leave the planet and I'm only half of who I am, and that's me getting personal and I don't need a sarcastic comeback."

"I can't deal with it. Too much other shit going on."

Jack's nearly drained IPA produced an animated look on his face.

"Miles, you can't go out on me. The loss would be incalculable. Why not at least get it biopsied?"

"Because I don't want to know," I exploded, hoping the sharpness of my words would end the subject, and now regretting I had ever mentioned it.

"Drink some of your terpene soda, man, and calm down."

I took a sip and nodded. I stroked Max's head, then massaged his whiskers with my index finger. "Max is going to outlive me," I said in an undertone.

"Don't say that, Miles. *Max is going to outlive me*," he mocked. Jack shook his head in disgust.

"His perpetual look of awe and wonder at the world does fill me with hope," I said to the passing countryside.

"You're losing your edge, Miles."

"May-be."

"Look, I have a confession." He waited for me to respond.

"What?!"

"You remember you gave me an early peek at your new book."

"Figured you wouldn't read it, so I wasn't worried about the reaction."

"I read, Miles. And not just doomscrolling and tabloid shit on the internet. Real books."

"I know you do, man, I know you do."

"And I also, as you know, occasionally produce." He looked at me with widened eyes. "And guess what?"

"What?"

"I've got Dan O'Neill attached to star in and direct *A Year of Pure Feeling*."

"What?" I said, that carrot-at-the-end-of-the-stick excitement rising in me once again for the umpteenth time, the way it does to us veteran Hollywood moths to the proverbial flame of cynical optimists. "Dan O'Neill. Mr. *Age of Uncertainty*?"

"Yep. And he flipped for it," Jack said. "Loved it!"

"How'd you get to him?"

Jack rolled his tongue over his front teeth, promoting the seed of a specious answer.

"Jack?"

"The stage-four clinger," he finally admitted. "She knows him."

"Oh, great."

"Doesn't matter. Dan said your story had so much depth and pain, and comedy, too."

"Dan O'Neill wants to turn *A Year of Pure Feeling* into a feature film?"

"Yep. Dan O'Neill, legendary Kiwi actor, multiple Oscar nominee, wants to do it, yep."

I swiveled my head to look out the window, a smile creasing my face and laughter of delight wanting to escape. I longed to be one of those lambs grazing on the radiant green grass. I longed to be a Kiwi bird soaring over these pristine landscapes. It must be what death feels like, I epiphanized.

"What are the next steps?" I inquired cagily, always on the qui vive for the prevarication designed to lift my mood.

"We start rounding up the usual suspects," Jack said. He turned to me. "Assuming you're on board." He cleared his throat. "I need you to sign on the dotted line when the team can get all huddled together."

"Aha! Multiple ulterior motives. The possible documentary of this book tour, the book-to-film deal . . ." I laughed out loud. "Always working an angle, Jack. Always trying to leverage something." I shook my head, delight and execration clenched in the talons of their holy marriage.

"Hey, don't be like that," he said, feigning hurt. "There's money in this for you, brother."

"Who's doing the adaptation?"

"You are, of course."

"Writers Guild minimum, I'm assuming."

"More than WGA minimum." He turned to me. "And it'll get you back on your health insurance so you can get that neo-thing looked at and don't have to be conscripted into marriage to stave off a premature death."

Believing him, I said, "I'll need it now that the marriage is off." I fingered the engagement ring bobbing on my sternum, looked at it wistfully. Dan O'Neill, if he put his weight to it, probably could get my book made into a film, and that's where the real money was. He could hoist me out of the doghouse of no health insurance and buy me another half hectare of Pinot if I decided to return. In the scudding of a single cloud, Jack had transited from a beleaguered wingman to an angelic savior.

Reality stomped open the door when Hana's voice crackled over the walkie-talkie: "We can shower at the venue," she trilled. "And park and camp there."

I reached for the walkie-talkie and hit the press-to-talk button. "Thanks for the update, Hana. A shower would be an improvement over last night's debacle."

Jack looked at me and nodded. "All right."

"All right. Hot showers. Movie deal. Mood definitely improving. I think I'm going to celebrate and pop that Quartz Reef bubbly I've had my eye on."

"Now you're talking."

I slithered into the back. "And you'd better keep fucking that stage-four clinger," I said. "Get a refill on those ED meds, if you have to. My treat."

"I'm not there yet." Jack tooted the horn to no one. "Cougars of Christchurch, here we come."

CHAPTER 12

It was nearing dark when we pulled into the tautologically named Christchurch. I didn't want to grill Jack too much on the Dan O'Neill connection and movie deal until I learned more details. Having to re-invent myself as a novelist in New Zealand, I felt a sense of uplift, a scintilla of redemption.

Christchurch had suffered a devastating earthquake a few years back and was currently in the process of rebuilding. Among construction sites scarred by cranes reaching to the sky, we glimpsed beautiful new, modern buildings that had sprung up in the renovation aftermath of the quake. New Zealand had come together and rallied around the destruction.

We followed Hana's Subaru up a tortuous, hair-pinning road too narrow for the hulking camper van to the top of Mount Pleasant and the house where the no-doubt self-deprecatingly, risibly named Cougars of Christchurch Book Club held their monthly get-togethers. Surely they couldn't be serious. Surely they were being humorous with the club's name alliteration and the blaring of attention to their ages. I had reached the point in life where nothing surprised me. Henry Miller once said at age twenty he thought he knew everything, but by age fifty he be-lieved he knew nothing. That's because life is too surreal. The accretion of lived experiences only produces more befuddlement, not more clarity.

We heaved the camper van into an enormous driveway that fronted one side of a two-story house cantilevered over the steep hillside, sprung white like a giant, ostentatious mushroom. In the driveway, our camper van competed for space with an enormous speedboat mounted on a trailer, the kind seafaring men pilot into treacherous oceans. Fishing rods rose from the rear and speared the twilight sky. Appeared the host's husband was an avid sportsman.

Jack and I—the Quartz Reef rosé bubbly demolished and feeling a little tipsy as a result—clambered out of the camper van and drank in the view. We were tired, our bodies straightened against the creaking of aching bones, but the champagne had lightened our moods, soothed what the depredations of age exacted on one with hours logged on the road in buffeting winds and blinding rains in a vehicle no one should be piloting in these climes. Apparently, Hana had noticed, because before we could get prepped on the Cougars event, she was holding up the empty Quartz Reef bubbly we had killed and shook it at us reproachfully.

"Getting an early start, lads," she mocked, thrusting the bottle in our faces as one shoves a puppy's face into its own poop.

"Three-hour sipping, Hana," Jack said. "Relax. We're fine. We just sandpapered the edges."

"Laid the Pinot base for the Cougars of Christchurch," I added for good measure.

Dropping the bottle to her side, Hana was unamused by our facetiousness. Her wide nostrils flared with an angry exhalation. She'd been warned of Jack's and my predilection for overimbibition, and in her expression was a downturned look of failure.

Jack swung around and faced the harbor, arms outstretched in a eureka moment. The sun spilled on his brown locks and highlighted where they were frosted with gray. The panoramic view overlooked an estuary that fed out to a cold ocean blistered with whitecaps from the unceasing wind. "These folks must have serious coin," he said.

"Come on, let's go, lads," said Hana, hustling us along. "Grab your clothes and toiletries." Jack and I faced her. "And wear something nice. Button-up shirt. Jacket. I want you to look like proper celebrities."

"Hana," I said, still feeling a little large from the half bottle of bubbly,

"I'm an artist. Artists don't dress up. If you show up sartorially sharp, they don't believe you're an artist."

"These are society ladies. Their idea of artists is different than yours. Besides, Hughie instructed me to advise you to wear your finest. He wants you lookingfuckingnice, all right?"

Jack and I looked at each other, smiled, shrugged. "Whatever you say, sugar," Jack said.

"Don't call me *sugar*, Jack."

"Forgive him. He reverts to the atavistic now and then."

Hana narrowed her eyes at me at the word *atavistic*. "I'm going to look that up."

Jack and I rummaged in our luggage for clothes and shaving gear and met Hana at the wide double doors that led into the hilltop estate. We were greeted by a diminutive mustachioed man smartly dressed in slacks, a shirt, and a blazer. He was introduced as Peter. "Right this way, Miles and Jack," he said, beckoning us in with an outstretched arm.

We walked into the house with Hana in tow, paused in the foyer, and marveled at the vast, high-ceilinged living room.

"Where are the Cougars?" Jack queried Peter. Hana elbowed Jack in the ribs. "Forgive me. The lovely ladies hosting this book club," he rephrased with affected emphasis.

"They're at the country club," Peter said, without elaborating. "Let me show you gentlemen the bathrooms."

"Gentlemen," Jack whispered to me and Hana, nodding. Hana smirked at him.

Peter led Jack to a bathroom downstairs, then returned upstairs to escort me to an en suite doozy in the master bedroom. A picture window looked out cinematically onto the ocean to the east and Christchurch to the west, now scintillant with multicolored lights pricking the night sky. A ceiling mirror suggested the couple who lived here enjoyed watching themselves copulating. I'll never understand that kink, I mused to myself. Who wants to look at themselves fucking? Apparently, men who go fishing for bluefin tuna. Or women with Brazilian butt lifts.

The showerhead was a foot in diameter and rained water over me as though Christchurch had never suffered a drought. I luxuriated under it, stretching my shoulders, pulling slow strokes with my razor underneath my beard, which I had moments ago taken scissors to and trimmed down to less primordial magnitude. I was feeling in a slightly ebullient mood, despite all the portents on the horizon—the face-the-music return to California; Ella calling it quits with me; the potentially cancerous neoplasm plaguing me with thoughts of mortality—and I thought it was high time for an adjustment in the hirsute department. I drew one hand over my face, and when it had reappeared, I didn't think I looked all that old, maybe even a few years younger than my age. Had New Zealand rejuvenated me somehow? Had a relationship with regular sex revivified me to my university virility? Despite his denials to the contrary, Jack was on the ED meds already, but not me.

"You look nice, Miles," Hana said approvingly as Jack and I emerged from the house, he in a designer navy bowling shirt under a black bomber jacket with *Washed-Up Celebrities* stitched on the back, a gift from the US production before its cancellation; me in a shawl-collar cardigan over a blue linen button-up shirt. With one foot on the stepladder, she beckoned us up into the passenger compartment for a run-through of the event.

Inside the van, Jack and I eased creakily into seats in the lounge area as Hana leaned against the stove, standing imposingly over us. She was wearing a simple combat boot with chunk heel and yellow threading that lent her more stature, not that she needed it. Her military jacket with the brass buttons had been paired with a different shirt, but it still conferred on her a look of authority. In the cramped space she also emitted a female hotness. Jack, in particular, was jumping out of his skin, but even he, too, was keenly aware those days where age wasn't a factor were in his past. We just grinned until it hurt.

"Okay," Hana said, clutching her hands together and shaking them twice to highlight her preamble and gain our undivided attention. "When I tell you it's time, we're going to go in. I want to make sure all the ladies are here so you can make a proper entrance."

"What's the big deal?" I said. "It's just a book club, right?"

"Right. But they want it to unfold in their orchestrated way." Jack and I exchanged puzzled looks. "They've never hosted an author of your stature before, so they've planned something a little different."

"I thought you said they had *The Luminaries* author Eleanor Catton back when? She won a Man Booker."

"They did. You're the first *male* author of prominence they've hosted, and the first non-Kiwi."

Jack caught my eye and nodded once as if saying, *Take the compliment.*

"Okay," I said. "To them, I'm a celebrity author."

Hana appeared nervous. She cracked knuckles on both hands, first one, then the other, the popping noises discomposing Jack and me. "This is Hughie's personal connection, so we need it to go smashing."

"How long have you been doing this PR gig, Hana?" Jack queried her, as her eyes were diverted to her ubiquitous phone.

"A couple years," she replied to the phone in an unconvincing tone.

"Ever do one with an author in a camper van?" I said.

"Nope." She barked a sardonic laugh. "This is a first for me." In her upbeat way, she added, "This could start a whole new trend in book tours."

"What's this *orchestrated* program?" I said. "Do you know?"

"I don't, no." She looked up from her phone. "They might have you read, they might just want you to field questions about your writing process, I don't know. Go with the flow. Wherever it goes."

"We like to improvise," Jack, dressed for damage, said with an impish grin. "We welcome the unexpected, don't we, Miles?"

Hana stabbed a bejeweled forefinger at the empty bottle of Quartz Reef on the counter. "And go light on the grape, lads."

"Everyone here can hold their mugs," Jack informed her. "No need to kill the vibe."

Hana ignored his reproval. "After the introductions, I'll be cutting out of here. You've got your camp spot here, you're all set." She glanced at a text lit up on her phone. "All right, they're ready for us." She looked up. "You boys behave now, okay?"

Jack and I rose cumbrously to our feet, heads bent to avoid the ceiling. Hana led us out of the camper van. We followed her across the asphalt driveway, past the mammoth powerboat with the two onboard Mercury engines, to the double front doors. She rang the chimes, and they seemed to reverberate inside as if activating sonorous bells in every room. Peter opened the door with a great flourish and a performative bow as if a prohibited substance had improved *his* mood, and let us pass by him with a dramatic sweep of an arm.

A raven-haired woman in flowy and silky print pants and an equally colorful halter top dangerously pulled down to a chasmic cleavage glided up to us, borne aloft on the magic carpet of obscene wealth. Bangles jangled at her wrists. Gold earrings with intricate patterns sparkled at both earlobes. Midforties, I guessed, put together and effervescent with personality. A flute of bubbly was held aloft in one hand, tilting precariously at an angle suggesting the festivities had already begun. "This must be Miles Raymond," she cooed through lips that looked unnatural.

"Miles, this is Eileen," Hana said.

I extended my hand.

She shook her head reprovingly. "Oh, come on, you can do better than that." With her free hand, she curled an arm around my neck and kissed me on both cheeks, reeking of champagne-and-cheese-scented breath. "I'm glad you agreed to come. We love living authors." She leaned forward and whispered, "Especially ones who risk the debauched." Laughter cackled out of her as my eyes widened in dismay.

Hana turned to Jack, who was smiling over my shoulder. "And this is Jack. *Washed-Up Celebrities.*"

"And other credits," Jack amplified.

"Jack," Eileen blustered, "there is definitely someone I want you to meet. A fellow thespian."

"Can't wait. Nice to meet you, Eileen." And they enthusiastically exchanged the European double kiss.

"Come on in," Eileen enthused, "and meet the Cougars of Christchurch." She cupped a hand around her mouth and insisted, "We're not really," with a twinkle of salacity in her eyes. "It's all for fun."

We trailed a traipsing Eileen inside, who skated across the foyer into her capacious house. Hana stayed back to exchange a few words with Peter standing sentry at the door. A dining room larger than most of the apartments I had lived in was centered by a baronial table littered with plates heaped with food: cheeses, cured meats, olives, quartered fruits, sliced baguettes, dips. Champagne from the eight unique wine regions of New Zealand sloshed in huge decorative pottery bowls filled with half-melted ice. A cork popped on one and foam spewed from its neck, but it didn't seem to bother the woman holding it. My eyes widened when I noticed a fat pâté formed into an arcing erect penis, cue ball and scrotum expertly crafted!

"Ladies, let me introduce you," Eileen said, a toggling beringed hand encouraging me to come closer to the table, her arm now hooked around my waist and pulling me nearer her warm, perspiry body. "This is the author Miles Raymond and his actor friend, Jack."

We were greeted by a chorus of "welcome" and "hello there" and other fulsome salutations from the well-dressed, 1 percent (I was guessing) Christchurch cognoscenti, the ones who supported the arts even in the face of catastrophic earthquakes and draconian pandemic lockdowns.

"Would you like some bubbles?" trilled a tall woman in a high-neck, structured houndstooth dress, accessorized at her voluptuous hips with an enormous black belt cinched by a gold buckle designed in the image of a roaring lion.

"We would," Jack said, beaming moronically, as if he had stumbled into a Kiwi salon of fin de siècle decadence on the heels of my book.

Two Baccarat flutes were produced and rosé champagne was poured and handed to Jack and me as Eileen launched into the introductions.

"That's Olivia," Eileen said, indicating the woman who had filled our flutes. Eileen threw her head to Jack with such force I thought her makeup was going to fly off: "She used to star on a soap up in Sydney, didn't you, dear?"

"I did," boomed Olivia in a baritone voice. "And I'm still big. It's the soaps that got small." Jack and I forced chuckles at the jokey paraphrastic reference to Gloria Swanson's famous line in *Sunset Boulevard*. She toasted Jack, who met her flute for flute with clinking gusto. "Yes, I used to be on TV. And I've done the boards, once with Geoffrey Rush."

"I'm impressed," Jack said, eyeing her with elevated interest. "We must . . ." He finished his sentence with a spiraling motion of his index finger inscribing an imaginary circle in the air saying *continue the conversation in private.*

Eileen directed our attention to the next woman in her book club soiree. "And this is my dear friend Sonia." Eileen pressed her mouth to my ear and whispered, "Recently divorced. Crypto queen extraordinaire, got out before the crash, not authentically Russian," before rearing up again. I shook Sonia's hand. She was wearing a one-shoulder silver dress, blinding to look at under the bright chandeliered lighting. From her ears hung pendulous massive gold panels encrusted with tiny glittering diamonds. A heavy choker of jewels shone around her neck, ostentatiously showing off her wealth.

"We need to talk," Sonia said over her flute. "Privately."

"After the book club," I said, chuckling nervously.

"*After* the book club," she echoed.

"And this is Colleen," Eileen continued the introductions.

Colleen, the youngest of the gaggle, perhaps late thirties, tossed me a vacuous smile, eyeing my wardrobe up and down with great trenchancy. "It's a pleasure to meet you, Miles. I confess I haven't read your book. But I want to! If only I could find the time." She tossed back half a glass of champagne, then broke into a smile that occupied half the real estate of her face.

I shrugged at her comment. Feeling uncomfortable in the setting, sweat trickling from my underarms, I discreetly sipped my champagne for liquid courage, then had my attention directed to Ava, a voluptuous woman shoehorned into a black pleather minidress and plunging-neckline sweater top. The pleather mini produced the same noises the blue penguins made on their journey to the Pacific when she adjusted herself in it. "I loved your book," she slurred. "*A Year of Pure Fucking.* How did you ever get that past the censors?"

"*A Year of Pure Feeling,*" I deliberately corrected her, growing uneasy in this throng of lubricious ladies.

"I know, silly!" She reared back in a gargantuan laugh that

disorganized her face, a face absent of expression because of all the peels and chemical injections it had been subjected to. "You need to tell me more about this book, wily Miley. I can't be expected to flip pages with a dirty martini in my hand." She roared with laughter at her own joke. "Kidding again."

Eileen bent to my ear. "Ava likes to drink."

"You think?"

Eileen straightened up with a derisive laugh. "You're funny, Miles." She turned to another woman next to sloppy Ava. "And this is Fiona."

Fiona, a leggy brunette, was draped in a loud pink strapless dress top-heavy with poufy shoulders. When she bent forward to shake my hand, it was impossible not to notice she wasn't wearing a bra, as her chest quaked in all directions. Her sharp, dagger-shaped earrings seemed to stab at her dress as her frame closed in on me. "What do you make of our little group?" she said, her eyes wolfishly casing me up and down.

"My writing has taken me to some interesting places," I said, trying to maintain a sense of decorum in the Babylon I had found myself imprisoned in. "I'm never surprised. That you ladies are interested in books makes me interested in you." Sounded saccharine coming from me, but that penis pâté still had me a wee unsettled.

Fiona, sensing speciousness, sighted down her champagne flute, which she tilted at me, her eyes narrowing devilishly. "After they finish the next bottle of bubbles, they'll forget they're married and you'll have a target sign on your back. And front, too." She pointed her flute at my crotch and some spilled out, playfully tossed or otherwise, I couldn't decide.

I lurched back a step and brushed champagne from my zipper. "No worries," I said. "It's all good."

Eileen extricated me from drunk flamingo Fiona, clutching my elbow with a clawlike grip and dragging me around the plundered table of gourmet hors d'oeuvres. Champagne bottles plunged in and out of the buckets with unapologetic regularity. Confabulation rose in volume until it felt like we were aswarm in an aviary of fledged female hominids who hadn't laid eyes on men in weeks. Jack was now nose to ruddy nose with the former soap opera star Olivia, grinning and laughing at her no-doubt-apocryphal anecdotes.

"This is Nadine." Eileen introduced me to a beautiful woman with dyed black hair, her face a furrowed field of tiny wrinkles suggesting time was running out but that hope sprang eternal the more "bubbles" she imbibed. She was wearing a light-blue linen wrap dress with a ruffled hem. The top of the dress clamshelled over her chest at a competitively low position compared to the other Cougars. The loose structure of the dress made me wonder whether if she uncrossed her legs too suddenly the whole ensemble would fly open and expose her to the crowd. Tiny silver hoop earrings coruscated down her cheeks, framing a pair of rapidly blinking eyes. A mauve-colored gem twinkled at her cleavage, held by a delicate silver necklace.

"Nice to meet you, Miles," she said in a deep voice. "I loved your book, but we'll get *deeper into it* later." She winked at me.

"What's the gem?" I inquired politely, motioning to her necklace.

"It's a pounamu, quarried in Central Otago, home to your beloved Pinot Noir," she whispered in a personal tone.

"You've done your research," I said.

She telescoped her head forward and breathed heavily on me. "I like to know my prey."

I sucked in my breath. An eavesdropping Eileen roughhoused me away in the nick of time and introduced me to a woman named Susan, the oldest of the group. She was wearing a colorful caftan, over which was strung a heavy wooden necklace with Māori ancestral designs inked in scrimshaw. Though judging by her Aryan physiognomy, I deduced her whakapapa was probably closer to Captain Cook's.

Susan extended her hand in a queenly fashion. "Hi, Miles. I'm probably the only one here who read your book all the way through."

"It should make for a lively discussion then," I said.

"When you give the Cougars this many bubbles"—she held up her glass—"the void has no bottom."

I laughed at her Baudelairean stab at poetry. "I like your description," I attempted to flatter her. "I might borrow it one day."

"I write, too, you know."

"Do you now?"

"I have a lot of titles," she told me, reaching for her wooden necklace with her thumb and forefinger and rubbing the scrimshaw for good luck.

"Just don't have the chapters," I said.

Her expression turned into one of scorn. "Smartass." She turned like a boat heaving into the harbor and reached for the nearest bottle of champagne, indiscriminate about whether she mixed her "bubbles." Champagne Meritage!

Eileen squeezed my elbow tighter and motioned with her eyes across the hors d'oeuvres table to a young woman sitting under a voluminous head of red hair, so voluminous her face was but a mere egg glowing red in its nest. "That's Robin. She doesn't read books, but we've taken pity on her because her inheritance didn't come through as she had hoped." She lowered her voice another register. "Husband absconded back to America and took his hedge fund millions. With a younger woman."

I widened my eyes at the intimacy. "Damn Yankees," I said, trying to make light of Robin's tragic divorce backstory. "I didn't get anything, either, but then I couldn't afford a family law attorney."

Eileen dissolved into a laugh so gratingly affected I had to wait for her to stop convulsing.

Susan with the wooden necklace, in a gesture of amity, asked with large eyes and an extended bottle if I wanted a refill, then sloppily refreshed my flute after I held it out with eagerness. I quickly came to realize Jack and I were drifting, rudderless and with busted engine, into uncharted waters, and libations were needed in lieu of a sextant.

"I didn't mean my comment," I attempted to apologize.

"Didn't offend me at all. You writers are all bitter fucks. My ex-husband was one, and a successful one, too, and then he shot himself."

"That's terrible," I said, wincing at the lurid image blossoming in my head.

"He left a note. 'Went out like Ernest.'" A hyena-like laugh surged up out of her, suggesting she was relieved he had left Christchurch in a final blaze of self-loathing. "As if he'll ever be remembered," she spat nastily, closing the chapter on that confession.

Eileen, our butterfly extroverted host, and owner of the hilltop mansion with her real estate magnate husband—in Fiji to fish, I was informed—clinked her flute with an hors d'oeuvres fork to summon everyone's attention. "Okay, Cougars, it's time to convene. *Grrr. Grrr.*" In unison they all *grrr*-ed back in a drunken chorus while simultaneously raising their hands in cat-scratch gestures like something out of *The Lion King* crossed with a football team performing a power chant before the big game.

Jack's smile was widening from ear to ear while I was teetering on the verge of one humdinger of a panic attack.

CHAPTER 13

Jack and I were led—more descriptively, shoved—down into the titanic sunken living room in Eileen's two-story hilltop affair in the ironically named Mount Pleasant. I was escorted by two of the women to a feathered couch. A few flutes of champagne had clouded the space-time continuum in my beleaguered brain, but I believe there was a bit of a tussle as to who would flank me, putative celebrity author that I was. In the end, Nadine with the blue ruffle dress and the fake Russian Sonia prevailed, their thighs pressed against me, creating a vise in which I was claustrophobically clamped tight, primed for the plucking. Other Cougars had kicked off their heels and were sprawled loose limbed on the remaining furniture. Hippie Susan sat cross-legged on the floor as if yoga and meditation were on the schedule but only she had paid attention. Eileen held court *Game of Thrones*-style, collapsed in a giant leather chair that accentuated her imperial air as host and founder of the club, and no doubt the one responsible for giving the book club its self-mocking name, an in-joke that bound them all together in a lascivious cabal—when their men were whoring away in Thailand. Jack had collapsed in a matching chair with a fawning Olivia, the actress manqué, sitting on the floor leaning against his side, one creeping hand climbing his knee like a drugged tarantula. They all had my book clutched in their hands or lying in their laps or employed as champagne flute coasters as if my suffering words needed the sweat of their warming glasses to come alive. Two had Post-its flagging multiple pages; some had the cover open to the title page ready to be autographed; flaming redhead Robin had her copy tossed aside like a sartorial accessory.

"Are we ready to begin?" Eileen addressed the Cougars of Christchurch Book Club as Jack and I stared nonplussed at this surreal nadir our lives had descended to, ironically at the highest point—Hana had informed us—in all of Christchurch.

"More bubbles," spluttered Ava, her face now as red as Robin's hair. Robin topped her off and the two teetered in place, toasted, and exchanged vacuous expressions.

"Anyone else?" Robin trilled, bottle held aloft triumphantly.

Almost every flute shot forward on thrust-out arms for refilling, and Robin had to fetch another bottle, her sashaying hips knocking over a vase on an end table in the process. These women can throw it down, I thought.

"So, what did we all think of *A Year of Pure Feeling*?" Eileen said, officially beginning the book club in a voice suggesting Jack and I wouldn't disparagingly judge them. The Cougars glanced at one another with blank expressions. "How many of you read it?" implored Eileen. Six of the seven hands shot up, some with champagne flutes so I wasn't sure if they were answering in the affirmative or requesting refills. "How many of you read it all the way through?" Three of the hands lowered and I was left with crystal-rubber Susan, know-it-all Nadine, and villainess Eileen to weigh in with any degree of literary credibility.

"I couldn't put it down," said Susan, firing the opening salvo. "The main character . . . that's you, isn't it, Miles?"

"It is. Yes. Wrote it in first person. As is my wont. Though my ex-wife begged me to shift to third to disguise my peccadilloes."

"That's why she's your ex," chimed in a voice I couldn't put a face to. Cathartic laughter enveloped her words.

Susan continued: "Miles exposes his soul in a way we don't get much from men these days. The few men who are left in our lives. The true men. The real men. The ones with hair on their chest you just want to rake your fingers through and *grr grr*." With one hand she made the clutch-and-scratch gesture.

Instead of laughter this time there were nods of approbation and even a pair of *woo-hoos*. A few of the Cougars replied in kind to Susan's clutch-and-scratch, semaphoring solidarity with her sentiment. Where was this going? Jack's face had broadened into an irrepressible smile. Olivia's arachnidan hand had advanced to his thigh and was coyly massaging it. Jack discreetly slipped something from his jacket pocket and placed it under his tongue.

"Even though I haven't finished it yet, I found some of the sex scenes to be more than titillating," effused Fiona in pink.

"Is that good or bad?" inquired Nadine, who imperceptibly squeezed *my* thigh with a hand.

"If you like your fellatio with wine," Fiona suggested, her remark accompanied by a profane grin.

"Eww," whinnied Ava in imitation of a sick horse.

"I found it, well, to be drawn from real life," critiqued Eileen. "Not that Ric would ever be so romantic. And on a golf course yet. Fore!"

The Cougars found this wildly hilarious and collective laughter erupted, quaking the group, a few of them jackknifing forward out of their chairs. Fiona in pink kicked off her matching pink pumps and tossed them aside with an insouciant sweep of her hand.

"I think we need to talk about the character of Jacob, who is clearly this rugged manly man here," Fiona said. She patted Jack on his opposite thigh, surreptitiously competing with Olivia for his attention. Olivia's eyes narrowed disapprovingly at Fiona's tactful enemy move, and she seemed to bare her fangs. Jack, stirred with desire, touched Olivia's hand in a reassuring signal but pulled discreetly away before others could see who he had chosen, because we both sensed a rugby scrum brewing, the Cougar hierarchy in active disassembly. "You did base it on Jack, didn't you?" asked Olivia in a bald-faced effort to draw attention to herself.

"I did," I said, hoping the book club would settle into some semblance of civility. "It's autobiographical fiction." I attempted to right the ship.

"I know fiction from fact," Olivia said, "and I think Jack's character is cut from the cloth of reality."

Eileen darted a look of silently thrown daggers at Olivia and Jack. "Olivia, how far did you get through Miles's book?"

"Far enough," she shot back. "And then I needed a stiff one." Laughter erupted at the blatant double entendre.

"What, Allen isn't performing his marital duties?" Eileen joked.

"You know Allen is off with your Ric in Fiji and we have the five-hundred-kilometer rule, Eileen," Olivia reminded, dipping her flute of champagne at her in mild contempt.

Jack and I exchanged bulging-eyed looks. His was bright and nodding; mine was downturned and disconcerted. I was disquieted by where this "autograph signing" was going. Soon I would be pressing ink to buttocks and attempting signatures and inscriptions. Where was Hana?

"When was the last time you acted on the five-hundred-kilometer rule?" Eileen challenged, not one to be derided in her castle.

"Excuse me a second," I said. I rose from the vise of Sonia and Nadine, who seemed to collapse together into the vacuum my rising had left.

"Bathroom's down the hall to the left," Eileen directed, assuming that could be the *only* reason I had leaped to my feet.

Over my shoulder, I thought I heard one of them say, "Get your condom on, author man," followed by exploding laughter. "Au naturel, Miles," joked another whom I couldn't distinguish.

In the palatial bathroom, I braced a hand against the wall festooned with framed photos of Ric posing proudly next to trophy fish suspended from huge gaffs. I don't know if it was nerves or the sudden fear of being smothered by a book club of libidinous, sexually aroused Kiwi women whose partners hadn't fucked them properly in months or what, but I was having trouble getting a stream going. Champagne had fluttered to my head. Since disembarking to New Zealand to teach in Dunedin, I had cleaved, with occasional exceptions, to the abstemious. Ella and I were both familiar with the dangers of drink in the wine world. The refrain was always: Did you bring your problem here or develop it here?

We had vowed not to go down that dark path, but I was off to a parlous start on this camper-van book tour. I blamed the camper van. I blamed the email from the mother of my daughter. I blamed the biblical New Zealand winter weather. I blamed the sorry state of literature. There was always a rationalization for a return to the Hadean depths Jack and I had often staggered in, potato-sacked to the bottle.

Out of habit I looked at my phone and noticed a text notification banner. It was from Hana. "How's it going?"

"The Cougars are on the prowl," I texted back with a pecking index finger. I tried to add the "shocked" emoji, but I wasn't adroit enough on a cell—bad eyes; unsteady hand.

"Do this one for Hughie," she texted back.

I texted her three question marks.

She texted me three dollar signs. I had no clue what she meant. Was Hughie hoping to shake them down for some development funds for the international expansion of the book tour he had envisaged?

I zipped up and walked out of the bathroom, then ducked into the master bedroom, plopped down on the Super Caesar bed, which swallowed me whole, and stared at my cell. I brought up Ella's contact and held my forefinger poised over the phone icon. She would hear the champagne in my voice and would be censorious. I could already form the sentences. "How much have you had to drink, Miles?" "I thought Hughie had talked to you about how dangerous this book tour could be for you with your history of relapsing. Huh?" I swiped out of Contacts and into Messages and texted her, "I miss you. All is well. Max is traveling like a champ. Jack is behaving." And even those innocuous phrases would be met with suspicion. A touch of sentimentality suffused me. What Jack and I had moralized about the need for women in our lives earlier in the day now resonated more strongly than ever.

I stowed my phone in my back pocket and rose from the monstrous bed. Before I could get my bearings, in the tenebrous light a figure appeared in front of me with daunting height.

"Where did you disappear to, Miles?" Eileen said in a seductive voice.

"Texting. I'm coming."

Instead of affording me some space, she vectored in, clamped both hands on the sides of my head, and kissed me with such velocity and carnal force I had to gently but forcibly push her away. "Eileen, what are you doing? You're a married woman."

She ran two fingers over her bulbous lips. "I didn't pay ten thousand for these lips for them not to be kissed." She planted another sloppy one on me, cheese and rosé and penis pâté lending her breath a dangerously miasmic scent. I have to admit it felt thrilling in the moment, if terrifying, too.

"Let's go back in," I said in a tone insinuating she might have a Hail Mary chance if I drank myself into a fugue, when in truth I was repulsed by the thought of kissing those collagen-bulbous lips again and in desperation was already hatching my escape plan.

We returned to the cavernous living room, Eileen clinging possessively to my arm as if to show off her celebrity author wildebeest she the lioness had slayed and dragged back to the pride for mutual feeding. When I blinked my eyes into focus, the dramatis personae had been rearranged. The moon had blazed through the storm clouds, and as if bewitched, the Cougars had shorn items of clothing: belts, shoes, wraps . . . Everyone was now seated in a circle except one: Nadine. She was lying supine and her ruffled wrap dress was unbuttoned and her breasts had tumbled out, held precariously in by a loose-fitting black bra.

"So, Miles, we have a game the Cougars play," said Nadine seductively, as I was pushed by Eileen, who now thought she had control of the narrative for the rest of the evening, back toward the feathered couch. I gripped the armrest and held my ground.

Sonia handed me a full flute of champagne as Nadine writhed peristaltically on the floor, aswoon in a trance. Was it my imagination or had someone dimmed the lights? Music had been introduced into the equation, a first for a book club I had (dis)graced. Bruno Mars's "Leave the Door Open" was playing at midvolume. For the romantics? Or to drown out my remonstrations? "You need to get to where we are, author man," Sonia said over the music in her thick Russian accent, patting the sofa next to her and motioning for me to sit down so they could begin the *real* festivities. Quailing, I obeyed. She leaned into my ear, her mouth emitting Beluga breath. "Are you looking for residency? I can help." Her elegant fingers brushed my wand and caused it to momentarily dowse.

Eileen assumed the position opposite me Nadine had vacated. "So, Miles," she said, "one thing our club is famous for is we like to reenact scenes from the book in question. Now, there's a bit of sex in your novel."

"Indeed there is," chimed in hippie Susan, lamenting, it appeared, the old days of the commune orgies of her misspent youth.

"I read enough to know," blustered a now-shoeless Fiona.

"I read a review of your book in the *Herald* that said it was *smut*," interjected Robin, wanting not to be excluded now that the festivities had shifted away from boring book critiquing and were getting exciting. I took this as a criticism from her until she added, "I love smut." Her appallingly lopsided mouth somehow managed a smile.

Robin's comment quickly vaporized, and the attention returned to a writhing Nadine in the middle of the circle. "Miles, you seem to have a fondness for oral sex." She widened her legs until her matching black panties were showing, a woman now wrung from lust rather than literary passion. "I bet you've pleased more women than have pleased you," she weirdly complimented, her eyebrows arched provocatively, her legs tantalizingly widening. "Don't you want a little taste?" She fingered the band of her panties.

I could feel my eyes bulging frog-like.

Jack, aroused by this, flicked his tongue like a cartoon iguana. Olivia looked up at him, her mouth wreathed in unspoken concupiscence.

"Come down here, Miles, and show us your technique." These women were seriously shit faced. I was suddenly beset by paranoidal fantasies of their husbands watching their partners on baby cams. But maybe getting aroused by it!

"I feel uncomfortable," I muttered ineffectually.

"Oh, play along," said shit stirrer Eileen, who already assumed she had dibs on me and didn't feel threatened by Nadine's looming vulva.

"I came to discuss and sign my book," I said, smiling feebly, wishing I had the walkie-talkie, could press SOS and summon Hana to rescue me.

Nadine produced her copy of *A Year of Pure Feeling* and opened it to a

Post-it-selected page and placed it over her crotch. "Come down here and read for us, Miles," she said, curling the fingers on one hand in a beckoning gesture that made me think of Lorelei of the Lake and all the other legendary anima figures who had destroyed men in myths and fairy tales.

Jack drew my attention and made a tight little circle in the air with his index finger as if: *Humor them, Miles.*

Eileen placed a hand on the middle of my back and shoved me somewhat aggressively down off the couch, indicating she and her Cougars wouldn't be denied.

I don't know if it was the champagne or the surreally transgressive stunt they wanted me to reenact, but I slid down off the couch and knelt in supplication. Nadine kept beckoning with her glittering bejeweled fingers as if calling me into a rotunda of pure female hellfire. I was on all fours now and approaching the book I had spent two years writing, revising, copyediting, and preparing for publication, and here it was, in all its ignominious glory, inches from a woman's pudendum, splayed open like a filleted fish for me to begin reading.

"Turn the music down, Ava," ordered Eileen, snapping her fingers.

"Oh, why?" Ava said. "Let's have some fun."

"Turn it down," Eileen said.

Ava, weaving in place, her mouth hung open, worked an app on her phone with clumsy thumbs and lowered Bruno Mars to elevator music level.

"Go ahead," urged Eileen, leaning forward off the couch and offering me encouragement.

To the Cougars' great collective amusement, reinforced by too much bubbly, I crawled lemur-like on all fours toward Nadine's inviting crotch and my opened book, no stranger to humiliation and blackout cunnilingus. Lavender scent poured from it—her crotch, not my book. I flipped the book over. The pages she wanted me to read were highlighted by a Sharpie in yellow.

"Here, do you need your glasses, Miles?" I heard Eileen's words stream over my shoulder, her hot breath baking my right ear. I craned my neck backward, and she fitted my reading glasses on. "There you go, genius," she said, then planted a slobbering kiss on my cheek, gave my beard a little scratch as if rubbing tinder to promote the start of a fire. And what a fire it could blaze into once I started licking!

With glasses askew on the bridge of my nose, my book came into focus, but the rest of the room went out of focus. I started to read. It was actually the only sex scene in my book, but Nadine had enthusiastically zeroed in on it. And no doubt she and villainess Eileen had conspired on the ideation of the evening's narrative and this luridly climactic moment. I was drunk on the bubbly, and still wounded by the breakup with Ella, I didn't care. I started reading. It was mortifying to read out loud the explicit scene. If I had before publication, I might have cut it. No doubt my ex-wife was cringing somewhere in Manhattan and hurling a martini at the wall—*Is this who I married and brought home to my churchgoing parents?* There are some passages in books that aren't meant to be read out loud. But not at the Cougars of Christchurch Book Club! I was frequently interrupted by salaciously double entendre comments like, "Was it *hard* to write, Miles?"

Ava, the sloppy party monster, lurched around and deftly undid two buttons on my shirt. "I like to see more of a man." She staggered to a standing position and threw out both arms to the Cougars and, with them, the world of Mount Pleasant. "Don't we all, ladies!"

An affirmative chorus rose from this tribe of privileged Christchurch women, all of them seeming to sink into a kind of collective delirium, having supplanted trance-inducing hallucinogens with champagne and sacrificial virgins with celebrity authors they believed needed—no, desired, hankered—to be fucked. In a bizarrely feminist reversal—born of pandemic horniness—they had turned the tables on the men, even if it took magnums of New Zealand's finest to propel them to the finish line.

Shirt unbuttoned, I soldiered on, fearing if I stopped reading I would be mauled. Nadine's thighs inched wider and wider apart, a maw of unadulterated darkness awaiting my rappelling into its sea anemone quivering with lust. She seductively fingered the band of her panties until pubic hair was efflorescing black against her alabaster thigh. The Cougars stirred with excitement, each in her own individually perverse proclivity:

nervous laughter; hands clasped over mouths; fists shaking encourage-ment; heads thrown back, fortifying themselves with more champagne.

"More bubbles!" cried a desperately drunk Ava, who had her flute hand extended and the unoccupied one pressed to her forehead, palm forward in a histrionic movie swoon. While Robin topped her off, Ava, looking increasingly pale and stricken, projectile vomited onto the plate glass picture window, and the lights of Mount Pleasant winked out. Christ had clearly left the church.

That was it! I clambered to my feet as Nadine made a raring, des-perate last attempt to grab my hair and yank my head into her crotch, where a mouth of pink now smiled at me through her feminine darkness.

When I looked up, I noticed Jack and Olivia had decamped from the lounge chair, my reading obviously having inspired them to activi-ties best conducted in private.

"You were simply wonderful," crooned Eileen. "Now kiss these lips again in front of my Cougars."

"Excuse me," I said. I extricated myself from Eileen's clutches and fled tangle-footed down a long walkway that led into an enormous kitchen hidden out of view from the great room of depravity. I popped on the lights and discovered, to my horror, Ava squatting over one of the crisper drawers she had pulled out from the open refrigerator, her pleather mini hiked to her waist and her panties pulled to her ankles, lustily urinating. How she had staggered from vomiting to peeing in such a short time span made me think I was already blacking out.

When she saw me she shot an *oops* hand to her small, pouty mouth. "Too much bitch diesel," she whimpered in a high-pitched voice. "Bath-room's locked. I had to go." She shut her eyes tight and started bawling.

"There must be one downstairs," I said, both shocked and humored by the black comedy of this demolished angel peeing in her wealthier friend's crisper drawer.

Ava excused herself with a whisper and the vacant expression of a cow. "Eileen'll never know."

Undeterred, I reached over her for an Antipodes sparkling water, New Zealand's ubiquitous and purest perched appropriately over one of its incontinent denizens. I chugged the water, pulled a hand over my face, and tried to get a grip on my mug as I staggered down the hallway to the bathroom. I was woozy. Voices were unintelligible.

A red-faced Jack juddered out of the bathroom, detonated by something powerful and intense—his expression was beyond disorganized. He saw me and immediately veered over to where I was standing trying to figure out what our next move was.

"Dude, you didn't tell me," he said with a flushed grin, his complexion colored red from the nitrous oxide the ED med had flooded into his face.

"Tell you what?"

"Fifteen K, dude. That is awesome. And they just wanted some entertainment. But what entertainment! Woo!" He made two fists and shook them in the air.

Over Jack's shoulder shambled out a disheveled Olivia from the bathroom, hurriedly trying to pull herself together, fumbling with her gold lion belt buckle and frantically combing her mussed hair with a raking hand, her lipsticked mouth and makeup an abstract expressionist painting.

"Fifteen grand?" I said to Jack, puzzled. "What are you talking about?"

"Appearance fee."

"Appearance fee? I didn't hear about any appearance fee."

"It's cool if you wanted to hide it from Hughie." Jack leaned into me, his breath fetid with hors d'oeuvres and something else I wanted purged from my nostrils. "Did you and Hana have a little action on the side?" Jack grinned crookedly.

"No!"

"Well, Olivia told me the Cougars paid you fifteen grand for your appearance."

"What?" I said, incensed.

"It's cool, man, it's cool," Jack whispered. "I wish you'd given me a heads-up. These little blue fellas take an hour to kick in." He patted the meds vial in his left front pocket.

Suddenly it was all making sense to me. Eileen's aggressive kiss and her half-hearted attempt to seduce me on the Super Caesar. Nadine's cunnilingus performance idea and my reading a passage from the book. *Washed-Up Celebrities* Jack going off with the one who wanted a taste of his celebrity the most. Hana wouldn't do this. Then it hit me like a light post I hadn't seen while speaking into my phone. Hughie had sold me out for fifteen grand and pocketed my fee!

I shook my head in disgust at the revelation. "If you worked up an appetite in the bathroom, I'd avoid the crudités in the fridge if I were you," I fumed to Jack. I pointed over my shoulder at Ava, who had wobbled to her feet and was pathetically trying to regroup but reeled clumsily about like a newly birthed foal.

Jack took a peek. "Oh my Jesus. That is fucked up."

I stormed back into the sunken living room. The music had been turned up full blast again, and all the Cougars left standing were dancing rhythmically, loose limbed and half-naked, the "book club" in celebratory full swing. With a Windex dispenser brandished in one hand and a rag in the other, mustachioed Peter was scrubbing the picture window dripping with Ava's vomit, but it seemed to smear in his obligatory attempt. Astonishingly, more champagne was being consumed; in the case of redhead Robin, straight from the bottle. As if they had all waited for a suitable occasion, the penis pâté was now being plundered with oversized spoons by one and all in a Grand Guignol finale.

"Turn the music off," I shouted to get their attention. "Turn it off."

"What's wrong, Miles?" Eileen said, signaling to Robin to turn the music down.

Weaving in place, Robin fiddled with the app on her phone, and the music abruptly cut out. The sudden silence seemed to hoist the Cougars out of their trancelike state.

"Bummer," said Ava, who had passed out on the couch, awakened, then lapsed back into a coma again.

Fiona and Susan rallied and evinced concern. "What's wrong, Miles?" Susan echoed Eileen.

I stood in the middle of the living room holding up Ava's copy of my book, which had absorbed spilled champagne and was bulging twice its size. "I spent the last two years writing this soul-baring personal book of mine. Now, I didn't expect all of you to read it. But what I didn't realize is that you paid my publisher—you, Eileen!—fifteen thousand dollars with the promise I would bring my actor friend Jack here and get down with you ladies. I don't give a shit this night turned into a Dionysian orgy and that some of you got what you wanted." I darted a furtive glance at disheveled Olivia. I could feel the blood blossoming hot in my face. "But the fifteen grand didn't go into my pocket. And whatever Hughie Martin promised, it was never run by me. I don't mind being sexually assaulted by beautiful women like the gaggle of you shirleys. Nor does Jack. In fact, if I'm being honest, we fantasize about it." Jack had sidled up next to me, and his head, taller on his shoulders than mine, was casing all the Cougars, admonishing them to back off. "My problem is the fifteen K didn't go into my pocket, and I didn't have a heads-up on the evening's narrative."

"Calm down, Miles," said Eileen with a raised hand, hoping to placate me.

"I'm out of here," said Olivia, disappointed apparently her fuck had been semi-pre-planned and wasn't born of her attractiveness to men. She stripped off her panties and threw them over her shoulder like the tossing of the wedding bouquet as if whoever caught them was the next one to get fucked in the bathroom.

"Olivia," Jack called out, "I want you to voice the audiobook of Miles's book. My offer stands."

"I've had better cock in the poultry section of New World." Olivia threw him a backward middle finger and thundered full commando out the heavy double doors.

"Did you two have sex?" shrieked Eileen. "In my bathroom?" I was shocked she was shocked. The mood had shifted seismically. The event had deteriorated. The enormity of the book club battlefield was now apparent in their frozen expressions.

"Let's boogie," urged Jack. "Nice meeting you, Cougars," he called out with a conciliatory little wave.

As Jack fishhooked me out of there, I got a dismaying glance of fake Russian Sonia holding up her camera phone.

As soon as Jack and I ejected ourselves out the front door and into the cold air, we bolted for the camper van on tripping feet. I commandeered the wheel as Jack had had more to drink. I started the engine, then made sure Max was okay in his carrier. He looked agitated; he could sense something was gravely amiss.

"Go go go," yelled Jack. He rolled down his window: "Bye, ladies," he called, waving a hand out his open window as the remaining Cougars left standing, fronted by Eileen, disgorged from the estate, their libidinousness undiminished.

"Come on back," cried Eileen. "We have you booked for another hour!"

Backing that automotive leviathan of a camper van out of Eileen's driveway was a trucker's nightmare. I ignored all the warning beeps on the overhead video and somehow managed to get us turned around while Eileen drummed her gnarled fists on the driver's-side window and pointed venomously to her watch, tapping it to prove she owned me for another hour. I ignored her entreaties. Reduced to the primitive, she spat on the window, fulminating something about how she didn't get her money's worth. Her saliva crawled down the glass like the slime trail of a snail.

"Go fuck your fucking hori," she screamed, growing smaller in my side mirror.

"What's a *hori*?" said Jack.

"The N-word for Māori."

"Jesus fucking Christchurch."

On the narrow road out of the top of Mount Pleasant (ha!), the camper van collided with a sturdy post with a mailbox mounted on it. We heard a loud bang, and it didn't sound good, because Max started hissing and meowing up a storm.

"There goes their new shipment of sex toys," quipped Jack.

"Seriously twisted sisters back there," I said, my heart racing.

"Why didn't you do Eileen?" Jack said, bizarrely sanguine. "She looked like she could go for hours."

"I'm not into sex with someone Hughie pimped me out to," I railed.

"You saw where the evening was going, why didn't you just go with it? Why the fucking outrage? The ladies were down to get brown."

"Glad you got *your* nut."

"We could have been bunked in, hosing them all night long, and you get on your high horse and read them the riot act. Fuck, Miles!"

"I don't like the bait and switch. First this"—I slammed my right hand on the steering wheel—"and then the Cougars and the appearance fee that was more than my advance and which I never saw."

"Miles. No one reads books anymore. You're a circus act. I'm a circus act. We're the freaks in the carny, okay?"

"Maybe I'm more gullible than you."

"Where are we going to camp tonight?" Jack said, shaking his head in disappointment.

CHAPTER 14

We woke in Edenic splendor at the Pegasus Bay Winery guest lodge just north of Christchurch. I had met winemaker Mat Donaldson at a wine event, and he had offered the accommodations if I ever needed a place to stay.

A climbing sun poured golden light through the windows. The biblical storm of the century had moved north, and the immaculate gardens below and the weeping willows enclosing them dazzled in the rain-soaked aftermath. A pond dappled with lilies sparkled in the lush greenery. Jack and I thought we had died and been resurrected in a heaven on earth.

The night before, we had regaled Mat with our Cougars of Christchurch Book Club story, and he couldn't stop laughing. Feeling generous, he led us down into his personal cellar on a rickety ladder and decided it was an occasion to pop some rare Burgundies. Vosne-Romanées. Puligny-Montrachets. Meursaults. Corton Les Renardes. And a Grand Cru Batard-Montrachet that hoisted us to new heights of vinous incredulity. Twenty and thirty years' age on some of them. Decadent beyond my socialist politics, we plundered wines from his dank cellar, bottles resting on their sides in wire racks. The viscous white Burgundies and cloud-ethereal Pinots eased our unsettled mood, and we couldn't stop laughing. Jack didn't go into explicit detail on how far things went with Olivia in the bathroom, but it had gone far enough, because the woman looked ravished beyond words when she had unceremoniously decamped.

During our Bourgogne bacchanal Hana's importuning texts poured in at an alarming, frantic pace. I ignored them because I was still angry about the appearance fee I never saw that she had to have known about, and I didn't want her busting up our debauched high-end wine tasting with another scolding.

"2015 Le Montrachet?" I remember Mat suggesting with a wicked grin, as he slowly—slowly!—slid a bottle out of his rack and mumbled something about how there were probably only a few hundred in existence.

"Bring it on," I said, needing the anodyne of the fabled libation, still a bit traumatized by the predatory book club at the top of Mount Pleasant. The Le Montrachet was beyond exquisite. It soared across the palate like an extinct winged creature, tasted of limestone and lichee and licentiousness. Never tasted anything like it before. But a memory. A book can be reread, a movie can be rewatched, but a Le Montrachet passes you by like Halley's Comet, a once-in-a-lifetime, singular moment only the abstraction of memory, employing the sacred power of words, can grasp onto and keep from evanescing. The only experience that can be likened to it, Jack, Mat, and I agreed, was the occasional mind-altering sex. And that, too, when they turn the stopcock open on the morphine and wave goodbye in ICU, is but a faded memory.

"You're one dark dude, Miles," I remember Mat saying, and we all shared yet another communal laugh. There was a lot of laughter, and a train car of Burgundy's finest, the kind of night where intemperance civilizes.

"Just reaching for the truth," I remember replying. "That's the problem with getting old. As our memory declines, we lose touch with the transitory, the light starts to go off on those epiphanic moments in life, and we no longer even possess our memories; they, too, no longer belong to us. It's back to carbon, from whence we came."

Before passing out, I had a final image of Jack and Mat staring fixedly at me, as if my grim philosophizing had disinterred something repressed in their discrete souls. Special wines can do that to oenophiles. But, rested, the next morning, sitting in a large leather-upholstered chair with the paradisiacal view, nursing a hangover, reality kicked in, and I started to scroll through Hana's desperate texts. "Where'd you go?" "Hughie's pissed!!!" "Why'd you turn the walkie off!!!" "Turn on your FUCKING phone." "Turn on your FUCKING walkie so I can come get you!!!" "WHERE ARE YOU?"

I set my phone aside. Now that it was powered back on, Hana, with the Share My Location toggled on, would be arriving soon. Max stood on his haunches basking in shafts of bright sunlight that had eluded us for days, craning his neck to take in all the colorful birds he fantasized preying on; he, too, had found himself in heaven. I knelt next to him and stroked his fur. He immediately started purring. I spoke to him: "Hi, Max man. How're you doing? Huh?" His purring intensified, and then he collapsed to a sitting position and continued staring out at the birds trilling in the willows.

A few minutes later Jack lumbered out of his bedroom. Unwashed, unshaven. "The stage-four clinger is coming out," he announced, running a hand over his scraggly face in hopes it would transform it into the one he remembered from before he had sold out to reality TV to rescue him from a life of ruin.

"What?" I said, alarmed.

"She saw something the Cougars posted on Instagram and now thinks we're up to no good."

"Oh, fuck," I said. I didn't have the heart, or the energy, to go online to hunt down the affronting video. I had a vague memory of the fake Russian Sonia and her iPhone videoing us. "You want some coffee?" I asked.

"Fucking school of piranhas," Jack muttered. "Yeah, something," he said, collapsing into the matching chair that was pointed toward the paradisiacal view, massaging his temples, trying to assuage his Burgundy blowout hangover, the paradisiacal view not so paradisiacal.

"That Mat's a cool guy," he managed. "If a bit twisted."

"Yeah, he'll go deep when the occasion warrants. He's doing a lot of interesting stuff with Rieslings and botrytis. But that's for another night."

"Don't get started on botrytis, Homes."

Chuckling, I padded into the kitchen on stockinged feet, boiled some water, and brewed Jack a strong pour-over, then brought it out to the view room and handed it to him.

He sipped it appreciatively. "These are damn good coffees, Miles."

"Ninety Plus Coffee," I said from the kitchen. "They send it to me for free because I promised to write the founder's biography one day."

"Beautiful here," he observed, his mind drifting elsewhere.

I picked up my coffee mug and joined him in the matching chair and luxuriated in the view. "Imagine what it's like in summer." We were staring at that male fixed point of reference on the horizon, not meeting each other's eyes, but locked in a struggle with the same ambivalences, the same neuroses, the same relationship issues. We didn't have to look at each other, didn't have to touch or hug or anything, and we could ineffably mesh over the tragedy of growing old, the mutual recognition we were, like a wine that had collapsed on its journey in time, on the downslope.

"We're always on the run," Jack observed. "You ever own property?"

"Other than my half hectare of Pinot, no."

"Me neither," he said. "Well, except the house I lost in the divorce." He brought his coffee to his lips and held it there, blowing on it, eyes staring penetratingly out the window. "We missed the boat," he said.

"Yeah, all my friends in SoCal are real estate rich," I said. "They live off the appreciation while you and I face steeper and steeper rents, and grimmer and grimmer futures."

"Yeah," Jack said. "And we're not getting any younger."

"Nope."

"I still can't believe last night. I would have thought it was going to be some quaint literary salon with tea and biscuits and polite talk about your book."

"How was that doll Olivia? You can tell me now that Mat's not present."

"Something about bathroom sex in a full house that turns me on."

"There's an urgency."

"And the thrill of being caught."

"Doesn't do it for me."

Jack shook his head and guffawed so loud it startled Max. "But peeing in the crisper? My Lordy!"

"She had to go. Too much *bitch diesel*."

Jack and I shared another cathartic laugh.

"And you were hogging the bathroom. Poor Ava. What? She was going to pee in her pants?"

"The crisper?" Jack said through eye-watering laughter.

"Woman friend told me to think of it as a dog's fire hydrant."

"Desperation, man. Get these gals on some pink bubbles and they turn into feral cats." He shook his head at the memory.

"Fifteen grand, huh?" I said soberly.

"That's what Olivia told me." He pointed his coffee mug at me. "In flagrante delicto."

"I sincerely hope you gave her her money's worth."

Jack flashed me a wicked grin.

"She is a former actress, you know."

"I saw the whites of her eyes, Homes."

"Happy for you." I shook my head in a tight pattern, the bitter taste of raw onion suddenly rising in the back of my throat. "Fuck, man, I'm going to have to read Hughie the riot act. I hate my celebrity—what remains of it—being leveraged."

"Get him to pay you, man. Tell him you'll plonk on the trip."

I nodded. "Is the stage-four clinger coming for sure?"

"She's threatening to," Jack confided somberly. "Fucking Cougar with her cell camera." He shook his head at the view. "It's tough being washed-up celebrities."

"Speak for yourself. I'm still relevant."

"After last night?"

"Point noted."

As the birdsong filled the silences, I thought of men and their own birdsong language. We talked in code speak, too, but we understood each other perfectly, like those birds.

"What does it mean Amanda's threatening to come out?" I inquired, not wanting to, but needing to know before Hana showed.

Jack narrowed his eyes over his steaming cup of coffee and didn't reply.

"Are you in love with this woman?"

"I don't know," Jack rasped.

"I mean, you cheated on her last night."

"Doesn't count."

"Bet it does to her."

"Some insane wines last night." Jack hoped to steer the conversation away from the unpleasant, as he was wont to do.

"Yeah, Mat went deep, and generously, with those Burgundies. We probably drank over ten grand in wine in those gems he popped."

"Seriously?"

I nodded. A peace, hovering over a colossal fissure in the earth, settled over us. In the ensuing silence, the singing of the birds accompanied the Pegasus Bay gardens with a heavenly soundtrack. But heaven never lasts on earth. Not on my earth. Not on Jack's earth.

A series of doors banged open and shut and then Hana barged into the guest quarters. She marched over to where we were slouched in our chairs, phone weaponized in one hand, walkie in the other, her youthful face a rictus of anxiety. She was wearing the same knobby black turtleneck sweater over fitted jeans and standing tall in her high-heeled combat boots.

"Where were you two?" she demanded, stomping one foot on the floor, loud enough Max woke up, turned, and glowered at her.

"Obviously here because you found us," I said.

"I wasted allfuckingmorning trying to find this PegasusfuckingBay place."

"Sorry, I powered off our devices."

"Why did you leave early?"

"You don't want to know, Hana," Jack said.

"Tell me. I *do* want to know."

"It involves a crisper and a penis pâté," I said, knowing it would bring a mystified look to her face. "Do you vet these book clubs?" I said sharply. "Or is this some fucking joke to you and Hughie?"

Hurt slackened her expression, but her black eyes blazed with indignation and absence of full understanding.

Feeling bad, I told her in a colorful narrative what had happened up on "Mount Pleasant"—sparing her the Jack-fuck-in-the-bathroom part of the program—and she transited through the rhythms of different levels of shock, her mouth alternately agape, her hand slapping her forehead, her head shaking back and forth in disbelief, finally landing on a look of mortification and fear for her job.

"The fuck," she said when I had finished the recounting, mirth restored in Jack's and my wounded personalities. She took a joint from her purse and lit it without explanation, sucked it in, held it in her lungs, then exhaled. The pungent smell of marijuana and tobacco permeated the room.

"Now, the question is," I began in a dramatically gentle voice, "how much did you know about the Cougars' true agenda? The depraved evening they had diagrammed down to the penis pâté?"

"Nothing," she protested. "I swear." She took another hit, then extinguished the joint on a saucer, replaced it in a baggie, and put it back in her purse. "I only smoke when I get anxious."

"No one's judging you," I said.

"Good."

"But back to the Cougars," I said in a rising tone. "If we were women and they were men called, say, the Cretins or Cavemen of Christchurch Book Club, they would be down at the fucking station answering some pretty hardfuckingquestions right about now would be my expat Kiwi guess. And probably indicted on sexual assault charges."

"Yeah," chimed in Jack, "but we don't mind being groped by women, do we, Miles?"

"The goalposts definitely got repositioned last night on this book tour."

"From ostriches to a harem of harlots," Jack finished my sentence. "You're on a roll, sugar." Jack winked at Hana and she grimaced in reply, nonplussed.

"Give half a dozen women more champagne than a rugby team

could down after winning the Six Nations World Cup, and out comes the unbridled libidinousness, damn the fucking book I spent two years pouring my heart into."

"What's *libidinousness?*" Hana asked.

I turned to face her. "Sexual desire in all its unapologetic, untrammeled, unhesitating efflorescence," I said, enunciating each polysyllabic word to rub it in.

"I had no clue," she said. "I was only following orders. That was Hughie's gig, not mine."

"We get that part," I shot back, the corroded wires in my befogged brain having sparked back to life, the rare Burgundies making the journey epic. "Hughie pocketed fifteen grand for our appearance and apparently told the Cougars we would be an entertaining pair, not realizing we were unwittingly auditioning for Chippendales Christchurch."

"What's *Chippendales?*"

"You probably don't have that here," Jack said. "Except in the bush." Jack and I suppressed a laugh at the tacit vulgarity.

Hana, ignoring Jack, as she was wont to do because I was her charge and he was her bête noire, swung her head to me. "All I know is Hughie's majorly upset because the Cougars are demanding their money back."

A mordant laugh spluttered out of me. "Want their money back? They got into the bonus round," I countered.

"Sans gratuity," Jack added.

"They're lucky I'm not suing them for a million quid."

"Dollars, not quid," Hana testily corrected.

"I could care less, Hana. It was a fucking stressful evening. A book-signing event I'll remember on my deathbed. As well as the realm of Persephone."

"You need to call Hughie," she said, her eyes burning a hole into me.

"Fuck him," I exploded. "I'll call him when I'm good and ready."

Hana's face had transited from anger to incredulity to crumbling into helplessness. Tears muddied her eyes and then poured down her cheeks in two raging rivulets. "And peeing in a crisper isn't all that aberrant for a woman. You men can autographthefuckingsand!" She threw

a hand to her face, turned, and went into the adjacent room and collapsed onto a bed and openly wept.

Jack looked at me with a pained expression. I locked my eyes onto his. We needed Hana, and we both knew it. Without her, we would be royally fucked, and not by the Crown. The evening had clearly deteriorated into a bacchanal where a bunch of high net-worth women just wanted to have some entertainment at my expense—and theirs!—but I believed it wasn't her fault, and guilt seized me in its taloned grips. Jack gestured with his head in the direction of where Hana had fled. I rose cumbrously from my chair and tiptoed into the adjoining room to comfort my book publicist, which for all you aspiring writers reading this, the hand-holding is supposed to be the other way around.

"Hana," I said, squatting down to her prostrate level on the bed, "I'm sorry. I'm sitting on a lot of shit. Maturity vacates me sometimes."

"It's okay." She swept a hand across her eyes, hoping to stanch the tears. "I'm under a lot of stress."

"I understand."

"No, you don't."

I ventured a hand to her shoulder but stopped short (times had changed; unapproved touch was forbidden). "Have you done this before, Hana? Be honest."

"Done what?"

"Shepherded a writer on a book tour?"

She gulped a few breaths before she admitted, "No. I took it because it was an opportunity. I love books. I want it to work."

"You didn't know about the appearance fee? Tell me honestly. I'm not going to judge you."

"I knew about it, but I didn't know your arrangement, or nonarrangement, with Hughie." She rolled on her side and turned to me with sodden eyes. "That's fucked up, Miles."

"You know, Hana, it is, but the life I've led, nothing surprises me. That's why Jack and I can laugh about it. Because you see, we've been down this fucked-up road before. We were annealed in the cauldron of Hollywood, cast in evil and the fucked up. We expect this duplicitousness and malefic shit, even if last night went to the Felliniesque." I raised my eyebrows and shook my head at the hallucinatory memory I was desperate to expunge.

She looked at me questioningly. "*Felliniesque?*"

"Forget it," I said. "Someday we'll sit down, reminisce, talk film and literature, and share a load of laughs over this . . . this . . . aberration. Problem for us, we're in the middle of it now, and I don't need any more surprises. I don't need some harridan chasing me down her driveway and telling me to fuck my . . . forget it."

"What?" said Hana, her face contorted with alarm.

"Learned a new N-word."

The word *hori* suddenly dawned on her. "Fucking rich white bitch," Hana exploded. She rolled her tongue around the inside of her mouth, gathered all her strength, and said, "Look, if you want to fire me . . ."

"Hana," I said, chopping her off, "who's going to replace you? I can't be out here all on my own. The Tough Guy Book Club, I admit, ended a little perverse, but that was creative. Kudos for that one. I'm starting to see my next novel. And even the Cougars'll get my creative juices flowing once I get enough distance from it." I moved my face closer to hers and made her meet my eyes. "Jack and I are in the middle of the South Island in the dead of winter, without a compass, rudderless as usual. We can roll with it. But if you bail, this tour ends."

She exhaled relief, then slowly produced her phone. "We have another problem," she said.

"What's that?"

She tapped and swiped a few times, then flashed her plus-sized phone in my face. There I was on Instagram reading the Cougars the riot act, the video Sonia the Russian had recorded when I had had my meltdown, the video the stage-four clinger saw that apparently had ignited her invidiousness.

"Oh, Jesus," I said, glancing away.

"Thirty-four thousand likes and counting," she said.

"And Hughie saw this?"

"Of course."

"You're my publicist, this is New Zealand, I'm an American, what do you want me to do?" I beseeched, exasperated, worried about my future, the retinal detachment I'd suffered in Italy that never got the proper ophthalmological care, the neoplasm, Ella, the daughter I didn't know I had . . .

"I'm getting requests from media," she said.

"For what?"

"To ask you what the hellfuckhappened," she sputtered. "You're a celebrity author, Miles." She glanced down. "Of a sort."

"Not tier one?"

She shook her head and smiled. "Thank God you're not Russell Crowe."

"Crowe could afford a team of lawyers to handle this damage control."

"I think we let it play out. I'll try to keep the media at bay." She brightened. "I mean, I'm loath to admit this, but Hughie noticed a significant uptick in book orders from indies."

"And is probably hoarding my royalties or not declaring them." I gripped my outer eye sockets with thumb and forefinger to massage the hangover and spoke to blackness. "Maybe I should run naked through the streets of Wellington."

Hana laughed in spite of herself, forearming tears from her face.

"A shame we didn't have video of those ostriches chasing Jack and me."

Hana's laughter hoisted her out of her misery. She was sitting on the edge of the bed. I wanted to lay an arm around her shoulders and pull her close to me and rake that dark curly beautiful head of hair of hers and tell her it was going to be okay but was afraid she'd misinterpret what I only envisioned as a conciliatory hug between author and publicist.

"What's on the agenda today, Hana?"

"Something *I* arranged."

"Hit me."

"Esses Wine in Kaikōura."

"Okay. I thought we agreed on no wineries."

"They bought your book, they loved your movie, and they're eager to meet you, Miles."

I nodded. "Anything else I should know?" I said, raising my eyebrows comedically.

"Kaikōura suffered a terrible earthquake recently, and they all lost their homes and are rebuilding. For now, they're operating out of campers."

"Sort of a wagon train book club?"

"Sort of."

"No ostriches?"

Hana tried to suppress a laugh. "No. I hope not. Maybe seals."

Hana straightened from the bed. Our eyes met in wordless conciliation. I sensed she wanted to hug me as much as I wanted to envelop her in my arms, but the distance between that happening and our nearness to each other was wildly incongruous.

"You're doing a great job under the circumstances, Hana," I said in lieu of a hug. "Books are being superannuated by your generation. If you spend all day on your phones and don't read, then books cease to exist. I've given my life to something your generation is obsoleting." I nodded, pretending to be deep in thought. "Thank you for still believing in literature, even if hope for the written word is fast approaching the usefulness of arrowheads."

"My generation still reads," she said. "It's not all doom and gloom for books." She looked down at her feet. "Otherwise, what is *my* future?"

I glanced away. Outside the sun had been consumed by swiftly approaching storm clouds and the grounds of Pegasus Bay Winery had darkened. Within minutes rain began dumping out of the skies, clattering on the patio and streaking the windows. Jack and I were still near the bottom of the world, literally and metaphorically.

"Look, Hana, I've got to make a call."

CHAPTER 15

"G'day, mate."

"What the fuck do you think you're doing pimping me out like that, Hughie? Huh?"

"Calm down, Miles." I could picture Hughie, a ruddy-faced man in his fifties, balding, overweight, short of stature, eclectically intelligent, headset clamped over his head, ensconced in his office. We had never met in person. The University of Otago fellowship and publishing deal had gone down over Zoom and emails. He was, he expressed, a "fanboy" of mine, but I've learned from painful experience that, deep down, every fanboy is out to leverage me, work an angle on me. Fame is a curse worse than failure, I once quipped to an interviewer, who then asked me to read his novel in hopes I would pass it along to my agent.

"Calm down?" I said. "I'm all over the fucking internet."

"And book sales are soaring. Congratulations."

"This isn't how I want to sell books, Hughie, being humiliated by a gaggle of horny Kiwi housewives whose partners stopped servicing them during the pandemic and didn't pick up where they'd left off. And where's my fucking fifteen grand?"

"It wasn't fifteen grand," corrected the parsimonious, first-time-publisher miser.

"It fucking-A was, and I have double confirmation on that, you Janus-faced hypocrite."

He tacked. "How do you think I'm footing the bill for this book tour?"

"I thought you were shooting wallabies to cull the infestation and funneling the funds to our operation." He chuckled sardonically, a fan of my derisive wit, no matter how personally derogatory. "I don't know how you're paying for the tour and I don't fucking care, Hughie. I want my fifteen grand, or I'm either going to bail, or when I get to Wellington I'm going to go on the news and tell them what a crook you are, then come over to your house and strangle you to death!"

"You realize that was my ex-wife your mate Jack had sex with?"

"I didn't know, and I don't care, Hughie. The thought repulses me. I hope she was finally able to enjoy climaxing for the first time in her miserable life."

"I'll ignore that."

"Let's get off the despicable night that shouldn't have happened. I want that fifteen grand, Hughie."

"The Cougars are demanding a refund because you and Jack cut out early."

"Oh, bullshit. And if they are, I'm positive you'll stiff them the way you stiffed me on this camper-van bait-and-switch nightmare."

"You don't like the camper van?"

"Lovely, Hughie. In this arctic weather?!"

"We'll work out a split if the Cougars pay."

"I know they paid because of the way that Eileen harridan came after me."

"We'll split it," he tacitly admitted his lie.

"This is *not* a negotiation. I'm the one who had to eat a penis pâté."

"A what?"

"You'd better wire the fifteen K into my account, or I'm going to snap."

"Looks like you already did."

"That was an appetizer, Hughie." I ended the phone call, seething.

Hana, eavesdropping, returned to the drawing room and said, "Everything okay?"

"No, nothing is okay. Let's go meet some shattered winemakers living out of their campers in where?"

"Kaikōura."

"Kaikōura. Did you ever see that film *Krakatoa, East of Java?*"

"I heard about it."

"It's actually west of Java."

"Oh."

"That's how fucked up the entertainment business is." Where was Max? I needed Max!

We packed up and drove out of Pegasus Bay. Hana led us north on Highway 1 to Kaikōura. The walkie-talkies were back on and crackling with life, and relations had seminormalized, despite the fractious call with Hughie, despite the portent of Amanda cutting us off at the pass. This time Hana didn't race ahead and kept us firmly in her rear-view mirror, not trusting my twitching finger on the walkie power-off button. Jack had reassumed the driving duties—his eighteen-wheeler experience coming in handy as buffeting winds battered us now that we were in an open area unprotected by mountains. He drove the Beast like a pro. I held Max in my lap and stroked him repeatedly, bent over so Jack couldn't hear, and whispered in his ear *I love you, little guy, I love you.* Thank God for Max because the past week had been emotionally harrowing.

Jack's cell, mounted on the dash tray, was incandescent with text messages, all of which he noted with a darting left eye, none of which he responded to.

We crossed the Jed River and noticed a billboard advertising what looked like a place to stop, stretch, eat a goat pie, and pee, preferably not in a crisper drawer.

"We need to pull over and you need to take the helm," Jack said in a solemn tone, eyes glued on the red badge on his Messages app, now alarmingly in the triple digits.

I radioed Hana about needing to stop, and her voice snapped back over the walkie with a better idea than the one advertised on the bill-board. "Number Eight Café. Follow me."

A few miles later we angled off the road into a dirt-and-gravel drive-way at Number Eight Café, a white, wood-framed structure in the comatose town of Cheviot. Charcoal-gray skies, whorling menacingly and painting an empyreal apocalypse, threatened more rain but had held off so far. As we climbed out of the camper van and stretched, we could make out snowcapped mountains to the west. Nowhere in New Zealand was farther than seventy-five miles from an ocean, or a short drive from a mountain range or folds of green drapery unfurling from hilltops and acned with dun-white sheep. Its sublimity was a stark con-trast to my agonistic self.

We found a table at Number Eight Café without any trouble. It was winter and the tourists hadn't poured in yet, and who would be as harebrained as Jack and me to be driving in a camper van on the South Island in the middle of July anyway? As Hana and I perused our menus, I could make out Jack through the café's windows, phone pressed to one ear, pacing back and forth, occasionally stopping to explain the inexpli-cable with an expressive face and windmilling of arms.

"Everything okay with Jack?" Hana asked.

"I don't know. He's a chaotic guy." I didn't want to get into Jack's complicated romantic entanglement with Amanda. She would have to be apprised of the distinction between an inveterate dog like Jack and a serial monogamist like me, and neither thumbnail sounded flattering in the inchoation of an explanation, so I chose brevity.

"Female problems?" she ventured.

"He's had female problems all his life."

"What about you?"

"*Half* my life. Mostly issues with my mother. Headshrinker said I turned to art because I wasn't breastfed."

Hana chuckled in spite of herself.

I pretended to study my menu, but Hughie's ripping me off still had me ragingly pissed.

"What brought you to Aotearoa New Zealand?" Hana asked

ingenuously. "I mean, I know you had a teaching gig, but why did you stay on?"

I stared at my menu and all the items went out of focus. "I needed to get out of LA. It's a miserable place, Hana. Decent people move there, but the ones who remain are the ones who turned savage, ruthless, pachydermic—thick skinned—and it eats away at your sense of morality and what brought you there in the first place."

"What did?"

"To write. To make movies. But the process sours you, corrodes you from inside until one day you wake up sucking the marrow of your own brain hoping this time, this project, will be the ticket out."

"To what?"

"Sanity." I looked up from my menu. "The pure pleasure of making art."

"Why New Zealand?"

"It was as far away as I could imagine, but of course the internet follows you like a mongrel dog. As a writer, I couldn't get arrested in the US. Unless you count the IRS—" Hana laughed; I was on a roll. "Hughie emailed me out of the blue, one thing led to another, the teaching job in Dunedin, the chance to write a book for Hughie and his fledgling imprint. So, on broken wings, I flew over. Fell in love with Central Otago, less so teaching creative writing. Cashed out all my few retirement accounts and splurged on a half hectare of my all-time favorite grape, Pinot, and thought I would hang it up, write the book you're promoting, pull down the shade. The End. And then I met someone, and she introduced me to the possibility of love again. But with love comes responsibilities, obligations, reciprocities, relationship shit I'm lacking in—ex-wife told me I wasn't raised right." I paused, narrowed my eyes, and looked off to a world gone out of focus again. "Then I got an email a week ago. And that changed everything."

Hana telescoped her head forward. "What email?"

I shook my head. "I don't want to go into it, Hana. I don't know you well enough."

"You don't trust me?"

"I trust you." I raised a flattened hand to my chin. "Up to here."

"Okay." She let it go and pointed at my menu. "Do you want to order?"

"Yeah, let's." I told Hana what I wanted, and she crossed the café to the counter to place the order.

A minute later she returned to the table and stood over me with a mortified look. "Do you have any cash?"

"What?"

"The corporate card's been declined," she said.

Disgusted, but not surprised, I blew air out my nose and reached back for my wallet and produced a hundred New Zealand dollars. "Tell Hughie to take some of that fifteen grand and fuel up his card," I scoffed.

"Thank you," she said, taking the money. "I will. He said it should be back up and working by tomorrow."

"Right. Along with the delinquent second half of the advance."

Hana returned to the counter with my cash. Now I was not only the monkey on the leash, the freak in the carny act, I was funding my own humiliating book tour.

Shaking off the cold, Jack blustered inside and wearily, noisily plopped down in a chair across from me. He shook his head with an accompanying sigh and raked a hand through his tangled mane of graying hair, the faded TV actor, without makeup and pep pills, in visible decline.

When Hana returned, I held up a hand to her to give Jack and me a moment, and she nodded assent, drifted off, instinctively reaching for her world microcosmically contained in her phone.

"What's going on?" I asked.

"Amanda's pissed off."

"What's the story?"

"That fucking video that Russian uploaded. Tagged me. Everyone saw it, Miles," Jack said in an aggrieved voice, and I knew he wasn't acting.

"That doesn't mean you were present," I said.

Jack smirked. "She fucking fingerprint ID'd me while I was sleeping

and has been inside my phone all this time." He closed both hands over
his face like a bivalve. "She read some of our texts. I wasn't straight up with
her about the book tour, and now with the Christchurch debacle . . ."

"What did you tell her?"

"She's got me geo-located, Miles. The truth. Sans Olivia. She said
if she couldn't join us she's dumping me into the Tasman." Jack leaned
forward on both elbows. "I can't lose her, Miles."

"Oh, Jesus. With all the shit we have going on, you're going to let
her join us? Jack!"

"I know," he said, "I know. I'm thinking it through. I'm trying to
talk her down. I mean, I would blow it off, but the Dan O'Neill connection for your book option is hanging in the balance. She'll scuttle
that, too." He looked off, a tongue pouching out one cheek. "And she
got me the *Washed-Up Celebrities* gig, as you know. It was her idea. I
can't fuck this up. She's all I've got between the comfort of Byron Bay
and tent city in Venice."

"But of course, you're, as usual, doing everything you can to fuck
it up."

"No one could have predicted last night. Seismically off the charts."

"No. That is true. We're in a different arena, Jackson. That shit that
went down in the Santa Ynez Valley a decade-plus ago couldn't have
happened today."

Jack smiled wryly. "I miss those days." He looked off. "Plus, she's
eager to start doing the documentary."

"What?!"

"To calm her down, I said she could do the documentary of this
tour, the one your publisher wanted to fund, the one Amanda got TV
One excited about."

"I can't believe all this shit has been going on behind my back."

"It's going to be great publicity for you, Miles."

"Yeah, but with Amanda in tow?"

Jack opened his arms up in resignation. "She's going to come and
make my life hell. Let's let her do the doc, and if it's awful, I'll figure a
way out of it."

I dropped my eyes to the table. "Can't we put that on hold? Do we need to document this new ignominy?"

Jack scratched his unshaven face. There were things he wasn't telling me. He, Hughie, and now Amanda had all been scheming behind my back. As usual, I felt pinched between two realities: mine and someone else's. There was never any purity in the work itself. There was *always* someone else. Fucking it up. "Not to dampen the romance of your bachelor trip nostalgia," I said, "but I was informed by Hana the corporate card just got declined."

"What?" Jack said, dropping his cradling hands from his head.

"It'll be back online tomorrow, Hughie promised."

"Fucking asshole. He's got fifteen grand of your coin burning a hole in his wallet."

"Don't remind me. If it isn't back on by tomorrow, his publishing house goes up in flames. He may have missed a payment."

"The guy's broke, Miles. He used you. He used your celebrity. You should let me do your deals. Your agent is a bloodsucking loser."

Hana returned to the table with our order number mounted in a little silver clip holder. I nodded for her to join us. She corkscrewed into a chair next to Jack, directly across from me.

"I got you steak and fries," she said to Jack.

"Thank you, Hana. I hope it doesn't break the bank."

"You okay? You look aggie."

"I'm okay and I'm not okay, okay?"

"Okay," she said, laughing.

The three of us had rallied in the cauldron of obloquy. I found myself, yet again, facing the treacherous world of money, corruption, false promises, dreams as vanishing as rainbows.

Our lunch orders arrived in a commotion of plates. Famished, we dug in. Hana ate ravenously, as if she hadn't had breakfast or was worried the corporate card wasn't going to come back online and was trying to pack in the calories in preparation for even leaner times in her maiden voyage masquerading as a publicist. Jack and I each had a beer to better shoulder our different burdens.

Glancing over the schedule, I said to Hana, "Kaikōura Quake Book Club?"

"That's right. Also known as 'the Long Drop Book Club.' Esses is pouring."

"Esses. What's their specialty?"

"Bubbles."

"Oh no," said Jack. "Not more bubbles. My head's still killing me."

The epicenter of a massive 7.8 earthquake had dealt seaside Kaikōura a tremendous blow a few years before the pandemic. Roads buckled. Houses and buildings pancaked and were rendered uninhabitable. Then the pandemic hit, New Zealand shut down, and local businesses were doubly, trebly, hammered. Kaikōura collapsed into a ghost town. Relief trickled in from the government, but many of the residents were still living in makeshift shelters: tents, campers, partially demolished houses roofed with plastic tarps . . . Hana explained all this to a dismayed Jack and me, who both feared this as our future, the odd couple, once marginally famous, now unsheltered, begging for alms from those who bore dim memories of our exploits in a movie that was barely a glimmer in the youths' cinematic memory.

I drove the short distance from Number Eight Café to Kaikōura, following Hana in her coughing and ailing Subaru. Max was parked on the passenger seat, head tilted up over the dash, darting glances this way and that at the surrounding countryside. He appeared to be getting acclimatized to being on the road. Jack was slouched in the back working his phone with propitiatory texts to Amanda. When it rang and he picked up, over the growl of the diesel engine, I made out snippets of conversation. "Look, honey, nothing happened. Nothing, okay?" "I do love you, and I do want this to work." "I know when Miles and I get together things can get nutty, but he's matured." I laughed and shook my head. "Nothing happened! Okay?" "Yes, of course, we want you to direct this documentary."

I tuned out, petted Max with my left hand, let my mind "have a wander," as Kiwis liked to say. Ella's beautiful apparition materialized wraithlike into the foreground. If I had told her why I was returning to

California, would she have had more compassion for my plight? But I couldn't tell her. It was too personal, too earth-shattering. It would raise too many questions. Jack, okay. He took it in stride. He probably had a few he didn't know about! Even I had yet to fully process the unwelcome news. I knew it was why I was once again adrift on the River Styx, the glorious wines of New Zealand providing an ameliorant, if ephemerally, as wine is wont to do. New Zealand had been my home for two blissful years. I wrote a book I had wanted to write, damn the attention-deficit readers, damn the political correctness, to hell with money and all the rest. But my past had surreally caught up with me. The bad drinking years. The Hollywood years. The celebrity years. I had needed the isolation and distance New Zealand vouchsafed me, but California was unwittingly pulling me back. I didn't have to go; I had to go.

Aotearoa New Zealand can fool you. Just when some piker publisher reneges on his promises, prevaricating to you like any motherfucking, scumbag, pathologically lying Hollywood producer would do without compunctions, you gaze out on the natural beauty of this extraordinary country and it ushers in a tsunami of absolution. One feels fortunate to be here. Even as the planet implodes—relentless heat waves, flash floods, droughts, Santa Ana wind-whipped conflagrations, island-obliterating hurricanes, revolutions—you deludingly hope that here, in New Zealand, the country down under will be spared all eco-calamities, all revolutions sprung from mass poverty and the horrible dictatorships that arise out of earth's ills. There'll be water. The hillsides are dotted with tasty lambs. Surely, vegetables are ripening somewhere. And if all seems hopeless, just pull up to Kaikōura Beach and drink in the resplendent coastline. As we neared the destroyed city, sea lions lounged on lichen-slick rocks. Waves clapped politely at the rocky shore. You would never think an earthquake had shaken this place to a gravesite of rubble and rendered its inhabitants in a gallimaufry of destitution.

Following Hana, we turned in to a makeshift seaside campground. A cluster of campers and tents were respectively positioned and pitched in a circle, a modern-day wagon train. A bonfire was roaring in a makeshift pit fashioned of bricks. Covering it was an iron grill, through which the flames flicked fiery tongues at the sky. Twilight was upon us when we

arrived, and the ocean was touched with a magenta hue painted from
the fading rays of the sun's brush. The snowcapped mountains to the
west shone incandescent against the violet spectrum of the empyrean's
nothingness. The highest peak is named Tapuae-o-Uenuku or, as Hana
translated as we climbed out of the camper van and I stared up at its
majestic height, "the footprint of the rainbow."

"The footprint of the rainbow," I repeated. "That's beautiful." I
pointed it out to Jack. "Footprint of the rainbow," I said to him.

"What?" he said.

"That mountain. That's its name. We don't have names like that in
America. Mount Shasta. Fucking soda pop."

Jack read a text and a smile brightened his face. "I think I've got it
sorted out, Miles."

"Great, Jack, because I can't lose you. I don't think I can drive the
Beast by myself. Certainly not alone with Max."

Jack, who seemed in a suddenly ebullient mood, clapped me on
the back. "The ship is righted." I was afraid to ask him what rapproche-
ment with Amanda he had brokered for fear I would have to have a
heart-to-heart with Hana about the documentary. She'd had a rough
night, too, and I didn't want to spring anything new on her.

"Ready for the Long Drop Book Club with Esses House of Bubbles
pouring?" Hana said, a smile emblazoning her face.

"We are ready for more bubbles," said Jack, putting his phone away
in a back pocket and clapping his hands.

"What's the etymology of the Long Drop Book Club?" I asked Hana.

"Ask them," she said, tittering, as if she knew but didn't want to
spoil its punch line.

Upon our arrival, from the camper vans, trailers, and tents emptied
a motley crew of North Canterbury–region winemakers. They ranged in
age from twenties to seventies and rose out of the murky light like refugees from a civilization that had gone nearly extinct. The hosts tonight
were Mel and Aaron Skinner and their Esses House of Bubbles, a minuscule winery that only produced sparkling wines. Mel, a woman, was in

a wacky sartorial getup complemented with colorful oversized eyewear. Her diffident husband, Aaron, looked like an accountant with his serious countenance but in reality was an esteemed viticulturist of the region. After the two back-to-back temblors that foundered them, literally and figuratively, to the ground, they had formed the Long Drop Book Club because, as they noted on their Facebook page, they wanted to reconnect with something real, something tangible, something palpable; they wanted to reestablish a sense of community on the destroyed ruins of Kaikōura, and a book club afforded them a cultural reason to assemble over a mutual ambition to reacquaint one another with the Luddite pleasures of reading and conversation, a return to the slow, a return to the days before the internet, which, after the earthquake, seemed to capriciously ebb and flow here in Kaikōura. It was a refreshing mission statement.

We gathered in canvas-upholstered fold-up beach chairs in a circle around the leaping bonfire. Giant crawfish one of the Long Drop members had trapped in the ocean lapping mere feet away from where we were assembled were speared on skewers and positioned over the fire, juices sizzling and hissing over the lava-red embers. They all had a copy of my *A Year of Pure Feeling* clutched in their hands and were eager to ask me questions. After the Cougars of Christchurch, this sedate clambake-style affair was a welcome respite.

"How long did it take you to write it?" one of them queried, silhouetted through the fire, her face obscured.

"It's hard to say," I said reflectively. "Do you count the years I suffered the ideation process or just the months I spent actually typing on my laptop?" I paused. "Or the years my ex-wife verbally abused me?"

Chortling laughter crisscrossed over the flames among the members.

Mel deftly uncorked a bottle of her Millésime 2016 Brut Cuvée, a stunning blend of Chardonnay and Pinot Noir that had spent five years maturing on the lees.

"How can you afford, with all this devastation, to keep a wine that long in bottle?" I asked, after she had introduced the sparkling wine.

Mel and Aaron looked at me with surprise. "That's how we make it," she said.

"Nothing changes for us," chimed in Aaron.

"Miles?" said a woman with a raised hand. "Do you think you'll write another one? I've read interviews with you where you bemoan the death of literature." She held up my book with a talismanic reverence. "We here in Kaikōura still believe in the written word."

"That's gratifying to hear. I don't know," I said, sipping the sublime champagne here, for me, at the end of the world, its inhabitants housed in temporary shelters, the disembodied sea lions plangently barking, pelicans gliding feet above the surface of the ocean in a primeval scene out of another epoch where humans had yet to plunder and rape the planet of its profuse resources and disrupt its harmonious natural state. "Novels have only been with us for five hundred years, movies for only a hundred. Who's to say what will last, what has to last? If no one reads, then my question to you is, does a book exist?"

Everyone looked at one another, baffled by my words. Coming from an author, I guess they expected a less pessimistic prognosis of literature's future. Crawfish were dipped in gravy boats of herb-infused butter. I noticed the tide flooding in and imagined it drowning a scholar's study lined floor to ceiling with books and could see the tomes floating in an aqueous room in an underwater city aswarm with fish and wraithlike ghouls of a doomed civilization.

"I mean, of course they exist, in a repository, like a relic, but are they actually alive if no one reads anymore?" I challenged them.

"If no one reads anymore," said the woman who had asked the question, "then what is the hope for humanity?"

I pondered her profundity, then asked, "Why do you call yourself the Long Drop Book Club?"

A collective snicker met my cold ears. Aaron explained: "A lot of us don't have working toilets, so when we have to—you know—we go to this shed"—he pointed—"and sit on a hole and take a long drop." His explanation detonated another gust of laughter.

I stood. "And where would I, famous author, be introduced to the long drop? We have a toilet in our camper van, but Jack and I are afraid to use it for fear it'll back up and we'll be stuck driving in a sanitation vehicle."

Laughing, Aaron gestured somewhere beyond the perimeter of the campsite, and I took off on foot in the direction of a crude wood-framed structure that faced the ocean, an astonishing view to accompany a defecation. The door swung open on rusty hinges. I perched myself over the dark hole of human waste, fixed my gaze on the incoming swells, and waited for relief. There was something utterly uncomplicated, so elemental in the act, I wondered why we didn't vacate our bowels like this more often. Ideas flooded me. I pondered again the email from Milena that had upended my world. Darker thoughts drifted to Ella and how much I missed her and whether there was hope we'd ever get back together again. Bleaker memories intruded as I propped my head in my hands, elbows on thighs, and waited for "the long drop" to come, the humor of the double entendre not escaping me. I needed the evacuation of my bowels as much as I needed some answers to my existential questions. The only thing missing was Rodin's *The Thinker* perched on the hole next to me, chin on hand, staring perplexedly at the world, immortalized in marble. Would that be me one day, sitting on this wooden plank, pants crumpled to my ankles, immortalized by the Kiwis as the writer who came here and was best remembered for taking a long drop?

I let go, waited a seeming eternity before I heard an echoic splash. I imagined it passing through the earth's core and landing on Hollywood, and that produced a laugh. I wiped myself with the provided roll, pulled up my jeans, then returned to the book club.

We camped on the beach in a prime location. Standing outside the camper van, Hana explained to me, holding Max while Jack snored away on the upper bunk, she was going to sleep in her car because she had consumed too much champagne to drive into Kaikōura and grab a motel. I didn't believe that was the reason. The bum corporate card was the culprit, but she was too proud, too Kiwi, to admit it.

"I'll pay for a hotel, Hana," I offered.

"No, that's okay," she said, puffing on a joint, relaxing after another long day on the road. "It's all good."

"It was a wonderful night tonight," I said as we sat on our haunches at the shore's edge, a bottle of Madame Sec 2012 Vintage Sec Cuvée, a sparkler that had spent an extraordinary nine years on the lees before Esses released it, planted in the sand between us.

"I'm glad you liked it."

"They asked intelligent questions."

"They did, yeah," she said, sipping the champagne.

"And they had all indisputably read my book. Which almost brought tears to my eyes."

"What else are they going to do in their campers?" she said.

"Good point. It sounded like they actually liked it."

"They did. You write with a forthrightness they can relate to." She turned to me with a sheepish grin. "You got a good review in the *New Zealand Herald* yesterday," she said. She produced her phone and started swiping with her index finger. "Want me to read it to you?"

"No," I said, fashioning a cross with my arms to hide my eyes. "When I'm done with a book, I'm done. I don't want to know anything about it."

"Are you sure? It's super positive."

"It's been such a perfect evening, let's not spoil it with anything positive."

She laughed. "You're a funny guy, Miles."

"Without humor, I would be dead. With humor, I can handle anything."

"Yeah." She sipped her flute of champagne. "Great bubbly," she commented.

"Ethereal."

She turned to me with her large brown eyes and locked them on me. "What's in California you might have to go back?" I looked away. "Jack said something about ending the tour with you flying back."

"Can't keep a secret with that guy." I rolled my tongue over my upper teeth and didn't say anything in reply. "I don't want to go into it, Hana." She looked away. A silence descended. Knee-high waves expired at the shore's edge, each its own spuming death.

After a moment, Hana produced a small jar from her handbag and passed it to me.

"What's this?"

"It's bee pollen. Māori."

"Why are you giving it to me?"

She pulled her upper lip into her mouth and exhaled through her nostrils. "I was talking to Jack the other night and asking him how you were doing, and he . . . uh . . . told me you were having a little problem down there." She gestured to my crotch.

"I don't have performance issues, Hana. Yet."

Her face colored and she stifled a laugh. "No, silly." She paused for seeming dramatic effect. "Your tumor."

"Jack told you that?"

She shrugged. "Try the bee pollen. It's curative."

"Bee pollen is no match for the Big C."

CHAPTER 16

Jack was lying in the upper bunk, his face ghoulishly illuminated by his phone, when I returned from the outside, having braved a pee in the howling winds and the beginnings of yet another winter storm of biblical proportions.

"What's up?" I said as I took two steps to the bed I had fashioned in the lounge area and climbed in fully clothed, bone cold, haggard.

"Amanda's on the way," Jack said.

"Batten down the hatches."

"I tried to talk her out of it," he bullshitted. "Can't believe she fingerprint ID'd me and can get inside my account and has been tracking my movements ever since I left Oz. Then when she saw the post on Instagram, she went DEFCON Two."

I pulled the comforter up to my neck, interlocked my hands, and pillowed my head in supplication to more madness. "Aside from the cockamamie documentary idea, what does this mean for us, I'm loath to ask?"

"Somehow she managed to get a copy of your book tour itinerary, saw the next one is near Blenheim and that it's a"—Jack looked at me with a puzzled expression—"couples book club?"

"I haven't looked at the schedule. I'm afraid to. From the Tough Guys to the Cougars to champagne connoisseurs who go in for the long drop when the alimentary canal starts rumbling, nothing would surprise me. We're moving in a strange world, my friend."

"She's thinking maybe we could be in the couples book club," he said.

I barked a laugh. Hearing me, Max crawled out of his carrier and climbed up onto my bed using only his forepaws, padded over to my chest, and curled up under my chin. "Little Max man," I congratulated him on getting up on his own. "Couples Book Club in Blenheim, are you ready for that?" I stroked the top of his head. Max began purring, but every time Jack started talking, Max would pause as if Jack's voice capsized his feline sangfroid. "Are you in love with this woman or what?"

"She's powerfully connected and she's made a lot of shit happen, including your book-to-film deal," he confessed, dipping his phone at me from the top bunk for emphasis.

"So it's transactional?"

"It's more than transactional," Jack said, offended.

"Then I suppose we have to humor her," I said, resigned.

"She will not be deterred. She is a force of nature."

"This book tour's got another couple weeks to go, Jack," I reminded him. "Where's she going to stay?"

"I'll work it out. I always do. She wants to meet you. She's excited about this doc." He craned his neck down from the upper bunk. "And apparently has someone she wants you to meet."

"Who's that?"

"Some writer friend."

"Tell her to forget it. I'm not interested in being set up."

"Could be a bridge woman to get you over your river of misery with Ella." Jack reached over to the control panel and tapped a few icons, and the camper van plunged into darkness. Wind whistled through its automotive bones. We were mere panels of aluminum and glass from feral animals, windblown oceans, ghosts of marauders, New Zealand's wild, barbarous South Island. I hugged Max close to me. He nuzzled his face between my clavicle and chin, seeking warmth.

The morning dawned ragged and raw. I fed Max, then stepped out of the camper. The step my bad eyes assumed was there wasn't, and I pitched forward and splashed into squishy, clayey mud. I clambered to my feet like a man with no hinges in his joints, my feet sliding in the clay in a desperate attempt at purchase, a mannequin robot controlled by a deranged and cackling puppeteer. When I had regained my balance, I shook my head at the step-down ladder that had been taken out by the mailbox post in Christchurch and how I still hadn't gotten used to its absence. I brushed myself off, scratched my beard, combed my matted locks with my muddied fingers, and wondered what an illustrious literary giant like Julian Barnes would make of this camper-van book tour. Not only would he not be subjected to one, he would scoff at the mere suggestion, let alone the appearance of it with, say, his wine-aficionado, wordsmith-extraordinaire buddy Jay McInerney. Imagine the two of them in a camper van! I laughed out loud to myself at the comical image. An Oxford-educated Brit and a dapper dresser married to the scion of the Hearst fortune in a camper van, on a book tour, in the dead of winter, on the South Island of New Zealand, hawking prestige, high-end literature to adoring fans. Celebrity author, my ass. Jesus! Inexperienced, first-time publicist. Maxed-out corporate credit card. Defecating in outhouses over a hole in a wooden plank. A special needs writer in love with a special needs cat. Best friend embroiled in yet another relationship shitstorm. "Fuck the one percent! I am who I am, right, Max?" I said to Max, who had ventured to the door's edge and gazed out at me with wonder and worry and whatnot.

Storm clouds had gathered over the ocean. A freezing wind had kicked up overnight, mottling the Pacific with churning whitecaps, making it look wild and downright dangerous. Nonetheless, a few fishing boats bobbed on the waters, a living to be made by their hardy captains, a habit to be exercised, a partner to escape from—who knows!

I closed the door to the camper van and ensconced Max safely inside and splashed through the puddles over to where Hana's Subaru was parked. Clothes had been hung in the windows to seal out the sunlight and were flapping in the breeze where they extruded. I craned my neck around and espied Hana in the back in a sleeping bag—had she known free camping was in the job description? Or did she always come pre-pared? Jesus, I thought, book tours have sunk to a new bottom when your publicist is sacked out in the back of her car.

I knocked on the windshield, and Hana sprang to life. A look of horror contorted her expression. A moment later the face of an attractive woman with purple-dyed hair popped up out of the sleeping bag next to her. I raised my hand in an *excuse me* and wandered off, chagrined I had caught her with her lover unannounced.

Twenty minutes later a gray SUV I hadn't noticed peeled away down the dirt road, and a sheepish Hana approached me where I was sitting on a cold, lichen-covered rock, cradling Max in my lap.

"That was my partner, Sofia," she confided.

"I didn't mean to interrupt you."

She shook her head, then rolled a cigarette with a mixture of tobacco and marijuana, open now about her habit. She scratched a match aflame, lit it, inhaled deeply, then held the burning joint up to me. "Want some chop?" she offered.

"What's *chop?*"

"Weed mixed with tobacco."

I waved away her offer. "I'll get the fear. Not that I'm not already possessed of it."

"We can't have that now, can we?" She laughed, then took another lung-expanding hit.

"Have you been getting stoned this whole trip? I noticed you smok-ing before."

"Stoned is normal for me. Reality is terrifying."

"I can only imagine."

She reared back and studied my appearance up and down. "What happened to you?"

"I took a dive into the muck." I jerked a thumb over my shoulder to the camper van. "We lost the stepladder on the Beast escaping from the Cougars. Took out their mailbox, apparently."

Hana threw a backward glance and narrowed her eyes at the camper van. "Hughie's going to be pissed."

"Fuck him."

Hana power-smoked her chop, her nerves rattled.

"Look, Jack's got a girlfriend who's coming over from Australia to join us for a few days. From all the information, she's a bit of a piece of work. I want to alert you to her presence."

"Why is she coming?"

"Jack, as you might have guessed, finds himself in these complicated relationships. I think it's what keeps his blood flowing." I set Max down on the fescue, petted him to make sure he stayed still. "She's a producer of crap TV, a former actress who sort of made it but sort of didn't, which is a volatile mix in the entertainment business when it comes to a person's sanity." I waited while Hana chortled at my cynical view of Hollywood, a world that both fascinated her and that she could have cared less about. "Jack is in her money purse—how deep, I doubt he possesses the humility to tell me."

"I see." She turned to me. "How does this affect me?"

"I hope it doesn't," I said without meeting her gaze. "I just wanted to alert you to her coming, that's all. She's going to shoot a little documentary that Hughie told you might be happening."

"I didn't know it was Jack's girlfriend."

"That's okay."

She took a few more apprehensive back-to-back hits, then extinguished the "chop" on the bottom of her boot, put it in its plastic baggie, and stowed it away in her purse for future psychoactive salubrity. As we watched the storm clouds darken and the blowing morning materialize, her dishevelment bore a pulchritude not difficult to fathom. A randy smell emanated from her.

"When's the last time you showered, Hana?"

"I get by with the campgrounds."

"You're not staying in hotels?"

"Hughie said he can't afford it."

"Cheap Kiwi fucker." I shook my head in disgust, turned to her. "As a Māori, do you experience persecution? Discrimination?"

She shrugged. "I was bullied as a child."

"How so?"

"Beat up."

"Really?"

"Really."

"By who?"

"A bunch of girls who schemed to ostracize me, didn't want me in their little social circle, I guess."

"When did that end?"

"High school. But it turned more subtly microaggressive."

"How?"

"It's harshly cliquish. White over here, Māori over there."

"How does it manifest itself?"

"Say I go shopping in a high-end clothing store. The employees will follow me."

I nodded, reflecting on prejudices I'd never been subjected to. "But Māori have certain powers in your country?"

"We do. And we're getting more and more. But we're not in parliament. We're not at the levers of control. We're getting there, though." She stirred the sand with a contemplative finger. Beautifully ornate tattoos decorated the backs of her hands and rode up her arms, narrating her ancestry in intricate scrollwork.

"Love your tattoos," I said. "I bet they tell quite a story."

"They do," she said, gently touching the tattoos on her right arm with the fingers on her left, sinking into their meaning, their memory. She grew absorbed in them and seemed to have been transported away for a few reflective minutes.

"Someone once did my ancestry tree," I said, to break the silence. "I'm positive yours is more colorful, if just as tragic."

"What is yours?" she said to her tattoos.

"I told the woman researching my ancestral tree to stop when she landed on some coal miners in Austria who had died of black lung disease."

That lifted Hana out of her trance. "Seriously?"

"I don't know. It was depressing. No English royalty, no famous artists, just some characters out of a Dickens novel who didn't make it past forty." I turned to her. "I'm faring remarkably well for a Raymond. Though the name dies with me, the ancestral tree goes dark."

"Why?"

"None of my siblings had kids. Parents were both only children and now both dead, thank God."

"Why thank God?"

"They were heavy drinkers, agoraphobes, depressives, miserable."

"No children with your ex?"

I shook my head.

"No children at all?"

That stopped me dead in my tracks. Milena's email flew up in my face. I dropped my eyes to the ground. "You googled me. You know my whole story."

"Not why you might have to go back to the US," she prodded.

"Like I said, it's too painfully personal." I fell silent.

Hana gazed off. The last ragged pennant of blue sky got closed off by clotting black clouds, and the landscape darkened. The wind kicked up and blew sand across the shore. We folded our arms around our torsos and shivered in the cold.

"Why so many book clubs in such a short span of time?" I wondered.

"Hughie wants to get you across Cook Strait. We need to be at Picton three days from today."

I stared at the ominous horizon. "What's with this Couples Book Club?"

She turned sharply to me. "Miles, you told Hughie you were willing to do anything to sell your book. Book clubs started out as real book clubs, but in truth they're merely excuses for like-minded people to get together over anything. You should thank me for not signing you up for the End of Life Book Club!"

"Seriously?"

"Seriously."

"Keep it in play. We might need to close on that one, the way this book tour is going."

Hana barked a laugh. Her large teeth gleamed white in a blunt instrument of hope.

"What's on the agenda for today?"

"Short drive into Blenheim. We're camping at this cool place called the Coterie. They're a collective of young winemakers." She turned to me: "They're excited to meet you, Miles. They say you changed the wine industry."

"I don't want to get pigeonholed as the Pinot guy. I like to believe I have other arrows in my quiver."

"They've read all your books but of course remember the famous one made into a movie. Be proud of it, Miles."

"I don't know," I said, stirring the black sand with an index finger.

"They supposedly make awesome wines." She looked away. "And they have bathroom and shower facilities."

"Sold." I turned to my left to pet Max, but he wasn't there! "Max?" I called out, jolting anxiously to my feet. "Max!"

Hana leaped to her feet. She whipped out her phone and started pecking frantically at it.

I cupped my hands around my mouth. "Max?" A light rain had begun to shower us. The wind gusted and blew harder, sandblasting us with the shore's debris. The catastrophic thought of losing Max was crushing my soul. If I lost him, I don't know what I would do. "Max?" I bellowed with overt dismay in my voice. "Max?" I swept the beach with searching eyes, evidencing no sign of him as I staggered along the shoreline in a panic.

A fog materialized out of nowhere, and visibility cratered to mere paces. All of a sudden I felt like the only human left on planet Earth—it was that eerie. Instead of calling out for Max, I cupped my hands around my mouth again and yelled, "Hana? Hana? Where are you?" I grew disoriented, a light plane pilot flying into a dense bank of clouds with no instruments, suddenly experiencing vertigo. In that moment I saw what Death must look like: a disembodied voice in a featureless world crying out hopelessly as the skies grew darker and darker until finally, at last, there was nothingness.

"Miles, over here," shouted an elated Hana.

I sloshed over the sand and fescue, my arms breaststroking through the fog, in the direction of her voice. Within a matter of minutes, I had transited from suicidal despair to believing in life again. There was little Max man perched on his haunches, growling and hissing at a pair of slumbering sea lions, one of whom was barking now at my intrepid cat. I picked Max up as Hana held out her phone and showed me, with enlarged eyes, the tracking device she had used to recover him.

"Aren't you glad I got this?" she exulted, looking at me, her eyes absorbing light and gleaming her triumph.

"I am," I said as I cradled Max in my arms and hugged him close to me. "I love you, little guy, I love you," I whispered into his whiskers.

"Use it, for fuck's sake," she said, "if I'm not here. I recommend keeping that little critter in the camper. If you're going to let him out, get himafuckingleash," she admonished.

I gave her my solemn promise I would in an upbeat tone now that Max was safe and sound and back in my arms.

We clomped through the wet sand and dense fog back in the direction of our vehicles. I cleaved close to Hana's side, as her eyesight was superior to mine and she seemed to know where she was going, following some instinctual sense of direction I had long ago surrendered to the geographical discombobulations brought on by age. In a weak moment I thought about telling her I had once had a numinous encounter with death, but it was early in the morning, and I didn't want to scare her with the prospect that maybe I was losing it.

As the fog parted into diaphanous curtains of dissipating gray, Hana and I came to a halt when we saw a shiny new black four-door midsize pickup truck with a small, box-shaped camper trailer hitched to the rear with a bright white logo reading: "Marlin Campers." Showing a chagrined Jack around the compact trailer was a tall, attractive woman with shoulder-length chestnut hair framing an angular face etched in perpetual circumspection. When she turned and smiled at Hana and me, she didn't show her teeth, only the age lines in her almost-for-sure-Botoxed face.

"Hi, mates," she called out in an Aussie accent, waving amiably as we anxiously approached, as if the ground were booby-trapped. "You're Miles, of course, and"—she turned to an anxious Hana—"and you must be Hana, the Māori publicist."

Hana scowled at her, preferring not to be singled out as an indigenous person.

"Meet Amanda," Jack said, breaking into the group, realizing everyone was nonplussed except for Amanda, who seemed to instantly fit in like we were expecting her.

I was still taking in the tiny camper trailer and all the repercussions of that vision when Amanda thrust out her hand. I took it. It was greasy with lotion and her handshake crushed my hand, as though it were fashioned from the bones of a songbird and hers from a corporate CEO on a fast track to a billion-dollar empire. The tan jodhpurs and the black riding boots that rose to her knees were a bit sartorially theatrical for my tastes. All that was missing was the fetish flogger, but no doubt that was stowed away in the Marlin Campers Cruiser Deluxe model. "Well, here we are," Amanda exulted.

Jack manufactured a smile from a long-ago TV show.

Hana stared stoically.

My stomach roiled with the stench of disaster.

CHAPTER 17

"If you hadn't had your epic meltdown at the Cougars, I wouldn't be in this mess," Jack roared.

"Oh, and how was I supposed to know some Russian double agent was going to video me, post it on Instagram, and that your paramour had face ID'd you in your sleep and was tracking your every move?"

Jack blew hot air out his nostrils like an exhausted bull in an arena of his own devising. He kept checking the rearview mirror with anxious regularity. I glanced in mine and shook my head in abhorrence. On our tail was the Honda Ridgeline pickup and the Marlin Cruiser trailer that no doubt expanded into a mini manor estate replete with a long drop and a bed overhanging a bluff to set the perfect outdoor romantic scene. I convulsed at the thought.

"When's the documentary crew showing up?" I asked, suppressing my anger.

"Soon."

"How compromised are you?" I asked the windshield, Max curled up in my lap, fortunate to be a cat and not a fucking human.

"She's producing the reboot of *Washed-Up Celebrities*," he reminded me for the third time.

"I know. You told me. And she got to Dan O'Neill to buy the film rights to my book?"

"Yep. She's a mover and a shaker."

"So," I started, in a rising tone, "if you fuck things up with her, you fuck yourself, then you fuck me, and we're fucked twice?"

"If you're thinking negatively."

"I'm always thinking negatively because it keeps me sane, it keeps me from having my expectations dashed."

"I've got it under control," Jack declared with conviction, his jaw jutting forward over the wheel, his words specious as fuck.

"I hope you've explained to your sugar mommy I can't be captaining the Beast on my own?"

"I told her." The lies were pouring out like lava over the rim of the Hunga Tonga–Hunga Ha'apai volcano. This is where the rift between Jack and me always started: the lies. The lies he had learned acting in, directing, and producing small films and cable TV shows in Hollywood. The pathological dissembling required to climb up the rungs of the ladder to the brass ring in Hollywood. The lies you had to wantonly strew to stay one step ahead of the game of lying in order not to get blindsided by even cleverer lies. The world Jack and I once moved in ran on the fuel of lies. I thought I had escaped it for good when I decamped for New Zealand. Apparently not. Only Max's purring and warm body suggested there was another way to live your life.

"And then there's Hana," I spluttered, emerging out of my cynical reverie. "She didn't bargain for this."

"She's a publicist, Miles. Their every waking moment is a shitstorm."

"She's a first-time publicist, and she doesn't know that," I snapped. "And a Kiwi one at that in a quaint country. Was not annealed in the shark-infested waters of Hollywood."

Jack looked at me aghast. "A first-time publicist. I should have guessed. Jesus! I thought you were famous."

"I am. Only the books got small," I lamely joked. My eyes and upset being traveled out the window to the hoped-for peace of twenty-five million sheep in harmony with nature's perfection of photosynthesis. We were lumbering along the Pacific in a camper van instead of a Stagecoach bus. Miles and miles of undeveloped beachfront property fled by, prime oceanfront property that venal real estate developers in California would slit their spouses' throats for.

"Well, the good news," I said to Jack as I emerged out of my bleak reverie, "Amanda's the one who's going to have to endure your snoring."

Jack shot me a quick, puzzled look. "Snoring?"

"Camper van was shuddering. I thought it was the wind, or maybe a wounded sea lion."

Jack laughed. "I've never heard that complaint before."

"It's thunderous. Window rattling. And unrelenting."

"Okay. Okay. I get it, Miles. I snore. It's probably the change in diet since we started this book tour."

"Oh, blame it on my book tour. Maybe women haven't wanted to tell you for fear you would leave them?"

"Not Amanda. She speaks her mind."

"That's what worries me."

I let that thought hang in the air and turned to the window. The hills were furred with green. Dotting them were the ubiquitous dun-colored sheep. They never seemed to move, as if forever fixed in a postcard. With one breathtaking view in New Zealand you can see a canvas of wind-swept ocean, snowcapped mountains, and verdant green pasture. I didn't know of any place like this in all of America. It's why my heart sank into this country when I came two years ago and why leaving would be trau-matic. Particularly since it appeared if I did decide to leave, I wouldn't be able to return. I feared America, but what was pulling me back was such a powerful magnet, and a surreal one to boot, I was still wrestling with it in my emotionally repressed way. Unbidden, it would thrust up in my mind, a geyser through a fissure in the earth, paralyzing me. Jack now knew, but he was cold comfort. I needed the analytical attention of a therapist, the deeper feeling of a woman, or the speechless sagacity and the one-way-current empathy of a cat.

We cruised along stunning, empty black sand beaches that con-trasted with the blue and gray of the storm-mirrored ocean. The protean, chiaroscuro skies remained dramatic; the weather was dramatic; our caravan of three now was approaching the dramatic! Growing up in

Southern California, I had come to detest the absence of seasons and the monochromatic skies. It softened the brain, pounded it like abalone into something ostensibly palatable, but in reality made it amorphous. I longed for dramatic weather. I had a theory that Southern California could never have given the world a James Joyce or a Virginia Woolf precisely because the weather doesn't test their limits, doesn't push their creative beings to the extremes they need to go to in order to dredge up the profoundly unique stuff. Maybe that's another reason why I had fled to New Zealand. I wanted to be tested in the maw of its dramatic meteorology. I needed a new lens through which to view the world for fear I would lapse into repeating myself, ending up an epigone version of myself, the writer I once was when I wrote my supposed legacy work a decade and a half ago.

Somewhere where the region of Canterbury bled into Marlborough, Highway 1 peeled away from the heart-stoppingly picturesque ocean and angled in a northwesterly direction. The thoughts churning in my head stayed there, crisscrossing and intersecting one another like cars on freeway cloverleafs. Jack had command of the wheel and command of his own thoughts, no doubt chewing over the repercussions of the stage-four clinger now, well, living up to her sobriquet.

"You know," I started, wanting to hear my voice over the roar of the diesel engine, "if you don't want to be with this woman, and you're just staying in it for me, whatever, don't do me any favors."

"I appreciate that, Miles." Jack took a sip of a soda. "When I came to Australia, I was pretty tapped out. This was a second chance for me. Well, a fourth chance—"

"Or a ninth—"

"—Or a ninth, or whatever, but I'm not getting any younger. We've been out of touch, but I got pretty close to the gutter back there after you had your brush with fame." He darted a glance at me. "And did I try to touch you up? No."

"I would have fueled you up."

"I know you would have, dude, but money ruins friendships. It ruins everything," he said, uncharacteristically philosophical. "But Amanda has some serious coin, she loves me, or so she claims, and I'm not about to turn a gift horse in the mouth to grits and collards," he said, the North Carolinian seeping out of him. He nodded. "Okay, so I risked it back in Christchurch and she busted my balls, but maybe that was a wake-up call."

"Again!"

"Again." He pursed his lips in defiance of life's fate. "We have a nice place in Byron Bay—well, she does—a hip little place, a lot of celebrities—"

"Washed-up celebrities?"

"Oh yeah, but my kind of people," he finished, winking at me.

"You need this to work is what you're saying?"

"I need this to work."

"Then why risk it?"

"I thought I was in the clear, but that fucking Tim Cook and his Share My Location feature. Fuck, man."

"Look, Jack, I don't honestly care."

The walkie crackled and came to life with Hana's voice: "Sending you the link to where we're going." I checked Messages on my phone, saw her text, then clicked on the link, and it routed me to Google Maps. I clicked to start directions.

"Where to?" asked Jack.

"The Coterie. It's a wine collective. Should be a rollicking night."

A horn blasted to Jack's right, and he whipped his head. Amanda had pulled up alongside us, driving in the wrong lane (!), and was motioning for Jack to roll down his window. He did.

"I need to take a pee," Amanda shouted.

At the next turnoff, Jack, Hana, and I stood outside in the cold, hugging our bodies, as Amanda emptied her bladder in the bathroom in the camper van. Hana had rolled a joint of chop, managed to get it lit with repeated—anxious?—match strikes, and was puffing on it fretfully. Jack and I stood next to each other in the pastoral barrenness, marveling at the wintry beauty of New Zealand.

"I see why you moved here," Jack said.

"As long as I keep getting opportunities to write, I can be anywhere,"

I said. "I don't need people." Jack threw me a look. "I've got Max, and he's all I need."

"I don't believe you."

"Max won't cheat on me. Besides, it's over with Ella."

Jack turned to me with that grooved face of empathetic concern. I wouldn't meet his beseeching eyes. "Then move on, man. Let Amanda introduce you to her writer friend."

"I'm not ready."

"Well, let's have a good time, because we don't have a long time."

I nodded at his rare moment of perspicacity. "You ever talk to your ex-wife?"

"Babs? Rarely," he muttered.

"See your boy often?"

"Now and then. I'm not a part of his life. Sadly."

"Maybe one day things will normalize."

"Yeah, maybe," he said with a downcast look, laconic to the point where he wished I hadn't recrudesced the scars of the past. He shot me a glance. "And you've got a daughter now. That makes us both dads."

I nodded. "Yep."

A moment later, in a whole other world, in a world that was now and brand new, Amanda came bounding out of the camper van. A solicitous Jack caught her a split second before she catapulted over the missing step and plunged into the muck. That's all I needed. I'm sure Hana would have gotten an irrepressible stoner's laugh out of that one. Instead we were witness to Jack with Amanda in his strong, gym-rat bulked-up arms swinging her around and kissing her passionately—though, as he's an actor, one never can be quite sure of the divide between the performative and the genuinely passionate. He set her down and she turned to Hana and me.

"I'm treating everyone to dinner tonight," she announced. "You mates look a little scrappy to me, look like you could use a gourmet meal."

"I'll get you set up at the Coterie and let you three enjoy yourselves," said Hana, the threat of Amanda's company palpable in her voice.

"Are you sure? Stay with us. I'd love to give you some beauty tips," Amanda crassly offered.

Hana, quietly seething, manufactured a smile but didn't say anything in reply, her nonresponse both a *no* and a repudiation of everything Amanda.

A traveling sun slipped behind a storm cloud as if a portent of things to come.

CHAPTER 18

The Coterie is a tall, white, windowless building standing sentinel on a knoll a short distance outside Blenheim in the Marlborough region of New Zealand. In it is housed a collective of young vintners experimenting with vinification methods, a quiet revolution, in rebellion against all things Kim Crawford and the monoculture of Sauvignon Blanc, a lesser grape variety Kiwis had grown dangerously dependent on. Hana had thought, given my first novel had explored a region of wine in California, this would be a marriage of my new book and a wine tasting with young, hip winemakers who all held me in esteem.

We parked the camper van adjacent to the Coterie structure on a patch of dirt. Close by, Jack was helping Amanda unpack and assemble the Marlin Cruiser into a tent habitat. On a first go-round, the setup appeared complicated, and bickering competed with the birdsong and the stunning vineyard vistas as they set about pounding stakes into the ground with mallets and unfolding canvas coverings in an abode I had trouble imagining them having sex in.

In the camper van, I fed a purring, neglected Max, then convened with Hana in the back.

Hana interlaced her fingers and sighed. "I don't think Jack's partner is a good idea for tonight," she said.

"We might have no choice." I lifted Max onto my lap and petted him until his purring grew audible.

"Then I'm going to let you handle it because I see a conflict."

"What, Hana?"

"Miles. These young winemakers see you as a rock star in the wine world. One word out of that woman's mouth and it's going to look bad for you." She reached in her bag for her half-smoked joint, then decided against firing it up. "I don't have a good feeling about this." Worry drew nests of wrinkles in the corners of her youthful eyes.

"I'll talk to them over dinner," I consoled her.

Hana glanced at her watch. "Be back here at eight," she said.

"You don't want to have dinner with us?"

Hana straightened to her feet in the camper van and smiled sarcastically. She opened the door.

"Watch out for the step," I said, but Hana had already gone tumbling out.

"Fuckingstepladdershit," she cursed, clutching a knee with one hand and employing the other to clamber back to her feet.

"You okay, Hana?" I called out, braced against the open door.

"Yeah, I'm okay," she said, brushing herself off. "I'm so fucking okay it's unreal!"

Max, hearing the commotion and seizing a rare opportunity, made a dash to scramble out the open door, but I managed to stop him by scissoring my legs closed, then picked him up by the scruff of the neck and reproved him by bouncing an index finger against his nose. "No, little guy, I can't lose you. Don't run out on me."

When the Marlin Cruiser tent had finally been erected and Hana had departed for the nearest public shower, Amanda drove Jack and me in her Ridgeback into the nearby town of Blenheim.

"You should move to Byron Bay," Amanda said to me with a backward look as Jack followed Google Maps to a Brazilian restaurant named Gramado's that Amanda had picked out based on a recommendation from one of her many Kiwi friends.

"I prefer it in New Zealand," I said from the back, querulous, itching for a drink.

"Miles might have to go to California after the book tour," said Jack, "in which case he wouldn't be able to return."

Amanda threw her head around to the back where I was seated to meet my eyes. "All the more reason to move to Australia. I know someone who would sponsor you in a heartbeat." She turned back to the windshield flooded with a full moon sweeping in and out of gathering rain clouds, haloing their penumbras. "You two would have a lot in common," Amanda said.

"What does she do?" I inquired faux-naively, knowing she was probably referencing the writer friend Jack had apprised me of.

"She's a novelist like you," she said without elaborating.

"Writers don't get along," I said, to be difficult because I was having difficulty warming up to her—I can't stand brash, fulsome, gushy actress types; they make my skin crawl; I don't trust them. "They're temperamentally—"

"Miles," Jack chopped me off.

"You'd like Jamie," Amanda said.

"How do you know her?"

"I produced the limited series of her *A Sorrow Beyond Years*."

"Okay, I'm officially impressed," I said, recognizing the title of the award-winning miniseries. "But I might need to return to the States."

Intrigued, Amanda threw me a backward look, but this time she telescoped it over the headrest, and I could smell her wine-scented breath. She and Jack had already started uncorking bottles in the cache of Prophet's Rock Pinot I had stocked up on before departing on this warped book tour. "Why?"

"It's personal."

"A woman?"

"It's personal. Only Max knows."

"Who's Max?"

"His cat," Jack explained.

Amanda cackled so loud and unendingly it turned me against her, even though, for Jack's sake, I wanted to like her. Jack locked his eyes on mine, brought an index finger to his lips to let me know he wouldn't tell her a thing I had divulged to him. I wagged an index finger at him in dire admonition he'd better not.

Gramado's is a small, family-style Brazilian restaurant in the heart of Blenheim. The waitstaff are overly solicitous. They pull up a chair to your table midmeal and try to engage the dinner party in a conversation about, for example, the spiciness of peppers. It's a rehearsed performance, it would never happen in the States, but this is New Zealand, and a lot of the people on the South Island are uptight Scots, and maybe the foodie interaction gives them a sense of feeling wanted—all that time alone with the sheep, you know.

After the young man had been shooed off by an impatient Amanda, she peered at me over her menu. "Miles, how can I help you on this book tour? You realize the young Māori girl doesn't know what the fuck she's doing, right?" I ignored the subtle racism in her undertone.

"It's her gig," I defended Hana. "Plus, I like her. A lot."

"Jack said you've hosted some pretty strange events. I mean, you're Miles Raymond, author of one of the most famous wine novels in literary history," she hyperbolized, "and you're on a beach as the guest of honor of a book club called the Long Drop?" She barked a laugh. "You should be in front of hundreds. Autographing books until your writing hand cramps."

"I appreciate the compliments, Amanda, but I'm loath to let Hana go."

"She's never done this before!"

"How do you know?"

"Because"—she held up her phone—"I googled her. There're no other authors on her résumé."

"I like her creative spirit," I said in further defense of the inexperienced Hana and because I had a soft spot in my heart for a publicist who camped in her own car in order to make the stingy budget Hughie had her on.

"The Cougars of Christchurch Book Club?" Amanda scoffed.

"That was foisted on her, but it turned out . . . interesting."

"Sounds disgusting." She leaned her head forward again in a threatening gesture. "What really happened there?" She swiveled suspicious looks between me and Jack for any catcher-and-pitcher signs. Jack's face went stoic and I stared fixedly at my menu. "Huh?"

"I sold a dozen books and got a handsome appearance fee," I lied.

Amanda drilled her dagger producer eyes into me.

"You produced the limited series of your friend's *A Sorrow Beyond Years*?" I said to get her off the Cougars disaster.

"IMDb it if you don't believe me."

"I truly loved that book."

"I'll let Jamie know."

"I'd love to meet her," I said, biting my tongue, thinking of Ella, and that thought competing with wanting to mollify inquisitional Amanda.

The performative waiter returned to take our orders, fake Brazilian accent on full display. Taking charge, Amanda selected a bottle of local Marlborough Sauvignon Blanc.

"Kim Crawford? Are you fucking kidding me?" I protested.

"I like it."

"It's industrial waste. Here, give me the wine list," I said, extending my hand. Amanda relinquished it, miffed I had rejected her decision by vilifying her taste. "We'll have a bottle of the Boneline Iridium," I said, then handed him the wine list back.

Chameleonic Amanda, not one to linger on a slight, shifted into a more ebullient disposition, produced a shopping bag, and hauled out two sweaters. One was brown embroidered with three white sheep with a black sheep in the middle. The other was blue with four white sheep handwoven into it. "Bonz Black Sheep jumpers," she said. She made a presentment of them for examination.

I reached out and felt one. "Soft," I said.

"They're handwoven out of llama wool. But the cool thing is the sheep are all woven out of a different yarn from a different animal. And they're not cheap. You should wear them. It'll be your uniforms. Social media will catch on to this—"

"—And I'll be the laughingstock of the literary world."

"It's quintessentially New Zealand, Miles. Kiwis will love you."

"I'll run it by Hana. But thank you, Amanda."

"Come on, be good sports, try them on."

I shook my head, but Jack made a face as if saying, *Come on, humor her, remember where our bread is buttered here.*

Jack and I clumsily pulled on the sheep sweaters. They were cashmere soft and warm . . . and kitschy as all hell.

Amanda reared back and clapped approval. "I think you two look cute."

Jack nodded at me. I nodded back at him. We kept them on to appease Amanda in hopes she wouldn't continue her inquiry into the Cougars of Christchurch fiasco.

Over dessert, Amanda got down to business. "I think this book tour needs to go bigger, Miles."

"Jack hinted you had something up your producer sleeve."

"I'm putting together a shorthand crew to come down and film it."

"He told me."

"And you're not using social media with enough posts. Your Hana posts a photo now and then. I'm talking about professionally produced videos."

Jack shot me a moronic smile as if: *See, Amanda's going to right the ship and you're going to learn to love her.*

"Let me think about it," I said. It was obvious what was happening. The producer in her was taking over, as producers are wont to do. She had grand designs for my modest, if off-to-a-rocky-start, book tour. But like all of her grand plans, there was an ulterior motive. And it was Jack. She wanted him to return to Byron Bay.

We drove back to the Coterie, Amanda talking a mile a minute about her documentary ideas, my meeting her famous writer friend Jamie, fantasizing two happily married couples down under in Byron Bay.

Back at the Coterie, Hana laughed out loud when she saw Jack and me, standing next to each other, wearing our black-sheep sweaters. "You're not going to wear those, are you?" she howled in execration, astonished, appalled, one hand clasped to her mouth to stifle her laughter.

"We are," Jack said.

"Who bought those hideous jumpers?"

"I did," snorted Amanda, eavesdropping a few feet away, her face lit up by her pesky phone.

Hana steered an expression of rebuke to her but, not sure about the dynamic, didn't say anything in response. Finally: "Okay. Whatever you guys want to do. Let's go inside."

The Coterie is a high-ceilinged barrel room, a custom crush facility festooned with winemaking equipment from barrels to stainless steel vats to cement eggs to basket presses and other winemaking equipment. Composed of a dozen young winemakers experimenting with grapes grown in Marlborough, they were undoubtedly the most avant-garde thing happening in the New Zealand wine world. Their respect for my first novel and the movie adapted from it was evident in their starstruck eyes. Had *A Year of Pure Feeling* moved them as much?

Seated in chairs, Mike Eaton, a Kiwi viticultural legend whom Hana had engaged to put this event together, introduced the young vintners one by one, and each stood to tell me their story and the wines they were vinifying. During the short presentations barrel samples extracted with wine thieves were poured into our wineglasses. All of them, men and women equally, were experimenting with extended skin contact on Sauvignon Blanc grapes of different clones to extract a flavor profile nonexistent in the commercial winemaking that had begun to dominate, and vitiate, the New Zealand wine industry. All the wines were unlike Sauvignon Blancs I had ever tasted before, and the future of New Zealand wines, I realized, was not only in the sublime Pinot Noirs coming out of Central Otago, but here at the Coterie in Marlborough, infamous for industrialized farming of Sauvignon Blanc for big producers making monochromatic swill for the masses. Kim Crawford. Villa Maria. Kono.

As the extraordinary tasting continued, Amanda grew increasingly intoxicated and belligerent. Hana, in horror, had retreated to the periphery, her female instinct about Amanda crucifyingly realized, evident in her downturned-mouth expression. Amanda, possessing only a smattering of wine knowledge, started critiquing some of the wines with offensively stupid comments like, "This tastes like dirt," before discarding it in a floor drain. Following it with embarrassing bombast like, "What did you blokes and shirleys think of Miles's new book? Fabulous, isn't it?"

I pulled Jack aside. "You've got to get her out of here, Jackson."

Jack looked nervously back and forth between the stricken face of Hana and the blowsy Amanda, who was now center stage impersonating a wine connoisseur. He moved toward her and grabbed her by the elbow. "Come on, honey."

"What?" she cried. "I'm enjoying my wine."

Against her vociferous expostulations, Jack frog-marched her out of the Coterie, much to the relief of Hana and the young winemakers.

I leaned against a barrel and turned to the nonplussed vintners and said, "I'm sorry. My friend Jack's partner has had a little too much to drink. You should shoot for a lower alcohol next vintage," I joked to their muffled laughter. I drew my hands together prayerfully. "You ridiculously young men and women are making some of the most cutting-edge, interesting wines I've tasted in a long time. I'm impressed. And I want to thank you for the extraordinary tasting. We don't need to talk about my new book," I finished.

"But we all read it," spoke up a young woman.

"Okay," I said. "What'd you think?" I sipped a Sauvignon Blanc that tasted of ocean and rare tropical fruits I couldn't identify.

The young woman winemaker stabbed a finger at her chest. I nodded at her. "Is it hard for you to write from such a personal place?"

I looked at her, blinked, sucked in my breath. "I'm taking risks," I started. "If I didn't take risks, if I wrote formula fiction or, in this case, a saccharine work of semiautobiographical fiction, I wouldn't be able to live with myself. And yet in writing confessionally, from such a personal place, I incur, unwittingly, oftentimes, not always, the condemnation and outrage of others. I could ask you the same question: Is it hard to be making wines so sui generis, so unfashionable, so seemingly uncommercial, you risk going bankrupt?"

They looked at one another, smiling at the truth of my words.

"Wine is one thing," spoke up a young guy with a patch of black hair embellishing his chin. "But you're writing about yourself."

"But your wines reflect you," I said. "And yes, I've taken the personal to the human, to real people in my life, but I'm still no different in terms of taking risks. Yes, I could be sued . . ." I waited for the explosion of laughter to die. "And probably will be," I said to more raucous laughter—the profusion of barrel samples liberating me to new heights—"especially that section about my ex-wife—all true, by the way." I stared at the wine in my glass. It was cloudy because it was unfiltered and swirling with the lees of dead yeast and the must of skins deliberately not racked off to add complexity and depth. "But I'm going for the quintessence of truth." I held up the glass. "Just as I believe you are going for the essence of this much-maligned Sauvignon Blanc grape."

"That was beautiful," Hana whispered in my ear after I had finished autographing all the winemakers' copies of my book and we were heading out of the Coterie back to the camper van.

"The wines were extraordinary," I slurred. "Thank you for taking me to this holy tabernacle of New Zealand wine. And sorry about Jack's paramour's embarrassing you."

"She's a live one," Hana said.

When we got back to the space where we had parked our vehicles for the night, Hana and I stopped. The tent that the unstable Marlin Cruiser had mushroomed into—tentpoles that looked like giant toothpicks—was rocking precariously back and forth, seemingly in danger of tipping over. A woman's voice was ululating in the throes of a cresting orgasm, shattering the quiet of the night. Jack was righting the ship.

I turned to Hana. "Oh, what an actor will do for the rent."

CHAPTER 19

A sharp rap at the camper-van door jolted me awake. Max bolted from the bed and scampered up the passageway and hid inside his carrier. I glanced at the time on my phone. It was 2:11. The rap came again, sharper, louder, and with a voice:

"Miles, open up. It's me, Amanda."

I clambered out of the convertible bed, hastily scrambled into a pair of jeans, and opened the camper-van door. Greeting me was the strained face of Amanda, makeup sex with Jack disheveling her countenance. Her bed-tangled hair looked like a tumbleweed had blown onto her head and somehow had latched itself to her skull. Whatever makeup and mascara she had started the evening with was smeared, or kissed, or fellatioed, off.

"I need to use the bathroom," she said through her oversized, lopsided mouth.

"What about the Coterie?"

"It's locked."

"We're camping, Amanda, it's the great outdoors. No one's looking."

"This isn't a squat-and-drip-dry situation, Miles. I have to bloody go!" she said with great urgency, stabbing an index finger alarmingly at her backside, which she turned to me for emphasis. Without waiting for my permission, using the hand grip she adroitly hoisted one foot up onto the entrance above where the treaded ladder step should have provided her a boost.

Overwhelmed and not processing the full impact of the emergency, I stepped aside and let her climb up into the camper-van passenger compartment. Max, sniffing trouble, was meowing discontentedly. I pulled him from his carrier and cradled him in my arms, fearing he would bolt.

Amanda stood before the door to the toilet/shower combo. "I need privacy."

I sighed, then leaped out the passenger door with Max in my arms. As I made my way into the night, a starlit sky provided a depthless contrast to whatever was happening in my new home. I found a picnic bench to park Max and myself on and plopped down. A shadow materialized out of the dark, startling me. Jack sat down across from me, raking a hand through his bushy hair. His mouth gleamed like a glazed doughnut from no doubt multiple sessions of cunnilingus. A zephyr sent the stench of his being wafting past my nose.

"She had to go," he said.

I nodded in thinly veiled disgust, and kept nodding to underscore my disgust, hoping to expunge the image of Amanda christening our camper van with a bowel movement, not exactly the champagne bottle smashed against the bow send-off.

Feeling protective or conciliatory, Jack moved around the picnic bench and sidled up next to me. We were both wearing our sheep jumpers and looked like a pair of Kiwi tourists, the Vladimir and Estragon of wine, literature, film, and TV, a sorry pair, still waiting for God to resurrect us from the indignities of our flawed lives.

"This isn't off to a propitious start," I said. "How long is this going to go on? And I have serious doubts about this documentary she and Hughie—and you—have been cooking up."

"Give me a few days, Miles. It's like hooking a bluefin tuna. You've got to give them some line and tire them out before you reel them in."

I turned to Jack. "What does she want? Ultimately? The doc is chump change."

"She wants me to put a ring on her finger."

"Well, fuck, then do it!" A light rain had begun to leach from the now-starless sky. Even with our sheep jumpers we were both freezing cold. I hugged a confused Max close to me and Jack had his arms criss-crossed against his chest while we waited for his future wife to finish defiling my new home. I turned sharply to Jack. "This isn't going to last, you realize?"

Jack remained stoically silent, wouldn't meet my withering gaze.

"Even after I had somehow wrapped my brain around the book tour in this camper van, and even after the surreal start, I was glimpsing redemption in envisioning my next comic novel. It was forming in my head. I was almost warming to more craziness if only for the rich loam of material this fucked-up book tour was vouchsafing me!" I jerked a thumb toward the camper van. "But she's not going to be a character in it, because then it wouldn't be a tragi-comedy, it would be a lurid spectacle murder mystery with a Grand Guignol finish no one would believe. Because that's all I'm feeling right now."

"Give it a chance, Miles. For me. Your ol' buddy Jack?"

"She's evacuating her bowels in my mobile home, Jack. Gives new meaning to shitting where I eat."

Footsteps crunching on gravel approached out of the dark. It was a sleepy-headed Hana in jeans, slippers, and some type of loose flannel top. "I heard voices. You guys look knackered."

"We are," I said.

"Don't move," she said, snickering. She raised her iPhone and snapped a series of photos from different angles, a perverse grin plastered on her face. "You look hilarious in those sheep jumpers. It's going to make for a great Insta post."

"Please don't, Hana," I said, shaking my head. "There's only so much humiliation I can handle before I tie one on the likes of which I promise you you don't want to witness."

"Heed his warning," Jack said.

"Great publicity," Hana said, ignoring us. "Hughie's going to love it."

"Go ahead then," I said, no longer caring.

"Warm us up on Photoshop," a vain Jack chimed in. He hooked

an arm around my shoulders and pulled me close to him. "Take a few more," he encouraged Hana. "Miles and Jack, iconic road buddies."

"The losers who could never win even when it seemed like they were winning," I said.

Hana obliged, moving about and bobbing up and down to shoot us from different angles, laughing uncontrollably for the first time since this misbegotten trip had launched. "This one with you two and Max and the camper van in the background is classic," she laughed.

All of a sudden, the camper-van passenger compartment door burst open and Jack sprang to his feet, rushed to gather his lover in his arms before she vaulted herself into a puddle of muddy water. He solicitously helped her down, then escorted her toward us. Hana, who felt toxicity in Amanda's presence, had already beaten a path back to her Subaru, wanting to avoid her.

"She's all yours, Miles," she said in a dismissive tone.

Jack waved to me as he helped a relieved Amanda back to the friable Marlin Cruiser, silhouettes weaving in the darkness to an uncertain future.

I rose to my feet with Max in my arms. I walked with him the few steps back to the camper van, set him down inside, then, employing the handhold of the door, hoisted myself up into the passenger compartment. The fetor of Amanda's bowel movement was like nothing my olfactory senses had encountered since a keg party and guys defecating jumbo bags of Lay's potato chips. Max kept sniffing the air as if he, too, smelled the end of the world, then fled into his carrier, where I swear, in the dim light, I thought I saw him covering his nose with his forepaws. Out of grim curiosity I checked the toilet to see if it had successfully flushed. Either Jack had forgotten to turn the water on or the tank needed refilling, because I was met with the most beastly sight I had ever laid eyes on. I quickly closed the lid, closed the toilet/shower combo door, then crept back to bed, nauseated, wrestling with insomnia knowing I was mere feet away from an unflushed toilet, a mephitic metaphor of my mostly wretched life that didn't escape me in that mirthless moment.

I was beset by broken sleep and disquieting dreams. My unconscious threw every repressed fear at me in a volley of warning: narratives of homelessness, imminent death, tsunamis, nursing homes, prison, and worse: loneliness so solitary a Tibetan monk would have deemed himself an extrovert.

The morning dawned auspiciously. Consciousness threw me a lifeline of hope. Ragged storm clouds had blown to the far edges of the 360-degree panoramic view where the Coterie stood sentinel. I sipped coffee outdoors as Jack worked on the unflushed bowel movement of his soon-to-be second wife. Looking more put together, Amanda joined me at the picnic bench, propped her elbows on the rough wood, and slanted her head toward mine.

"You don't like me much, do you?"

"Why do you say that?"

"It's just a feeling." I didn't say anything. "You think I'm crashing your party, don't you?"

I glanced off. Hana was perched cross-legged on the hood of her Subaru, smoking chop and engaging the world with her phone. "No, you're a welcome addition," I lied.

"This book tour is a joke, Miles, you know that?"

"It is what it is."

"It's a roadshow joke."

"Okay, it's a joke." I tossed open my hands, inviting her to continue.

"It doesn't look good for the film deal with Dan O'Neill," she said with conviction. I waited. "I think what's going to keep his excitement is if we film this and turn it into a comedy."

"Turn my life into a comedy?"

"That's right," she said. "Because it is a comedy. And you and my Jack are the stars."

"A reality TV show?"

"Yeah. It's my specialty. As you know."

"I don't know, Amanda. I know you mean well. I know you and Jack are building a production company . . ."

"You'll all be characters in it," she said, ignoring me. She swept her arm to a forlorn-looking Hana trying to overcome her apprehensions with copious amounts of cannabis. "Including your little Māori publicist. No one has done it before. A reality TV show of a book tour. Two guys in a camper van in the middle of winter in New Zealand. One's a once-famous author and the other is his Man Friday, his Sancho Panza to your Don Quixote."

"I thought it was only going to be a documentary, that that's why you're here?"

"Fuck the documentary. This shit show is the show. After talking with Jack, I realized this could be much more."

"You've thought this through, haven't you?" I said in a monotone, hoping to capsize her enthusiasm.

Amanda opened her eyes wide and nodded. "Give it a chance before you become too judgmental." She grabbed my wrists and held them tight to the picnic bench, pinning me down. "I know we have different personalities, I know we're polar opposites, but we have Jack in common, and I care about Jack. I love Jack. And he loves me. I want what's best for Jack. That means I want what's best for you. Your publicist is a nice girl, but she's a pot-smoking intern at best, Miles." I rolled my tongue around my mouth, bearing the brunt of her lecture full on. "And she's fine as a PA, but somebody has to take charge here. You've got a great book about your life story, it's going to make a fabulous movie with Dan, and this is an opportunity to ramp up the publicity for it." She glanced anxiously at her phone. "My film crew are on the ferry now. They should be here in time for the Couples Book Club."

"Amanda," I feebly protested, growing alarmed.

She gripped my wrists tighter. "I know what I'm doing," she insisted. "Just go along with it. The book isn't going to make you shit as a book because nobody reads anymore, but the reality TV show of your tour is going to make you a fortune. And *then* you might sell some books."

I smirked at her probably true commercial assessment of her self-aggrandizing proposal.

Our impromptu tête-à-tête was broken up by a converging of vehicles on the property. The Coterie crew shambled in. Nancy, their house chef, had prepared a breakfast spread on a large picnic table that overflowed its planks. Homemade breads and jams, sausage and eggs, delicious coffee.

Afterward, Amanda's plans pinging around disconcertingly in my sleep-deprived brain, I caravanned off with viticulturalist Mike Eaton. He wanted me to meet someone at a place that was special in Marlborough called Wrekin Vineyard. It was a small but newish custom crush facility, and one of the winemakers working out of there was a legend in New Zealand.

The Wrekin facility was perched on a hill with untrammeled views of rolling countryside in all directions, an apposition, if ever there was one, to what I was feeling and experiencing. Everywhere one journeyed in New Zealand was hallucinogenic in its splendor, whether the sun was obscured by the clouds or burning brightly in an intensely blue sky. Peace was promised everywhere but seemed delivered nowhere.

Inside the high-ceilinged facility, Wrekin was outfitted with all the winemaking equipment one would expect in a proper winery: fermenters, barriques, destemmers, even a high-tech stainless steel, computer-controlled basket press.

Hätsch Kalberer was a diffident man in his sixties, a saintly-looking guy with stringy, long graying hair and a sallow face. He made Pinot Noir with grapes sourced from all over. We barrel-sampled wines that went back in time over decades, which was unusual. The wines were spectacular: pure, perfumy, alive, and fresh as if new releases. Even though my heart was in Central Otago, Hätsch convinced me there were sublime Pinots from Martinborough south to Cromwell. The ones in his neck of the woods tasted plusher, more bright red cherry, whereas the ones in Central Otago were denser, more mineral driven, possibly more complex, splitting hairs.

"Pinot didn't begin in New Zealand in Central Otago," the soft-spoken Hätsch explained to me. "It began in the north but found its footing in Martinborough. Eventually, it gravitated to Central Otago. I didn't think it would flourish down here in Marlborough, but I was wrong, so I came."

"These wines are spectacular," I said. "Pinot expresses itself, wherever it can ripen, in the place of origin." Hätsch nodded assent. "Little or no intervention here?" He shook his head. "Pure Pinot Noir?" He nodded and smiled. "Destemmed?" He smiled at my knowledge.

It was a moment of quiet, an eye in the proverbial hurricane of my surreal book tour. Hätsch asked me about the process of writing, and I told him it was no different than winemaking. With wine, you have one year to get it right. It's not like beer or distillates where you can throw out a bad batch and begin over. "With a book," I lyricized, "you start with what you're given, and then you begin the alchemical process, with words as the only tools at your disposal. Like you, we make subjective choices, and we have to live with those choices. Both entertain the hopes and aspirations for poetic heights. Both have the chance to collapse and fail and end unpalatable. The only difference is that some books have more aging potential than wine," I concluded. "Though of course many don't."

He smiled wryly. "And books are not consumed like wine either," he said. "With wine, you're always drinking a memory."

CHAPTER 20

I was napping in the back of the camper van parked outside the Wrekin wine facility when the ringtone on my phone jangled me awake. Popping up on my screen was the lovely face of Ella, the toffee-colored hair, the penetrating green eyes. It seemed like weeks since we had last spoken.

"Hello," I said.

"How's it going?"

"Okay," I said groggily, massaging the low-grade Pinot Noir headache I was nursing, trying to compose myself in the frame with my shaky hand.

"I saw your meltdown on social media."

"Did you?"

"What's going on?"

"I thought because I might have to go back to the States you didn't want to know me anymore?"

"Are you?"

"I don't know. I'm still undecided."

"What's the reason for the ambivalence?"

I closed my eyes and fell silent. I couldn't meet her inquiring eyes.

"Why won't you tell me? It's another woman, isn't it?"

"Don't start. I've been faithful to you from the beginning of our relationship, and that's not a lie."

"Anyone would think, as close as we've been, the plans we've mapped out, you would tell me."

"I will when the time is right. You will know everything."

There was silence on her end. She looked off camera. "How's Max?"

"He's fine. He's had some experiences."

"I bet. Like, for instance?"

"Jack's Aussie girlfriend showed up unannounced."

"Gee, I wonder why."

"Ella, if this is going to be an interrogation, I'm not in the mood. I've got the Couples Book Club tonight, and there's a documentary film crew coming . . ." I trailed off.

"What? The Couples Book Club?" She snorted a derisive laugh.

"Yeah, our industrious young publicist has come up with some creative events, not all of them to my liking."

"I see."

"It's where the arts are today, Ella. Nothing is what it was like before. Book clubs are big in New Zealand, so . . ."

"*Are* you flying back to California or not?" she wanted to know, uninterested in my book club tour.

"I honestly don't know, Ella."

"If you do, what're you going to do with your Pinot lot?"

"I'll gift it to you." She didn't say anything. "Do you know a guy named Hätsch Kalberer?"

"Of course. He's a legend."

"I met him this afternoon and sipped some of his Pinots with him. He said drinking wine was drinking a memory."

"Is that what you think our relationship is?" she deliberately tacked. I deliberately didn't answer. I had been on the planet for five decades and I understood women less than I ever had. Or, perhaps, I now realized I understood them less and had been deluded in my youth. There was always hope, but I cynically didn't think the chasm would ever be bridged in my lifetime.

I glanced at my watch. "I've got to run, Ella. I'm glad you called."

"Have you been drinking, Miles? I mean, really drinking again?"

"It's been a rough journey. I've seen things even God hasn't."

"And that's your excuse for relapsing? God?"

I shut my eyes again and exhaled wearily out of my nostrils.

"Are you going back to the States, Miles? I want to know." Emotion vibrated in her voice.

"I don't know, Ella. I love you, but there's some music I have to face, all right? And if I can't get back into the country, then I guess it's curtains, but I don't want it to be curtains, and I know that sounds paradoxical and inscrutable, but I'm facing something I never thought I would face in my lifetime."

We ended the call on that unresolved note. Ella was not one to beat a dead horse, and that's one of the things I loved about her. It was selfish of me not to tell her why I might have to go back to California. My partner of the last year and a half. The soon-to-be creator of my maiden vintage of Pinot. The warmth of my winter. The love of my second half on this planet. I sensed in her voice the chasm was widening, and in sensing that my heart was sorrowing.

I needed a shower, but I couldn't stomach the one in the camper van after Amanda had defiled it. Fortunately, Jack had fixed the issue ("water was turned off"), and he was able to get it to flush, thank God, but the progenitor of the problem was still the problem. And here it came:

When I stepped out of the van, I was met by a three-person film crew. There was a cameraperson with a shoulder harness and a serious-looking digital camera in front of her face, a sound guy wearing a beret, and a digital imaging technician, rail-thin, pencil mustache, staring at a tablet, all of them in their twenties. They backed up, filming me as I emerged from the camper van. Behind them stood a tall, beaming Amanda, dressed in tapered black jeans and a royal-blue sweater, hair billowed on her lollipop head, looking like the producer, now director, who she was. Jack was conveniently nowhere in sight.

Amanda introduced me to the pubescent crew, but their names went in one ear and out the other because I was still grappling with the potentially damaging repercussions of this expansion of my book tour, not to mention the sour note Ella and I had ended our conversation on.

"Where's Hana?" I said, the first thought that came to mind, worried she had bailed.

"She's inside setting up the book club," Amanda answered, in charge of the book tour now and sounding like it.

"Excuse me," I announced to the documentary crew with a raised index finger, and turned sharply toward the Wrekin facility. "Don't go in the camper van, you'll scare my cat, Max, and then I'm going to be royally pissed off."

I accosted Amanda. "I didn't approve of this. I have not signed on the dotted line. Nor seen a fucking contract."

She ignored me, like a typical producer for whom the means justify any ends, including lying, blackmail, payola, extortion, and worse. "Wrekin! What a great name," she enthused.

"Yeah," I chuckled, not immune to the fact that producers could also show flashes of mordant humor in the interstices between their pathological lies. "I'm going to go inside now. Do not let them shoot at will," I said. "Or I will disappear."

Inside the Wrekin barrel room Hana had set up a couple dozen fold-up chairs. On a small table for the author (me), she had dutifully stacked copies of *A Year of Pure Feeling*, which I wasn't, ironically, feeling anymore.

Hana turned to me and spoke sarcastically, tonelessly, like the PA she had been relegated to be. "Jack's *partner* wanted to move it here from the farmhouse where it was supposed to take place."

"How are you holding up, Hana?"

"You're good," she said, worry in her shifting eyes.

"Yeah, but are you good?"

"Hughie's thrilled about the reality TV show idea."

"Yeah, because he's probably sold me off for spare parts. What about you?"

"It's your career, Miles."

I gazed off. Wine and couples for a book signing . . . I was growing nauseated by the inching minutes. "Amanda's been in touch with Hughie all along about this?" I said offhandedly.

Hana cast her eyes down. "Yeah. He even offered to raise my salary if I would stay on."

"You threatened to quit?" I said, thrown by the prospect of losing Hana.

"I'm a publicist, not a PA," she said, "but Amanda promised me a coproducer credit on the show."

"On the show?"

"She said she sold it to New Zealand TV One, contingent on a sample episode." Hana threw out an arm like a live snake. "Welcome to *Washed-Up Writers!*"

"What? This has all been in the works? Fuck me with a hot poker."

"She said it was a working title and not to tell you."

I brought both hands to my face in a wordless declamation of disgust. Then I started laughing. I laughed so hard my beard follicles ached. When my laughter had subsided, I looked at Hana, and she was staring at me questioningly. A sadness fleetingly enveloped us in the fog of uncertainty. I espied the unbelievable bottles of Pinot Hätsch parked on one of the upturned barriques, found a glass from the white-cloth-covered table Hana had laid out, and poured myself a near-full glass. Hana's eyes bulged. She had literary experience of my benders.

Things happen when you start drinking subsequent to when you've been hewing to an abstemious course for as many years as I had. First came the roar of rationalizations: the troubling call with Ella and the heart-piercing ostensible end of that solid relationship and all the memories of ends of relationships which had seared their immutable scars on my soul. I remembered most of the women, even their names, and I still genuinely ached for a select few of them. Then there was the book tour: the Tough Guys luring Jack and me out to some ostrich pen, the Cougars of Christchurch and their salacious literary boudoir high up on Mount Pleasant, the Long Drop Book Club, and the great champagnes of Esses and the depressing, but weirdly uplifting, sight of those stragglers in paradise all hanging precariously to some crumbly edge of life subsisting out of their camper vans and trailers. And then there was me: once an ephemerally famous writer behind the jet wash of a critically acclaimed hit movie, but who had descended too deep into hedonism, shipwrecked on the shoals of destitution (again!), then despair, then the Sisyphean climb out of the Hadean realms, miraculously resurrected on a winery property on a hill overlooking sublime nothingness, reborn with a new partner, a half hectare of my beloved Pinot, a fresh start, and then launched on a book tour with a new book born from the pain and ashes of that ephemeral celebrity I never leverage in my behalf, an autobiographical novel/quasi-memoir I probably shouldn't have published, a book tour so monumentally fucked up an Aussie producer had pitched it as a reality TV show and incredibly managed a flickering green light for it to go forward. And abstainers wonder why the siren call of wine is so powerfully magnetic.

I don't know how many glasses I downed as the room filled up with the members of the Wrekin Couples Book Club. I had an image of Hana, stiffened, a dark cloud of concern hovering over her. Amanda, taking charge, cracking the whip, in her element, seemed to be encouraging me to keep drinking. *Washed-Up Writers* indeed!

The timeline of drinking is about ellipses, the events you remember, those you don't remember, those you regretfully remember the next morning: the parked car you backed into and left the scene without leaving contact details; the woman you woke up next to whose name you couldn't recall and who cried in protest, "But you said you loved me?"; the zigzagging drive to the wine emporium to purchase more wine, "the most expensive bottle you have!" you dimly remember roaring to the smiling floorwalker fantasizing a monster bonus.

The people of the Couples Book Club started arriving. I was feeling large, growing loud, on the two bottles I calculated I had consumed. The three-person camera crew hovered like giant bumblebees over moving stamens, scouring for any shots, any material, that would build into a great episode.

When the four couples were settled, and wine had been poured, Hana introduced me. I was leaning back in my chair on two legs, imminently about to fall. Jack sat close to Amanda, his arms pretzeled around hers. They seemed to have resolved their differences (I thought!) and were conspiring against me (the paranoid me being me).

The couples introduced themselves. One was a middle-aged pair. The woman ranched three thousand head of sheep and six hundred head of cattle. The man oversaw a vineyard. She couldn't care "fuck-all" about his vineyard, and he said at one point if he didn't see another sheep in a hundred years, it would be too soon. Clearly, they had differences. Another was an attractive winemaking couple. He worked for a conglomerate making sure vintage no longer mattered in producing wine commercially, and she worked for a small producer of artisanal wines. They fought about things like "no intervention," "no filtration," "basket presses over gigantic bladder presses," "mechanized harvesting over hand harvesting." The third couple had been in the wine business in Marlborough for years, but she wanted to retire, and he feared being bored under an umbrella on an equatorial beach in Fiji if stranded there with her. If memory serves.

"Hi, I'm Miles Raymond. Thank you for coming." I held up my glass, perhaps the fifth one, though I had clearly lost count. I had gone up the wine ladder and found a plateau of momentary lucidity before the great plunge into the void. "This is certainly a unique event for an author. We're used to book tours to bookstores, but since bookstores have closed over the years, we authors—is it *us authors*? Oh, whatever!— have to intrepidly venture where the readers are, and I presume all of you have read my new book, *A Year of Orgasmic Fuckin'*." I remember uneasy laughter. "Kidding," I said, reaching for my glass. "I don't know what the decision was to write an autobiographical novel because I feel like I have years yet to live—" I raised my glass of wine. "Maybe I don't, but I wanted to tell my story before some fan on two bottles of Merlot T-boned me."

More uneasy laughter greeted my drunken attempts at humor. Amanda bounded in like a kangaroo and addressed the attendees. "And we'd like to hear your stories and how they relate to Miles's book."

I remember the couples seeming to be uncomfortable with the camera crew and spilling their guts for a potential reality TV show, even though Amanda had implored Hana to get them all to sign release forms. Amanda encouraged them to "drink up," not that they needed the encouragement. A woman named Mary, who was the host and had made the introductions, turned the event over to the winemaking couple. Amanda wasn't getting the sizzle she wanted, so she motioned for Jack to come over. Jack dutifully rose and moved into the center of the barrel room, he himself looking bemused and chagrined.

"Jack and I have been together"—she turned to Jack—"what has it been, honey?"

"Six months," answered Jack, "maybe less," as if he didn't want me to know how long they'd actually been a couple.

"Sit down," said Amanda. Jack plopped back down. Amanda poured him some wine and then some for herself. "You disappeared on me a week ago, right?"

"I didn't disappear," Jack said. "I told you I was going to help out my longtime friend Miles on his book tour."

"You disappeared." She held up her phone, weaponizing it. "And then you did this book club with a gaggle of horny women and fucked one of them, isn't that right?"

"No, no, Amanda . . ." Jack protested, red faced with embarrassment.

The Couples Book Club members seemed taken aback, stiffening in their chairs, their Kiwi reserve on full alert.

"See, we're opening up," Amanda said to the couples, swiveling her head around to make eye contact and be sure they all absorbed her words. "We need for you to get down to the nitty-gritty, express your true feelings about your partner. Isn't that right, Jack, you lyin', cheatin', no-good, good-for-nothing, washed-up celebrity?"

I didn't know what any of what followed had to do with my book. But goaded on by an ambitious Amanda, seeing a winner where only a neocon, money-thirsty homunculus like Mark Burnett would, the wine-maker couple proceeded to unleash their true feelings.

Sarah, or whatever the hell her name was, wearing a black T-shirt that had "Harden the Fuck Up and Have a Riesling" stenciled on it and apparently no bra (!), rose to the occasion, unleashed by some of the finest Pinots in all of Aotearoa. "Rob hasn't fucked me in months." Whoa! I staggered in place. And as if to underscore her point, she picked up a bâtonnage stirring rod and started flogging the shit out of one of Wrekin's expensive Damy barriques maturing exactly 308 bottles of some of Marlborough's most prized Pinot.

"Why would I fuck anybody who won't pick until her refractometer readings are just perfect?" shot back her husband, slurring his retort.

Sarah paused her beating of the barrel and turned to him red faced with indignation. "And you wonder why I've been having a romance with Mike over at Clos Ferdinand."

"What?" shrieked her newly anointed cuckolded husband.

"You want to see some wand work, huh?" screamed a seriously intoxicated Sarah. And she punished the barrel with another vicious lashing with the stirring rod.

I ducked out for a pee. The starlit sky was no longer stationary; it looked like it was mounted on a colossal gimbal and was pinwheeling around me. I staggered over to the camper van to check in on Max. He was asleep in his carrier. He came awake when I passed a fishy-smelling treat under his nose.

I returned to the now aptly named Wrekin barrel room. Sarah had, if my recollection serves, tossed the stirring rod, and her husband had sullenly turned away from her. But that ugly performance hadn't deterred the sheep/viticulturalist couple from having a go at it. They, too, were sitting on great mutual hostility that had gone unvoiced until Amanda with her producer prodding had ignited their deep-seated resentments toward each other like something out of an ancient episode of *The Jerry Springer Show*.

After it had mercifully concluded and enmity was contaminating the barrel room, I vaguely remember signing my books and Hana hustling me out by the arm. Slumped in the passenger seat of the camper van, having imbibed more than I had in years, Hana drove us what seemed like a long way. I kept slurring, "Where are we going? Where are we going?" but she ignored my entreaties and kept her focus on Google Maps, which she had mirrored from her iPhone onto the dash screen.

"We're going to where you're not going to getfuckingarrested."

CHAPTER 21

I woke in sodden clothes in the middle of the night to the sonorous music of insignificant waves slapping an unseen shoreline. Feeling shaky, I disentangled myself from the twisted covers, stumbled a few steps in the passageway, and found an opened bottle of Prophet's Rock Chardonnay I had stowed in the refrigerator. I uncapped the screw top and filled a drinking glass and drank half of it down like water, badly needing to take the edge off.

"You okay, Miles?" said a woman's voice, staggering me by how close it was to my one exposed ear.

I raised my eyes. Hana's head poked out from under the covers of the bed above the cabin, where Jack had been sleeping before Amanda had crashed our party and spirited him away to the Marlin Cruiser. "No, not really," I said, blinking her into focus. Her face was lit up by her phone, and she looked spectral. "Where are we?"

"On the West Coast. A beach north of Nelson," she said. "Get some sleep."

"What happened?"

"You don't want to know."

I found Max in his carrier, beckoned him out, and carried him back to bed. I lay on my back and stared at the ceiling. Hana's breathing, Max's purring, and the Prophet's Rock Chardonnay combined for a salutary feeling. Two Advil fished from my Xanax vial assuaged my sledgehammer-pounding-a-pier-piling headache. If only I could remain like this forever, I imagined. *Unfortunately, life's respites are temporal, there is no peace, there's only the next storm on the horizon,* I wrote in my head as I fell asleep with Max's warm soul next to my depleted one.

Morning dawned on a rocky shoreline at a place named Boulder Bank Scenic Reserve. A vast flock of silver-back gulls was shrieking murderously over caught fish. The surface of the water was watercolored in hues of gold and orange. My brain was trying to piece together the previous night when Hana emerged from the camper van, combing out her long, black, curly hair with an oversized bristly brush. Had she risked a shower in the combo bathroom? Seemed like it from the sweet scent of soap that emanated from her when she sat down next to me.

"How're you feeling?" She directed her question to the waves, slapping politely at the shore, her voice competing with the shrieking silver-back gulls, who knew no satiety in their ravening for fish.

"Not too hot." I glanced at her. "So, what happened?"

"Amanda got the Couples Book Club all riled up, I guess for her sizzle reel, and, well, it spiraled out of control from there, and everyone was confused about what was going on, and you had another one of your epic meltdowns and went to the dark side before passing out."

"And it's all on camera, I presume?"

"I presume." She faced me with an earnest look. "I had to get you out of there. This may be good for publicity, but it's not good for your reputation," she said. "Or mine."

"I've only done one book tour. Nothing like this. Jesus FC. I *have* hosted some large wine festivals where things went a little sideways."

A silence fell over us. When I glanced at her, Hana looked like she was screwing up the courage to say something. "We've got to be in Picton by one o'clock," she finally said.

"What's in Picton again?"

"It's where the ferry docks." She turned to me. "I promised Hughie I would get you across Cook Strait to Wellington . . ." She trailed off.

She picked up a small, jagged piece of driftwood and drew a design in the sand.

"How are *you* doing, Hana?"

"Not well," she started, lighting a joint she had been meditatively rolling, and inhaling it deeply.

"I'm sorry. It's my fault."

Hana hung her head and struggled to gather herself. "I realize this book tour has been kind of a disaster," she began.

"Kind of?" I barked a mordant laugh.

"Okay. A total disaster. I did my best. With no money, little lead time, and a first-time publisher who doesn't know whatthefuck he's doing."

I nodded. I didn't like the sound of her preamble. "You know I've never met Hughie in person."

"Seriously?" Her expression displayed surprise.

"Seriously. It's all been email, text, and Zooms."

"Well, you'll be meeting him in Wellington."

"Right." I shuddered at the prospect.

She crossed out her design in the sand with a show of futility. "Ever since Jack's producer partner showed up, it hasn't been the same for me."

"I understand." The sun was rising over the hills to the east of us and the ocean shimmered, blinding me. I reached into my pocket for my sunglasses and shielded my sensitive eyes.

"We're booked for the event in Wellington at the Welsh Dragon Bar. It's a little touristy now but it used to be a public toilet."

"Sounds metaphorically perfect."

"Their book club is called—"

"Let me guess," I chopped her off. "The Public Toilet Book Club?"

Hana laughed. "You're smart."

"Actually, I'm the dumbest dude on the planet. I gave up a beautiful woman for the writing life. And now a brilliant winemaker for a dark secret I'm holding inside."

Hana blinked her large dark-brown eyes. "There'll be a lot of young people there, people who'll want to hear your story, hopefully buy your book." The new design in the sand was taking shape. It looked like the ouroboros, the dragon eating its tail, the symbol of eternity and regeneration. "And then there's the big Featherston Booktown event outside Martinborough. That promises to be great," she consoled. "You'll get to experience a pōwhiri."

"What's a pōwhiri?"

"A Māori welcoming ceremony. You'll see when you get there." She threw back her mane of coal-black hair, grappling with something unspoken. "I would have loved to have been there to talk you through it, but . . ." She lowered her head, sighed, and paused dramatically. "I'm leaving the tour."

"What?" I said, panicked, turning to face her.

"I can't take Amanda. She's got a streak of that Aussie bigotry we Kiwis are all too familiar with." She looked at me. "And I'm notherfuckingPA."

"I'll talk to her," I said, "straighten it out."

"I didn't want to say this, Miles, because I like you, I respect you. But it's either her or me, but if she's got a deal for this reality TV show, I don't want to be a part of it. I don't want to be in it. Period." She threw her drawing stick away to underscore her decision. "I could recommend other publicists, if you want me to," she offered.

"I don't want another publicist. What other publicist would crash in her own car? You're a team player, Hana."

"Yeah. A team player." A dark shadow crossed her face. "I'm not sure I'm cut out for this profession. I might take out a loan and go back to school and get my masters in theater, or business. Figure out my life."

I exhaled through both nostrils, resigned to her decision. "Yeah, being a book publicist today is like being a restaurant critic in the postapocalypse."

"Funny. You've got all these great expressions."

"They keep you sane in a dwindling cultural universe where books are going the way of lacework, where movies have diminished in magic by having been dragged to the internet and our ubiquitous devices. The world I came of age in is no more, Hana." I turned to her. "But your life is just beginning."

"Do you think there's hope?"

"Not as long as the Amandas of the world are puppeteering it." She laughed. "If there isn't hope we've reached a cynical nadir, haven't we? Even if we don't think there's hope, we have to believe there is hope because in believing we maintain a conviction to live, if that makes sense."

"You don't believe there's hope?"

"No. But paradoxically, I'll believe there is in order to keep fuel in my tank, because if I lose all hope, then I might as well off myself."

"You couldn't off yourself," she said.

"Why?"

"Because of Max. He would miss you. His eyes would guilt-trip you out of it. I might understand, but he wouldn't. It would be perceived as a great absence of someone he's bonded with."

I was impressed with her perspicacity. "A friend of mine told me when I got Max and found out about his metabolic bone disorder he would bankrupt me." I paused and chuckled to myself. "And then I realized he wouldn't necessarily financially bankrupt me, but if I lost him he would emotionally bankrupt me. You're right, I couldn't off myself unless I could find a good home for him." I nudged her shoulder with mine. "If something happened to me, would you take him?"

"No! Because then I would be left with the guilt I gave you permission to kill yourself."

"You've got a brilliant sense of logic." I bent my head to her profile. She wouldn't meet my eyes. She had already left, and I tried one last time to bring her back. "How are you doing, Hana?"

She shook her head, then looked down. "You want to hear my story?"

"Sure."

"When I was fourteen I was caught stealing in a high-end clothing store. I was fingerprinted and booked. It was beyond humiliating." She raised her head and met the Tasman Sea of her despair. "I knew I was going to be persecuted beyond anything I had ever experienced before, so I . . ." She paused, her words stalled on the cusp of a painful memory. She sucked in her breath. "So I, uh, went into the bathroom, got in the bathtub . . . and slit my wrists."

"Jesus."

"My parents found me, called 111, and they saved me." She nodded contemplatively at the memory. "After that my parents slept outside my bedroom on the floor for six months because they were deathly afraid I was going to attempt suicide again."

"What great parents," was all I could manage.

"I had to leave the private school I was attending, which I loved, because the arrest meant I would be expelled, plus the ostracization was going to be too much when everyone found out about my stealing expensive clothes and jewelry. As penance, I had to enroll in public school, which I hated, and that's where I was bullied beyond belief."

"You don't have to tell me this, Hana."

"No, I want to. I want you to know who I am and where I come from, okay? Before I leave this tour and never see you again." Emotion choked her words.

"Okay."

"I started realizing I was not physically attracted to men, but rather to women. I met a girl named Claire, and I fell in love with her, and she made me feel good, proud of who I am." She took a hit off her chop and blew smoke. "Of course I had to come out to my parents, you know, and tell them I was gay." She paused, her story hobbled by her recounting of it.

"How did they take it?"

"Not well. I waited until I got accepted into university and had moved out before telling them." She took another dramatic pause. Tears leached from the corners of her eyes. "They didn't speak to me for three years. Completely shut me out." When I glanced at her, she was drying her tears with the knuckles of one hand. "I got my degree in marketing and communications from Victoria and found a job working in publicity for a government agency, but I fuckinghatedit." She nodded. "Then I found this job. Publicist for a famous writer on a road trip."

I smirked an exhalation.

"You are, Miles. Anyway, I thought it was an incredible opportunity. I've worked my ass off to be creative with these book clubs. I've endured declined credit cards, sleeping in my car, trying to look presentable, but

I realize I'm a failure, that I've failed you, Miles." Her words tumbled into sobs. She clasped a hand to her mouth.

"You haven't failed me, Hana, that's ridiculous."

"Yes, I have," she said, her words muffled by the hand covering her mouth, her tears running over her tattooed fingers. "I wanted to be good at something, and I failed, and now I have to start all over again, reinvent myself as something else, and I don't know what that is." Weeping openly, she sounded like someone who felt all alone in the world.

I gazed off into the distance.

"I'm sorry," she said.

"Don't be."

"You understand why I have to leave the tour?"

"I wish you would reconsider."

She glanced at her iPhone, started to clamber to her feet. "Look, we've got to get to Picton."

I nodded and rose, shakily, to my feet. At that moment, the sky suddenly closed off with a massing of black clouds.

Hana tented her eyes with a flattened hand and scanned the horizon. "There's a massive storm on the way again," she said. "A bomb cyclone. There're rumors the ferry will close. I hope we make it."

We climbed into the camper van, Hana at the wheel, me in the passenger seat, too hungover to even consider driving. Her confessional story, her excavation of a painful time in her life and what she was going through on the tour, had produced a somber, unspoken understanding between us. Thinking of all Hana had said about Max, I lifted him out of the carrier and set him on my lap. He immediately began purring.

The Hana driving the camper van seemed like a different person from the one I had met in Cromwell. It was as if she had everted her soul and confessed everything and now, like me, was naked to the world. If only I could live in the moment like Max and not ruefully dredge up the past all the time, or dwell on the asteroid vectoring Earth's way and the sixth extinction, the cosmic event that would wipe out mankind. Maybe it would be a blessing if we could all start over tabula rasa.

The storm worsened as we headed north out of Boulder Bank Scenic

Reserve. It was too generous of Hana to wrest me out of Wrekin and away from the disaster of the Couples Book Club and Amanda's first day directing *Washed-Up Writers*, perhaps feeling guilty she had arranged it.

"Someone taking care of your car?" I said.

"Yeah, my girlfriend, Sofia."

"What does she do?"

"She works in the government," she said, without elaborating.

"Are you getting along with your parents now?"

"Better," she said, smiling for the first time that morning.

"Hana, look, you didn't fail anybody. And, plus, you have youth on your side." She turned to me. "Look at me. Washed-up writer. The sands are mostly in the bottom of the hourglass. I maybe have two more books left in me. You have time to write an entire oeuvre, star in a dozen plays."

"I appreciate that, Miles."

"I wish you wouldn't leave."

"I wish I didn't have to."

Hana cranked the wipers up. Looking tense, she gripped the wheel with both hands and slanted forward and peered through the blurred windows. She bravely navigated the six-ton automotive leviathan on the narrow two-lane road through wooded countryside in the direction of Picton. The pouring rain obliterated the passing landscape from view. If I closed my eyes, I could imagine a summer of glittering blue estuaries, flocks of migratory birds hurtling their small bodies in fierce upper-atmosphere winds, guided by the galaxies, to this verdant, supernal paradise that was New Zealand. But all I saw was leaden gray. All I heard was windshield wipers swishing back and forth, locked in a fierce battle with the torrential rain.

"If this keeps up, I'm not sure I'm going to make it all the way to Auckland," I said, fearful now that Hana was leaving the tour.

"You'll have Jack. And his girlfriend."

"Are you joking?"

"It'll be better on the North Island."

"I appreciate your sharing your story back there," I said. "I'm glad it didn't end in tragedy."

"Then you never would have heard it."

"Point taken."

She turned and smiled at me. "I like you, Miles. I hate to do this to you."

"I understand, Hana. You and Amanda are on different tracks. It would never work. It's demeaning to you. I'm sorry."

All of a sudden we heard the sustained blaring of a horn. A large truck swerved, nearly sideswiping us. Hana jerked the wheel to the left to avoid a collision. We heard a BANG, the camper van shuddered . . . and then Hana shrieked, "What was that?"

Hana braked and pulled over to the side of the road at the first available turnoff. We climbed out together. I touched down gingerly because the remaining passenger-side step on the destroyed ladder was dangling from exposed screws. Shivering in the rain and cold, we inspected the vehicle. The left wheel well and step had struck some-thing, and the fiberglass housing was smashed in. I followed a wordless Hana backward to the scene of the impact. We deduced the left side of the camper van had struck a waist-high, sturdy, round mileage post at the side of the road. The post was still standing, but paint scraped from the wheel well had streaked it in white. In the pouring rain I picked up a piece of the headlight housing, a jagged shard of orange plastic, and stared at it with dejection.

Back where the camper van was parked, Hana started viciously kicking the back of it. "Shitfuckshitfuckshitfuck!" she screamed angrily.

"Come on, Hana," I consoled. "It's not your fault. Accidents happen. At least we're okay."

She turned to me with a pained look. "This whole book tour is my fault," she wailed.

"Come on, Hana, don't beat up on yourself. It is what it is. It was what it was." I threw my arms toward the skies pouring rain down on us bedraggled two and gave it two middle fingers. "Fuck you, God!"

Seconds later we saw a jagged fulguration of lightning light up the storm-occluded skies, followed by a low growl of thunder. I kid you not.

"Miles!" a bug-eyed Hana shouted.

I leaned back and tilted my head to the heavens. "IS THAT ALL YOU GOT, MOTHERFUCKER?"

Seconds later, another incandescent bolt of lightning tore open the sky, this time closer. Thunder pealed to underscore the threat.

Hana and I, both superstitious, raced back inside the van, me having to hoist myself up since there no longer existed a step, and closed the doors. Hana locked hers. Max was meowing up a storm. We didn't say anything for a long moment, and then I snorted a laugh at the absurdity of everything. Then Hana laughed. We shared a cathartic, eye-watering laugh.

"And right there is the argument against atheism."

"I can't believe you did that," Hana said.

"It was an inexplicable coincidence!"

"I don't think so," she said in all seriousness. Hana looked at me with bulging eyes, then shook her head in repudiation of my explanation.

I felt like pouring a glass of wine, but I knew Hana would reproach me. She looked tense, upset, and a thousand things I had no clue about were ping-ponging around in her head. She turned the key in the ignition. The engine turned over on the first try and Hana steered us back onto the highway.

We continued on the sinuously narrow road into the small, charming town of Picton, the disembarkation port for the Interislander ferry that would take us across the fabled Cook Strait to the North Island and whatever new tragedies and ignominies lay ahead for this pathetic book tour.

In Picton, Hana found public parking off London Quay and pointed to a coffee shop across the street. "Cortado café. That's where everybody is. We have a couple hours before the ferry leaves."

Edging up closer to Hana was her girlfriend, Sofia, behind the wheel in Hana's Subaru. She parked and climbed out. She was a beautiful brunette, a tad heavyset, with a round face broken into a welcoming smile. She was eager to talk to Hana, so I backed away.

"I'll meet you back here in an hour," said Hana.

I waved and marched across the rain-slick street to Cortado café. It was spacious inside. Two tables had been dragged together, and Jack,

Amanda, and the three-person documentary crew were clustered around a laptop, gales of laughter erupting from them every few seconds.

Seeing me, Jack waved me over. "Miles, come here. You've got to see this."

Wincing, I shook my head, waved him off, not wanting to relive a moment I was blissfully oblivious of. I crossed the café to the counter and ordered a flat white with a triple shot of espresso. The young female counter attendant handed me a silver holder with a number mounted at the top—13! No!—and I retreated to an empty table and plopped down, the weight of Hana's words about leaving the tour bearing down on me, trying to process the repercussions—Jack and me? Jack and me and Amanda?—shaking my head at her suicide confession, trying to understand how hard it must have been growing up Māori in a land of mostly rich white descendants of marauding invaders.

A moment later, Jack approached and sat down across from me. He sensed my downturned mood. "Where were you? We thought you had gone on a walkabout."

"Hana drove me to the Tasman Sea. There we rested, got down, watched prehistoric birds clamoring for prey, a sun lifted by the hand of God and spilling liquid gold onto an ocean so pristine I wanted to Virginia Woolf in it and meet Poseidon."

"Are you okay, Miles?" Jack knew my waxing lyrical was sarcastic doomsday opining and not because I had found the way, the truth, the life. He waited.

"God threw a lightning bolt at me, and I had an epiphany."

"Oh no."

"I'm going to retire from writing. I'm wrung out, Jack. I have nothing left in me. No more stories to tell."

"All because you saw some lightning?"

"It was heavier than that, but I'm keeping it a secret between Hana and me."

The server brought my flat white over and set it down. He wordlessly took the number holder away.

I took a few sips of the strong coffee, then raised my head to meet

Jack's beseeching, bloodshot (drink + sex + sleeplessness) eyes. "Hana's leaving the building."

"What?"

"She's not interested in being your girlfriend's PA, is essentially the gist of her reason for bailing."

"We still need her for scheduling the events. Just because we're doing *Washed-Up Writers* doesn't change anything."

"To her it does! And *Washed-Up Writers*? Really, Jack? Really? Is this the nadir we've sunk to? I mean, I get *Washed-Up Celebrities* and you hosting that. It sounds like kitschy fun and a hefty payday, but this is me, Miles Raymond. This is my life."

"It's only a working title. And if it's a hit, it's going to sell books—come on."

"It hurts me deeply we alienated Hana."

Jack glanced back at Amanda and the reality TV crew, who were still laughing their asses off over the footage from Wrekin they were screening on a MacBook. "This show's going to be a hit," Jack said, grinning.

"I could give a fuck." That silenced Jack. I sipped my flat white, the caffeine helping make visible my blurred view of the world. The rain slashed at the windows. More Kiwis streamed into the café to take shelter from the biting cold, the gathering winds, blowing hard now, colorful flags snapping audibly, trash pushed along the gutters in eddying currents, the Picton inlet white capped.

Jack slid two white pills across the table. "Here."

"What's this?"

"Dramamine. I'm told by our crew to fasten our seat belts. It's going to be a bumpy ride."

CHAPTER 22

Jack grimaced when he examined the fresh new damage to the camper van. "I hope Hughie's got insurance."

"Probably not," I said. "He's got a publicist sleeping out of her car and fifteen K of mine in humiliation money."

"I hear you," Jack said.

We climbed into the camper van and caravanned with Hana and Sofia, Amanda in the Ridgeline with the camper trailer, and the film crew in their SUV, to the vehicular lanes with cars lining up to board the Interislander ferry. Jack and I didn't converse much. With both arms planted on the steering wheel, he was doing his best to hold fast to the road as the winds gusted over forty miles per hour.

We angled into one of the lanes to check in with the booking agent, impervious to inclement weather, beaming from her booth. She checked our names against a list on her computer and motioned us on our way.

The treaded ramp that led up into the hold of the massive ferry barely accommodated the camper van. The mirrors on both sides had to be folded in, otherwise we would have sheared them off along with the footsteps and the left headlight shroud.

Before the corporate card had gone kaput, Hana had thoughtfully booked seats in the Plus Lounge. No way, she said, was I going to make the nearly four-hour Cook Strait crossing in steerage, and no way was she going to either. In the uncrowded upper deck lounge, I selected a table away from Amanda, who was grating on my nerves, and the film crew, who seemed to be getting a kick out of my wanton willingness to humiliate myself on camera. Hana and Sofia sequestered themselves in a booth as far away from the rest of us as possible. No doubt they had a lot to talk about.

The crossing was equal parts sublimely beautiful and terrifying. New Zealand is a developed, high net-worth nation, but it has an unexplored quality to it, a frontier openness, a place where you could bushwhack for days without crossing the path of another human being, which greatly appealed to me at the moment. But the skies were black mixed with every hue of gray, the diagonal rain blown by monsoon winds unrelenting. The ferry rocked, port to starboard, bow to stern, sometimes both ways simultaneously. Anxious, I straightened on unsteady feet and walked out onto the deck, where a few hardy Kiwis were taking in the storm, to breathe some fresh air. The gale-force winds nearly knocked me off my feet. I was afraid to take pictures with my iPhone for fear the wind would shear it from my hand and send it hurtling into the strait. Maybe that's what I needed! The waters were white capped and the swells rose fifteen to twenty feet, causing the ferry to list violently. All of Nature's fury was on display in that crossing. I later learned we were the last ferry and it had been shut down until the weather improved.

Safely back inside the Plus Lounge, I brooded over Hana's leaving. Despite my brush with God, the planets were not aligning. I wondered if I could talk her out of it, but she seemed unyielding in her conviction to leave. I knew I couldn't convince Jack to dispatch Amanda because the three of us were inextricably bound together in an unholy triune of various mercantile enterprises. Milena's email, which I had practically memorized, played in my head like an insidious earworm, which wouldn't stop playing and leave me in peace. I shut my eyes to its reality, summoned all my experience at suppressing emotional turmoil, and tried to fit all the broken pieces of my life together into some kind of recognizable whole. If I was smart, a part of me divined, I would pack it up, jet from Wellington back to Queenstown, reunite with Ella, ask her to marry me, secure my residency card, and live happily ever after in Aotearoa, forever gazing in awe at those snowcapped mountains from my Prophet's Rock redoubt, knowing I was blessedly at the end of the world, the last place on earth that would succumb to lawlessness and revolution. But if I didn't return to California, I would never know the child I had fathered. The book tour? The book tour. I was on a purgatorial ride that at least promised an end.

The "sailing" across Cook Strait was so rough car alarms kept triggering and announcements came frequently over the loudspeakers politely identifying cars by their make, model, and license number—"And would the owner please return to their vehicle and disable their alarm. Thank you." By the tenth announcement, I almost wish they had come on and yelled, "And would the fucking idiot who didn't turn his car alarm off please get his ass to his vehicle before we drive it off the ferry into Cook Strait!"

"Come on, Miles, get up, let's go," Jack said, his hand on my shoulder shaking me awake.

"What?" I said groggily. Night was falling and the city of Wellington, perched on a hillside reminiscent of San Francisco, coruscated with lights. "We're here?"

"We're here," Jack said.

Max was meowing when we got to our vehicle. I fed him a few treats, then took him out of his carrier and climbed into the passenger seat. Jack started up the camper van. We waited in a long line of cars to disembark.

The winds were monsoon strength when Jack rolled the damaged camper van off the ferry ramp. Jack and Amanda, who had been apprised of Hana's giving notice, had taken over command of the tour and booked hotel rooms, as the weather was too severe to consider camping. Amanda, of course, viewed all of this as drama for *Washed-Up Writers* on a book tour from hell, taglines she and her doc crew were already spitballing with one another, ideating new ways to exploit my misfortune.

The hotel was located in downtown Wellington. It felt comforting to be inside the enclosure of a real room protected from the elements with real walls, with a hot shower, a proper bed, high-speed Wi-Fi, and a working toilet, and, most importantly, all alone, all alone with my eddying thoughts and apprehensions and catastrophist prognostications that were now sapping all my strength.

Together, we trooped in the buffeting winds and slashing rains to nearby Ortega Fish Shack and feasted on a scrumptious meal of blue cod and other delectable dishes, a vast improvement over the fare we had stocked in the camper van and the various fish-and-chips shacks we had frequented due to Hughie's dodgy credit card and Hana's tight budget. If I weren't ruing the departure of Hana, I would have surmised the tour conditions were improving, but they weren't. At some point I was going to have to apprise Amanda of my not wanting to go forward with *Washed-Up Writers*, but I was too exhausted from the ferry crossing, too emotionally wrung out from Hana's early-morning confession, the stiff-legged march through barbarous winds to a restaurant Amanda had selected, I didn't have the energy to spill my concerns and have to listen to her, being the producer she was, expostulate, convince me we had a winner.

Hana wasn't with us at Ortega Fish Shack and her absence, to me, was palpable. How I had let Jack insinuate Amanda into my life, my book tour, my realm, was further cause for disquietude. I needed to sleep on it.

The morning dawned a cold cobalt blue, the sky ragged with torn banners of swiftly moving clouds. Tree branches and debris littered the streets of quaint Wellington. The winds were still maritime and end-of-the-world fierce, and the overhead cantilever stoplight poles bowed and juddered and creaked in the face of the bomb cyclone's fury.

I fed and petted a meowing Max and told him I loved him a hundred times, because that's how emotionally vulnerable I was feeling, until he quieted, and then, assured he was settled, I went into the bathroom. When I came out of the shower, towel knotted at my waist, there was a voice text from Hana on my phone: "Hughie was taken to urgent care last night, but he should be back home later today. We have the Welsh Dragon Bar tonight."

The storm continued, unabated. Placid New Zealand was testing me. Was it retribution for its beauty?

From my carry-on bag, I produced my hand grinder, Panama beans from an Arrowtown roastery that had served me well, filters, and V-60 dripper and, with the supplied water kettle, brewed a nearly perfect pour-over. Provided milk—those Kiwis think of everything!—added the right creamy touch. I went online and surveyed the news on my few media subscriptions. Floods, droughts, species of all ilk going extinct at alarming rates, political unrest, wars with thermonuclear connotations, human rights abuses, microplastics in oceans and marine life. I closed my laptop, ambled over to the window, and gazed out. Tattered patches of blue were being consumed by another wave of storms, and soon the sun had returned to memory. No wonder Hughie had been rushed to urgent care. His author was in town. His publicist had quit. The Cougars of Christchurch had probably lawyered up to sue him for a reimbursement of their hefty appearance fee. Dude was sitting on some serious kakapo guano.

An email notification appeared on my iPhone lock screen. I glanced down at it, and my heart performed an ellipsis in beats. I picked the phone up and swiped to the email and read:

"Dear Miles. Have you thought any more about coming to California? I need to know. —Milena."

"I will let you know in a few days," I typed with a single tremulous thumb, then archived her email so it wouldn't be importuning me from my inbox.

I met Hana at nearby Peoples Coffee, a small café catering to the Wellington version of the Gen Z and Y crowd. She was late, reminiscent of the first time I met her a week ago—felt like a month!—tapping on her phone with both thumbs but moving forward as if she had eyes on her forehead and insect antennae to prevent her from tripping over obstacles. When she saw me she smiled without showing her teeth, held up a single finger, then angled over to the counter to place an order. She kept glancing at her phone. There was the real world, and then her other real world, and the two were locked in perpetual combat.

A few minutes later, Hana sat down across from me with a cup of tea. "How are you, Miles?"

"Finally got a full night's sleep. Shockingly didn't open any of Prophet's Rock's finest when I got back to my room." I held out both hands. "Steady as she goes."

She chuckled. "That's good." She sipped her tea, squinted, and gazed out at the street. "You're going to be in Freedom Campground tonight," she said. "It's on the outskirts of Wellington."

"This was Hughie's decision? Because I'd prefer to stay in the hotel."

"It was Amanda's. For the TV show. She *loves* the idea of you in the camper van. Especially you and Max."

"Lovely." I sighed, nodded, drank my triple-shot flat white, debated a remonstrating email to Jack and Amanda on the Freedom Campground executive decision, but my mind was focused on Hughie and the upcoming visit. "How is Hughie doing?"

"Doctors thought he was having a heart attack, but it turned out it was low blood pressure. They're conducting tests."

"Hughie has low blood pressure and I have high blood pressure. How ironic."

Hana laughed. "He wants to see you, though." I nodded. "I'm not sure I'd bring up the Cougars appearance fee."

"Or the camper-van bait and switch, or the declined corporate card . . . How convenient, that hospital visit," I said, sarcasm biting into my voice.

Hana stared into her tea, waiting for the leaves to report deep insights back to her. "Hughie knows I'm leaving the tour, but he wants me to tell him in person," she confided. She raised her head and blinked at me. "He knows Amanda, though, so you should be in good hands from here forward."

"Is this what you wanted, Hana?" I said, anxiety clawing at my stomach with its sharp talons. "I did not engineer this, you realize. Jack's producer girlfriend crashed the party, took over, like producers tend to do, and I feel awful you were sidelined. Can I make it up to you?"

"It's okay," she said. "Hughie said he would pay me through the contract. Plus, he gets Jack's partner for free, and a TV show out of it. It's a win-win for everyone."

"Except for me."

"Why? Didn't you think I was doing a shitty job?"

"No, Hana, I didn't. You've been pulling amazingly creative things out of that big brain of yours, and my God, looking back, what a tour it's been."

Hana blinked back tears. "I thought you thought I was a loser."

"You're not a loser, Hana. You rescued me from Wrekin and drove me to the Tasman. In the Beast!" She chuckled at the memory. "I will always retain fond memories of that. I would hire you in a heartbeat, but I'm retiring from the literary game."

"No."

I nodded in resignation.

Hana dropped her eyes back down into her tea, stirred it aimlessly.

"It's not going to be the same without you at this Freedom Campground." I looked at the passersby on the sidewalk, trying to suppress an emotion welling up in me, feeling it tinge my voice with sentimentality. "All alone in that camper."

"You've got Max."

"Yeah." I threw back my flat white and rose noisily from my chair. "Speaking of which, I need to gather him up before Hughie's. I can't leave him in the hotel room. I forgot his cat Xanax."

CHAPTER 23

With Max tucked safely in his carrier situated in the rear of Hana's Subaru, we drove into the hills outside of Wellington, climbing a narrow, single-lane road with the only indication of residences in the wooded enclave mailboxes mounted on weathered posts planted next to turnoffs to dirt switchbacks leading up to properties hidden away from view in a bedroom community that looked like a magical, fairy-tale forest where *The Lord of the Rings* was shot.

Hughie's house turned out to be a sprawling single-story compound that had been added on to in an aesthetic absence of architectural oversight as his hedge fund firm had prospered via risky investments in mining and fisheries. Children had been reared and spirited off to college. A second wife had departed, I learned from Hana, for more fertile pastures in New Plymouth with a retired rugby player, legally taking savings that might have bought much-needed renovations the now-neglected and semidilapidated home required. The fifteen K appearance fee no doubt got swallowed up by the renovations.

An epicene-looking housekeeper, a woman in her forties, possibly Filipina, met us at the door. "You must be Mr. Raymond?"

"Yes."

"Come this way."

She ushered us into the main room of the house, then down a

tenebrous passageway to a rear bedroom. It was freezing inside. Was Hughie trying to save on utilities? Even creepier, the murkily lit corridor's walls were hung with blown-up framed photographs of me: at awards shows of my past success; newspaper and magazine clippings; book covers; photos of me taken at various public appearances where I had, for a court jester's fee, performed the dog and Pinot show. It was a veritable shrine to my unremarkable, single blip of a career. In walking down this Kubrickian hall, I was going back in time to meet the madman who had, he believed, resurrected me from the dustbin of anonymity.

"You've been here before?" I said to Hana, throwing her a backward look.

"Yes."

"You should have warned me."

A complicit laugh flared from her nostrils.

The housekeeper stepped away from an open door that led into a darkened room that was twenty degrees warmer than the other rooms composing the eerie compound. Hana and I stepped inside.

Hughie was lying supine, propped up by massive pillows, on a motorized, adjustable hospital bed, a remote at the end of an extended arm. As seen virtually, he was, indeed, in his fifties, balding, a short, stout man who had cashed in his chips and was bankrolling a fantasy dream of reinventing himself as a publisher to bring, I could only assume, some excitement into a life squandered in finance, but whose flame was flickering in a candle whose wax was but a puddle in which the wick was swimming. He wore a T-shirt that was stenciled with the title of my novel over a pair of rumpled, urine-stained boxer shorts. Three giant Apple cinema screens mounted on a desk on the opposite end of the room glowed at him, the only sources ghoulishly lighting up the bedroom. Playing on them were clips from the Wrekin Couples Book Club, and Hughie was laughing so hard, his eyes pinched shut, he almost didn't hear our approach.

"Turn it off, Hughie."

He jerked his head in the direction where Hana and I stood and, pressing a button on his remote, switched off the videos. The screens all reverted to screen savers showing the cover of my novel. "This is great stuff, Miles," he enthused. "Orders are going to pour in when this airs." He gestured to the right side of the room. My eyes traveled to where teetering towers of *A Year of Pure Feeling* were hastily stacked. Their pillared tenuousness, a breath of wind from toppling over, sank me into a depression I hadn't experienced since my loneliest moments at Prophet's Rock when I was blocked on the damn novel and wasn't sure there was a way forward.

"Hi, Hughie," Hana said. "How're you feeling?"

"Fine," the broken, epigone publisher replied. "I'm sorry to hear you're going to leave the tour." He turned and shot us both a wide grin of bleached white veneers. He looked like a third world dictator holed up in a windowless fortress running his country through a network of modern communication systems unaware of the populace closing in on his derelict palace.

"I wanted to tell you in person," Hana said.

Hughie nodded. "You did a great job, Hana. A great job."

Hana smiled but didn't say anything in reply. She stepped backward with her hands prayerfully folded. "I'll let you two convene." And she disappeared into the cold and shadows of the house.

I pulled up a chair next to Hughie and eased into it. As my eyes adjusted to the darkness, I could make out more stacks of my book, along with messy piles of embarrassing merch (hats, T-shirts, even wines!) abjectly unloaded and warehoused haphazardly everywhere in the room, none of which had had my imprimatur of approval, let alone contractual autograph. It was obvious he was running a one-man operation, and despite his professional-looking website and falsehoods to the contrary, it was a shoestring operation, sans the assistant (the in-home nurse?), the internet making him loom like Penguin Random House ANZ. The bedroom itself had been transformed into a home assisted-living facility. Narrow surgical tubes snaked from an oxygen concentrator device to his nostrils and were secured with an elastic band around his head. Vials of medications, a digital blood pressure machine, and other medical-related items littered nightstands flanking him on both sides of his medical bed.

"How're you feeling, Hughie?"

"Better," he said. "Good to meet you in person, mate." He extended a hand from an arm half the length of mine.

I took it in mine. It had the feel of a sea anemone exposed too long to a hot sun. I shook it once and let it go. "Yeah," I said, glancing dejectedly around at all the *A Year of Pure Feeling* marketing materials scattered about. "What happened to the shipping department?" I inquired.

"Jasmine does it all for me," he said, waving a hand at an imaginary gnat.

"So, you had what you thought was a heart attack, but it was in actual fact . . . low blood pressure?"

"Yeah, just plummeted all of a sudden. Tests were negative for a coronary. They're running others." He rotated his head to me. His eyewear made his eyes bulge frog-like, permitting him extrasensory vision for this life in the dark. "I hear the tour's going brilliant," he croaked, completing the image of the amphibian he had presented himself to be.

I looked off. Laughter and despair were locked in combat in my increasingly unsound mind. "I want that fifteen grand, Hughie," I said.

"When the tour's over."

"Now! And I don't give a fuck if the Cougars of Christchurch stiffed you." I reached a hand toward the control panel of the oxygen concentrator device and performatively placed a finger on the on/off switch. "I swear to God, Hughie, if you don't write that check, I'm going to turn this off and watch you choke to death, you fucking slimeball."

"Don't be like that, Miles. We're business partners."

"Half a dozen women tried to rape me, motherfucker."

"I would have thought you and Jack would have enjoyed it."

"Jack maybe. Not me."

"Sorry it went south, mate."

"The check, Hughie, or your face is going to turn cyanotic."

"I don't know what that means." He grinned stupidly, hoping it would defuse the escalating situation.

"You're about to find out." I started to press the button ever so perceptibly.

"No, no, don't do that, Miles, it'll kill me."

"Only me and God will know."

A look of terror scudded across his face. He raised his heavy head with great effort. "Jasmine?" he bellowed. "Bring me my check ledger."

In the ticking silence that followed before Jasmine reappeared, I stared at this pathetic man who had conned me by funding the writing of a book—my first in years!—so he could begin his publishing empire. True, he had given me an advance to keep me solvent, and for that I was grateful, but now that the squeeze was on, I was in no mood for excuses and pleasantries. This was as raw and personal as it gets between writer and publisher. Usually an agent threatens death.

A wraithlike Jasmine slipped into the bedroom and handed Hughie his check ledger and a ballpoint pen, then left without a word.

"I'm going to make it for seven-five," Hughie bartered, clicking the ballpoint into action. "Split the difference."

"Fifteen," I said in a rising tone, "or you aren't going to see your daughter's graduation from Victoria." I reached for the oximeter on/off switch, this time with more resolve.

"Twelve. Or it'll bounce," he said with a quaver of desperate pleading in his voice.

"If it bounces, Hughie, I'm going straight to the authorities. In the US if you write a check for an amount you don't have, it's fraud. I'm guessing in Aotearoa, with so many pikers, it's a jailable offense. And I will fucking put you behind bars for what you pulled on me in Christchurch, I swear to fucking Tangaroa."

He wrote out the check in hurried cacography, tore it off, and handed it to me unhappily.

"Now write me a second one for twenty for the second half of the advance and postdate it."

He did as instructed, tore that one off, and waved it at me. "Don't try to cash this until the date, please."

I plucked the second check from his fingers. "What is your deal with Amanda Robinson on the TV series?" I insisted, folding the two checks and tucking them into my hoodie pocket.

"Nothing," he said. His eyes wandered around in their sockets, and I knew he was lying.

"She's going to tell me, Hughie, so you'd better be straight with me."

"Fifty grand for the upfront rights and a per-episode fee of five," he confessed in a guilty undertone. "We'll split it."

"No, we won't. We're not splitting anything," I screamed in exasperation. "I'm tired of you fucking Kiwis wanting to split everything. It's specifically stated in our agreement you have no contractual rights to anything film or TV. My entertainment attorney"—admittedly now in jail for tax fraud and embezzling royalties, but Hughie didn't need to know that—"was adamant about that when we drew up the contracts."

"You're right," he said, resigned to the fact I wasn't a naïf when it came to book deals. "I'm sorry Hana had to leave. I guess she has some family obligations she can't get out of."

"I think it's because she was sleeping in her car, the corporate card was repeatedly declined, and you had inveigled the poor woman into a job she wasn't trained, or ready, for." I threw up my hands in a show of bonhomie. "But she did a commendable job with the hand she was dealt."

He nodded, exhaling noisily through his mouth. "Sorry I can't be at the Welsh Dragon Bar tonight." He smiled broadly. "You know, it used to be the public toilet."

"I heard," I said, straightening sickeningly to my feet. The unsteady piles of my book were demoralizing me. I had what I had come for. Maybe one day my book would be discovered by a new civilization, birthed out of the ruins of this one, who believed in the sacredness of literature and the written word. And the moment I had that thought, it crepitated and died at the penumbra of hope.

"Take it easy, Hughie." I pointed a finger at him. "And I don't believe the near heart attack for a second. You knew I was coming for you, you pathetic rat, and you were hoping to buy my sympathies."

"Let's stay friends, Miles," he said to my back as I turned and walked out.

I patted my pocket, where the two checks were. "If these don't bounce."

Grinning until it hurt, I walked back outside in a huff. I found Hana leaning against her car, staring into her cell. She extinguished a joint of chop on the bottom of her black boot, stood, and climbed into the driver's side of her Subaru when she saw me approach across the weed-overgrown yard with two yowling dogs guarding the entrance to a garage stacked with bags of guano—another Hughie enterprise gone up in smoke? I settled in next to her. She started the engine, shifted into drive.

"How'd it go?"

"I threatened to turn off his oxygen machine if he didn't write me a check for that appearance fee and the second half of my advance." I waved the two checks in the air. "Mission accomplished."

Hana laughed harder than I had ever heard her laugh. Maybe it was the THC launched into her bloodstream; maybe it was cathartic because it was the end of the road for her; maybe it was because she, too, had wanted a measure of retribution from the man who had set us up for failure.

We drove back into Wellington, Max in my lap, Hana immersed in her music.

I checked out of the hotel and Hana helped me transfer my luggage and Max back into the camper van. With a missing mirror and stepladder and a battered front left side and a flora-lashed exterior, the Beast had taken a beating.

I followed Hana out to the Freedom Campground. The skies had cleared again, but the monsoon winds of the Cook Strait crossing hadn't subsided. The sun was lowering in the sky as I parked the camper van next to the rocky shoreline and climbed out, stretched, drank in the depthless view of the horizonless Pacific. The ocean was blistered with whitecaps, the sea an aqueous blue-gray color. I glanced over and noticed a rusted metal blue-and-white sign that read: "Wellington welcomes responsible campers."

"Where's Jack and Amanda?" I called out to Hana in a voice loud enough to compete with the howling wind. She pointed to a spot nearby. I turned and saw the Marlin Cruiser unfurled and pitched precariously on an escarpment, the tent's bed cantilevered practically out over the waves, obviously in an effort to afford them the most spectacularly un-obstructed, and romantic, view. I shook my head. "Figures."

When Jack saw us, he waved and trudged down the slope to where we were parked. As he approached, his smile slowly changed into one of solicitude toward Hana, the actor in him reaching deep into his method bag of tricks for the platitudes, the empathy, the specious mea culpas. "Are you sure about leaving the tour, Hana? We're going to miss you."

Hana smiled a reply. "I'll help you get set up at the Welsh Dragon Bar," she said in an appeasing tone.

Jack, as usual, didn't want to crawl hands and knees into the weeds of the ins and outs of why she was leaving, so he turned to me. "How'd it go with Hughie?"

I pulled the checks from my hoodie pocket and let them snap in the breeze. "The Cougars of Christchurch," I said, kissing the check. "Sans cunnilingus."

Hana cringed. Jack laughed. "There'll be more of that coming," he enthused. "Lots more."

I nodded, wondering what fresh humiliations I would be subjected to in the pathetic quest to transform this book tour into a financial success.

"I've got to run," interjected Hana, starting to back away. She pulled her walkie-talkie from her coat pocket and handed it to Jack. "Here's the other walkie. Stay in touch with each other, promise?"

It saddened me when she handed Jack the walkie. It seemed to symbolize the end of our relationship.

"Goodbye, Hana," I said.

Hana, fighting back tears, withdrew a few strides. "If you have any questions about the schedule, text me," she said. "Bye, guys," she added, half turning, throwing a backward wave. "Enjoy the rest of the book tour. I'll be thinking about you. See you tonight." Hana pivoted in place, walked the few short steps to her car, and drove off, gravel and dirt funneling out behind her car, in either anger or relief.

Amanda came bounding down the hill wearing a beaming smile, in an exultant mood. Ignoring Hana's departure, she said, "Miles, did you know the Welsh Dragon Bar used to be the public toilet?"

CHAPTER 24

The Welsh Dragon Bar was situated in the middle of a main street where the road bifurcated in the city center of Wellington. Inside, it featured a classic pub atmosphere festooned with a disordered clutter of brightly colored blinking signs advertising trendy beer and distillates. Positioned opposite the bar was a main room furnished with lacquered tables and hard wooden chairs. When I saw the toilet Amanda had arranged with the book club perched on a platform six feet in the air at the head of the room, I hurried to the bar and ordered a double tequila.

"You're going to read from the toilet," Amanda informed me with a gleeful grin on her face, her cerebral hemorrhage of the imagination of adding a real toilet to my performance in her producer mind a creative contribution to the *Washed-Up Writers* reality TV show, additional footage for the sizzle reel to showcase my increasing descent into literary ignominy, the developing theme of the show.

"It's going to be hilarious," Jack, now my Benedict Arnold and Amanda cheerleader, chimed in, slapping me on the back hard enough he nearly knocked me over.

I pointed at the toilet. "Clearly not Hana's doing?" I shot back with a note of anger at her having left because of Amanda's brazen, premeditated commandeering of my book tour.

"Amanda riffed on Hana's idea," Jack gloated. "I told you not to dismiss her so easily."

"Hana thought it was a great idea," Amanda course-corrected, but between an actor and a producer I couldn't ascertain who was the chief pathological liar of the two worst fabulists the entertainment world had ever given us.

I cast my eyes away from the porcelain throne. A holy trinity of flat panel TVs mounted to the ceiling and angled downward were broadcasting a rugby game between New Zealand's beloved All Blacks and Australia's poorer team, the haplessly—and aptly—named Wallabies. I knew nothing about rugby when I expatriated to New Zealand, but I had watched a few games with the Prophet's Rock winemakers and had come to see American football as a video game played by helmeted gladiators concussing one another for a paycheck, and rugby, contrarily, as a more primitive, and therefore purer, form of the American version.

The crowd in the bar swelled as the game revved up; the rabid fans sardined in shoulder to shoulder, cheek to jowl. I ordered another double shot of tequila, then a glass of wine to take back with me into the event room. Patrons for my autograph signing were drifting in. I had been on the book tour for over a week, and I had yet to be inside a proper bookstore. Had they disappeared from the face of the earth? Well, of course not, but apparently I, and book tours in general, had sunk to a circus side act nadir. Once I had signed so many books at a wine festival my hand cramped. Now, here I was, in the public toilet of Wellington, rebranded as the Welsh Dragon Bar, for a reading before the Public Toilet Book Club, a fitting end to my literary career. "Let's get it on," I roared to Jack and Amanda, the tequila hypodermically launched into my bloodstream and enlivening me to breathtaking heights of extroversion. "Let's kick some book butt." Jack threw me a cockeyed look. He had an innate sense of when I was recklessly ascending the alcohol ladder and free-falling into the realm of the unwell.

In a bustle of discarded puffer coats and scarves and boxes of equipment, the film crew burst in late to the Welsh Dragon Bar and the cinematographer moved erratically about the pub shooting B-roll footage. "This is so cool," Kylie, the DP, kept saying over and over. The crowd was composed of mostly young Kiwis. Many were tatted up and down their arms and even in some elaborate cases decorated with tattoos rising up their necks like flames reaching for the sky. Some members of the Public Toilet Book Club were clutching dog-eared copies of my legacy work in their hands, and others came to purchase and have me autograph my new book, which Amanda had stacked on a table beneath the toilet where the humiliating read would take place.

Amanda, gripping my elbow tightly, sat me at the autograph table, where I signed books for the patrons. In a gesture of magnanimity—or stupidity—I waved off their money. Word spread quickly in the packed bar author Miles Raymond was giving away free books, not that that inflamed a stampede to the autograph table. Regulars arriving for the All Blacks-Wallabies contest kept crowding in, making it falsely appear like my book signing was a smash hit.

"Free round for everyone," I shouted, both arms raised aloft. "Put it on my credit card."

A cheer went up with raised fists. I don't know if the All Blacks had successfully executed a try or if my offer of an open bar had ignited their cheering approbation, but the mood had turned festive.

The line for autographed copies of my book grew, snaked out the bar and onto the sidewalk. I was peppered with all manner of well-meaning questions I'd been asked before. "How long did it take you to write this?" ("My whole life.") "Why did you decide to become a writer?" ("I didn't choose it; it chose me.") "How are you finding New Zealand?" asked a thoughtful young woman with owlish spectacles improbably clutching a copy of Bret Easton Ellis's *Less Than Zero*. ("Beautiful. Brutal. Bizarre.") "How has fame changed you?" ("It's worse than failure because at least with failure you know where you stand, you know who your friends are," I answered in a moment of lucidity, "and besides I'm not that famous," I finished, pointing to the raised toilet awaiting the spectacle of my indignity). And the questions kept coming. The Public Toilet Book Club was an unforeseen crew of bookish intellectuals. I was surprised to discover I had such a fan base in the cracks of Wellington.

Maybe I needed to get back into an urban environment and out of the sticks, and I could be one of those shambling writer celebrities who gets stopped on the street with, "Hey, aren't you . . . ?"

Amanda and Jack were all beaming smiles. Jack's producer girlfriend, it appeared, now had two hit shows in preproduction, and the smile plastered on her face was the greedy grin of someone fantasizing investing in additional beachfront property. To Jack, his woman had saved the day.

The glasses of Central Otago Pinot kept coming, sousing me up for the slaughter. Jack's expression kept whipsawing from the worried (me) and the gleeful (Amanda having taken over and winning). From the Cougars of Christchurch to the Wrekin ball of disaster, he knew the switch could flip in me at any moment, my mood could sour, and I was capable of outrageous behavior. On the other hand, he knew Amanda was compiling great footage, and it was obvious from their frequent hugs and stolen kisses their relationship was firmly back on track, infidelities had been placated with lies and passionate, all-night fucking, courtesy of Big Pharma and endless bottles of bitch diesel—boy, could that Amanda drink, I thought at one point, and could she hold her liquor!

When the books had been signed, Amanda had arranged for four young men, impersonating pallbearers, to hoist me up to the toilet where I was scheduled to read, as per the Public Toilet Book Club's tradition to reverse the order—first the books are signed, then the author reads. In the main bar, the rugby game was neck and neck, coming down to the wire; my bar tab was ticking upward into another stratosphere, which I would regret in the morning, but at least it was a book signing with more than a dozen jaded attendees, and even if I had to buy their patronage, literature was, for the moment, having its moment in the, well, uh, toilet.

I was half in the bag, but still sentient enough to read, when they plopped me on the toilet on the dais. The view of the packed crowd, squashed together like the front rows of a concert, was galvanic, even, dare I say, life affirming. The owner of the bar, a guy named Gary, accepted a microphone from Amanda and quieted the buzzing crowd with his booming voice.

"From all of us here at the Welsh Dragon Bar, I want to thank the members of the Public Toilet Book Club for coming out on this beastly cold night to hear Miles Raymond, Oscar-winning American author, who has been on a book tour on the South Island, read from his new work, *A Year of Pure Feeling*." He turned to me. "And boy, is he feeling it tonight!" A cheer went up. Wineglasses were raised in a toast, libations I had splurged on the fumes of my credit card. "As a bonus," Gary continued, "Miles will be featured in a new reality TV show titled *Washed-Up Writers*, so look out for that in the coming months." He drew his attention to Amanda. "Now, I want to turn it over to the host of this event, Aussie film producer Amanda Robinson." There was a mixture of cheers and amiable boos, given that her national team was locked in a close match with New Zealand's beloved All Blacks.

Amanda snatched the microphone from Gary, who stepped aside. She towered above the crowd with her imperial presence. "Thank you all for coming out." She threw out an arm in my direction. "Ten years ago, Miles Raymond wrote a book that became an Oscar-winning movie that some of you might remember." Cheers went up. Did they remember it? "Then he disappeared. Like J. D. Salinger and Thomas Pynchon, he fell off the face of the earth." Her voice rose in volume in an effort to compete with the raucous cheers and collective groans of disapproval that came from the bar where the rugby match was in the tense waning seconds of a close contest. "Rumors abounded. Where did he go? Was he holed up in Northern California working on his next masterpiece? Had he fled to Mexico like B. Traven and was now writing under a pseudonym? Had he given up the quill for the bottle and was never to be seen again? No! He surfaced in Aotearoa New Zealand with a new book and a new look," she boomed, holding up a copy of *A Year of Pure Feeling* as evidence of my sordid resurrection. "Like Lazarus, he has risen from the ashes of his former self and written this marvelous novel which all of you have been gifted. And tonight he is going to read from it." Again, the crowd roared encouragement. Cheers don't resound at authors' events in the US at bland Barnes & Noble outlets. "The Welsh Dragon Bar," Amanda continued, "as you all know, used to be one of the glorious public toilets of

Wellington until it was transformed into this smashing pub. Tonight, the Welsh Dragon Bar, in conjunction with Wellington's own Public Toilet Book Club, honors one of the great authors of his generation, Miles Raymond." Amanda raised the hand holding the microphone and passed it up to me. A packed roomful of young literary types broke into cheers and whistles as I accepted the microphone and raised it to my mouth.

"Thank you, everyone," I said as the film crew snaked in and out of the crowd. I looked into the ruddy faces of these New Zealand youth. "First off, before I read a passage or two, I want to thank Hana Kawiti, my publicist, who made this night happen." I took a long quaff of my wine. "She couldn't be here tonight because she had a nervous breakdown on this book tour from hell, which is now being documented"—I swept around and pointed to the film crew—"by this film crew you see here tonight." Orating on my toilet-cum-soapbox, I held up my book. "I didn't think I would ever write another book, not because I didn't have another book in me, but because I didn't know where the readers had all vanished to. And then I thought: maybe I'm writing because only in holding a mirror up to yourself do you have any hope of understanding yourself." I produced a pair of reading glasses and donned them, opened my novel to a page Amanda had bookmarked with a Post-it, and began to read: "Darkness had descended once again . . ." and I read for about ten minutes to a rapt audience of Kiwi youth who, thanks to Hana, had argued her generation hadn't all abandoned literature for the ubiquity of cell phones and social media. To prove her point, she had managed to round up fifty young people on this bitterly cold night to listen to an American author who had expatriated to their country to revivify his love of the written word.

I closed my book and was greeted by avid—drunken?—applause. "Another round for everyone in the room!" I roared. "Including me." A wineglass materialized from Gary, and I was restored to my effervescent self. Hands bolted up in the air to ask questions.

"Do you think this will be your last book then?" a young woman inquired.

"I don't know," I said thoughtfully, quaffing my wine. "I have to return to California, my home state, for reasons I can't divulge. Something deep and troubling is calling me."

"Tell us," random voices called out. "What is it?"

Over the heads of the young Wellington literati, a fight broke out in the main bar area. A disputed call in the close rugby match seemed to be the cause of the scuffle, which was more of a pushing-and-shoving match than an all-out brawl with fisticuffs. Soon, it appeared there was the Welsh Dragon Bar's version of a scrum. Men—and women!—clad in their teams' jerseys, were down on their knees on the sticky floor, closing ranks around the two who were pugnaciously wrestling and throwing punches. Amanda directed the film crew into the bar to get B-roll footage of the melee.

I took the cue and stood from the toilet. Raising both hands in the air, one with my novel and one with a glass of wine, I addressed the crowd. "Thank you all for coming out. Thank you." I stepped down from the stage and the young people surrounded me, thanked me politely as their compatriots duked it out over a fucking rugby match.

An elated Amanda poured her delight out to me over the headrest as Jack drove us through the freshening new storm back to the Freedom Campground, windshield wipers on high, rainwater streaming across the streets.

"You were fantastic, Miles, brilliantly fantastic," Amanda blustered.

"I didn't appreciate your taking credit for what Hana had worked hard to arrange," I said.

"Oh, get off it, mate. She had barely a dozen committed until I worked my contacts," she countered, probably lying.

"Still, the Welsh Dragon Bar book signing was her idea," I said, still peeved about Amanda having alienated Hana and being the reason for her sudden departure.

"Let's not fight," interrupted Jack. "It was a great night, the highlight of the tour. The footage is awesome." He threw me a backward look replete with a flashing grin. "We've both got hit reality TV shows in the making," he said, as if those successes would bind us together all the way to the grave.

"Another smashing episode," Amanda exclaimed, chameleonically shifting to her boyfriend's changing of the subject.

I settled back in my seat and checked my phone. Max's picture blossomed on my home screen, gazing soulfully into my eyes. I worried because he had been left alone in the camper van for more than three hours and would be meowing for food and company, wondering where I was, every strange noise unnerving him.

Amanda threw her mane of hair back at me, her creamy face pinched in its middle. "And I have a surprise for you."

"What's that?"

"Dan O'Neill is going to be joining us at the campground."

"Dan O'Neill?" I brightened.

"Yes," said Jack. "He wants to talk to you about your book."

"Tête-à-tête," added the more linguistically educated Amanda.

"He's attaching himself to the book as a movie?" I said, incredulous.

With enlarged eyes, Amanda nodded enthusiastically.

CHAPTER 25

The wind had strengthened when we arrived back at the Freedom Campground, and that was saying something. Storm clouds raced across the empyrean, backlit by a traveling moon. Rain had begun to fall in heavy droplets, obscuring the view.

I fed Max and held him in the back of the camper van, missing Hana, when there was a rap on the door.

"Come on in," I called out.

An already tipsy Jack and Amanda clambered in. Amanda took a seat across from me in the lounge and promptly uncorked a bottle of champagne, amateurishly letting foam spew out of the top. In the crowded space, Jack stood in the passageway in front of the cockpit where the two of us had begun this journey. We had managed to make it to the North Island and were on the home stretch. Jack produced champagne flutes from an overhead compartment. The wind pitched the camper van back and forth. Amanda poured three glasses of Esses champagne I had been gifted in Kaikōura and raised hers in a toast.

"Here's to our two shows. May they go on for season after season."

"Hear, hear," cried a smiling Jack, having resolved all improprieties with Amanda, and sensing he might have a future, that there *would* be security in his dotage. I wasn't as convinced, but I was too drained from the event to protest.

"Hear, hear," I said.

We clinked glasses all around.

"TV One *loved* the footage of you on the toilet." Amanda beamed, seeking congratulations for her Hana-riffing event production, me the one who would have to endure its images on the internet for all eternity.

"No doubt," I said. "There is no bottom to where culture will go for the media's venal chasing of ratings. I'm a victim of my times. Imagine F. Scott reading from *Gatsby* on a toilet?"

"It's going to sell books," Amanda said.

"On the back of humiliation or merit?"

"Does it matter? As long as you get a deal to write the next one, and the one after that."

I stroked Max, grew introspective, my eyes fixed on his fur, but looking through it to an ignominy I hadn't envisioned when I started writing *A Year of Pure Feeling*, my creative fires aflame for the first time in years, the world having passed me by and by the time I had surfaced I had awakened to a shithole of superficiality.

"You talk about truth," Amanda said in a belligerent tone. "Well, isn't this the truth of where books are today?"

"Sadly, yeah."

Jack, wanting to be closer to the conversation in case it erupted into a full-blown argument, eased onto the cushion next to Amanda. They were in a giddily exultant mood, my morosity over the mortifying event evoking scant sympathy in them.

"In the end you hope the money will come from the merit of the work and not the performative abasement of yourself," I said matter-of-factly, without rancor.

"You're going to make more money off this show than you would ever make off your book," argued Amanda, dollar signs locking in the slot machine of her eyes.

"I preferred the humiliation, but the documenting of it takes it out of memory and stamps it with certification for the few inglorious years I have remaining on this foundering planet."

"It's promotional gold. Your publicist didn't know what she was doing."

"Maybe she had a different plan for me," I said, growing testy.

"Miles," Jack said, "they're going crazy over the footage."

I raised my eyes from Max's fur and his calm purring in the face of the many storms, inside and outside, battering me. There was something so pure about Max and the current of feeling that poured from him, but when I looked into the ruddy faces of well-meaning cash-grabbers Amanda and Jack, I glimpsed a side of Jack I hadn't wanted to believe or witness realized. He could be the most fun person on the planet. To go through the wars with him could be a cathartic laugh riot, as it was years ago in the Santa Ynez Valley wine region, as it was recently at the Cougars of Christchurch Book Club. But there was another side to Jack, as there was to almost everybody I had ever met in Hollywood: he was, at the end of the day, a two-bit hustler for whom the prospect of fame and fortune, however realized, outflanked true friendship. With Jack's thigh pressed to Amanda's and their twin grins in treacherous concert, it was the corruptible Jack I was seeing, and it soured me on everything about our relationship.

Hollywood is a magnet for all kinds of aspirants, but, in my experience, it seemed to, inevitably, reduce people to a kind of low common denominator of greed, despite their at-times exalted claims of wanting to make art, move people's souls. But to maintain that homeostasis, one had to always have access to the blackest regions of their debased hearts. And if it took an aggressive, overachieving money whore like Amanda to educe it and, even better, make it happen, then the dark heart follows the dark path, and the besmirched legacy that dishonorably trails it. Hollywood doesn't draw the degenerate and the corrupt to LA, but when the dust settles, it seems that's all who is left standing in its perfidious center of power. Jack and Amanda, swilling expensive champagne, on the brink of success, needing only one last dowel to finish assembling the Ikea desk at the liminal edge of usurping my soul, what tattered ribbons in the void remained of it.

"I haven't signed on the dotted line," I reminded them.

Amanda threw Jack a troubled look.

With a nod and a wink, Jack mouthed, *I'll talk to him and it'll be okay.*

"It's a celebration of you, Miles," Amanda reassured me.

I nodded up and down, having made my point. "Where's Dan O'Neill?" I said, clapping my hands together, shifting the conversation, pretending to brighten.

We trooped outside into the lashing winds and slanting rain pelting us unmercifully. Gusts of wind were so powerful we had to widen our stances, tilt into the teeth of it, and shout to hear one another, mariners on an ill-fated voyage to intercept a galleon weighed down with gold.

Amanda pointed an extended index finger to a nearby knoll where a lone camper trailer was parked, aglow from inside. "He's up there," she yelled. "Don't talk about the book option. He's going through a divorce," she confided.

Jack hooked an arm around his windblown girlfriend, helmet of hair now a riot on her head. I hoped for Jack's sake it wasn't a wig. "Come on, honey, let's celebrate," Jack said, flashing a profane grin that ate his face whole.

I watched the two of them, bent forward against the wind gusting in off the harbor, trudge up the steep incline to their Marlin Cruiser stationed in its primo-view location.

With nothing to do except read Julian Barnes out loud to Max, I took off on foot in the direction of Dan O'Neill's trailer. As I drew near, I could hear wailful weeping issuing from inside. It rose and fell with an alarming amplitude. Normally I would have turned to go back, but I was emboldened by all the tequila and wine coursing through my bloodstream and clouding my sense of reason.

I banged on Dan O'Neill's camper-van door. "Dan? Dan! Are you in there?"

The door flung open and I jolted backward. Dan O'Neill had the large, craggy, handsome good looks of almost every male movie actor I had ever met. But instead of beaming a greeting—because we're accustomed to seeing famous actors either smiling or spuriously laughing—an aggrieved look furrowed his face.

"Who are you?"

"Miles."

"Who?"

"Miles Raymond, the author." I pointed over my shoulder. "Friend of Amanda Robinson's."

He peered over my shoulder into the dark with squinting eyes, tenting his forehead from the torrential rain with both hands.

"Are you okay? I heard crying."

"I'm fine," he roared. "I'm researching a character. I'm an actor."

"I know."

"I'm playing a Catholic priest who has been indicted on charges of pedophilia."

"Oh."

"Come on in. What did you say your name was?"

"Miles."

"Miles who?"

"Miles Raymond."

Dan's camper van was twice the size of mine, but the disconcerting squalor of clutter inside made it seem smaller. No doubt he was rehearsing a difficult new dramatic TV role, but it looked more like the digs of a newly minted bachelor who was accustomed to having someone cook and clean for him.

"Sit down." He beckoned. "Would you like a drink?"

"Sure."

"What's your poison?"

"Wine."

"You're in luck. I own a winery."

"I heard. And you make some awesome Pinots and Chards."

Dan, teetering in place, unscrewed a cap on a bottle of his Schist Soils Vineyards Pinot Noir. I glanced around the capacious interior of his camper. In a cubbyhole repurposed as a bookshelf, I noticed a copy of both of my books, the legacy one and the latest, and I smiled to myself.

"Miles Raymond? Miles Raymond?" He snapped his fingers a few times. A flare went off in his head and his ruddy face brightened. "You're the bloody bloke who made Pinot famous," he said in his gravelly voice, setting a glass in front of me.

"The movie did, yeah. It was years ago, Dan."

"But your movie began with a book. And you wrote it."

"True. It wasn't the Immaculate Conception."

Dan roared with laughter. "Cheers, mate," he said, raising his glass. We clinked, then settled into broken, desultory conversation.

"I loved you in *An Age of Uncertainty*," I said.

"That was a good one," he croaked. "They don't make them like they used to."

"No, they don't," I said. "Those lovemaking scenes would never get past the intimacy coordinators."

Dan threw back his head and laughed so hard I thought his head was going to explode. "No!" He leaned forward. "And guess what?"

"Don't tell me. You made love in front of three remote-controlled cameras as per the gossip?"

"And Judy was amazing," he said in a lowered voice. "Shh." He looked around for paparazzi brandishing recording devices.

"She did it for the cameras?"

"No, mate, we were in love." He gazed backward into the tunnel of years and the movies he had starred in, but here he was, Dan O'Neill, in a camper trailer parked at the Freedom Campground outside Wellington, no different than me, or any of the rest of us sad-sack souls braving this ferocious bomb cyclone. He held up his wineglass. "What do you think of my wine?"

"Ethereal. In ten years Central Otago will be the new Burgundy."

"That's what everyone's predicting. I hope so. My soon-to-be ex is soaking me, Mike."

"Miles."

"Miles. Sorry." He dropped his eyes to the Formica table and rested them there. "It's been a rough year. I got one kid in rehab, another who wants to transition to a boy, wife is leaving me because she says I'm not around enough, I'm working my butt off to keep my lifestyle going, my damn winery"—he held up his wineglass—"is bankrupting me." He swung an arm around his camper trailer. "This is my new home." His booming voice reverberated in the small space.

"She's getting your chalet in Queenstown?" I said, remembering something I'd read about Dan online.

"That's merely the opening salvo." He pointed a finger at my nose. His bleary, bloodshot eyes, nested in a face colored red and purple with burst capillaries, tried to focus on me. "Don't get married, Giles."

"Miles," I corrected again, realizing he was too far gone to even remember the conversation.

"Should have just cohabitated," he said, shaking his head, his curly locks that looked like they hadn't been shampooed in a week tumbling onto his sun-weathered forehead and sticking where the sweat from frequent night terrors in the trailer had made them into a kind of human glue. "And the lawyers, they'll kill you. They'll bankrupt you before the kids."

"You still have your career, Dan."

"I don't know. That could go next," he said bitterly. "Not getting any younger."

I forced a smile. "Well, we have our project," I said.

He jerked his face up at me. "Huh?"

I stood in place, reached over him, and pulled down my book. "*A Year of Pure Feeling.*" I set it on the table separating us. "I'm fired up to begin the adaptation."

He picked it up and leafed through my book with an absent look in his eyes that seemed to swim with mystery and confusion. Then, as if a memory had been disinterred deep in the geology of his mind, he boomed, "Oh, the book the producer Miranda wanted me to read!"

I fell into a funk. After trading a few depressing film industry anecdotes, I extricated myself from O'Neill's blackout camper-trailer bender and plunged back out into the stormy night. Incensed, I trudged through the wiry fescue and blowing sand in the direction of the knoll where Jack and Amanda had pitched their Marlin Cruiser tent. I came to a halt when I grew close. Amanda's orgasmic cries pierced the night, through the whistling wind, right through all her motherfucking blatant lies. The tent that had blossomed out of the Cruiser was in violent motion as Jack celebrated his twin successes by plundering her in their romantic overlook. The flimsy tent was swinging back and forth with alarmingly increasing periodicity, a foot this way, a foot that way, then two feet this way, two feet that way, Amanda's shrieks rising histrionically in volume until my anger turned into horror as the Marlin Cruiser, catching a sudden gust of wind at precisely the wrong angle, toppled over the edge of the knoll and disappeared from view.

Then I heard different screams in the storming night.

CHAPTER 26

"Well, you sure fucked her to death."

Jack lolled his head in my direction. He was lying in a mechanical hospital bed, eerily reminiscent of Hughie, the two men in my life reduced to convalescence by a book tour! His left leg was elevated and encased in a white plaster cast due to a compound fracture in his femur, a nurse had explained as she escorted me to his room. His handsome face bore cross-hatching of scratches. From the tumble over the knoll or the sharp fingernails of an overexcited Amanda? It was hard to know. "What?" he said in a narcotized voice through chapped lips and a look of despair.

"Amanda died," I said solemnly.

"What?" His eyes welled with real tears.

I let that sink in for effect. "Just kidding. She told the doctors it was the best sex of her life."

"Don't fuck with me, Miles, I'm hurting here."

My eyes traveled along the plaster cast. "Must have been painful." I shook my head.

"Are you joking?"

"You must have caught a gust of wind right at the exact moment she flipped you over for the sideways straddle."

"Not funny, Miles; not funny."

"I guess this is the end of the road." Jack looked at me with questioning eyes. "Amanda said she was taking you back to Byron Bay to rehab."

Jack lowered his chin to his hospital gown. "Yeah, I fucked that one up."

"You've still got *Washed-Up Celebrities*." Jack pouched out a cheek with a defiant tongue. "I wasn't going to sign on the dotted line for its bastard cousin, FYI."

"I had a feeling," Jack said. "It's all for the best." His eyes traveled to the ceiling, searching for heaven. "I love that woman," he said. "I know you think she's a drama queen, but she fills me with life."

"Yeah, we all have our predilections in the partner department," I concurred.

"You probably don't remember this, but a year before I came here, I was cast as Willy Loman in *Death of a Salesman* at the Taper. Okay, it only ran fifteen performances, but I got great reviews and it was damn rewarding." He brought a hand to his heart. "It brought me back to what I love about acting. But it didn't pay the rent."

"I don't remember you telling me about that."

"You say books are dead; well, so is theater, so is acting. It's all garbage now. We're just scavengers, Miles, foraging for the crumbs."

I don't know if the fall off the cliff and the near-death experience had dislodged a rare moment of profundity in Jack or what, but we were on the same wavelength again, our trajectories no longer asymptotic, a polysyllabic I spared him. "Yeah, it's not fun being superannuated," I said. Jack furrowed his brow at *superannuated*. "Dated," I defined. "Sunsetted into irrelevancy."

Jack looked reflective as he nodded solemnly at my words. "What about you?" he finally managed, throwing me a sidelong glance.

I shrugged. "Just me and Max now, I guess."

"Hana won't come back?"

I shook my head. "The love of your life performed a pretty thorough job of alienating her."

"I feel guilty about that."

"Don't. You tried. With *Washed-Up Writers* and Dan O'Neill. And I appreciate that, Jack. I know you have my back. And I have yours."

"I got you up the South Island and across Cook Strait," he said, sadness in his voice.

"That you did. And what a ride it was. More memories for the archive."

"Don't journal this and put it in the Miles Raymond Papers," he half pleaded.

I laughed through my nostrils. Out Jack's hospital window, I could make out our home for the past week parked in visitor parking. Max was ensconced in there, waiting patiently for me, as he always did.

"Are you going back to California to meet your daughter?"

My gaze remained out the window. I nodded.

"It's going to be fine."

"Maybe I'll meet the person who's going to take care of me when I stroke out, the way I had to with my mother."

"And that was some trip," he said, referring to a four-thousand-mile road journey we had recklessly undertaken with my wheelchair-bound mother to get her to Wisconsin and reunite her with her sister. "What's next? Are you going to abort the tour?"

I shook my head no. "I've still got a few more events Hana had penciled in and committed to, and I don't want to disappoint those folks. I'm a professional."

"I'm sorry it didn't work out," Jack said, his rheumy eyes fixed on me.

"I'm tempted to write about this trip, but you remember what my former agent said to me when I told him a scene in my manuscript he didn't believe had actually happened in real life?"

"I know. Sometimes reality is more fiction than fiction." I was fond of repeating my most sententious lines, and Jack was fond of teasing me about my repeating myself. Then he squeezed his eyes shut and winced in pain.

"I'm going to miss you, brother," I said. "This might be the last time I see you in a while."

Jack pried his gaze away from the ceiling and rolled his head in my direction and looked at me with imploring eyes. "Get the neoplasm checked out, Miles. It might only be a wart. For me. Your buddy Jack."

I nodded. Whenever I went to the dark, Jack went to the light; whenever I went to the serious, Jack went to the playful; whenever I drank heavily, he slowed down; whenever I was having relationship complications, he ignored his for mine and was there for me; whenever I was broke, he loaned me money, even if I know sometimes he shaved it off a girlfriend's debit card; whenever Jack needed important self-reflection, I was there for him because that's usually all I was capable of rationing from my meager cache of provisions. Once he told me my "wisdom" was "priceless" and I felt cherished by his loyal friendship.

"I'd get back with Ella," he suggested. "She sounds like she's one in a million. And we're running out of time, Miles."

"It's the one thing we have in common, Jack. Just when you find the supposed ne plus ultra of women, you dream of another, someone who has more to offer, when in reality it's only a treadmill of a fantasy, and the truth is we're both afraid of commitment because we're terrified the other door will never be opened, that the door that did open just slammed shut on us and we're now immured in that selfsame fate."

"Is that such a bad thing?" Jack wondered, my musings eddying around his drugged brain.

"I don't know. I don't think so. If you can resign yourself to it." I didn't want to leave. I knew when I walked out of Wellington Regional Hospital I would be all alone on the North Island, bracing for a long drive to Auckland. I started to grow panicky. All alone in a six-ton camper van. With a special needs cat.

"What's next on the schedule?" Jack inquired.

"Featherston Booktown."

"What's that?"

"I don't know. Probably some small-town Kiwi scam to gin up tourism dollars."

Jack rasped a laugh. "Sounds intriguing," he said, wanting us to part on a felicitous note.

I nodded, thinking many things. Jack could discern in my expression

I was thinking many things because his eyes were bright with thoughts and ideas and big-brotherly advice.

A young nurse came in wearing a warm, apologetic smile. "How are you feeling, Mr. Manse?"

"Well, as you can see, I won't be going out dancing with you tonight," Jack said with a sad glint of salacity twinkling in his eyes.

"No, I don't think so," she said, oblivious to his tomcatting history, the many women he had seduced and forgotten. "The PT will be coming in a few minutes to outfit you with crutches and get you started on some physical therapy so we can get you up on your feet and out of here as soon as possible."

"Good," said Jack.

The nurse backed away toward the door. "I'll let you two be alone." She squeaked away on rubber slippers.

I shifted my attention back to Jack. The painkillers launched into his bloodstream were taking effect, and he was struggling to keep his eyes open.

Jack glanced at his cell. "Amanda's going to be here in a bit."

I nodded. As happened once before at his wedding years ago, a woman, his soon-to-be ex, had torn a chasm between us. My lingering antipathy toward Amanda was abating slightly, but I didn't feel the need to bid her adieu.

I leaned forward and extended my hand to Jack. He hooked his thumb around mine in the old-fashioned peace shake of our youth and gripped it tightly. "Take it easy, brother," I said, holding his hand tightly. "I'll be watching for your show."

With all his waning strength he gripped my hand tighter and wouldn't let go. "If you need anything, call me. Anything," he underscored, fixing his eyes on mine.

"I will. Good luck."

"I don't need luck," Jack said.

When I walked out of the hospital room, I knew I had left a vacuum Amanda couldn't fill. But heteronormative men like Jack needed women. Me? I wasn't sure. I was too neurotic for them in the end. I think I had reached the grim conclusion my fate was to be eternally alone, wandering, the habitual *puer aeternus* chasing words in the dark cosmogony of my brain for answers to why I would never grow up.

I left the hospital, crossed the street, and climbed back into the camper van. Max was curled up in his carrier, his safe cave—one I didn't have!—but he came out on wobbly legs when I unlatched it, and began plaintively meowing. I fed him a few treats, then set him on the seat Jack had occupied for the last week, the irony, the symbolism, not lost on me.

"Just you and me, buddy," I whispered out loud to Max as I climbed in behind the wheel, a deep sadness suffusing me.

Hearing my voice, Max stood up on his haunches and tried to peer over the dashboard to the vast world outside. The mysterious, unknown world outside I was heading out into once again all alone. Then he performed something miraculous. He flexed his hind legs, debated for the longest time, then, in a great effort of will and courage, leaped up onto the dash, clawed with his forepaws to get a grip on the slick plastic, and settled, having stuck the landing in a warm sliver of sunlight he had his heart set on. Max had never once before leaped up onto anything—a bed, a couch, a table, nothing. I clutched a hand to my mouth and tears fogged my eyes.

"Magic Max man," I said. "What the hell did you just do?"

He turned and looked at me with his owlish eyes and ears pointed to the heavens and that ineffable look of awe and wonder he always wore, as if saying to me, *Don't ever give up, Miles.* I wanted to text Ella a picture of Max on the dash and inform her of his great accomplishment, but I feared rejection, so I showered Max with complimentary pets and whispered words of congratulations.

With Max settled comfortably on the dash, and a lifted feeling in me because of his miraculous leap to a patch of sunlight, I rooted my phone from my back pocket and typed in "Martinborough." I wasn't sure where I would be staying for the night, as I hadn't anticipated my entire support base deserting me, wittingly and unwittingly. But I had Max! And obviously no fear of death, having already given the middle finger to God and survived his bolts of lightning. Was I losing my mind?

Driving solo, I navigated the camper van out of Wellington in a northerly direction. Right off the bat things were different. My dodgy eyes were betraying me. When I heard tree branches suddenly scraping the passenger side of the vehicle, I realized with exacerbating consternation captaining it all alone was going to require greater concentration, a degree of focus I feared I wasn't capable of.

Out of Wellington, the road steepened, narrowed, twisted, and turned like never before. A dense fog was lying in wait for me, and I ascended into it without warning. By some freak of nature, I was winched up out of the known world and, quite literally, had soared into the clouds. Visibility fell to a few car lengths. I don't know if it was the crazy week on the South Island, the sleepless nights, the resumption of my overimbibition, seeing a dispirited Jack in the hospital with his leg in a cast, losing the irreplaceable Hana, Jack and Amanda and their turbulent fuck, or finding myself all alone with Max, but I pulled off at the first emergency turnout I could make out on the shoulderless two-lane highway, braked to a halt, put the shift lever into park, bent my head over the oversized wheel, and started crying softly to myself, one hand resting on the purring Max.

Perusing the New Zealand Traffic Authority website this morning to prepare for driving alone on the country's rural roads, I had come across the following advice: "Drive with recognition of your skill level and your understanding of how your vehicle interacts with these types of roads. There probably won't be police on these roads, and chances are, no one will find you for a few days if you crash off the road and are rendered unconscious."

CHAPTER 27

I glanced at my phone, but there was no return text from Ella, nor Hana, nor anybody else in my ever-shrinking world who I had drunk-texted. I turned to Max lying next to me on the bed in the Royal Hotel, a two-story colonial built in the late 1800s in the town of Featherston, north of Wellington in the Wairarapa region of New Zealand. If you blinked, you would have missed the tiny rural town driving through. Max's fur felt comforting under my cadenced petting. I could still see him jumping onto the dash, and every time it unspooled in my mind, I grew tearful.

I had wended my way to Featherston as one of the last events on the book tour planned by Hana. Booktown, as it was dubbed, was some kind of weekend festival of all things books, but with Hana gone, I had lost all interest in the tour and was now going through the motions, performing things obligatorily. I had no idea what I was even there for. Book signing? A reading? Without Hana I was rudderless, adrift in a country I had not come to know so much as expatriate to in order to escape my life in America.

A text notification popped up on my phone from Mary Biggs, one of the founders of Featherston Booktown, the official name of the festival. She and her husband were waiting for me downstairs in the restaurant.

I rolled off the bed and staggered wearily to my feet. Every bone in my body creaked, every muscle ached, every archetype in my psyche advising me how to live this life of mine demolished. The world had gone permanently out of focus, and I was weaving blindly, rudderlessly, in a fog of my own devising. Driving the camper van alone had exhausted me, depleted me emotionally, left me drained and plundered of energy. All alone now, I worried about making it the remaining five hundred miles up the North Island to Auckland and my ambivalent, still undecided, flight back to California.

I picked up Max from the bed and administered his oral supplement of calcitriol. Once in every five applications he threw it up, and this was one of them. That meant something was upsetting him.

"Oh, Max man, what's going on? Huh?" His back arched, he retched a foamy substance onto the carpet for the third time. I found a towel in the bathroom, soaked it with hot water, returned, and cleaned up the minor mess. I petted Max on the head. He always felt better after throwing up. "Okay, no calcitriol today," I said, lifting him up and placing him back in his carrier. I reached a finger in through the wire mesh door and touched his nose. "I won't be long, little guy. I love you."

I showered, shaved, said goodbye to Max one more time, then, slipping into my only decent coat, trudged down the groaning wooden steps to meet the docents orchestrating my next event on the New Zealand book tour. A part of me had wanted to cancel, but given the Biggs were hosting me in their historic hotel and I had somehow made it all the way to Featherston, Pyrrhic victory though it was, it seemed like a shitty thing to bail on them.

Mary and Peter Biggs were waiting for me at one of the restaurant's tables. It was in between lunch and supper, so the dining room was empty, ghosts of its past eerily shifting about on its faded trompe l'oeil walls and ceiling. The Biggs were a couple in their sixties, and they seemed excited to meet me. Peter, the more gregarious of the two, stood to greet me with an outstretched hand.

"You must be Miles Raymond?"

"I am," I said, taking his hand in mine briefly.

"Peter Biggs." He gestured to his wife, who dreamed a warm smile up at me. "My wife, Mary. We're the founders of Featherston Booktown. Have a seat."

I settled into a chair, trying not to appear jaded, but the strain must have shown in my expression.

"How's the book tour been going?" Mary said.

I performatively enlarged my eyes and shook my head as if: *You don't want to know.* "Quite an adventure all in all," I finally said. "I haven't witnessed the end of the world, but I have glimpsed it," I added.

They looked at each other and chuckled nervously (had they seen the social media posts of the Cougars of Christchurch and Wrekin debacles?). Mary returned her gaze to me, the gentle wrinkles lining her face suggesting wisdom and deep-rootedness in Featherston. "Where's your publicist, Hana? Such a bright, beautiful young woman."

It was as if someone had slid a knife into my heart and twisted it a quarter turn. It wasn't until Mary Biggs had mentioned Hana that I realized how much I missed her. "She . . . had to leave the tour for reasons too complicated to go into."

"That's too bad," said Mary. Peter drew an accompanying, complementary expression of empathy.

"What did she tell you about our festival?" Peter said.

I shook my head. "Not much. Something about a Māori ceremonial thing." I upturned my hands and showed them the symbolic emptiness of my palms. "After that, I assumed there'd be a book signing at one of your local bookstores, and that was it."

Mary and Peter exchanged looks of surprise bordering on alarm.

"What is the agenda?" I said in a tired voice.

"Well, we have a lot planned for you," said Mary, leaning forward on her elbows and smiling.

"You're our celebrated international guest of honor this year," Peter added, sitting back in his chair, straightening tall and proud.

"I am?"

"Hana didn't tell you?" Mary said, taken aback.

"I lost my support crew. I'm a soldier of one on a battlefield of books." They chuckled at my mordancy. "All I had was an address and a brief description. I typed the address into Google Maps, and somehow, through a treacherous fog and on narrow roads, without my copilot,

Jack, I made it here to Featherston and your lovely Royal Hotel. To be truthful, I don't know how I made it."

"It's been quite a journey for you, hasn't it?" observed Mary, laying a comforting hand on my forearm for the briefest but sincerest of seconds. "A book tour in the dead of winter in New Zealand, my Lord."

Peter got down to business. "Miles, as our honored guest this year, we'll be taking you in a few moments to the main venue for the opening ceremonies. There you'll be given a pōwhiri."

"A pōwhiri?" I said, squinting my eyes in incomprehension, vaguely recalling Hana had mentioned it the fateful morning she told me she was leaving the tour.

"It's the traditional Māori welcoming ceremony, the one your publicist alluded to," Mary explained. "Hana worked with us and the local iwi to make it happen."

I recognized the term *iwi* as Māori for *tribe* and nodded assent, not aware approval was required.

"After the pōwhiri, we'll be brought in," continued Mary. "I'll give a few opening remarks, and then you'll be introduced and give a talk."

"Pardon?" I patted my pants pocket to ascertain my vial of Xanax was where I always kept it secreted.

"Hana didn't describe to you how the pōwhiri works?" said Peter.

"No. She's a woman of few words. She was fond of springing things on me at the last moment. What do you want me to talk about after this pōwhiri? Who's the audience?" I said, waking up.

"Talk about Aotearoa New Zealand," Peter counseled, "and your impressions of it."

"Remember," said Mary, "you're the honored guest of this year's festival. People are looking to your opening remarks as a celebration of the future of books."

A celebration of the future of books? I spoke in my head. *What the fuck am I going to say?*

Anxiety jarred me awake as Peter and Mary drove in a clock-ticking silence from the Royal Hotel to the venue for the opening ceremonies of Featherston Booktown. A light rain had drawn curtains across the landscape, and an icy wind was blowing in from the south off Lake Wairarapa, a sizable body of water south of Featherston.

Peter parked in a special VIP space in front of a large, windowless facility, and together we climbed out of their vehicle and started up a short flight of cement steps. A large banner, snapping horizontal in the freshening wind, announced "Featherston Booktown." We were met on the pathway to what I surmised was an auditorium by a Māori woman in her thirties.

"She's the kaikaranga," Mary said.

"She starts the pōwhiri, the welcome," Peter explained.

"What do I do?" I said, hands thrust nervously in both pockets, digging for purchase on reality.

"Nothing," said Peter. "Go with the flow, you'll be all good, mate."

"Hi, I'm Manaia," greeted the woman, extending her hand. "You must be Miles Raymond?"

"Yes," I said, taking her hand in mine.

"We are honored to have you here this year."

"I'm honored you would have me."

"Peter, Mary, good to see you," said Manaia, addressing them. "Shall we begin?"

"Let's do it, Manaia," Mary said, clapping her hands together and holding them prayerfully.

Manaia turned to the auditorium and, with hands cupped around her mouth, blasted out a call in a Māori dialect, a language I obviously didn't understand a word of. It was more of an ululation than a call per se, the beginning of a spoken-word song, quite beautiful in its hauntingly sonorous, heart-piercing expression. Then, issuing from inside the auditorium, came an echo of her call in the same strange ululating voice. Manaia called back, her reply call seeming to grow in both volume and intensity. Her call was again responded to from inside and a sung dialogue broke out, one in my ears and another calling from seemingly the catacomb of the auditorium.

"This is the karanga," Mary whispered into my ear. "The call to be accepted from the iwi."

"What if I'm not accepted?" I joked to assuage my nervousness.

Mary laughed. "I don't think it's ever happened."

As the karanga continued, we followed Manaia up the footpath, inching closer and closer to the auditorium's entrance, drawn by the powerful magnet of the disembodied singing voice. Soon we were in the foyer, and the karanga's ululations from inside were loud and filled my ears with a ballad of reverberant mystery. A few back-and-forth calls later, and our small party was led down the left aisle into an auditorium that seated some five hundred high school boys and girls dressed in uniform! Their youthful faces all turned to me in unison with expectant expressions when we entered and were escorted down the aisle to the foot of the stage. My heart pounded uncontrollably. There was a powerful buzz in the auditorium, the walls holding the moment in a kind of human pressure cooker.

The leader of the iwi, a tall Māori man, stood up from a chair where he and a few other prominent tribespeople were seated. Pressing his mouth to a microphone on a stand, he introduced Mary Biggs.

Mary stepped up to the stage, accepted the microphone from the Māori leader, who towered over her, and commenced a rehearsed speech. "Welcome, everyone, to Featherston Booktown. Twenty years ago, before you were born, Featherston was going through a hard time. Drugs, poverty, crime. The town's leaders decided to do something about it. So we created Featherston Booktown. The idea of a booktown had its origins in Wales back in the early sixties and has spread to many countries, but it had never been done in Aotearoa New Zealand before." She cleared her throat. "A tiny town that gives itself over to all aspects of the written word. In short, to books. The writing, the production, the selling, the entire process. We didn't know if it would succeed. But here we are, alive, thriving, with over ten thousand expected this week to celebrate authors and their books and the people who publish them and the folks who sell them. Featherston has turned a corner. By embracing the culture of books, we have transformed this town, once ravaged by drugs and crime, into a cultural magnet of what we like to believe is a burgeoning pilgrimage honoring the written word."

Polite applause greeted her when Mary paused to gather herself. She held up her hand to signal the students to quiet down.

"This evening we have a special, honored guest. A decade ago, when he, in his own words, 'had nothing to live for,' he wrote a novel that was turned into an internationally famous movie. Since then he has re-located to Aotearoa on our South Island and has been writing a new book. That book, *A Year of Pure Feeling*, has been published. When we found out he was planning a book tour, Biggsy and I"—she turned to Peter and they exchanged triumphant smiles—"decided he should be our guest of honor this year."

I turned ninety degrees and stared into the sea of faces of the high school students. Shockingly, a number of them had copies of my book clutched in their hands! It stabbed me in the heart again Hana couldn't be here to sit next to me and feel what I was feeling and to know she was the sole reason for that rhapsodic feeling. I had come a long way from the Cougars of Christchurch to this moment, and I wondered if it had been her grand plan all along, to cap this tour with such a moving tribute to someone as misanthropic and mistrustful of the world as me.

Mary interrupted my musings and snapped me back to attention. "And so without nattering on, I want to welcome California author . . . Miles Raymond." Mary turned to me and began clapping and beckon-ing at the same time for me to come up onto the stage.

Peter gave me a nudge and I ascended the stairs with shaky steps, my legs vibrating in nervousness. Mary stepped back from the micro-phone and I approached it with mounting anxiety. I was greeted by thunderous applause, and I waited for it to subside. Even a raised hand by me didn't quiet the students immediately. I had no idea where it was coming from. Were they applauding enthusiastically, the cynic in me reasoned, because the tradition of the opening ceremony of Booktown Aotearoa called for it?

"Hello." I brought a fist to my mouth and cleared my throat. "Yes, I'm Miles Raymond. I'm not sure I'm as internationally famous as Ms. Biggs here introduced me as, but that's no way to begin a speech, is it?" I paused, blinked and nodded, and then almost went blank. I blinked back tears welling in my eyes. "I've given a few talks in my day, but tonight's has me feeling the most nervous I have since my mother gave birth to me in a taxicab." Raucous laughter greeted the admission of the truth of my birth. "I had no idea about this, this gathering with all of you, when my publicist signed me up for Featherston Booktown. It wasn't until moments ago that I realized what a pōwhiri even is." Scattered laughter relaxed me. "It's quite poetic in its otherworldliness, and I mean that as a compliment." I inhaled deeply. "When I look into all your fresh youthful faces, I think back to when I was your age, and now knowing what I know, what I've experienced, what I've accomplished, and how I've often failed, I'm loath to say anything for fear I will scar you for life," I finished in a rising, exclamatory tone, gaining confidence from the positive audience reaction. I gazed into the eager, young, blushing, and ruddy faces of New Zealand's future and was suddenly at a loss for words. "If I told you what I thought about the future of planet Earth, you might leave here with a feeling of hopelessness." I turned to Mary and fixed my eyes on hers. "But after Ms. Biggs's speech about how books, the culture of books, an art form I have suffered for and given my life to, has transformed your town and revitalized it and summoned it hope, it would be churlish of me to lay on you a bleak, dystopian lecture. This—I'm just now realizing!—is a festival of hope, however microcosmic it is in your tiny town of Featherston. Like all hope, only a seed needs to be sown somewhere, anywhere, and it has the chance, if watered, if attended to, to grow into something that spreads across the oceans to other countries and becomes a permanent fixture. And to think books—books!—are at the center of this revolution . . . I cannot in all good conscience go to the dark side here tonight. I simply cannot." The audience went blurry as I stood there blinking back tears. "I have a special needs cat. He can run but he can't jump, but yesterday he did something remarkable. He leaped from the passenger seat of my camper van up onto the dashboard . . . across a chasm of hope. He took a risk and he made it. And now *risk* is etched in his brain as a plausible strategy going forward. If you don't take risks, you won't live life, you won't cross that chasm like my cat, Max. Like me."

I bowed my head and stared down for a moment at my scuffed shoes and denim pant legs. I realized I was wandering into the realm of the unwell and tried to regroup. Hesitancy about whether I should continue or politely thank them and wish the festival a great success lowered me to a moment of uncharacteristic speechlessness. With great effort, I gathered myself. In the cauldron of emotion I was experiencing, there was something else I needed to say. "A couple weeks ago, a young woman named Hana Kawiti showed up at Prophet's Rock Winery, where I was staying, and announced herself as my publicist for this book tour I've been on in your sublimely beautiful country." I chronicled the book tour in a synoptic but humorous narration, omitting the profane parts, at Mary and Peter's behest when they had instructed me on the drive over how R-rated I could go. There were moments I had the students jackknifed over in their chairs laughing uproariously, but all along I kept reeling it back to Hana. "And then Hana had to leave my book tour for reasons I profoundly regret. To not have her here tonight evokes in me a great sorrow, is a hole in the sun of her being." I cupped a hand over my mouth and raised my eyes to the ceiling. "This was her doing." I gestured to the iwi members sitting alongside me. "You are her people. This beautiful pōwhiri you have extended to me and her not being here to experience it with me lances my heart with an ache I'm at a loss of words for." I closed my eyes and tears leached from their corners, coursed in rivulets down the sides of my face. The five hundred strong could feel my emotion emanating out to them in waves of irremediable grief, and it was transmitted back to me in their hushed countenances, their mesmeric stares, their blinking eyes. "Instead of tonight being about my story, my journey," I soldiered on in an emotionally trembling voice, "I want tonight to be about Hana Kawiti, in absentia, and this extraordinary Māori pōwhiri you've staged on my behalf, and which I don't deserve, and which I had no idea was forthcoming when I drove into Featherston last night." With closed eyes, I looked inward. Hana's visage loomed in my imagination, and I could clearly see her wry, radiant smile effloresce and suffuse me with its warmth. "Thank you, Hana, for making this wonderful tribute happen. I'm not sure I'm deserving of it, so I'm dedicating it to you. Thank you from the bottom of my wretched heart."

I waited for the applause, but the cavernous room had instead fallen eerily into silence. Had I said something inappropriate? Baffled, I started away from the microphone, but Mary held up a hand and motioned me with a wagging index finger to return to where I had delivered my speech. Stupefied with confusion as to what was next in the program, I did as instructed.

A moment later, one of the iwi's other luminaries stood from his chair. He raised a wireless microphone to his mouth and called out to the audience in the Māori dialect of their iwi. There ensued a great, collective commotion as all five hundred uniformed teenaged men and women rose from their seats. From the crowd another iwi member, a young man with curly dark locks, standing off to the side, flanking the packed auditorium, raised a microphone to his mouth. He called out something in Māori, and the five hundred young men and women began to perform what the Biggses told me was called the *haka*. All the students' movements now were in sync. Their chanting voices harmonized into one unified whole. The haka burst out as a kind of warlike address, fierce in its bellicosity. Their eyes were fixed on me as they pounded their chests and arms with their fists, alternating their blows. They seemed to descend into a collective trance. Several of them had their tongues stuck out and wagging grotesquely. The thunderous chant, or song, in Māori, was powerfully emotional. At first I thought they were assailing me in a kind of tribal derision of my foreignness, but as it continued, in rises and falls as the leader on the floor urged them on to spectacular heights of loudness and fierceness, I realized, in a moment of transformation, riveting me with its sonic power, the haka was a demonstration of their respect, a bonding with their honorary guest, the closure of the pōwhiri.

The students poured their hearts and souls into the ceremonial rite in a performance both breathtakingly surreal and palpably moving. The stomping of their feet, the guttural voices that rose from their souls, the sheer expenditure of energy, the letting go of all inhibitions, the booming noise of the words they were chanting I didn't understand; after all I had been through, it sheared my heart in two in a way I have never experienced in my home country, in my life. It was beyond a polite applause.

It transcended cheering. In its ritualistic enactment it gathered up the recipient of the haka and swept them (me) off their feet, thundered me into a kind of ineffable submission.

Tears, unbidden, sprang to my eyes. What a moment! Two minutes of ear-deafening acclamation sundered in seconds to a thrumming silence, the auditorium vibrating. It ended abruptly, not with a decrescendo but rather like a cleaver slamming into a block of wood. All one could hear was their collective exhalations from all the energy they had expended. At the leader's instruction the young men and women, spent from the two-minute, exhilarating performance, sat back down in their seats in unison, their foreheads perspiry, their expressions fixed in a theatrical ferocity. It was an astonishingly cathartic moment. Every anxiety and ambivalence and dark dagger of depression had vacated me. I felt like I belonged to the world again, a world I never felt like I belonged to. Here, in the tiny town of Featherston, a town that had decided to revitalize itself on the foundation of the written word, my faith in humanity had been unexpectedly, if temporarily, restored.

When the haka had ended, the silence that ensued was more profound than any I had ever experienced. Not even death, I concluded, would be this transporting.

CHAPTER 28

The Featherston Booktown festival sprawled over a sun-splashed Saturday and Sunday in a storm window of blue and wet verdure that seemed to meteorologically align for the Biggses. Thousands of booklovers of all ages were drawn to this annual book festival in a pilgrimage the likes of which I had never witnessed. Once a town with only one bookstore, now it had nearly a dozen dotting its mere three-block main street, most of them selling used, rare, and antique books. In an array of venues, events of all kinds were staged: panel discussions, book signings, demonstrations on how books were printed on robotic machines, poetry slams, author appearances with wine tastings hosted by some of Martinborough's finest vintners. I cohosted one with Monty Petrie of Gladstone Vineyard, a small producer of exquisite Pinots. I returned again and again to my room at the Royal Hotel to check in on Max. At one point I took Max out with me to one of my scheduled events and let him rest on the table while I autographed and inscribed dozens of copies of *A Year of Pure Feeling* for young fans of my work, my favorite being: "What you're doing is what you're becoming; what you've done is what you've become." Where did these young booklovers come from? What cracks in the earth had they risen from? Never has my cynicism been so repudiated.

It was heartwarming to witness so many bibliophiles swarm this tiny town to bestow their unified love for books and the written word, disgorging from buses driving up from Wellington, streaming in and out of bookstores, talking books, listening to Kiwi and Aussie authors opine on the writing process, a veritable orgy of books with seemingly no sense of satiety. I'd been pessimistic about the future of books, but this festival brought me an astonishing glimmer of much-needed hope, especially given that not only had I seemingly lost all hope, but I had lost everyone in my book tour caravan to boot. I met wonderful young people who peppered me with questions. Even *if* there were more events on the schedule, without Hana, this was the end of the book tour for me.

And then it was time to leave Featherston. I asked Monty about a beach where I could free-camp for the night, and he recommended a place called Ngawi along Cape Palliser Road. "Beautiful," he said. "You'll meet a lot of great people there. Wanderers like you."

"Thanks, Monty. Love your Pinots. You're the next wave, dude."

I gathered my belongings, little Max man, and packed up the camper van. I said goodbye to the Biggses and thanked them profusely. They seemed genuinely puzzled I would feel the written word was not alive and well. But Kiwis, far from the chaos and madness of the rest of the world, replete with their twenty-five million sheep and abundance of water, had ample reason for hope.

I departed Featherston early in the afternoon. The Biggses had warned me there was a polar vortex approaching from the south that would be bringing strong winds and freezing rain that would make what I had experienced on the South Island seem like a passing squall. I didn't care. I needed to get away. I needed to get to an ocean.

"It's you and me now, Max man," I said to my constant, most trusted, faithful companion, my best and only friend in the world, as I steered the six-ton automotive leviathan, severely damaged on both sides, in a southeasterly direction vectored for Ngawi and the promise of a desolate beach where I could camp and assess my once-again-uncertain future.

As I rode out into open farm- and ranchland, the wind kicked up with a terrifying savagery. I had to grip the steering wheel tightly with both hands until my knuckles had truly, not metaphorically, turned white. With its high center of gravity, the camper van was pitching back and forth on the narrow single-lane rural road. Thank God it was empty of passing traffic—but who would be this insane to be out in such inclement weather? A part of me wondered if I shouldn't turn around, return to Martinborough, check in to a hotel, and hunker down and wait out this polar vortex bearing down on me from the frigid Antarctic. Storm clouds bruised the sky and soon had closed off what streaks of blue remained. Rain began beating the windshield with a machine gun–like mercilessness, and I switched the wipers on to little avail. No way was I turning back, I exhorted myself. I wanted to get to that beach, park the Beast, and just feel myself at the end of the world because that's where I had come to, and I wanted to feel it, I wanted to feel fucking something, anything, because the Featherston haka had left me emotionally gutted.

Cape Palliser Road is the beginning of a narrow, shoulderless two-lane road that snakes sinuously along the Pacific in curving turns so acute it is dizzying. It makes the world-famous Big Sur Highway 1 drive seem like a midnight run up the I-405. The beginning is auspicious: the coastline, the black sand beaches, and the white-capped seas bloom into view as if J. M. W. Turner had painted New Zealand in all its maritime fury. But offsetting the coastline splendor was the ruthless, otherworldly power of the wind, a force greater than any I had experienced before, and that was saying something given where I had been of late. According to my weather app, I noticed to my disconcertion, gusts were exceeding sixty miles per hour. Undeterred, with reckless abandon, I soldiered on.

The descent to the beach on tortuous Cape Palliser Road was heart-palpitatingly harrowing. At one point a gust of wind slammed the camper van so violently a piece of my luggage flew from the upper bunk and crashed to the floor with a bang. The dismaying noise caused me to lurch in my seat. At the first emergency turnout I braked to a halt, crawled through the passageway to the passenger compartment, and replaced my luggage in the rear, securing it under a pile of blankets. With no step-down ladder, I hopped outside to take pictures for my archive, the Miles Raymond Papers now enshrined at my alma mater, UCSD, where future scholars would study a life in eye-popping, unmitigated terror. The moment I stepped out of the camper van, the wind hurtled me three steps before I could regain my balance and brace myself for another blast of the polar vortex's might, assailing me now with all its violence. The ocean was a cyclonic turmoil of gray and white. Boats, ubiquitous in New Zealand, even in the worst of weather, were nonexistent. Marine life no doubt clung to the ocean's bottom, quaking in fear.

Back inside the relative warmth and calm of the camper van, I took a deep breath. I stroked an increasingly anxious Max (head darting, eyes unblinking) and debated for a moment if I shouldn't secure him back in his carrier, but I preferred to see him riding shotgun, sparing him rattling around in that tiny enclosure. Maybe *he* would give me the signal to turn back. But as I kept descending the twisting Cape Palliser Road, I knew, for me, at this moment in my life, there was no turning back. I was determined to make it to the Cape Palliser Lighthouse, where the road dead-ended, park, and ride out the storm. "Are you a man or a mouse?" a Mexican dentist in Tijuana once said to me before filling three cavities without Novocain when I was ten years of age.

The total absence of cars unsettled me. Kiwis knew something about the polar vortex I didn't, knew something about treacherous Cape Palliser Road Monty hadn't apprised me of. I had seen white-capped oceans aplenty in California but nothing like what these barbarous winds were whipping up in this South Pacific Ocean. The entirety of its vast expanse churned ferociously. There weren't whitecaps per se; the whole ocean was now nothing but a sea of white. I had never seen a body of water this furious, so lost to its primeval forces it just surrendered to the Antarctic elements lashing it.

I thought it would improve when I reached sea level, but the winds had grown even stronger, as if the storm were vectoring in on me, just me, haranguing me, some malignant god exhorting me to pack it in and go home. The cold, heavy rain only exacerbated my state of discomfiture. Now and then I had to jerk the wheel to offset the force of a powerful gust. At one point—or was it my imagination?—I sensed the wheels on the right side had momentarily left the pavement!

"We're in it now, Max man," I said to Max in a gleeful, roaring, death-wish tone. "We're in it now!" I started laughing uncontrollably, a madman, reduced to this craziness by the storm of the century and the life I had lived that had led me on this insane search for a desolation that would obliterate my past, and I, tabula rasa, could begin life anew, reborn, reborn with the chance to fix all the mistakes I had made that had brought me to this shattering end.

Pounded by the wind and rain, I stubbornly drove on, along the ocean necklaced with its black sand beaches, in the direction of Cape Palliser Lighthouse, the terminus of this treacherous finger of a road that now seemed but a Fata Morgana. Black sand can look exotically beautiful, or ominous and portentous when the skies are storming. From land to sky it's a cavalcade of blackness parading at you. Monty had lied to me. The free camping grounds were empty. Surely he wouldn't have sent me to my doom and was now cackling at my misfortune. I did nothing but extol his delicious Pinots. I kept on. Fully stocked with provisions, I didn't need to find a general store on this barren stretch of coastline, not that I would have had such luck.

Tremendously strong gusts of wind continued to pummel me. Assailed by one violent gust, a locked upper cabinet sprang open and a bottle of Monty's Gladstone Pinot sailed to the floor, shattered, and spewed wine everywhere. I fingered the vial of Xanax in my left pocket. Wine was not going to be the anodyne tonight. Nothing was. Naked to the world in all its fury, there was no ameliorative, only a capitulation to the elements and fate.

I started passing ominous black-and-orange hazard signs: "Be Careful of Slippery Road." More alarming: "Washed-Out Road." Moving at a crawl now, I couldn't believe my eyes. I thought I was hallucinating: the right side of the road had collapsed into the ocean about twenty feet below. Only the left lane, my lane, remained, and it didn't escape me that in a six-ton vehicle it wouldn't take much weight pressing down on that foundering asphalt for the rest of the road to give up the ghost. And there was no shoulder on my side! Should I keep going? I got out and took pictures of the sign because I thought Jack would get a kick out of "Washed-Out Road." Humor and suicide were locked in combat in my embattled psyche! But the wind was so strong now, rain slanting in on me from the south and striking me with thousands of watery projectiles, I had to race back inside for fear the hurricane-force winds would blow me off the crumbling road and carry me out to sea—wouldn't that be a dream?! But as I opened the driver's-side door, the wind, in a perfectly timed gust, caught it and slammed it into my face. I reeled back and struck the pavement. My prescription sunglasses skittered on wet asphalt. I flew a hand to the outer side of my left eye socket, looked at it, and saw blood running freely.

I retrieved my sunglasses and clambered inside. But the wind was so powerful I had trouble closing the door. I inspected the injury in the rearview mirror. An inch-long gash had opened up next to my left eye. As the camper van rocked violently in the gale-force winds, I braved the passageway into the back, located a box of Kleenex from the road map of my memory, snatched a handful, wadded them up, and pressed them to my eye. I found duct tape in a drawer and affixed the Kleenex to the gash under my eye because I needed desperately to get my prescription sunglasses back on, without which I would be visionless as a bat. The shattered wine bottle and the purple spread of wine on the floor didn't improve my sense of impending doom. I cleaned up the mess the best I could manage, fearing Max getting cut.

With my heart in my throat, I continued in a crawl past where half of Cape Palliser Road had toppled into the sea. In America, they would have closed the road. Fire trucks and emergency Caltrans vehicles would have swarmed the area. Helicopters would have been hovering. Not in Aotearoa New Zealand. You were on your own, mate! (". . . There probably won't be police on these roads, and chances are, no one will find you for a few days if you crash off the road and are rendered unconscious.") Proceed at your own risk. Wanting to find a clearing and seeking to get out of the terrible winds and torrential rain, I frantically kept going, believing, as I always deludingly had, salvation somehow was awaiting me around the next corner. Max was on his haunches riding shotgun, tremulous with fear. Another cabinet door exploded open and a bag of foodstuffs clattered to the floor. Jars rolled and collided with cabinets.

I kept on. If the wind was coming from the southwest, perhaps, I reasoned in my crazed mind, if I got farther up Cape Palliser Road, the beaches would be shielded. I could find a place to park the camper van for the night, prepare a meal, comfort Max—but no such luck. The wind howled fiercer than ever. I gripped down on the steering wheel as the camper van took on the brunt of the winds. At a blind turn I debated turning around—for the hundredth time—but stuck on a narrow sliver of road, there wasn't enough room to execute a one-eighty! I could have inched it backward in reverse, but that seemed as insanely perilous. Onward I went, heaving at low speed around the blind turns on the road folding away from me in horrendous sections as it crumpled underneath me into the encroaching, predating sea. Laboring around another curve, I came upon yet another section of asphalt that had tumbled into the ocean as if the coastal highway were nothing but a play toy road for the forces of nature assailing it.

Terror had me clutched firmly in its grip. It was me and Max now and this friable road crumbling into the ocean like some dystopian movie produced by rich Hollywood fucks and watched by young men screaming and cheering in an air-conditioned movie theater, oblivious of the world coming to an end. But this was not a movie. The world *was* ending right before my terrified and now-bleeding eyes. Rising sea levels, eroding shorelines, monsoon rains, cyclonic winds, oceans heaving their waters on fragile shorelines where roads shouldn't, in hindsight, have been constructed. There it was on Cape Palliser Road, the end of the world, come vividly to life.

The road straightened for a bit, but all it did was cause me to realize my heart was beating like a small animal trying to escape the prison of my chest. I saw another camper van, this one more like a luxury RV, and a man standing outside, his thinning hair blown to one side of his face. I pulled over and clambered out.

"Hey!" I shouted over the din of the wind. "Are you headed back that way?" I said, pointing in the direction I had come from. I drew closer, leaning into the headwinds.

He shook his head, then shouted back at me. "Road's closed, mate.

They sent out the warning." He flashed a phone at me, where he had received the news.

"What about north?"

"Dead-ends at the lighthouse. No way out." And without another word, he climbed back into his RV.

Stunned, I staggered back to the camper van and scrambled in. I circled back onto what remained of the collapsing road. The skies were night-darkening, somewhere a sun was lowering. The wind was beating down fiercely, the exhalations of a demon. I switched on my lights, vowing to pull over at the next turnout where there was nobody and no one and nothing.

CHAPTER 29

With my escape route now officially closed off and my options to make it back to civilization running out, where Cape Palliser Road leveled with the ground, I pulled over onto a black sand beach as night fell in starless terror. Instead of opening up the camper van to a favonian view of the Pacific, bathers frolicking in the warm waters, dolphins leaping on incoming swells, I battened down the hatches. When I went outside to turn on the gas valves for the heat, bent over, bracing into the buffeting wind, I felt like I was wading thigh high in quicksand to make it to the rear of the vehicle, where the control hatch for water and gas was located. My mittenless hands froze as I desperately tried to screw open the valve handles on the propane tanks.

Inside, I finished cleaning up the wine and glass on the passageway floor so that Max could safely move about. The van rocked violently, and often I had to grab a handle or grip a counter edge to keep from falling. I checked all the cabinet drawers to assure they were secured. I fed Max by hand because his bowl was shifting on the floor with every intense gust of wind. He looked confused, scared, helpless, in his smallness, marginally sheltered as we were from the big world outside assailing us. I assumed he had never experienced a weather event like this in an exposed camper van. Having grown up in Southern California, I for sure hadn't. "We don't have monsoons in Hollywood, Max man," I said out loud to maintain some grip on my sanity as the polar-vortex-driven storm outside raged unabated.

My phone kept saying "No Service" when I glanced at it. Which meant there was no way to get online and ascertain the severity, or the duration, of the road closure. With both walkies in my possession, what was I going to do? Radio myself? Although the camper van was equipped with satellite Wi-Fi, there was no way in my discombobulated state I was ever going to be able to figure out how to get it operational. Damn middle age, bring on the youth with their tech savvy! And even if the road hadn't been closed and the guy in the RV was lying to me like Rob way back when, with the slashing rain and cyclonic winds there was no way I was going to brave Cape Palliser Road back to Martinborough in the dead of night, no streetlights, me and Max on a hell journey through New Zealand's unconscious.

As the wind pitched the van from side to side in intermittent gusts, I whipped up a crude meal out of sesame crackers, smoked salmon, and feta cheese, and washed it down with one of my terpene sodas. I badly wanted to drain a bottle (or two) of wine, but the Prophet's Rock Antipodes had crashed to the floor and left me sans alcohol. All I had left for comfort was Max.

I've spent the majority of my life alone, sleeping alone, hermetically sealed off from the world while I pounded keyboards in the illusional hope writing would be my ticket to salvation and a life filled with people, but being alone on a strange shore in the middle of nowhere, in the middle of a polar vortex with winds in excess of fifty miles per hour, was something I had never experienced before. When gusts slammed the camper van, the force of the blows was so strong there were moments I feared it was going to be blown over. But there was nowhere to go. It was my only shelter from the elements. If I had had an internet connection, maybe I could have assuaged my growing fear with bulletins on the weather, texts and emails to friends who would have responded with *Hang in there, Miles. Ride it out, you've lived worse.* But I was completely cut off from the world.

Once, a long time ago, I visited a sensory deprivation chamber in

Santa Monica because I had read a famous screenwriter had visited there on a weekly basis for inspiration, and he had made millions and won Oscars and attributed his success to these submarine-like containment vessels where you floated in a saline-heavy, body-temperature water and were supposed to experience a sightless, soundless void of free-floating where it was only your imagination staring in wide-eyed terror at your mind, sucking the marrow of your own brain. But it didn't work for me. All I remember was being inundated with sexual fantasies, then banging the containment closure with my fist to summon help because I was experiencing a panic attack due to acute claustrophobia. The mind—or my mind—cannot exist without a fixed point of reference, I reasoned at the time, as some white-uniformed attendant came to rescue me from the horror of being exiled with myself.

But here I was, in the same situation. Cut off from everything, nowhere to go, the night loaded with fear! Somehow I had found myself in God's own sensory deprivation chamber, and I felt small, insignificant, a grain of sand in a cosmos of trillions of planets.

I lifted Max and hugged him close to me, his whiskers against my cheek comforting me. "Max man," I started, as the van rocked on its wheels, "the world is ending. We are at the end of the world. I have seen and done things most humans haven't. I've written books. Most didn't get published. One did. It made me semifamous, until fame, always fleeting, forced me to New Zealand, where, among other things, I met you, little guy." I lay back on the cushions in the dining area and positioned Max on my chest, holding him tightly for fear he would be catapulted off with the next titanic buffeting of wind. He wasn't performing his normal purring, and I sensed he, too, was terrified of the night unleashing upon the both of us the fury of the heavens.

"I've had girlfriends, Max. Beautiful ones. Crazy ones. Kinky ones. I've sampled them all. I was even married once, but that seems like ages ago, but wouldn't it be nice to have someone in my life right now? She would have talked me out of driving the Cape Palliser Road to Ngawi on this insane serpentine stretch of godforsaken highway disappearing into the ocean. We would be in a hotel somewhere; we'd be at a gourmet restaurant with candles lighting our faces; you'd be in the room with your preferred foods and your favorite toys. Instead, I'm here all alone and I've forsaken you, Max, because this isn't what you bargained for. If I die, I deserve it, but you don't deserve to die because I'm some crazy fucking ass writer who goose-stepped off the edge into the amplitude of this void, into the holy terror of this godforsaken night we're now cast adrift in together, the two of us, only the two of us." I kissed Max's whiskers and petted his head.

I bolted upright as a tremendous gust struck the camper van full force, shook it, and knocked it sideways what seemed like a few feet at least. The blast caused all the cabinet doors to creak on their hinges and challenged their locks and knocked everything inside them around with a terrible clamor. The most petrifying aspect of the infamous '94 Northridge earthquake on my rent-controlled house in Santa Monica was the noise: the shattering of wineglasses, the explosion of my TV as it toppled from the mantel and crashed to the floor, the vases that slid across the dining table and shattered and burst into shards. What went on for two minutes felt like an hour as I clambered between mattress and box springs to prevent the debris from the ceiling from caving in on me. This camper van was a miniature version of my house during that earthquake, but this wasn't two minutes of shaking. This had been going on for hours and was evincing no signs of letting up.

BANG! A gust punched the side of the van with a giant fist and jolted it to one side. Everything inside juddered. I could feel Max tense in my arms and try to escape. I hugged him tightly and refused to let go of him, even as he bit and clawed at my hands in fear.

"My father wanted me to go into the family business, Max," I babbled maniacally, not feeling his biting, actually happy he had chosen to sink his fangs into me. "He wanted me to sell coin-op laundry equipment, and I would have made millions because he had the table all set—the exclusive Whirlpool distributorship; the business clairvoyance to predict the evolution of Laundromats to laundry rooms at apartment complexes in a fast-expanding San Diego—and I told him, 'Hell no, I'm going to Hollywood to write and make movies,' and it crushed his

soul, Max. He died on the operating table, and my mother was felled a
year and a half later by a massive stroke that left her with the mind of
an infant and full left-side paralysis. They never got to witness my success, Max. Then Victoria tried to change me, tried to turn me into the
vanilla artist she hoped I would become, so I had to divorce her, Max,
because when people try to co-opt your talent, colonize your unconscious, and mold it into who they want you to be, then it's over. You've
lost your voice. You've become who someone else wants you to be." I
was dealing the cards in the deck of my past, charting in vain the lost
continent of my wrecked life.

"I followed my own path, Max. I detoured down a dark road. Weathered bankruptcy and artistic failures galore and landlords chasing me
down the alley for rent, an agent who suffered a nervous breakdown and
left the business and had to be institutionalized, a younger brother who
stole my modest inheritance from our stroke-addled mother, a girlfriend
I thought was the one but who ended up being bipolar and undergoing
electroconvulsive therapy. I'm here in New Zealand, at the end of the
world, Max, because I refused to listen to the advice of girlfriends and
agents and managers and all these people who want to co-opt what little
talent you have so they can make a buck or show you off to Daddy or
whatever their fucking ulterior agenda is . . .

"I'm a failure, Max. I had one fleeting moment, but I never made
it. I've never owned a home and realized obscene appreciation or had a
family or did anything contemporaries of my generation did that now
seem prudent even if their lives are sinkholes of spiritual desolation.
And yet they tell me they would like to be like me! Imagine that, Max.
Would you want to be me now? Here on Ngawi Beach, in the middle
of a fucking hurricane, in a camper van, with less than ten grand to my
name? My belongings in public storage somewhere in San Diego? I don't
mean to scare you, little guy, but my future is looking grim."

Struck by a new onslaught of terrifying winds, the camper van convulsed so violently I thought it was going to be blown to smithereens and
leave me exposed on the chassis, naked to the elements. I reached down
and could feel the heater vents dispensing warm air, and that calmed

me momentarily, nearly brought tears to my eyes! Heat. Something so basic. "We have heat, Max. Something does work in this world," I said aloud, cackling softly like a madman, some Rasputin of the past channeling their lunacy through me.

I continued to take inventory of my aberrant life, needing to hear my voice, my only audience a special needs cat and the maw of God. "And then there were all the bad decisions, Max. The bloodsuckers twisting my arm, to write this book for this publisher, this screenplay for this corrupt producer or production company. And then that went away and with what little I had I came here because I was vouchsafed a fresh start, a place to bivouac, a place to write, because that's all I ever wanted, Max, was a place to write, and free time. Free time is everything, Max. I didn't care about fancy cars or houses in Laurel Canyon or vacation homes on equatorial islands. If only my mind, my imagination, was unfettered, that's all I cared about. And I found it here in New Zealand. But like all things, Max—movies, books, plays—it, too, had to come to an end, the tent had to come down, the circus, the circus of my life, had to roll on to the next stop, the next handout, the next way station for this inveterate roustabout."

The camper van shuddered violently again, its bones creaking in every corner and compartment, and I cleaved Max closer to me and waited it out. I peeked out the curtains, but when there's no ambient light, when the cosmos are closed off by storm clouds, night is total blackness, and I wondered how primitive peoples kept from going mad. Or did they?

"What have I got, Max, except my freedom, huh? And you." I hugged him tighter with both arms enveloping him, fingers stroking the top of his head to comfort him. "I sacrificed so much, and I had my one success, but then like all successes that evaporated and I was left with nothing. Sure, there's Ella, but if I go to California, I won't be able to return." I nodded to myself, thinking how selfish I was, and could be, and how often I had been harangued for my self-centeredness, my solipsism. My hand unconsciously petted and comforted Max, over and over, my last grip on reality. Had I been alone, I'm sure authorities would have found a man who had lost his mind, wandering a driftwood-strewn beach, hair blown wild, babbling senselessly.

"No, I'm a failure, Max. I wasn't much of a carbon footprint, that I can boast of, but then, too, I wasn't much of a footprint at all, was I? Did I only have one book in me? If we get out of this alive, will I wring something else memorable out of this aging mind and body of mine? I can't retire. No pension. No savings. No one to take care of me. I've got to keep moving, Max man." I petted his head. "Will you promise not to abandon me?"

Another series of wind gusts slammed the camper van in cruel succession, a cannonade of Nature's unbridled fury. We were in the middle of the polar vortex, I theorized. The Beast rumbled, it convulsed, it shook violently in all directions. A cabinet drawer flung open and its contents rattled to the floor, unnerving me. Max tried to bolt from my arms, but I wouldn't let him go. He sank his fangs into my forearm this time, but I still wouldn't let him go. Once he knew he was held fast to me, he released his teeth from me, and now I was bleeding from my left eye and forearm, but it seemed the least of my worries. The wind howled and blew with such force I imagined waking to a world extirpated of its flora, boats washed ashore, capsized on their shattered hulls. BANG! BANG! BANG! It was not one continuous buffeting, but an unrelenting series of ferocious blasts. Even eerier than being alone was hearing that monsoon wind whistle through the nooks and crannies of the Beast. Whistle and shriek and caterwaul as if it were trying to get me and Max and disintegrate us, sweep us out to sea on a raft made of balsa wood and a sail torn from the underwear of a monster.

I drew the vial of Xanax from my left pocket, where I always kept it. I took a one-milligram tablet, pulverized it under my tongue, and hoped it would buy me relief from my crippling anxiety. Here in New Zealand, I didn't fear serial killers or nosy, revenue-generating police arresting me for vagrancy. No, I only feared two things: the elements and losing my mind.

"Who's going to remember me, Max?" I continued to babble in an effort to ward off the encroaching madness engulfing me. "Huh? I mean,

I know you will, but who are you going to convey that to because language is thought, and the written word is our only true, lasting legacy? And even then if there're no civilizations left, then the written word is merely an artifact in a repository and I've just returned to carbon from whence I came. I came in with nothing and went out with nothing, but . . . I guess I was able to live the life I wanted to live, I loved the women I was fated to love and not the ones I should have loved, who would have taken care of me now, in my moment of need, all alone here in this storm, the two of us swept out to sea.

"No, I won't be remembered, Max, but does it matter? Does it only matter we had this blip of a moment, and in that blip of a moment I did glimpse what I thought to be God, the fulgurations of my imagination put down in ink to paper? For future civilizations to excavate and study the ruins this generation made of the planet?

"And where am I going to go if I don't return to California? I'm roofless. I'm rootless. I'm ruthless." I laughed at my alliteration, laughter and my hold on Max the only thing keeping me from a full-blown psychotic breakdown. At one point I looked down at Max and he was staring up at me, wide eyed, unblinking, his expression fixed in both innocence and wonderment and possibly even dismay at my lunatic laughter. I petted his head. "I'm sorry, little guy, I'm sorry. You don't deserve my destitution."

The Xanax started to kick in with its narcotizing and anesthetizing effects. The storm no longer felt as immediate, even as it continued to rock the camper van back and forth. But after an hour or two of monologuing to Max, the fact that we hadn't tipped over comforted me slightly with the realization that maybe it would hold its ground, the storm would pass, and Max and I would wake from a broken sleep to live another day.

CHAPTER 30

Troubling dreams stalked me through a night of fitful sleep. I was having to move again, pack up, the situation was all wrong, people I didn't know were crowding into my rooms, I was running low on money, and then I was traveling with a caravan of lost souls in a futuristic world where populations had been depredated by great mortalities, food was scarce, warmth and shelter fleeting. Now and then I jolted awake, but peering out, I saw only blackness and a starless sky. "No Service" still showed on the banner at the top of my iPhone. The feeling of being cut off from the world weighed down on me, and it felt like there was no escaping my predicament.

Finally, mercifully, morning crept in through the windows with a timid light. The wind, still gusting, had calmed. The cacophony of the storm was absent. Max was meowing for food, so it seemed we had endured the worst of it and things had normalized.

I heard a strange noise: a rhythmical slapping against the camper van. Opening the side door, I saw to my horror that the tide had come in and the ocean had risen three feet, nearly to the level of the camper van's floor. *Fuck*, I muttered to myself. *Fuck!*

"Come on, Max man, we've got to get out of here before we're swept out to sea." I pulled on the knee-high Red Band Wellingtons that had come with the camper van, gathered Max up and secured him in his carrier, packed my carry-on bag with all the essentials it would carry, and, with my electronics bag slung over my shoulder and Max firmly in one hand, climbed out the driver's-side door, where there was still a stepladder remaining. Thank God I remembered the Red Band boots, because I landed in water halfway up my calves.

I heard a splash and lowered my eyes. Lying face down in the water was a copy of *A Year of Pure Feeling* that had fallen out of my unzipped carry-on. As I reached down to retrieve it, a sudden surge of ocean water lifted it up, then, on its ebb flow, carried it out to sea, Kon-Tiki in miniature heading on an El Niño current to North America, where, I laughed to myself, it might find a US publisher, a message in a bottle. Careful not to drop Max and the rest of my only belongings, I trudged nearly a hundred paces through seawater and muck to dry land. Barking fur seals were scattered on the sand and rocks as I approached the shore. They paid me no mind.

On dry land, I set down my belongings and looked back into the sun with tented forehead. The Pacific Horizon camper van was rocking back and forth in the tiny waves that broke at its wheels, clearly not the promotional social media post the company who had sponsored me was hoping for. How I had come to park it so close to the ocean I could only chalk up to my poor eyesight and discombobulated state of mind, the fact it was night and I had not factored in the tide tables. Why a surfer boy like me from Southern California hadn't foreseen the radical tides was confounding. The Beast looked whipped and beaten. Its mirrors had both been clipped off, and it looked like an earless woolly mammoth. The side that presented itself to me was tree and shrub abraded from too many brushes with the edges of the narrow roads I had dangerously navigated. Floating in the rising ocean, it appeared forlorn, an abandoned military vehicle in the aftermath of a battlefield where no side had won, soon to be set adrift and sunk for future marine archaeologists to discover and wonder about. Or not.

Then something miraculous happened. When I got to Cape Palliser Road, I stopped to catch my breath. A numinous force had pulled the clouds apart with enormous cosmic hands and revealed an azure-blue sky. Within moments a resplendently iridescent rainbow emerged and colored the empyrean. From the far reaches of the Pacific to the hills of Cape Palliser and Ngawi, the miracle rainbow arced, growing brighter and more vibrant with every passing second. I don't believe in spiritual anything, I don't even like the word *spiritual*, but there it was, magnificent, a gift (a sign?) from Nature, a breath of blue sky and a colossal rainbow that seemed to be pointing the way to salvation. And I desperately needed a ray of hope for salvation, because all that was left of me was a few items of clothes, my laptop, and Max.

Across Cape Palliser Road a tiny community of trailers came into focus, and I trekked in that direction. At one point I walked past what appeared to be a graveyard of tractor trailers parked on the sand. But on closer inspection it appeared some of them had fishing boats in tow.

A hundred yards inland, on slightly higher ground, I stumbled upon a general store called Sea Trader. Inside, I explained my plight to a middle-aged Kiwi woman with a sea-weathered face and a circumspect mien minding the store. My story sounded cockamamie, even to her, and at this far-flung outpost, one had to imagine she'd heard her share.

"Cape Palliser's closed, love. Caved in yesterday about twenty kilometers from here."

"I heard. What do I do? I . . . I parked too close to the ocean and my camper van is now stuck in the ocean." I pointed out the window to the vast, glittering Pacific in the distance, and her eyes traveled with my finger until they reached the nothingness of an image because Max and I had trekked too far to see it anymore.

She looked at me pitilessly. "There're no motels here. You can try knocking on doors and see if anyone'll put you up until the road is reopened. But that could take days."

I bought a coffee from her and sat down at a planked table. I powered on my phone. My heart skipped a beat with excitement when I noticed it was showing one bar! There was only one person in the world to call.

"Hello?" Hana said, picking up seconds before I ended the call.

"Hana, it's Miles."

A silence greeted me.

"Hi, Miles," she finally said. "Where are you?"

I explained my situation in as calm a voice as I could manage.

"My God," she said. "Ngawi. Cape Palliser. What possessed you?"

"I needed to get away from the tour. Anyway, the road's closed. Capsized into the sea. I thought I was hallucinating. What do I do?"

After a moment when I assumed she was googling, Hana spoke up. "Sea Trader? Ngawi?"

"Yes."

"Stay put."

"Where am I going to go?"

The phone went dead in my hand. I looked around. It was only me and Max and the proprietor behind the counter. My pant legs were sopping wet, but otherwise I was warm and dry. I didn't know what Hana had in mind. Was there another way into Ngawi? I considered calling her back, but she sounded definitive about a solution when she had hung up.

"Is that your camper in the ocean," a crusty fisherman said to me as he banged into the Sea Trader.

"Yes, it is."

"Do you need a tow? I can get one of the tractor trailers to pull it out." My look of utter consternation must have prompted additional explanation, as he went on to say that because there was no pier or marina at Ngawi, this was how they launched and retrieved their boats, the packed black sand of the beach acting as a natural boat ramp.

"I'm in touch with people in Wellington," I said. "I'll let you know. But thanks."

"It's all good," he said, then trudged his way to the counter to place an order.

Morning eased into afternoon, the minutes slow as earthworms on hot asphalt. The sun now burned a bright hole in the sky, dispersing the last remnants of storm clouds. The rainbow had evanesced. I texted Hana several times and all she texted back was, "Stay put."

The sun finally went over the hills, touching off fires on the other side of the planet, and I started to worry where I was going to stay for the night. Locals who had come in and out of the Sea Trader offered advice, most of it unhelpful or tinged with apocalyptic mordancy. Then this stunningly beautiful, wraithlike figure with long, dark, curly hair trudged up the pathway and approached the Sea Trader. I could see her through the windows, and my heart leaped with joy. Hana!

She trooped inside, spotted me at the table with Max and my laptop. "I'm glad you're okay," she said, rushing over.

"Yeah. It was quite a night."

"I'll bet. These all your belongings?" She pointed to my carry-on and electronics bag.

"Yep. All that's left of Miles Raymond."

She gathered up both, then said, "Get Max, let's go, follow me."

We trudged together down an unsealed road to Cape Palliser Road, crossed the closed highway, then met a red-and-white-colored rescue boat that had been piloted up onto the black sand. Outfitted with foam pontoons, it had amphibious capabilities. Two New Zealand Coastguard personnel, a stoic-faced young woman and a smiling middle-aged man, helped Hana, Max, and me into the raft-like boat. They motioned for us to get inside the cabin. With their powerful twin engines, they rotated the craft a hundred eighty degrees on a dime and steered back out into the white-capped Pacific.

"Miles Raymond, rescued by the N Zed Coast Guard after failed book tour," I joked to Hana. "One-of-a-kind publicity."

She smiled a weary smile.

"Thank you for rescuing me."

"It's what we do. You're in New Zealand, Miles. We take care of people."

"Tell that to Hughie."

The Coast Guard crew piloted the boat out into open waters. The seas had calmed from the night before, but it was still a bumpy ride back into Wellington's harbor.

As we neared the marina, Hana, who hadn't spoken much during the boat journey, turned to me:

"When's your flight back to California? Have you booked it?"

"Day after tomorrow. Red-eye."

"How're you going to get there?"

I shrugged. "I'm at a loss without my publicist."

"I'm driving to Napier to visit my parents. You can hitch a ride with me, then catch a flight to Auckland from there."

CHAPTER 31

"Twenty-five years ago, I was house-sitting for a friend in Del Mar," I started, turning to Hana, who was at the wheel of her Subaru. Twilight had descended, and we were on the road heading north to Napier, on the East Coast of the North Island, en route to Auckland. "Del Mar is a little beach hamlet north of San Diego. Anyway . . .

"It was back in my naughty drinking days, and desperate for some socializing, I walked to this bar at L'Auberge Hotel, a swanky place on the ocean." I sipped from my bottle of terpene soda to clear my throat. Nodding to myself, I debated whether to continue or not.

"You don't have to tell me if you don't want to," Hana said to the windshield through dark sunglasses, both hands gripping the wheel.

"No, I do. I have to tell someone. It's been gnawing at my soul ever since I found out. I mentioned it to Jack, but I didn't want to get into it with him. It's a deeper conversation than he's capable of absorbing." I gathered myself with a lungful of air and a sighing exhalation. "Her name was Milena. When she came into the bar, I thought I was hallucinating. She was tall, stunningly beautiful, my age, wearing a black dress, having come from a formal event, a wedding or something. She had four men in tow, all professionals in suits. Being young, in a bar, newly separated, on three or four glasses of wine, I have to admit she commanded my attention."

Hana smiled and chuckled a laugh.

"I was shocked when she elbowed up to the bar, surrounded by her entourage of obviously way more successful men than me, a failed writer, about to be divorced, house-sitting for a friend. But we struck up a conversation. She worked for a high-end software company, held a PhD in physics from MIT, but was a big reader; hell, had read *The Golden Notebook* by Doris Lessing. I was shocked when I realized our literary, and film, tastes intersected at so many junctures. She thought *An Angel at My Table* was a masterpiece, and so do I, naturally."

"Naturally," Hana said, effortlessly passing a tractor that was holding up traffic.

"I bought her a glass of wine with what little money I had on me. Turns out their company had enjoyed a banner year and the trip to Del Mar and this luxury hotel was to reward the employees with a beach-front junket retreat, and she was in a mood to let her hair down. After her second glass of wine and the fact she hadn't drifted away from me, after a shoulder had pressed against mine, after more than one hand had grazed my forearm and given it a squeeze whenever I said something funny—and I had her laughing with some of my Hollywood stories—"

"I bet you did," Hana said.

"Anyway, I asked her if she would like to take a stroll on the beach. She lived in Manhattan, grew up in an upper-class family, private schools, Bard, then MIT for her doctorate. An intellectual. Albeit in the sciences. But hey, a guy like me at that time could appreciate anyone with an educated background romantically interested in me, especially after all the deadbeats and wannabes and charlatans I had dated in Hollywood . . ."

Hana smiled ruefully and snorted a laugh through her nostrils.

I nodded, dropped my chin to the buttons of my shirt, and continued with my story: "I told her about growing up in San Diego, escaping the grappling hooks of my father luring me into the family business, surfing my youth away until I discovered, I don't know, Dostoevsky and Raymond Chandler and Patricia Highsmith, Wenders and Fellini and Mizoguchi . . . It was a balmy night. My memory wants to fabricate a full moon lowering on the horizon, but that might be a romantic embellishment. We ended up back at her suite at L'Auberge. A suite. I'd never been in a hotel room that big. The windows had been flung open and the curtains gently billowed from an ocean zephyr. It was something out of a movie." I nodded, my mind now suffused with the memories of twenty-five years ago and trying to give them voice.

"Did I venture a kiss on the beach? I might have. But it turned intense once we got back to her room. She had to be married. She had to have a boyfriend back in Manhattan. She was that beautiful, smart, successful; surely she couldn't be interested in me. She was the kind of woman I would never approach, knowing my chances would be dim at best. But no, she informed me, she was unattached, the men who accompanied her to the bar were colleagues at her company, and she would never start up anything with a coworker, I remember her telling me."

Hana glanced at me. I could see her out of my peripheral vision, and I wanted to believe her soulful eyes behind her sunglasses were forgiving ones, not reproachful ones.

My confessional story tumbled out irrepressibly: "Later she would tell me she wished I had kissed her as soon as we left the bar. Things men don't pick up on. Anyway, her company was in town for a week, and we spent every night together, enveloped in each other's arms. And every night I was transformed by this magically beautiful woman in unimaginable ways. When we weren't entangled in the sheets we talked and talked. Her father was a famous journalist for the *Times*, and her mother was a ceramist who'd had her work shown in galleries internationally, if memory serves." I paused to let the memories deluge me now that it was all coming out.

"Parting after a week of unbridled passion was painful. She implored me to move to Manhattan and live with her. She offered to support me while I wrote my way to fame and fortune. She owned some incredible co-op in the West Village, argued it would be good for me as an *aspiring* writer." I paused and joked, "Aspiring? I had already aspired, then expired ten times over, but she saw in me the chrysalis of talent, someone she wanted to commit to, mind, soul, and body." I shook my head in memory of her naked body, rued the cruelty of aging. "She didn't care I didn't have money, once I had opened up to her about my situation when things turned serious. She didn't care I'd been married and was on a fast track to divorce. She wanted a relationship, and apparently she was fixated on me."

Pinpricks of headlights bloomed at us in the dark. In telling my story, I hadn't been conscious of night falling inexorably around us.

I continued on to a patiently listening Hana: "Back at work in Manhattan, she traveled a lot. San Francisco. Chicago. Austin. London! And she had all these frequent-flier miles and she would FedEx me a ticket on a whim and I would fly to her and rush into her arms and everything would be paid for and the hotel rooms were spectacular, and, well, I don't want to sound unseemly, but hotel rooms and romance go together like Pinot and roast salmon."

Hana laughed lightly and I took another sip of my soda. My mood dropped, and Hana could sense it because I had paused longer than I had since I had begun.

"You don't have to tell me any more, if you don't want to, if you're not comfortable telling me."

"I need to get it off my chest." I sucked in my breath. "Milena called me one night from the East Coast," I began in a solemn tone, "I don't know, two months after this torrid, cross-country affair began and said in what I can only describe as an ebullient tone . . . 'I'm pregnant. We're going to have a child, Miles.'"

Hana looked at me when I went nonplussed for a full minute. "What'd you say?"

I cleared my throat. "Well, first off, when the affair started, I asked her if she was using birth control, and she told me she couldn't get pregnant, which I automatically interpreted as her being on the pill, or whatever. But no, as it turned out, she explained to me, she hadn't had her period in a year and had *assumed*—I stress the word *assumed*—she couldn't get pregnant. So to her, I suppose, getting pregnant was some kind of victory, that she was *not* infertile and that I would welcome this child into the world because we were destined to be together. And she wanted me to celebrate that victory with her. But of course, to me, it wasn't a victory. I didn't want a child. It wasn't the right time for me. I like children, but being a writer, it was never in the cards for me, and I always had to have this difficult conversation with prospective partners when things got serious. I viewed parenthood as an impediment to my trying to make it as a writer, I guess was always my selfish explanation." I turned to Hana. "You need all the obstacles out of the way if you have any hope of making it as a writer, unless you're a nepo baby or you're F. Scott Fitzgerald, and I'm neither."

"I see," said Hana, if only to punctuate my increasingly difficult-to-voice confession.

"Marathon phone calls ensued," I finally uttered, sighing. "This was when cell phones were first coming in and it was terribly expensive," I added, remembering the bills that resulted in getting my phone turned off. "I told Milena emphatically that I wasn't ready to be a father, that it wasn't fair to me for her to want to have this child. She vehemently—and I mean vehemently!—countered that I didn't have to have anything to do with the child's upbringing, that she would bear the financial responsibility all the way. And I argued to her, in many fervently contentious calls, that I would still know I had a child in the world, and I wouldn't be able to ever let that go. Forget the fact that this chasmic rift had dramatically altered the course of our love affair. As I was coming to grips with being an absentee father, I was also coming to grips with losing her."

"She didn't want to give up your child?"

"No. At first. And these calls were nightly, dragged on for hours on end, back and forth, the same redundant argument—she would assume all responsibility; I didn't want to know I had a child regardless of the financial arrangement. This went on for several fraught weeks, always ending in tears on her end and utter dismay and terror on mine. A father? I didn't want to be a father. I had a mother who didn't want to be a mother. She once told me she wished she had aborted my younger brother if she had had the option."

"What?"

"Complicated other family story." I inhaled deeply and exhaled slowly. "The calls got heated. She grew hysterical. Sometimes she would hang up, then call me right back. 'I'm having the child.' Then call right back and, in a violent whiplash, 'Okay, I'll . . . I'll terminate the pregnancy.'"

"Seriously?"

"Obviously, if she wanted to have the kid, there was nothing I could do. I tried to appeal to her wanting me, to be with me, to live with me in a committed relationship—and I did want that, though less and less with these hysterical calls. I told her, if there was any hope of that happening, she would have to terminate the pregnancy, that although I took responsibility for being the father—and never once questioned that—I didn't want to *be* a father; I didn't want children, a family. I was in my early thirties and I still had novels and screenplays to write, and if there was any hope I was ever going to make it and not throw myself off the tallest building in frustration, she had to do the right thing."

"You threatened to kill yourself?"

"I don't remember, Hana. It was a terribly stressful time in my life." I inhaled and let go two lungfuls of painful memories. "After two or three weeks of marathon phone calls, insomniacal nights, I was overwrought, I was desperate, I was pulling my hair out." I paused, measuring my words. "I came of age in a generation where abortion was commonplace, no big deal, you went to Planned Parenthood, but I had always been careful, and I had managed to avoid what so many of my contemporaries went through and had their futures changed forever in some cases. I'm not making light of it, but the pregnancy had transformed Milena into another woman, one I no longer recognized. At times on the phone she seemed crazed. Anyway, after three weeks of this fruitless tug-of-war, weeks went by and I didn't hear from her. And this from a woman who called me *every* night for a solid month!"

"What were you thinking?"

"I don't know. I traveled to a dark place, Hana." I exhaled sighingly. "Finally, she called. She wasn't hysterical. She was calm, matter of fact. She said, 'I went to the clinic with my sister and . . . took care of it.' I tried to pry details from her, but she refused to elaborate. I asked if I could pay for the procedure, but she didn't want my money. Or me either, for that matter." I nodded to myself. "In one phone call, she ended the pregnancy, and us."

"How did you feel?"

"Relieved." I paused dramatically. The night poured in through the front windshield in a river of black memories. "Until a few weeks ago."

Hana snapped her head in my direction and locked her enlarged eyes on mine for a brief few seconds.

"She wrote me an email out of the blue. Hadn't heard from her in over two decades." I threw a hand to my mouth and flashed back tears spilling from the corners of my eyes. "She said, 'Miles, you have a daughter, and she's getting married.'"

Hana stared through the windshield with her bulging eyes.

"She explained in the email she had gone to the clinic with her sister but couldn't go through with it. But because I had been adamant about not wanting to be a father, she had kept it from me all these years, but now that she is grown and getting married . . ." I raised both hands to my eyes and covered my face. "I lost a whole part of my life."

CHAPTER 32

"You've got to go back," Hana urged over breakfast the next morning at her parents' modest house in Napier on the North Island, situated on the placid harbor. "You'll never be at peace with yourself," she counseled. She leaned forward across the table. "You'll always be wandering and wondering."

I smiled wryly to myself. "All last night I kept thinking what it would have been like to have found this out when my daughter was two, or ten, or a teenager, or . . . But to find it out now, after all these years, I'm not sure how I feel. She's a grown-up, her adult life has already begun." I widened my eyes and raised my head to keep from tearing up again. "She's getting married, for God's sake."

"It'll worm itself into you and gnaw at your soul for the rest of your life if you don't meet her," Hana said.

"But how do I explain not wanting to have her?"

"Her mother wanted her, and that's all that matters to her."

Hana's father, Frank, came in, interrupting us. He was a stout man with the identifying features of a full Māori. "Well, I'm off," he announced. He taught English and te reo at a local high school. He extended his hand to me. "It was a pleasure to meet you, Miles."

I stood and took his hand. It was large and bearlike in mine. "The pleasure was all mine. Thank you for letting me stay here."

"We enjoyed the conversation," he said. "You live a most fascinating life."

Frank walked off. A car started and motored away. It was now only Hana and me looking at each other over the table. She said:

"I booked your flight to Auckland." She handed me back my credit card. "Have you decided?"

I stared at my card for the longest moment, then nodded up and down. "Yeah. I'm going home."

Hana smiled, stood, and, for the first time ever, took my hand in hers. "Come on, Miles, let's go," she whispered, squeezing my hand and then letting it go. "You've got a date with destiny."

"Her name's Leila."

CHAPTER 33

The Napier regional airport is small, and this being my first flight in two years, I needed to gird my loins for the long-haul transpacific one back to California.

Hana parked her Subaru in visitor parking and helped me with my luggage into the airport.

When we got inside the terminal, she said to me, "You've got everything?"

"Yeah."

"Passport?"

I patted my electronics bag. "Right here."

"Laptop? Phone?"

"Yep."

"And Max."

I squatted down and inserted a finger through the wire mesh door, and Max rubbed his nose against it. I flashed on my past flying issues—a deplaning due to a panic attack; leaving airports before boarding . . . "Yeah, I've got Max. I don't know if I could get on the plane without my little guy." I locked eyes with her, and we stared into each other's for the longest time. "Thank you, Hana, for everything."

"It's good."

"I'm sorry the book tour was, well, if not a failure, interesting."

"It was interesting."

"And sorry to have unloaded all that stuff about finding out I had a daughter on you."

She shook her head, and her dark curly locks tumbled over her shoulders. "It's okay. You had to tell somebody to get perspective." She paused. "And I'm glad you're going back to meet her."

I nodded, still ambivalent, but my mind made up. I bent down and picked up Max by the carrier handle, stood there in front of my young Māori publicist—the same age as my daughter!—and wished it all could have been different. "I guess this is it."

"Yeah," Hana said. "You should have plenty of time for your lay-over in Auckland."

An announcement blared over the loudspeaker, something about my flight to Auckland being on time and beginning early boarding.

"You'd better go," she said.

I nodded, not moving. Blinking back tears, I said, "Is it okay if I give you a hug?"

Hana raised her tattooed arms to horizontal and looked at me with beseeching dark-brown eyes. "Of course, Miles. Of course."

I set Max down and we came together in an awkward but feeling embrace. She held me tightly, wanting to communicate something ineffable. I whispered into her ear, "I would never have made it this far without you. And that's the God's truth." I could feel her hug me tighter, reassuring me the compliment wasn't necessary, but appreciating nonetheless.

We disengaged. Her hands clung to my forearms. I reached for Max's carrier handle, our eyes never unlocking, hers watery with tears, mine blurring with hers.

"God, I'll miss you, Hana."

CHAPTER 34

The Ritz-Carlton, San Francisco, is located on Stockton Street in Nob Hill, in a magnificent, old, majestic stone structure around the corner from the Stanford Court Hotel, where I honeymooned with Victoria three decades ago. We were young, we were giddily in love, we did what hip literary/film people did in San Francisco: visit City Lights Bookstore; traipse across the Golden Gate Bridge; explore the Haight; dine at Chez Panisse. We collaborated on two movies, and then our marriage soured on the acrimony brought on by failure. It always starts on the top of Nob Hill, I chuckled sardonically to myself, as I lay in my deluxe suite with a view of the city. All alone.

I had flown in late the night before, a brutal fourteen-hour hurtling of my tired body, but Max endured it like a champ, business class our friend thanks to the Cougars of Christchurch. A room had been reserved for me, but according to texts, Milena irrationally worried I was going to be a no-show. The Ritz-Carlton was the headquarters for the wedding. I could only imagine my daughter and her fiancé's financial situation if they could afford this apotheosis of California luxury.

As I lay in bed, hands interlocked and propping up my head, I thought about my return to the States. It had been two years since I left for New Zealand and its rural beauty to teach, then research and write a book, my first in years. America felt strange to me now. The airports were more congested; its citizens more harried; the brusqueness at the front desk at the Ritz—as if I maybe had cabbed it to the wrong address; i.e., the wrong social class—was different from the absence of circumspection you find in New Zealand. But unfortunately, now that I had gotten on the plane, having overstayed my visa, the probability of my reentering New Zealand was slim. I did it for . . . *my daughter*. It felt surreal to acknowledge that, that I had . . . a daughter.

A text notification lit up my iPhone. It was from Milena. "You made it! See you downstairs at the JCB Lounge in an hour?"

"Ok," I texted back.

I rose from the bed and all the worthless articles the media was inundating me with on the internet and crossed the large room to the picture window. What if I had stayed married? I wondered. What if I hadn't decided to strike out on my own to become a writer and had gone into the coin-op leasing business with my father? What if I had known I had had a daughter? And where was I going to go now that I was back in California? Hollywood didn't want me with their algorithms and data-driven decisions about what films got made. My antihero books with their unlikable, if roguishly lovable, characters weren't going to be fodder for their jejune streaming fare.

The JCB Lounge sparkled with quiet, if obscene, luxury. Jean-Charles Boisset seemed to want to marry the idea of a French cabaret with the opulence of Nob Hill and the exquisite taste his brand stood for. It was all dark colors and velour fabrics and an upmarket bar and, sitting on a stool, a beautiful woman: Milena. I don't know if it was the chic black cocktail dress apparel and the clutch of pearls, or the way her hair was styled, or the perfume that scented timidly from her that unlocked memories of our tangled bodies, or what, but she had grown into a middle-aged woman I wouldn't have imagined. I felt out of place in a black sports coat, faded jeans, and brown loafers, but that's the finest I had, the chicest I could afford.

She smiled warmly. "Hi, Miles."

"Hi, Milena."

Our greeting casually crossed chasms.

We stood a few feet apart from each other, and then she reached out both arms and invited me into an embrace. I let her envelop me in hers, then slowly reached my arms around her and hugged her, a little more tightly with each passing second, the concatenation of recognition forming a ghost train that bridged the quarter century.

She whispered in my ear, "I'm glad you decided to fly back."

We let go of each other, nervously corkscrewed onto stools at the bar, and settled uneasily next to each other. Our shoulders grazed. The tasting room manager, a young woman, approached us with a rehearsed smile.

Milena turned to me and whispered, "Should I tell her who you are?"

"No," I said. "Spare me. Please."

"Okay."

"Have you had a chance to look at the tasting menu?" the woman said.

I ordered a glass of the 2019 Puligny-Montrachet, and Milena echoed my selection.

"Good choice," said the tasting room manager.

"How was your flight?" Milena said, making conversation, marking time, the bigger questions hanging in the air.

"Long." I looked at her tiredly. "Exhaustingly long." I smiled. "But I'm glad I came."

Our wines floated over to us in Riedel crystal. Puligny-Montrachet is perhaps the greatest terroir of all Chardonnays grown in the world. The limestone soils, the destemming without crushing, the sixteen months in medium-toasted barriques, the native yeast fermentation, the beautiful weight and viscosity, it winches one up to empyreal heights, those many centuries of monks honing and refining their vinification methods and making me realize New Zealand still had a long road ahead of it.

"This is a gorgeous wine," I said, holding my glass up to the light and studying its ambrosial color.

"It is," said Milena, moving it around in her mouth. "Exquisite." She turned to me. "I guess you of all people would know."

I stared into the Baccarat crystal wineglass it was served in. This is the life I could have had if I had forsaken my calling, but once I'd read Dostoevsky, I never had a choice.

"I suspect you have some questions," Milena said, interrupting my digression.

I nodded, shrugged, still had difficulty meeting her eyes. Our worlds had cruelly bifurcated two and a half decades ago, and it seemed like whatever questions I might have were moot. "You lied to me," I said in a nonthreatening tone.

Milena turned away and stroked her glass of one of France's finest. "Yes," she said matter-of-factly. I nodded to myself. "I knew it wasn't what you wanted, so I made the decision not to involve you." She raised her fashionable eyewear and dabbed tears forming in her eyes with the back of her hand. "It was the best decision I've ever made in my life. Under the most intense circumstances." She turned to me: "Are you angry with me?"

"No, Milena. No." I stared at a point of nothingness. "Just numb."

"That you have a daughter?"

"How did Leila find out?"

"After you and I . . . went our separate ways, I started dating another man. He eventually moved in with me, and, naturally, Leila regarded him as her father, and she was too young and innocent for me to explain what she never would have understood at that age. This surrogate father of hers and I broke up a few years back. When she announced she was getting married to Mitul, I decided to tell her, so she wouldn't go on some internet search and accuse me of keeping her in the dark all these years. I, too, wanted closure."

I nodded in resignation. "How'd she take it?"

"After I told her who her father is, she surprised me by asking me to implore you to come to the wedding." Milena glued her eyes on the side of my head. "She wants to meet you, Miles."

"What does Leila do, Milena?"

Sensing my reservations assuaged, Milena threw out both arms and said, "After graduating from Stanford, she got a job as director of HR for a big wine company here in Sonoma. You two will have a lot in common."

I snorted a laugh and shook my head.

"She knows who you are, Miles, and she's proud of that fact."

"What about her fiancé?"

"He works in product development at Apple." She flattened her hand and raised it like the mercury on a barometer in a heat wave. "High end."

"Maybe they'll buy me an ADU to put on my patch of dirt in New Zealand," I joked.

"Are you going to emigrate?"

"I don't know if I can get back in." I shook my head in self-recrimination. "Overstayed my visa."

"Do you have someone there in your life?"

I shrugged, didn't shake my head no, didn't nod my head yes. I turned to Milena. "I haven't been successful with relationships. The writing always seems to get in the way."

A silence fell. Inane wine chatter and bottles being uncorked filled the void. Floor-to-ceiling wall mirrors everywhere wouldn't let me escape Milena or myself.

"I thought about you a lot over the years," Milena said, absently examining a painted nail. "When I met you, you were so intense, so at loose ends, so . . . suicidally depressed. I was convinced you had done yourself in."

I laughed at my youthful cynicism and occupational self-loathing. "Success is a great deodorant," I quoted Elizabeth Taylor.

"I'm relieved to see you're doing okay. I didn't know what to expect, frankly."

"I'm still at loose ends." For a moment I thought about bringing up the neoplasm on my groin, the broken teeth in my mouth that had gone unattended to, the book tour from hell, Jack screwing Amanda off a cliff and into the ocean (for a sliver of humor), the grim fate of the written word, and my love for a special needs cat, but I didn't want to open a Pandora's box on my personal life and have her start worrying about the father of her child all over again. Besides, there was a wedding tomorrow. Perhaps age had rationed me a smidgen of maturity.

There was a clock-ticking pause, and then Milena turned to me and said, "Are you ready to meet your daughter?"

CHAPTER 35

Milena and I rode the elevator to the top floor, then walked wordlessly down a carpeted hall. We stopped at a door with a number Milena recognized, and she knocked. A moment later a young woman opened the door with a smile that fissured her makeup and beckoned us in. Milena quickly introduced her as Courtney, one of the bridesmaids. She seemed to have been alerted to the solemnity of the moment, because she excused herself and left the room.

In front of a floor-to-ceiling mirror, Leila, in her flowing wedding gown, was being fitted with the final jewelry placements—tiny pearls at the neckline. The middle-aged seamstress who was marking where the pearls would be sewn in and studying the distances with a practiced eye, also apprised of my visit, retreated and left the room to afford us some privacy.

Leila turned to me. Like her mother, she was tall, brunette, willowy, lovely, her eyes animated with personality and intelligence.

Milena stood between the two of us as a bridge to an awkward meeting. "Leila, this is Miles." She paused dramatically. "Your father."

Leila stepped down from the fitting platform and turned to me. "Hi, Dad."

"Hi, Leila. You look beautiful." Searching with eager eyes, I could see the palimpsest of me, and it ghosted back at me from across the years.

There was a self-conscious moment when time had momentarily stopped, and then she floated toward me, and we embraced. "It's good to finally meet you."

"Yes," I said. "I never knew," I started haltingly, then stopped. I nodded slowly, acknowledging the gravity of the moment with my silence. "I never knew."

"You're coming to the rehearsal dinner?"

I cracked a smile. "Well, you know we writers never turn down a free meal."

She smiled a laugh. The chasm inside me wasn't our age difference, it was also the years I had not seen her become the woman who she had grown into. The huge lacuna was heart shattering, unfathomable, non-addressable, ineffable, soul gutting.

CHAPTER 36

I repaired to my room on a borrowed heart, lifted Max up, lay down on the bed, and let him nestle on my chest. He instinctually started purring, then nuzzled his snout against my cheek, which he loved to do before settling into a long purring session. He brought me a serenity life had not, did not, could not, because of who I had set out to become, what I had set out to achieve. I read somewhere a cat's purring performs a self-healing function, the sound-wave frequencies building bone and confidence. Was his incessant purring keeping us both alive? Had it put the spring in his legs that gave him the courage to leap onto that dashboard into the sun?

After half an hour of Max and meditation, I set him down on the floor, pulled on a coat, and ventured outside. It was midsummer here now in the Bay Area, and most of the grapes in famed Napa-Sonoma would have been harvested, a diametrical contrast to antipodean New Zealand, where winter was winding down.

I walked a mere block and turned a corner into another chamber of my past. San Francisco evoked memories because my ex-wife, Victoria, and I used to vacation often. The Stanford Court Hotel, another majestic old stone masonry building standing sentinel on the top of Nob Hill, looked the same as when we had honeymooned there decades ago.

As I stood on the sidewalk and stared at the grand entrance to the

Stanford Court, I reflected on how swiftly the years had been consumed by the flagitiousness of time. And where had they gone? When you're young, the years stretch out before you like the greatest of all journeys yet to be embarked on. When you grow older and look back, it's always: How did I get here so fast? What did I accomplish? And who was I to arrogantly think I could buy immortality with a book or a movie?

And then there are the regrets. The bad decisions, the invidious people who stole from you, your soul, but not your legacy. And now the new regrets: Leila. My God! I lost twenty-five years of a life I had given the only contribution a man can give to a life. I of course didn't blame Milena for her last-minute change of heart. It was her body, her monumental decision, and she had clearly made the right one to abjure mine . . . and give birth to this lovely woman.

How would my life have been different had I capitulated to Milena's wishes and been a part of Leila's life? Time holds no answers, but time is the harshest critic. Would I have been a writer? Would I have written that legacy work of mine that transcended its puerilities to become so iconic? Or would I have drifted into another profession in order to support my daughter? *My daughter.* My God.

CHAPTER 37

"And to my daughter, Leila, and her fiancé, Mitul," said an emotional Milena, "I want to wish you two all the happiness in the world."

The two dozen attendees of the rehearsal dinner were seated around a white-cloth-draped, rectangular, baronial table in an event room at the Ritz, crystal chandeliers, ludicrously expensive champagne, more Boisset Burgundies sourced from every region in the Côte d'Or. Milena paused with a hand clutching her mouth. I imagined in that moment she, too, must have wondered how different it would have been had I been in Leila's life.

"And now," she continued, "I'd like to introduce someone none of you have met, only a few of you know about." She extended an arm in my direction. "Leila's father, Miles Raymond."

I sat back in my chair, stunned. I looked around from the back of the table. Faces had turned to me and were waiting on me. Smiling faces, bemused faces. After years of Hollywood meetings, I was not used to smiling faces. Not this many anyway.

"Come on up, Miles." Milena beckoned with an outstretched arm and piano-motioning fingers.

I rose slowly from my chair and edged my way to the head of the table. Milena gave me a perfunctory hug. I turned to the faces now slanted up at me.

Addressing Leila's fiancé, I said, "I know, Mitul, you work at Apple, so you might appreciate this story. Some thirty years ago Steve Jobs learned he had a sister. He contacted her. They reunited and became extremely close. Her name is Mona Simpson. She's a successful writer. But not so successful she lives in a Craftsman-style home in Santa Monica Canyon with a view of the California coast all the way up to Malibu!" The incipience of laughter relaxed me. "Maybe this is my Mona Simpson moment." More, louder laughter followed. I gazed down at the table and grew reflective, the faces a blur now. "All my life I've taken journeys," I started, raising my head, "journeys of the imagination. But sometimes reality is more fiction than fiction." I glanced down to my left and glued my eyes on Leila's. "Two weeks ago—" I cleared my throat. "Two weeks ago . . . I learned I had a daughter." My words drew a collective hush from the crowd. "And that she was getting married." I nodded repetitively in an effort to quash the emotions welling up in me. "It's not important, nor appropriate, at this moment, to divulge the whys and hows. The past is the past, and it's implacably irremediable. I've learned the hard way. There's only the present and the riches the future holds, or doesn't." I turned and caught Milena's eyes. "I want to thank Leila's mother for having the courage to reach out to me. It could not have been easy." I turned to Leila sitting opposite her mother. "And I want to thank Leila for having the courage to . . . allow me into her life." I raised my head and looked up at the back of the room and fixed my gaze on a painting hung on the wall. "I don't have family. Parents, brothers, wife, all gone now. Just me and my special needs cat, Max, and he's, trust me, been with me these past months through serious thick and thin." Uneasy but seemingly knowing laughter broke my train of thought. I soldiered on through the emotion threatening to capsize me into speechlessness. "It's almost a miracle to learn then I do have family, I do have someone who will wipe the drool from my mouth in assisted living." Mordant laughter erupted from the tipsy group. I raised my wineglass and held it out to the bride and groom. "To Leila and Mitul. Invest in real estate. Don't become a writer."

CHAPTER 38

Buena Vista Winery is the oldest winery in Sonoma. A narrow cobblestone pedestrian-only pathway leads up to an ivy-covered three-story stone structure built by Chinese immigrants in the mid-1800s. It has been witness to many weddings.

A fleet of vans caravanned from the Ritz-Carlton to the property. I elected to go alone in my rental. Driving through the vineyards, leafed out in green, now pendulous with grape clusters, I couldn't help but reflect on the wintry New Zealand vineyards and the brown, leafless rootstock I had left behind, the country I would now presumably not be able to return to.

The wedding was held outdoors. There were several hundred people in attendance. In the tuxedo rental I was fortunate to score at the last moment, I stood in the back, all alone, feeling uncomfortable, sweat dripping from my temples as the hot sun beat down on me—the first real warmth I had experienced in months. Other than immediate family and those at the rehearsal dinner, the majority of the attendees didn't know who I was. Once again, as I had been most of my life, I was blissfully anonymous, and existentially alone.

A hand clutched my wrist and drew my attention to my left. It was Milena, in a green dress and bedecked with a luxurious necklace with a jade pendant. "Miles?" she said.

"Yes?"

"Leila wants you to escort her to the altar. It's tradition." She fixed me with a beseeching gaze. "Will you? Please?"

"Okay," I said, not feeling qualified.

A few minutes later the wedding procession made its way up the center aisle between the flanks of fold-up chairs. Pachelbel's Canon played over the amplifiers, ironically the same music they played at Victoria's and my nuptials. In shimmering white, my daughter approached me and reached out her hand. I took it in mine and escorted her up the aisle, a surreal experience for a guy who didn't know he was a father until a couple weeks ago.

At the lectern, a man clad in colorful vestments and white turban was awaiting our approach. As Mitul, the fiancé, was Indian, the religious figure hired for the ordination was naturally decked out in the traditional sartorial costume of his sect.

As we neared the altar, Milena, who had been trailing me, instructed me to let go of Leila's hand. I did. She turned to me and flashed a resplendent goodbye smile. Flummoxed now without her hand, I didn't know what to do or where to repair to. One of Mitul's siblings, who I had met at the rehearsal dinner, noticed my confusion, stood, and whispered into my ear:

"It's customary to give advice to the groom."

"Pardon?"

"Some words of wisdom from the father giving away his daughter. You know, like 'Be good to her or I'll kill you.'"

I chuckled in spite of the solemnity of the occasion. I didn't feel like her father all of a sudden and felt out of place saying anything. Then, caught up in the spirit of the moment, I turned to Mitul, standing to the left of my daughter, his future wife, my future son-in-law. He glimpsed me out of the corner of his eye, then, expecting the tradition to be honored, slanted his head toward me over his fiancée's shoulder and looked at me quizzically. With the wriggling fingers of one hand, I motioned for him to come closer. Understanding the gesture, he leaned in. I cupped a hand to the side of my mouth and drew it next to his ear. He waited, head bent toward me. I paused dramatically, then whispered:

"No fucking Merlot."

EPILOGUE

The first season of *Washed-Up Celebrities* was a hit in Australia and New Zealand. Apparently, audiences couldn't get enough of the humiliation of their once-famous—even Dan O'Neill made a guest appearance!—who had fallen on hard times. Jack boasted it was his charismatic hosting, and maybe it was, but whatever the reason for its success, it was re-upped for a second season and Jack was, in his own inimitably upside-down way, back on top, married for the second time, enjoying the luxe life of fashionable Byron Bay.

My novel *A Year of True Feeling*, for whatever inexplicable reason, was picked up by a US publisher and became a minor *Times* best-seller—"auto-fiction at its most soul-baring," crowed one critic—and the royalties trickled in. A real movie deal—not the Dan O'Neill fiasco—materialized, and it fueled up my bank account like it hadn't been topped off in over a decade. If a movie was made—a big *if*—it would probably afford me the opportunity to pull down the shade and enjoy the quietude of books and ripening of Pinot in Miles's Lot.

Owing to my book's success in the US, and given that Hughie had launched it on a wing and a prayer, I buried the axe with him. Using his extraordinary range of governmental connections, and no doubt the passing of the white envelope, he was able to secure me a return visa to New Zealand. Hell, if a movie adaptation of *A Year of Pure Feeling* ever went into production in Aotearoa, its author had to be there, right?

The Prophet's Rock Winery owners agreed to let me station a small mobile home on a pedestal of cement overlooking my half hectare of Pinot Noir. The double-wide was spacious and had everything I needed or ever wanted in life: hot running water, propane stove, high-speed satellite Wi-Fi, extravagant views of Mount Pisa across Lake Dunstan. Max seemed happy there. He delighted daily in looking out the window from his cat hammock at the diorama of all the colorful birds that visited the vineyard, now in harvest bloom, my Pinot Noir hanging pendulously from the vines, the summer sun warming him. Now and then, without using his cat stairs, he would leap up onto the couch to cuddle up next to me, defying his disability. Every time he did, it filled me with an ocean of hope. The little guy never complained, never gave up, he kept trying, trying . . . because that's all he knew. Studying him, I learned more about life than from any human being. Without him, I'm positive I would have ended it on the beach at Ngawi.

At Hana's urging, I visited an oncologist in nearby Cromwell. I explained to the bespectacled doctor I had noticed what I believed to be a neoplasm in my groin. "Let's have a look," he said. I removed my pants and underwear to allow him to examine me. He peered at the area closely, looking all around, then glanced up at me with a bemused look. "I don't see anything. When did you last see this tumor?"

"Six months ago. I was too petrified to look at it, or dare touch it, again."

"Well, I don't see anything," he repeated.

Hana's Māori bee pollen? I drew a hand to my mouth, closed my eyes, and for some reason flashed on the emotional haka the young men and women at Featherston had performed for me.

I was sitting in a fold-up chair on my makeshift porch under a retractable awning with Max purring contentedly in my lap, both of us drinking in the sun, when a dark ray crossed the vineyard and stopped. I heard a familiar voice:

"Didn't think I'd ever see *you* again," called out Ella.

ACKNOWLEDGMENTS

I'd like to thank Youssef Mourra for having the idea for me to come to New Zealand and bring my alter ego, Miles, down under. To the many people in New Zealand who helped me, wittingly and unwittingly, to bring this next installment of the Sideways series to life, especially the folks at Prophet's Rock Winery, where much of the first draft of this book was written. Rick Bleiweiss and Josh Stanton of Blackstone for believing in the continuation of this story. Madeline Hopkins, my inestimable and assiduous editor. Ananda Finwall for setting me straight on commas and more. To Kate Saeed and Marco Mannone for providing me some crucial early ideas. To the legion of *Sideways* fans who inspire me to keep writing, and to Alexander Payne, who made this writer's dream come true. And last, and hugely, to Joy Murphy, without whose support this novel never would have happened.